"A powerful read...I loved seeing the characters develop their relationships with God."
—*Julia Wilson, christianbookaholic.com*

"The weaving of three disparate, seemingly unrelated stories into cohesive, joined narrative is a tough feat to pull off. Paul Thomas Anderson, for example, does this brilliantly in film. So too does Jess Lederman in his novel of historical fiction, *Hearts Set Free*."
—*IndieReader.com*

"*Hearts Set Free* walks confidently along a winding path, weaving together friendship and family, struggle and failure, love and faith into a master tapestry of redemption stretching across generations."
—*Pastor Ashley Brown, Wasilla Bible Church*

"*Hearts Set Free* is a fascinating mixture of history and fiction woven together by a strong cord of truth. The novel takes one on an adventurous ride through the past and present, but what makes it a must-read are the thrilling spiritual stories of how people come to faith in Christ. This is a story about the grace of God and how His prodigals find their way home. It will stay with you for a long time."
—*Pastor Stephen Carney, Retired, Church of God (Anderson), Brookville, OH*

"Complex, heart-wrenching, and beautiful."
"An awesome read!"
"I finished this book crying in the middle of the night with my soul feeling the love of God like I hadn't in a while."
"Kept me engaged from beginning to end. I love and serve my Savior Jesus Christ and this book was such an inspiration for winning souls to Christ."
"Over and over again, I was taken by surprise by the unexpected twists and turns of events. Mr. Lederman's fascinating inclusion and interweaving of historical events and characters allowed me to believe it all!"
—*Reader Reviews on Amazon*

Hearts Set Free
A Novel

Jess Lederman

This book is a work of fiction. Any references to historical events, real people, or real places are used fictitiously. Other names, characters, places, and events are products of the author's imagination, and any resemblance to actual events or places or persons, living or dead, is entirely coincidental.

Except where noted below, scripture quotations are from The ESV® Bible (The Holy Bible, English Standard Version®), copyright © 2001 by Crossway, a publishing ministry of Good News Publishers. Used by permission. All rights reserved.

The scriptural quotations on pages 175 and 313 are from the King James Version. The epigraph at the front of the book is from the NIV.

All rights reserved. This book or any portion thereof may not be reproduced or used in any manner whatsoever without the express written permission of the author except for the use of brief quotations in a book review.

Copyright © 2018 by Jess Lederman
Cover art and design by Alexander von Ness, nessgraphica.com
Interior design by Booknook.biz
Published by Azure Star, LLC
ISBN-13: 9781098511098

For my wife, Ling, devoted mother of my children,
whose goodness and love have helped me to grow
beyond what I thought possible; and for David,
Daniel, and Tim.

Special thanks to Ashley Brown, Sharon Edel, and Julia Zhu, whose comments and encouragement were invaluable during the writing of this book.

In my anguish I cried to the Lord,
and He answered by setting me free.

—Psalm 118:5

TABLE OF CONTENTS

PART ONE

THE FALLEN MAN

One
Luke and Yura: The Alaska Territory, 1925

My father deserted my mother and me when I was thirteen years old. He had become famous that winter on the Great Race of Mercy, one of the Athabascan mushers who brought diphtheria serum to Nome and saved ten thousand lives. He'd done the impossible, a blind run in the howling darkness, crossing the open ice of the Norton Sound, the temperature falling to sixty below, the sun a distant dream. He was our hero, our North Star.

And then he was gone.

He left us, of course, for a woman. A blizzard had hit him at Unalakleet, a storm so powerful that it travelled four thousand miles, till at last it reached New York and froze the Hudson River. The woman lived in just that far-away land, on the wild island of Manhattan, and her name was Kathleen Byrne. The Hearst papers had been giving the Great Race front-page headlines; Kathleen was a reporter, lean and hungry, she'd go to the ends of the earth for a good story, and one day she got her chance.

No one in my hometown of Nenana had seen anything like her, a slender redhead with emerald eyes, smoking Lucky Strikes and exhaling expertly through her nostrils, this coolly confident young woman with fiery hair.

She wanted details that would bring the story to life, so Father brought her to our home to show off his sled dogs. At least, the ones who'd survived, for three he had raised since they were pups had died on the trail. Somewhere in the madness of that journey he'd forgotten to cover their groins with rabbit skins, and they'd perished of frostbite in the unfathomable cold.

I gaped at her stupidly.

"Excuse my son," said my mother. "He has no manners."

Eighty-six years have passed since that time, but from old photographs I understand just what my father must have felt. She seemed audacious and yet fragile, and she had the sort of smile that made men who'd known her barely fifteen minutes want to say, *if you smile that way at any other man I'll lose my mind.* I'm not talking about lust, you understand; rather, a sort of greed combined with something barely distinguishable from rage.

And what did Miss Byrne want with my father? Ah, but what an outrageous trophy to bring back from the Arctic frontier! His native name was Taliriktug, strong arm, but he went by his English name, Victor. He was sinewy, powerful, and, for an Athabascan, unusually tall. His maternal grandfather had been an Orthodox priest, a Russian who came to Alaska as a missionary and proceeded to lose his faith in a strange new world. He joined some fur traders, then married a native woman, my great-grandmother. All local legend, all stories overheard when my father and his friends had been drinking, for the Russian and his wife both died years before I was born.

When Kathleen left, my father went with her. He said there'd be interviews with *The Saturday Evening Post*, and on something called radio that could send his voice into a hundred thousand homes, maybe more. He said Miss Byrne had reason to think the Lambert Pharmaceutical Company might pay him a lifetime's wages for endorsing a product called Listerine. He said he'd write letters and be back in just a few months.

But I was the only one he fooled.

⌒⌒

"When will Father return?" I asked incessantly.

"Soon," my mother said at first, and later, "When the winds that took him blow him home," and finally she answered me only with silence. I stopped asking, I never spoke of him, though a great grief lay on my heart.

I heard mutterings around the village, but no one dared to say anything against father, for my mother was fiercely loyal to him and loved him with a warrior's heart. The months passed, winter came again and turned into spring. One day, the Angakkuq paid a visit, and in the low murmuring of voices I heard my father's name. I saw Mother turn from the old man, her eyes bright with anger. The Angakkuq could commune with spirits, with the elements and animals; had one such spirit snatched away my father's soul?

At dinner that evening I found the courage to speak.

"Why doesn't he love us anymore?"

Her eyes met mine and wordlessly we shared our pain. That night, I watched as my mother packed our clothes and valuables; the last thing she packed was her ulu knife, a knife she'd received from her father, its handle of musk ox horn.

"Are you going to kill Father?" I asked her.

"Don't be stupid," she said. "I'll bring him back with us in one piece. Everything will be just as it used to be, the two of you will be off hunting caribou when the leaves turn, and of what has happened we shall never speak. But the white woman must die."

Have I told you my mother's name? It was Yura, which means beautiful. As for me, I was born Uukkarnit Noongwook, though I have lived here in the Nevada desert for lo these many years, and men have always called me Luke.

Chapter Two
David: Paris, 1914

"Do you think a loving father could ever be persuaded to slit his own son's throat?" asked David Gold, a tall, broad-shouldered young man with a boxer's chiseled physique. It was a beautiful fall morning, and he and his two companions were lingering over coffee and croissants at Les Deux Magots. "Even if God Himself commanded him?"

"What a horrid thing to bring up at breakfast, Davey!" Lucille Johnson exclaimed. She was twenty-one, plump and plain, and dressed in the latest Paris fashion. "What is he talking about, Jack?" she asked, turning to her husband.

"Abraham and Isaac. It's in the Good Book," Jack Johnson explained, patting one of Lucille's jewel-bedecked hands. He had recently defended his title as heavyweight champion of the world, prevailing, at the age of thirty-six, in a fight staged not far from the Eiffel Tower.

Everyone in the café was angling to get a look at the famous pugilist, a black man resplendent in a white linen suit, derby hat, and a silk tie that shone like sunlit daffodils. Although not as large as David, who'd been his sparring partner for the past two years, Johnson had an aura of happy confidence which overshadowed the younger man. No one cared that he was black and Lucille was white; those backwater Americans might get worked up about such things, but to the Parisians, he was a hero, the first of his race to take the title. One great white hope after another had been pitted against him, and he'd battered each into oblivion without breaking a sweat. His allure was further enhanced by reports that he was an outlaw, a fugitive from justice in the United States. He'd been sentenced to a year and a day in prison for violating the Mann Act, which, the French discovered, prohibited transporting a woman across state lines for immoral purposes.

"In America, that is a crime?" asked the Parisians, nonplussed. "How completely absurd!"

Of course, they would forget him the moment he lost.

"Did God really command the slaughter of Canaanite women and children?" David continued. "Did it warm His heart when the Psalmist prayed for Babylonian babies to have their brains dashed out against the rocks?"

"Oh, please!" said Lucille, setting down the morsel of pain au chocolat she'd been about to consume.

"Mr. Moody should've set you straight on all that, seems to me," said Johnson.

"D.L. had long since passed when I showed up," David responded.

He had spent three years studying at a college founded by the great evangelist, D.L. Moody. David had grown up on the Lower East Side of Manhattan, a wild, brawling boy with a quick and restless mind. In 1908, at the age of sixteen, he heard the booming voice of a revivalist who'd set up a tent in the Bowery and was preaching to prostitutes and Skid Row bums. He stood at the tent's edge for a long time, then finally came in and sat down, listening as the man preached a virile message of hope in the midst of ruin and despair. The words reached to the depths of the boy's soul, and he answered the altar call. David remained after all the others had left, and the preacher, intrigued by the powerful-looking youth, the emotion so evident on his face, asked if there was something he needed. "The Lord Christ Jesus," David answered. "God the Father and His Holy Spirit." A great thirst had risen up inside of him! He wanted to know—he *had* to know—more about the Word; everything there was to learn! The revivalist, impressed, promised to help, and six months later David hopped a freight train bound for Chicago, where he'd been accepted to the Moody Bible Institute.

"My teachers—well, it seems there are many *mysteries* in Scripture," said David, with a touch of bitterness. "They said I ask too many questions."

"Just might be some truth to that," said Johnson. "What you need to do, you need to emulate your betters, which of course would be me. Now, where would I be without my bass viol, can't even imagine. You ought to take up an instrument, learn something by Wolfgang Amadeus. Memorize some of Shakespeare's sonnets, relax your mind so you don't go insane. Otherwise, boy, you're going to end up like Hamlet;

you'll be agonizing over which appetizer to order while the rest of us are polishing off desert."

The champion slathered butter and jam on yet another croissant.

"But surely you see how troubling these questions are," said David. "I mean, unless I *understand* God, how can I love Him with all my heart, and soul, and strength, and mind?"

"Sometimes, my man, you need to stay focused on what's right before you," said Johnson. "Namely, my fight in Barcelona next month with Baltasar Reyes. You know, they asked me if I would stay on afterward and do a turn as a matador, did I tell you that?"

"Yes, you did," said Lucille. "Honey, the Luxembourg Gardens are ever so close, and you promised me a stroll."

"Patience, girl," said Johnson. "Now, the thing about Reyes, he's six-eight, got seven and a half inches on me. You ever fight a tall man, Dave?"

"Not *that* tall," David replied.

"Everyone knows you got to get inside on him, or that long reach'll chew you up. The question is, *how*. See, your tall fighter, he relies on his jab, uses it to keep you away. But when he pulls that arm back, you come in behind it, throw your left hook, let your body follow to get inside. Then you use his height against him, 'cause he's having a tough time blocking your body blows with those long arms. Best of all, the surest way to knock a man out is a mighty jab to the jaw, thrown from *below*. Tall man's brains bounce around and he passes out cold for the count."

David hadn't seemed to be paying much attention, but something in his mentor's last words caught his interest.

"Suppose you weren't just fighting for money," he said, "What if you were battling, bare-fisted, to the death?"

"Well, I've been there, just about," answered Johnson. "Nothing much changes, 'cept you got to understand the kill shot, know human anatomy. Attended an autopsy one time for just that reason. Some poor chump had been thrown from a car, and the coroner opened up his skull, let me have a look."

"Honestly!" Lucille protested, to no avail.

"There's something much like a celery stalk," her husband continued, "connects the brain to the spinal cord; separate 'em and you've got a dead man on your hands. Easiest way to do it is a rabbit punch, though I've heard it can be done with just the right blow between the eyes."

"Satisfied, Davey?" asked Lucille.

"Sorry," said David, blushing.

"Cheer up," said Jack Johnson. "We're going to have a good ol' time getting to Barcelona. I'm thinking, leave next week, loll a bit on the Côte d'Azur—you two can watch me win big in Monaco—then on to this dockside bistro in Marseilles which Marcel the cutman told me 'bout, makes the best bouillabaisse in all of France. Ahh! It's a stew of spider crabs and conger eels and scorpion fish, with a great slug of Pernod that's the magic touch." He smacked his lips in anticipation. "And I haven't yet told y'all *how* we're travelling, which of course will be in fine style. Day after tomorrow I am taking delivery of a Sheffield-Simplex, epitome of motoring magnificence, puts Rolls Royce to shame. Same model the Russian Grand Duchess Anastasia purchased just a few months ago, with the driver's seat fitted precisely to the dimensions of my derriere. Behave yourself, Dave, I'll let you have a turn at the wheel."

The champion leaned back in his chair with a broad grin, confident that his sparring partner would perk up at the prospect of embarking on such an exhilarating adventure.

An awkward silence ensued.

"I can't go with you to Barcelona," David said at last, sitting up straight and looking his mentor in the eye. "I've made up my mind to enlist in the French army. I'm a fighter, Jack; I just want to take on the biggest bad guy in town."

"You want to punch Kaiser Wilhelm in the nose," Jack Johnson said dryly. "Okay. Foreign Legion, though, ain't that a five-year stint?"

"They've opened up the regular army to all comers, now that the war's on," David replied.

"You're really leaving us?" asked Lucille.

"Your daddy should've taught you to finish what you start, Dave; you seem to have a problem with that," said Johnson.

That stung. David had dropped out of the Moody Bible Institute early in his senior year. He'd been in a state of pure euphoria as a freshman, soaking up the lectures and reading in the library until they turned off the lights. But questions began to haunt him; he'd find himself awake in the small hours, thinking things through. At the revival tent, he'd been inspired by the forcefulness of the message, by the power of the Cross. "Put on the full armor of God," the evangelist had thundered, and it had thrilled him to the core. To stand firm against the powers of darkness, with the apostle Paul himself urging him to run the race and press on! But it wasn't clear how all the pieces fit together and applied to real life. When the Kaiser's armies stormed across the border, were the French supposed to turn the other cheek? Most troubling of all, what was the meaning of the message Paul had received from the Lord, "my strength is made perfect in weakness?" Just how did that work?

He who had knit him in his mother's womb had made David a powerful man, a natural fighter. Was he to turn away from that, forsake what he did best? During his second year, he started visiting Chicago's boxing clubs, just to watch the men spar; it wasn't long before a trainer, impressed with the youth's powerful physique, asked him if he wanted to put on a pair of gloves and step into the ring. He began working out at the club every night, and at first the crowd snickered when word spread that he was studying at a Bible college. They didn't laugh for long.

By the end of his third year, David had won six of eight bouts, four by KO. That was when Jack Johnson heard about the big college kid who moved with grace, knew how to cut off the ring, and had a mean left hook. Johnson was tired of hanging out with palookas who couldn't tell a bass viol from a raw side of beef, and within weeks of their first meeting, the boy from Grand Street quit school to become sparring partner to the heavyweight champion of the world.

But an emptiness had been building inside of him for the past two years.

"My father ran numbers when I was growing up, Jack," said David. "One time, maybe I was twelve, some guy tried to horn in on his ten square blocks and pops went after him with a crowbar. Oh, *he* finished what he started, all right. Doing twenty-five in Sing Sing for his trouble."

"You want to compare hard-luck stories, boy, I got you beat."

"But Jack," said Lucille. "Talk to him, and don't be mean. Davey, we don't want you getting yourself killed. I think you're just lonely, spending all your time with *this* big lunk. Can't you marry one of these pretty Paris girls, instead—have little French babies, get yourselves a shadow in the countryside and settle down?"

"She means *château*," Johnson explained. "We toured the Loire Valley last week and visited Chenonceau castle. I'd have bought it, but it wasn't for sale."

"I appreciate your concern, Lucille," said David. "But I can't bring someone else into my life when I'm still trying to figure out my own."

"What is it exactly you need answers to?" asked Jack Johnson, not unkindly.

David leaned back in his chair and thought for a minute or two.

"Can I love God, not as I want Him to be, but as He is; and what is His will—what does He want of me?"

"Ah. Well," said the champion, and he downed the last of his café au lait. "Good luck with *that*."

Chapter Three
Joan and Tim: New York, 2011

The lovers lying beneath the sheets of a midtown Manhattan hotel bed were talking about God.

"You were lucky," said the man, whose name was Tim Faber, "that you lost your faith when you were still young."

He was in his early forties, an executive producer and one-time *enfant terrible* for a cable network devoted to all things scientific, a man with the dawning awareness that he was slip-sliding into middle age. Just the other day, Tim had found himself squinting at the small print that listed the ingredients on a cereal box at Whole Foods. He was sure people were noticing what a long time he'd been peering at that stupid box, and to cover his embarrassment made things worse by loudly declaiming, "Organic, my ass!" And what had he done to deserve the spite of that salon stylist who had held up a mirror behind his head, forcing him to gaze upon the ever-encroaching bald spot in the middle of his curly black hair?

Tim was divorced, a man who'd never had a problem attracting women and had been single for nearly ten years. He was sometimes haunted by the memory of his former wife; he could barely recollect the woman for whom he'd abandoned her. Why had he left? But thinking about that only depressed him, so he turned his mind to another matter: how much longer did he have to make his mark on the world?

"You never had faith," responded Tim's lover, "so what do you know about its loss? When I was small, kneeling in prayer at bedside with my father—before I lost *him*—those were perfect moments. That was bliss."

Her name was Joan Reed, and she worked for Tim as the producer of their network's hit series, *Mysteries of Modern Science*. She was a decade his senior, but wore her years well, a woman with short blond hair and blue-gray eyes that, when the light caught them, flashed violet. There was a beautiful sadness about the wrinkles at the corners of her eyes, and a few extra pounds had given her curves absent from her youth. Joan's husband had divorced her just over a year before, leaving for a younger woman, and she found herself wondering what she was doing in bed with the man she worked for, something she never could have imagined years ago.

"You once believed in Santa Claus," Tim said. "You don't miss *him*, do you?"

"Now you're just being asinine."

"Oh, come on." Tim could feel her body tensing, but this was too important a topic to compromise merely for the sake of romance. "You say I never had faith—but I have faith, faith that man can create a moral, meaningful world *despite* the yawning emptiness of heaven. We exist in an indifferent universe, knowing the human race will one day cease to exist, yet still invent the ideas of morality and beauty and honor while staring into the abyss! Now *that's* heroic. Compared to it, Christianity, taking orders from Big Daddy, is pale stuff. And the same goes for every other notion of the divine."

"So you think mankind is making moral progress?" Joan was looking at Tim's profile—he was a handsome man, there was no getting around that!—but when he became excited about something, Tim looked everywhere *except* his companion's eyes.

"Well of course. The slavery and polygamy so eagerly embraced by the writers of the Bible are now anathema to all but the most degraded souls on the planet."

"Still," said Joan, "I think six million Jews might question your hypothesis. Not to mention the mountain of corpses under Stalin, Mao, Pol Pot and other atheist worthies."

"Well, the trend line is jagged, I admit." Tim gave his lover a rueful glance. "But that only makes the struggle more impressive. Look, this is why the work we're doing is so important. If the common man doesn't understand science, then the technocrats will rule; people will make decisions based on emotion, superstition, and stupid misconceptions. They'll be ripe for manipulation. The pace of change is shifting into hyperdrive, Joanie, and people are being left in the dust: nanobiotechnology, evolutionary algorithms; how can people come to terms with the ethics of artificial intelligence, of moral outsourcing to military drones and to medical software that can make better and faster decisions than the smartest human minds—"

"You're in favor of robots that decide who lives and who dies?"

"*Robots* didn't commit the My Lai Massacre or slaughter the Lakota at Wounded Knee. How many of man's moral decisions are in fact made out of stress, exhaustion, rage, or simply because someone's eaten a bad bit of beef? Your question only proves my point!" Tim sat up, agitated and intense. "I need you focused on fleshing out my idea for a series on why God is *not* the answer—to mysteries or anything else. The fact that nature is mysterious is what gave rise to religion in the first place. But we no longer need a thunder god to explain thunder, do we? This is why I'm not so excited about your ninety-nine-year-old Eskimo."

"It's not about him and you know it. This is a story about one of the greatest advances in human thought in all of history—and yet most people know nothing about it. A young man challenges Einstein, sets him straight, and utterly changes how we understand the universe! He proves that there was a day when yesterday didn't exist! You just can't stand the fact that he was a priest. And then that narcissistic jerk, Hubble, gets all the credit and has the space telescope named after him. Oh, we're doing this story, sweetheart."

"I grant you the tale's not entirely without interest," said Tim. "But it just bugs the crap out of me how the God crowd plays it. Pope Pius the twelfth, a veritable Nazi tool, went into a perfect ecstasy over your priest's ideas, and announced that science had proven Genesis true! *Fiat lux!* It makes me want to puke."

"That had nothing to do with my story's hero, Tim! For him, religion and science were two entirely separate paths to truth. I'm doing the story, period, case closed, and it is going to blow people's minds. The man I've tracked down—Professor Noongwook—may have unique knowledge; but he's old, ill, and there's no time to waste." Joan's eyes narrowed as she gave her lover a baleful look. "You're going to support me on this."

The two looked at each other in silence.

"So—" Tim said at last, allowing himself a smile, "it seems we're chasing down an aging Eskimo who lives in Las Vegas. And what makes you think you'll learn anything that we can use from this gentleman?"

"Aside from his having been a professor of astrophysics at Caltech? You're just going to have to trust me on that. But even if I learn nothing, it'll still be the best show we've ever done."

"Well, fine, who am I to get in the way of our next Emmy. Or argue with an expert in the martial arts." Tim lay back down into the softness of the hotel bed, hands behind his head. "I'll have Elise book tickets for both of us, then, it's been forever since I've been to Vegas. Let's stay somewhere decadent, none of those family-friendly joints, what do you say?"

But when Tim turned to Joan, he saw she was averting her eyes.

"What?" he asked her. "You don't want me along?"

"It's not that," she said, meeting his gaze. "I just have some personal business to take care of when I'm there, that's all."

"More mysteries, how intriguing. Well don't worry, I'll figure out some way to entertain myself while you're taking care of whatever. And I won't even pry. Honest."

"It's nearly two-thirty," said Joan, "and there's a staff meeting at three. You go back first, I'll just be a few minutes late."

Tim Faber, executive producer *extraordinaire*, sighed and stretched and reluctantly rolled out of bed to get dressed. He'd likely work till late into the night; what did it matter if he took the occasional three-hour lunch?

After her lover had gone, Joan sat for a while with her head in her hands, then rummaged through her purse for a pack of Camels and lit up. What a wonderful feeling, she thought, holding fire in one's hand. The ninnies could whine and wag their fingers about cancer all they liked, but Ayn Rand had understood; the spot of fire alive in the mind, mirrored by the burning point of a cigarette. Still, it troubled her, not being in charge, being addicted to nicotine.

And what was she doing in that hotel room?

I wasn't going to sleep with him again, she thought. She'd always despised women who slept with their bosses. What a cliché! But there she was. Joan walked to the shower, then turned the water as hot as she could stand it, leaned her head against the tiled wall and let the water cascade over her while steam filled the air. On a whim, she'd recently taken up Krav Maga, the Israeli self-defense system, and her arms and shoulders were sore from the previous day's workout. Would sure be a lot easier to just carry around pepper spray, she thought, and then tried to banish thought in favor of wordless meditation. But all the while, a Bible verse from long ago kept running through her mind: *I do not understand my own actions. For I do not do what I want, but I do the very thing I hate.*

Paul, she thought. Now there was a man who understood her through and through!

Chapter Four
The Physicist Priest

The young man at the center of Joan's story was Georges Lemaitre, a Belgian who, fresh from the battlefields of World War One, became both a physicist and a Roman Catholic priest. He was fascinated with understanding how the equations that Albert Einstein had recently set forth in his general theory of relativity could be used to understand the universe. Ever since the time of the ancient Greeks, Western philosophers and scientists had believed in an unchanging cosmos that had always been and would always be. Aristotle wrote of the perfection of crystal spheres, one nestled within the next, and Newton saw the heavens as an infinite and eternal expanse of comets, planets, and stars. Even Einstein, who had astounded the world with his radical ideas—parallel lines meeting on the curved surface of spacetime!—had a deep affinity for the idea of a universe without beginning or end, and even modified one of his most famous equations so that it described the world in just that way.

But Georges Lemaitre was coming to a very different conclusion. The more he studied them, the more Einstein's equations told him that the universe was changing, evolving—from what, at first he wasn't sure. Eager to see if astronomers were finding any evidence to support what his calculations implied, Lemaitre traveled to England and America and found bits and pieces of tantalizing evidence that other galaxies were speeding away from our own. That was exactly what he expected; for, by 1927, the thirty-three year-old Lemaitre was the only man in the world who knew the truth: the reason those galaxies appeared to be moving away was that *spacetime itself was expanding*.

The universe was growing larger by millions of miles per day!

Lemaitre published his revolutionary findings that year, turning twenty-five hundred years of Western thought upside down. His paper, however, appearing only in an obscure Belgian journal, caused not even a ripple. The young priest met his idol, Albert Einstein, in Brussels that fall, but their meeting was to no avail. "Your calculations—they're all correct," Einstein told him. "But your physics—achh! Abominable!" Theories should be beautiful, the great man insisted, and the thought of an expanding universe was grotesque! No matter; Georges Lemaitre was unfazed.

Meanwhile, fifty-five hundred miles away, atop a peak in the San Gabriel mountains near Pasadena, California, two astronomers were meticulously documenting the rate at which other galaxies—or nebulae, as they called them—appeared to be fleeing from Earth. They were Edwin Hubble, an Oxford-educated American with pretentious British mannerisms and a monstrous ego, and his assistant, Milt, an eighth-grade dropout and former mule skinner and janitor who did much of the actual work using Mt. Wilson's 100-inch telescope. In 1929, only months before an epic stock-market crash would usher in the Great Depression, Hubble published his findings, which decisively validated Lemaître's theory.

But his paper contained no mention of the Belgian priest. Nor did Hubble put forth any ideas of his own about *why* the nebulae were receding before his eyes. Lemaître had already shown that the expansion of the universe was a consequence of Einstein's equations. But no one knew!

At least not until 1930, when Lemaître's mentor, Sir Arthur Eddington, a brilliant physicist and a Quaker whose pacifism had nearly landed him in jail during the war, found himself and the rest of the physics world perplexed at how to reconcile Hubble's findings with Einstein's theories. When his former protégé, hearing of his confusion, explained that he had already solved the problem three years before, Sir Arthur was both mortified—Lemaître's paper had been languishing at the bottom of a towering stack on his desk—and electrified. The world must know! An English translation should be prepared forthwith!

In 1931, as Depression deepened in America and construction began on a colossal dam where the Colorado River cut through the desert of Nevada, the English translation of Lemaître's paper finally appeared. Two years later, Einstein traveled to Pasadena and announced he'd been mistaken; the Belgian priest had been right all along!

But there was something mysterious about that English translation, something Joan felt a keen desire to understand: the paragraph containing what had come to be known as Hubble's Law—that the more distant a galaxy, the faster it appears to be fleeing from us—and the rate at which the universe was expanding, which became known as the Hubble Constant—was missing! The evidence that Lemaître had been the first to establish that the universe was expanding—surely one of the most momentous scientific breakthroughs in all of history!—*had been erased.*

But by whom? And why?

If his 1927 paper had been Lemaître's only contribution to science, Joan thought it would still be shameful that he was unknown compared to Hubble. But the young Belgian had only just begun. In the early 1930s, he concluded that all the matter in the cosmos must once have been compacted into something he called "the primeval atom," which then began to disintegrate. Joan was struck by one of his quotes, describing what came next:

"The evolution of the world can be compared to a display of fireworks that has just ended: some few red wisps, ashes, and smoke. Standing on a cooled cinder, we see the slow fading of the suns, and we try to recall the vanished brilliance of the origin of the worlds."

Lemaître was the father of what came to be called the "Big Bang." He had laid out a convincing scientific argument that there was, in fact, a beginning of time itself. A day without a yesterday! A moment when the universe, as we know it, began to take shape!

But wait a minute, thought many a skeptical mind: isn't it just a bit much that this outlandish theory, which smacked of the Biblical story of Creation, was the invention of a priest? It made atheists like astronomer Fred Hoyle gnash their teeth! But the priest, who in fact never mixed his science with his faith, would be proven correct.

And hardly anyone outside of the astrophysics community had even heard his name! This, thought Joan, was positively a crime. Who was responsible for Lemaître's anonymity? Hubble had always been hungry for glory; over the years, some scientists whispered that he or one of his minions had been the culprit responsible for the missing language in that English translation, ensuring that the credit for the discovery of the expanding universe would go to him alone. Well, if there was a way to prove that, Joan was going to find it.

There was something more she'd learned while tracking down even the most obscure references to the physicist-priest, though it was sufficiently bizarre that Joan had decided not to say anything to Tim until she uncovered more facts. Not quite everything can be found on the internet, and, while searching through records on microfiche at the New York Public Library, she'd come across an item that caused her heart to skip a beat. In 1933, a Sheriff Stone of the Las Vegas police department had contacted the FBI office in San Francisco to report his "suspicion based on thirty-two years in law enforcement" that underworld figures had a hit out on two scientists: Milton Humason and a Belgian citizen by the name of Georges Lemaître. If she could back that up and find the reason for it, she'd have both the sizzle *and* the steak! An Emmy would be hers for the taking.

Joan knew that Professor Luke Noongwook had met Lemaître in Las Vegas when he was a young man. Might he hold the key to both mysteries?

She could only hope.

Chapter Five
Seattle, 1926

"That your sister you're travelling with?" asked a man old enough to be my grandfather.

My mother and I had travelled nearly a thousand miles from Nenana to the Panhandle of Alaska, and in Skagway we'd boarded the S.S. Yukon, a steamer bound for Seattle. It would be two days before we reached port.

"She's a pretty one," he continued. "I was twenty years younger or ten thousand richer, I'd ask her to marry me." His hair and beard were long, and his clothes were ragged with age.

"You are talking about my mother, mister," said I. "We're on our way to meet my father in Seattle. I expect he'll be there to greet us when we arrive."

"Oh, well, no offense meant, boy. Name's Slade, Sourdough Slade."

"Uukkarnit Noongwook," I responded.

"That's a mouthful." Sourdough stroked his beard. "How 'bout I call ya Luke?"

That seemed reasonable to me, so we shook hands.

"Had me an Eskimo bride once," he went on, "fine gal, loved her dearly. Lost her in a poker game to none other than Skookum Jim, hope he's treatin' her decent, though I rather doubt it." He looked me over. "You seem a good sort. I like your people, I do; y'all just need some good ol' American gumption 'n grit. Untold riches in your land and you'd never 'a known it, we Yankees hadn't shown up."

That baffled me. "Do you think we know nothing of the caribou," I asked, "of the beaver and bald eagle, the brown bear that feasts on berries and grows fat on the salmon who come home from the sea?"

He seemed similarly nonplussed by my response.

"Gold, young Luke, I'm talking *gold*. Nuggets as big as my thumb!" Sourdough showed me an impressively large digit. "Imagine you got bags 'a gold dust, so much you pour it out on the bar counter like it was sand and call out, *Hey, boys! Whiskey, champagne, and brandy for every man jack 'a ya! Drink your fill, drink 'til ya don't know if you're drinkin' or dreamin', it's on me tonight!'"*

"Are you rich, then?" I asked him. "You don't appear so, but the Angakkuq says things are not always what they seem."

"Hmm? Oh, your medicine man. Well, bully for him! Luke, you could say of late I've had me a run of bad luck. But oh, my boy, back in '97 and '98! Pannin' placer gold in Bonanza Creek, then raftin' the Yukon to Dawson City, so flush I stayed in the Fairview for six months when she first opened her doors—and un'erstand, you couldn't find a finer hotel in all 'a Gay Paree, no sir. Slept in a brass bed, dined on bone china under cut-glass crystal chandeliers. Drank myself silly when they tol' me the money'd run out, woke up stone sober one morning to find they'd laid me outside in the mud, buck naked, and damned if there wasn't a Malamute lickin' my nose."

Sourdough smiled, revealing a sorry set of chompers but for one glorious gold front tooth.

"So what'ya say, son, think my hopes 'n dreams are blown to smithereens? Hell no. I'm makin' what you might call a *strategic retreat*; gettin' my grubstake together 'fore I head back north." He put his big right hand on my shoulder and looked at me intently. "See, nothin's more important in life than havin' a dream, somethin' you want more than anything else in the world."

I thought that over for a bit.

"But what is it you want, Mr. Slade? To sleep again in the brass bed? It must have been more comfortable than I can imagine."

"No, son, you're not hearin' me. I ain't hardly happy 'less I'm hip deep in some feeder creek off the Yukon. It's the nugget you ain't got yet, the one that's out there whisperin' your name—findin' *that* one, that's the dream."

"But what would you do if you found it? Would there be something else you wanted more than anything in the world?"

Sourdough shook his head. "Maybe you're just too young ta un'erstand. But how about *you*, boy, got somethin' ya want with all your little heart?"

"Oh yes!" I said, without pause. "To find my father, and know he loves me."

Why hadn't I said, "and Mother, too?" It was the first time that I had become aware of my own selfishness, and my face flushed with shame.

"Thought you said—" Sourdough checked himself, then ruffled my hair. "I had a daddy, once upon a time, or so my momma tells me. Never did meet the man."

"I'm sorry, Mr. Slade," I said, and my eyes filled with tears, but words escaped me. It was nearly six o'clock in the evening, so I thanked Sourdough for sharing his story and went to find my mother in the dining room.

⌒

Things started to go wrong the moment we arrived in Seattle. Two men who did business with friends of my father were supposed to meet us, make sure we were well supplied, and send us safely on our way to New York. Instead, a sad-looking youth, not much older than me, was waiting for us with a message: the men were very sorry, but their plans had suddenly changed, they'd left for San Francisco earlier that morning. We were to go to the Takhoma Trading Post, where a Chinook named Ray would pay a fair price for the sculptures and masks that my mother had brought with us. At least that was something to cling to, for money was an urgent matter; we had sold father's sled dogs to raise the cash for our voyage, and there wasn't much left.

The young man handed us a scrap of paper with the Trading Post address, then vanished into the crowd.

The two of us must have looked a sight, dressed for life in Central Alaska, with large packs strapped to our backs and battered suitcases in our hands. It took a while to find anyone who would give us directions, but at last we spotted one of the deckhands from the S.S. Yukon who was just starting his shore leave. Our destination was in Alki, eight miles away. I studied the map he unfolded and then closed my eyes, visualizing the route. We would walk; we'd trekked longer trails in the featureless tundra back home.

~⌐

By the time we reached Alki, night had fallen and the Trading Post had closed. We could hear the faint sounds of music and laughter, so we followed them to their source, a ramshackle establishment that billed itself as McSorley's Roadhouse and Inn. Famished, we pushed open the saloon-style front doors and went inside.

It was a popular place. I was startled by the sight of something I'd never seen before: a player piano, banging out *Yes Sir, That's My Baby.* We pushed our way through the raucous crowd and found a small table near the kitchen, where my mother counted out the last of our cash, two dollars and eighty-three cents, just enough for us to order two baked-chicken dinners and pie for dessert, pay for the night's lodging, and have breakfast in the morning. Beyond that, we were counting on Chinook Ray.

We were still waiting for the pie to arrive when trouble showed up instead. Two men who'd been eying my mother ever since we'd sat down pushed back their chairs and sauntered over, one large, dark, and glowering, the second slender, with a pencil mustache and an evil grin.

"Say, honey, you look a long way from home," said the smaller man. "Me and my buddy reckon you could use some company. I'm Billy Goat Gibson—" he held out his hand—"and this here is Gil. Never has tol' me his last name, ma'am, I'm beginnin' to think Gilbert don't have one. But it is a comfort indeed, havin' him around."

My mother raised her head just enough to look Billy Goat in the eye, but didn't say a word. His hand hung in the air for a few moments before he let it drop to his side.

"Well that ain't real friendly, sister," said he. "You bein' alone, and me and Gil offerin' our comp'ny and protection and all."

"My mother is not alone, mister," I said. "You better go if you know what's good for you."

Billy Goat laughed; I was a skinny fourteen-year-old, barely five feet tall. From out of the corner of my eye I could see my mother's hand slipping into the bag by her side, where she kept her ulu knife.

"Oh, I got a pretty good handle on what's good for me, sonny boy. Now, 'bout your pretty momma not bein' alone, let's remedy the situation." He reached into his pocket and pulled out a Mercury dime. "Why don't you take this and buy yourself a big ol' egg cream at the soda fountain 'cross the room?"

Billy Goat put his hand on my shoulder to encourage me to move.

"Don't touch my son," said my mother, and her voice wasn't especially loud, but suddenly the hubbub of voices in the roadhouse was stilled. A moment later I realized it wasn't because of her words; a short, wiry woman carrying a shotgun had come up behind Billy and Gil. Her gray hair was pulled back in a tight bun, and her eyes looked huge behind thick glasses.

"Oh, you sons of Satan," said she. "Defilers of my temple! You dare to have designs on a sojourner who comes to my door?"

"Now watch where you point that thing, Miss McSorley," said Billy Goat. "We're payin' customers, just having a chat with this fine young lady. And you surely don't want to get Gil here riled up."

With a sudden move that was faster than my eyes could take in, Miss McSorley slammed the shotgun's butt into the side of Gil's head, and the big man collapsed on the floor in a spreading pool of blood.

"Aw, what did you have to go and do that for," Billy Goat said softly. "Now there's blood all over my brand-new shoes."

The only sound in the room was the player piano thumping out *Sweet Georgia Brown,* until someone kicked it hard enough that it, too, fell silent. A moment later Billy Goat had a switchblade in his hand and in the moment after that the barrel of the shotgun was in his mouth and Miss McSorley was using it to shove him up against the wall. His eyes were wide and his face was white and there were pieces of his front teeth on the floor.

"If I see you again, I *will* send your soul to the flames of hell," said the proprietress of McSorley's Roadhouse and Inn. "Now take your friend and go."

With a rough jerk, she removed the shotgun from Billy Goat's mouth and he sank to his knees with a moan.

Seattle, 1926

"Hugo!" called out Miss McSorley, and a swarthy man with a gleaming shaved head stepped out of the shadows. "Kindly expedite their exit and expunge any sign that these devils were ever here."

Hugo gave Billy Goat the bum's rush and then hauled Gil outside—alive or dead, we couldn't tell.

"I smelled sulphur when they walked in the door," said Miss McSorley, addressing us for the first time. "Our Lord cast such demons into swine; for me, cruder measures suffice."

We had no knowledge of the Christian Bible, but understood well enough what she meant.

"My son and I are capable of defending ourselves," said my mother. "But thank you, nonetheless."

Hugo arrived with a bucket and mop for the gore, and we followed Miss McSorley to a storage room that doubled as her office.

⁓

"You'll stay here as long as you like, and I won't take a penny for your lodging," said the warrior woman, as I had come to think of her, after hearing our story. "How I wish I could go with you—what a lovely avenging angel you will be!"

Hugo had brought in pie and hot coffee, and my spirits were starting to rise.

"We do not need charity," Mother replied, "though I appreciate your kindness. Once my business is done with the Chinook, we will stay only until it is time to leave for New York, perhaps just one more night." Her eyes shifted to a metal safe behind Miss McSorley. "I hope to receive a good sum of money tomorrow—may I leave it with you while we are here?"

"Of course," said the proprietress. "That would be wise." She seemed lost in thought for a moment, and then added, "I want you to wear this, Yura dear," removing a small silver cross from around her neck.

"I cannot take your amulet," said Mother.

"Guard yourself, darling woman," Miss McSorley insisted. "Trust no one; the human heart is deceitful above all things, and desperately

26

wicked. There is danger on every side."

Her huge eyes peered into a dark corner of the room in a way which sent a sudden shiver down my spine. After a moment, my mother accepted the necklace, though I knew she only put it on to avoid showing disrespect.

Miss McSorley's face suddenly brightened. "Hugo and I engage in Bible study every evening at this time. So refreshing for the soul. Can I tempt you to join us?"

"Thank you," said Mother, "but we are terribly tired and must sleep."

"Of course! How thoughtless of me." Our benefactress called Hugo, who helped carry our luggage to a small but pleasant room that turned out to be just down the hall from the suite Miss McSorley called home.

Sometime after we had turned out the lights, I slipped out of bed and walked down the hallway to a bathroom shared by the guests. The door to the warrior woman's room was open, and I could see her standing at a dining table with a large Bible open before her, lecturing Hugo, who gazed at his employer, slack-jawed. After finishing my business, I stepped outside to breathe in the night air and think about the events of the long day. On my way back, I sneaked another glance; the Bible study was still going on, though Hugo's chin had sunk to his chest and Miss McSorley's voice could barely be heard above his snores.

Early the next morning we hauled the largest of our suitcases to the Takhoma Trading Post and met Ray, the Chinook. His wife, we learned, was one of our people and had been raised in the shadow of Denali, the great mountain, not far south of our village. Ray heard of most of the comings and goings between Alaska and the States and knew that father and Miss Byrne had passed through Seattle the previous year. He had been awaiting our arrival.

My mother began unpacking the contents of her suitcase onto a large table Ray had cleared for this purpose. First came her sculptures, many carved from walrus ivory, some from the antlers of caribou, others fashioned from soapstone or serpentine, black streaked with olive, and yellow with flecks of gray. He watched in silence, arms folded across his chest.

On the tabletop was an assembly of the Inuit gods in all their wondrousness, vainglory, cruelty, and lust. Tatqim, moon god, master of the hunt, ever in incestuous pursuit of his sister, Seqinek, goddess of the sun. Sedna, the sea goddess, who spurned every proposal of marriage, choosing instead to copulate with dogs—hence the origin of the white race. And Sila, breath of the world, god of wind and weather, of story and song; mother showed him whittling a walrus tusk, the shavings falling as snow. The sculptures, finished with a coat of hot beeswax, were luminous, as though lit by the first rays of dawn.

Then came masks like those my mother had created for the Angakkuq when he danced near bonfires that burned through the long darkness of the winter night. They were made of driftwood, animal skins, and feathers, and colored with red ochre. These dancing masks were revelations of the spirit world and showed the faces of bears and eagles and strange men whose mouths were frozen in teeth-baring grins.

Ray squatted by the table and looked for a long time at each of the gods, picked up some with a handkerchief and turned them this way and that, then peered through the eyeholes of one of the masks.

"Where did you get these?" he asked.

"I made them with my own hands," Mother replied.

"It is unusual for a woman to do such work."

"My father, who learned from his father, taught me to carve and to sew masks. I was my parents' only child; he raised me like a son."

Ray lit a cigarette and was silent for a while.

"These are not figurines to sell for a song," he said. "They are for rich men who delight in rare beauty, collectors who have heard tales of the art that comes from the top of the world but have never seen it with their own eyes. Such men will pay a great deal, but I need time to seek them out."

"How long?" Mother asked.

"Months, if you want what they are worth. Perhaps many months."

"Impossible. I cannot wait that long."

The Chinook stubbed out his cigarette and took his time lighting another. The smoke he exhaled drifted among the gods and masks like fog.

"I understand," he said at last. "There is money in Seattle; the Frye family and some others might take the best of your work, for the right price. Perhaps I can quickly get enough for your transportation to New York."

"I would be grateful to you," Mother replied. They agreed on his commission, shook hands, and we left the Trading Post. Whether the decision was foolish or wise, there was no choice but to trust Chinook Ray.

~

So we waited, living in limbo in a strange land. Mother wanted us to stay to ourselves, but I couldn't bear being cooped up. Every chance I got, I watched the people who came in and out of the Roadhouse: women with hip flasks in their stockings, lawyers and loggers who ogled newspaper pages filled with stock market prices in tiny print.

Ray showed up with our share of the proceeds from his sales several times over the next few days. He'd created a list of the statues and masks and crossed out each as it sold: Kinak, god of the north winds, along with an eagle mask, twenty-five dollars; Tornarssuk, polar bear god, fifteen dollars more. We gave the money to Miss McSorley, who stored it in her office safe while Mother watched and Hugo stood guard.

The dayshift waitress taught me the words to *Hard-Hearted Hannah* so I could sing along with the player piano, but I did that only when my mother was in our room, taking a nap.

Leather is tough, but Hannah's heart is tougher,
She's a gal who loves to see men suffer!
To tease 'em, and thrill 'em, to torture and kill 'em,
Is her delight, they say,
I saw her at the seashore with a great big pan,
There was Hannah pouring water on a drowning man!

Was that what had happened to my father? Was Miss Byrne like that, like the Vamp of Savannah? At night I dreamed of father, struggling to come to the surface of the sea, but to no avail, for Sedna held him in an iron grip. Hard-hearted Sedna, who chose to spawn with dogs instead of men.

～

Ray sold almost everything within two weeks. I was good with numbers, so mother had me do the sums: there was enough to travel by train to New York and bring Father back to Alaska, even if he hadn't a dime.

Our bags were packed; we had only to go to Miss McSorley's office to collect our money, then take Ray up on his offer to drive us to King Street Station. He was grateful for the money he'd made.

The office door was ajar.

"Miss McSorley?" she called, but there was no answer.

She stepped into the empty room.

My mother stifled a cry, and I followed her gaze. The door to the safe was open, and even from a distance we could see there was nothing inside.

"Come," Mother said, regaining her composure, "stay by me."

But when we turned, there was Hugo, framed in the doorway, his eyes red and his dark face streaked with tears.

"What has happened?" asked Mother. I knew that her right hand was grasping the ulu knife, unseen.

Hugo turned and headed down the hallway. We followed him to Miss McSorley's room.

Inside it was dark and smelled of sweat and strange sweet spices. Hugo sank to his knees by a large sofa where the warrior woman lay covered with blankets. Her hair, which I had only ever seen tied into a neat bun, had been let down and was long and wild; years later, when I first read of Medusa, this image of Miss McSorley came into my mind. She seemed lost in a deep, troubled sleep, and her breath came in weak gasps.

"My mistress!" Hugo moaned. "By Satan once more ensnared!" He turned to us with a pitifully hopeless look. "Laudanum. Morphia. And worse, far worse…"

"The money," said my mother. "Where did she put it?"

"All gone," said Hugo. "When the thirst for the demon elixir comes upon her, she empties the till, pawns her weapons, spends every cent."

"This cannot be," Mother insisted. "Impossible. I am going to search these rooms."

Hugo shrugged. "She won't stop you."

My mother began opening drawers, going through the kitchen cabinets, looking under every book and box, anywhere cash might have been hidden. I stayed by Hugo's side, staring at Miss McSorley's ghostly white face.

"Will she be all right?" I asked him. "Should a doctor be called?"

"No doctors," he said sharply, "or we will all be in great trouble. I have seen her like this too often," he added, his voice softening, "though this time is the worst. But I think she will live."

My mother returned and felt under the blankets to see if Miss McSorley had kept any of the money on her person. It was her right; what else could she do? Yet I felt ashamed.

"You," she said to Hugo. "For all I know, you are a thief as well."

He looked at my mother with his sad, dark eyes.

"If you wish me to empty my pockets, I will do so. Here—" he offered her a key. "You may search my quarters if it would ease your mind."

Mother's shoulders slumped, and her energy seemed to drain away.

"Come," she said to me.

I followed her back to our room.

Night had fallen, but she did not bother to turn the light on, only sat at a small table by the window with her head in her hands. Suddenly, my mother remembered the necklace with the silver cross that she'd been wearing, tore it off, and threw it across the room.

"The white man's god," she cried, "—it is only Raven, who has had his way with us again!" Among our people, Raven is a powerful, magical bird, a trickster, a shape-shifter, who thinks nothing of ruining lives to satisfy his gluttony and lust. "Oh Taliriktug, my husband, you who swore to share my joys and sorrows, to warm me with your body until your dying breath, why have you forsaken us?"

I threw my arms around my mother's neck, which grew wet with my tears.

"Please don't be sad, Mother," I whispered to her. "I will never leave you."

But she was inconsolable.

"There should be someone to look out for us, Uukkarnit," she cried, in the most desolate voice I had ever heard. "But there is no one! No one!"

Chapter Six
Flanders Fields, 1915

"If you could have anything at all for dinner," said David Gold to the Belgian soldier he'd stopped to rescue, hoping to distract his companion's mind from the pain in his leg, "what would it be? Because I'm famished." At least that was what he attempted to say using the broken French he'd absorbed over the past six months.

His regiment had recently reached the killing fields of Flanders, near Ypres, a beautiful Medieval city that was rapidly being reduced to rubble. Their orders were to reinforce the French troops fighting alongside the small Belgian army to stop the German advance. An order had come to fall back to defensive positions on higher ground two hundred yards to the rear, for there were fears that the *Bosches* were going to once again unleash the monstrous new weapon, deadly chlorine gas, which they'd used against the Allies two days before. David, noticing that the young, bespectacled Belgian was injured, had hopped into the soldier's trench, intending to carry him to safety. But now they were pinned down by machine-gun fire from a gun emplacement that had just been set up in a stand of willow trees only a few hundred yards away. They were done for if the Germans advanced; still, there seemed no choice but to wait for nightfall before making a move.

"If we are going to speak of such intimate matters," said the Belgian, "then introductions are in order. I am Georges."

"David," said the American, relieved that the other had replied in fluent, though heavily accented English.

"You wear the French uniform," said Lemaître, "but I think perhaps you are Canadian?" Both the British and Canadian armies were fighting immediately to the south.

"You're not too far off—I'm from Grand Street in New York City, we're known for acting impulsively. I was in Paris when war broke out, and volunteered; a friend of mine says it was because I want to punch Kaiser Wilhelm in the nose."

"I should like to see that," said Lemaître, laughing as he thought to himself that this David looked rather more like Goliath. "But to answer your question, that is very simple. My mother's carbonade flamande, it's a stew of beef and onions, like the French boeuf bourguignon, only made with good Belgian beer instead of wine, which tells you quite a bit about the difference between Belgium and France. But I am now finding myself torn, for there was really nothing better, when we sat down to dinner, than to feast on moules-frites; which is to say, mussels steamed with onions and celery and served with what you call 'French' fries, though in fact they were invented by the Belgians." Lemaître's nostrils flared, as though if he breathed in deeply enough he would be able to smell his mother's cooking. "And what would you have, mon ami? What do they eat on your Grand Street in New York City?"

"Never mind the cuisine of Grand Street, I'd give about anything to have again the meal I had not long after I enlisted. To amuse themselves, the French put me in with a Moroccan detachment of the 45th—they don't think much of them, or the Algerians, either, though it was all the same to me—and I became good friends with one of the men, Karim. On our one day of leave, he and I went to his cousin's restaurant just outside of Paris. I ate the food of the gods, Georges; lamb in saffron rice with turnips, eggplant, carrots, prunes, apricots, and pickled lemons, washed down with sweet mint tea." David smiled ruefully. "All night we talked, as Muslim and Christian, of reconciling man's free will with the sovereignty of God, though I'm sure both of us made a muddle of it. But Karim might well have the answers now; he was killed during our first engagement, at the Aisne."

"My sympathies," said Lemaître. "I fear to count the friends I have lost since the war began. But I must tell you, it seems we have something more in common than our fight against *les Allemands*. You have an interest in theology; I shall become a priest. I am studying Thomist philosophy—and engineering too, for my family has been in coal mining for many years, though I've nearly made up my mind to change that to physics and math."

"You might be the only man in the world more confused about his calling than I am," said David. "I left Bible College for *le boxe*."

"Ah," remarked Lemaître. "So you would strike the Kaiser's nose an artful blow."

"Let's hope. But your story is more interesting than mine—I can punch people hard enough to drop them for the count of ten; but you, you must be awfully bright. So, which path do you think you'll choose, the priesthood or science?"

"But why should I choose? I shall do both—I told my father so at the age of nine."

"Huh! And how did he react to that?"

"Patted me on the head and said he'd be proud." Lemaître blushed. "They are practical people, my mother and father, but very much love the church."

"You're a lucky man," said David. "If I'd said something like that to my father, he'd either have sneered at me or whipped me, depending on the take from the numbers that week." Seeing Georges' puzzled look, he added, *"C'est un escroc, un filou."* It felt good to describe his father with the French the Moroccans had taught him for swindlers, rogues, tricksters, and crooks.

"I am fortunate, yes," said Lemaître. "But we have a perfect, loving Father, both of us."

"I wish I could believe that with all my heart," said David.

"Ah, but you must, you must!— *By this we know love, that He laid down his life for us.* You have seen death and horror, and so you doubt? I think perhaps I have seen worse than you. Last August, my little brother Jacques and I were making plans to bicycle through the Tyrol; two months later we were fighting house-to-house not two hundred kilometers from our hometown. I have fought in these fields for the past six months, and it is all savagery and madness. But we are not the first to suffer, nor will we be the last. Only, I pray, let me face my death like St. Ignatius awaiting the lions."

Both men instinctively turned their heads in the direction of the German lines.

"Did you witness the gas attack?" asked David. Ashamed of his own doubt, and envious of Georges' faith—which only added to his sense of shame—he was unable to respond directly to his companion's words.

Flanders Fields, 1915

"It must have happened just before we arrived."

"I saw enough. We came to reinforce the French position after the slaughter. They say over five thousand French and Canadian died; I think closer to ten. You could see that men had clawed their own faces, trying to breathe; some had shot themselves to escape the agony. Nothing had survived; not the horses, chickens, rabbits, or rats. Everywhere I looked there was only death. And the strange scent of the chlorine gas, like pineapple and pepper, lingering on the few bushes that were left."

"What drives me to my wits end," said David, "is how to reconcile something so evil with the sovereignty of God. Those men who were gassed—did He dream their tortured deaths before the beginning of the world?"

"*Nothing* evil is of God. He gave us the gift of free will, that we might love—love each other and love Him. This gift came with an incalculable cost, for it allowed sin, our sin, and that could be dealt with only by the Cross. Yet will He bring about good from every act of evil, even from all of this—" Lemaître gestured to the devastated landscape that lay beyond their trench—"and there, David, you find the sovereignty of God. Most of all, He is Emmanuel, He is with us; He is the fourth in the furnace. He is right here, with you and me, even now."

The American was silent for a while. Georges' arguments were nothing new, but hearing them stated so simply and earnestly by a warrior on the front lines of Hell made a deep impression on him. At last, he startled himself, breaking the silence by quoting from the Psalms.

"*God is our refuge and strength, an ever-present help in troubled times. Therefore we will not fear though the earth gives way, though the mountains fall into the sea...*"

"*He breaks the bow and shatters the spear; He burns the chariots with fire,*" Lemaître quoted in return. "*He says, be still, and know that I am God. I will be exalted among the nations, I will be exalted in the earth!*"

"*The cords of the grave entangled me, the snares of death confronted me.*" David felt himself filling with a strange joy as he gave voice to the ancient words. "*In my distress I called upon the Lord; to my God I cried for*

36

help. From his temple He heard my voice, and my cry to Him reached his ears."

"*The Lord is my light and my salvation; whom shall I fear?*" Lemaître, too, seemed joyful. "*The Lord is the stronghold of my life; of whom shall I be afraid?*"

"*Make me know the way I should go, for to you I lift up my soul.*" How grateful he was, David thought, that the Lord has led him to commit these words to his memory, to his heart. "*Deliver me from my enemies, O Lord! I have fled to you for refuge.*"

"Indeed, our lives are hidden with Christ in God," said Lemaître. "But listen. Something has changed."

From the French and Belgian lines came the sounds of distant shouting. David peered over the top of the trench; from the German lines, under the clear blue April sky, were coming billowing clouds of green-gray death.

"They've released the gas," said David. "They didn't dare advance when our men could pour down fire, but now they've got the wind at their backs. If we lay flat against the earth, do you think it would pass over us?"

"No, their gas is heavier than air," replied Lemaître. "But there is something we can do: I have heard that the ammonia in urine will neutralize the chlorine. If we can urinate in our underwear, they will then function as a sort of gas mask."

David smiled grimly.

"As easy as I would find it to 'urinate in my underwear' at the moment, I have a better idea. The gas will serve as a smoke-screen; if I stay low, I can carry you to safety. But we need to go right now."

"Go yourself, mon ami," said Lemaître. "Don't be foolish, your chances will be far higher. It would be better for one of us to survive than for both to be lost."

"Hah! Listen to you," said David, hoisting Georges Lemaître onto his back as effortlessly as if the young Belgian were a small child, and setting off for the safety of the Allied lines. "You've already forgotten why God gave us the gift of free will."

Chapter Seven
Las Vegas, 2011

"'Ozymandias'—isn't that the name of a poem?" asked Tim. He and Joan were descending the escalator to baggage claim at McCarran International Airport amid the bedlam of slot machines and the glare of the electronic billboards which towered overhead. Tim was looking at the largest, most garish of them, which read:

Ozymandias Unveiled!
Only at Babylon West

Babylon West, the latest addition to the Las Vegas skyline, was the hotel they'd booked for their stay on the advice of Luke's nephew, who had also volunteered to pick them up at the airport.

"Yes, by Shelly," Joan replied. "Maybe the poetry lovers convention is in town!"

"Ha ha. That's not exactly what I had in mind, coming to Vegas." Tim grinned, and Joan felt another wave of regret that she was still in the midst of an affair with the man.

"That must be Daniel," Joan said as they reached the bottom of the escalator, and she waved to a man holding a sign bearing their names.

"Looks like the bad guy in a Bond flick," Tim muttered under his breath.

Luke's nephew was a tall, powerful-looking man, perhaps fifty years old. The lines of his face were strong, but his skin was mottled and crisscrossed by rope-like scars. "He's been terribly burned," Joan thought, and felt ashamed that she had averted her gaze after their eyes met. Tim, she noticed, had no such problem; he looked the man straight in the eye, walked up, and offered his hand.

"Mr. Gold, I presume?"

"Yes, indeed," said Daniel, shaking Tim's hand. "But I go by Dan. I've been looking forward to this, Tim, I'm so pleased to meet you and Joan."

Before she had waved at him, Joan thought that Daniel's face had a still, resigned sadness, but when he smiled, there was a joyful warmth that almost erased the disfiguring scars.

The travelers had made do with carry-on, so Daniel led them to his old Ford pickup in the parking garage, and they started off for Babylon West, at the far southern end of Las Vegas Boulevard.

"So, Dan, are you a scientist, like your uncle?" Tim asked.

"Science fascinates me—especially cosmology, which Uncle Luke loved to teach. But no, I'm a pastor. My church is adjacent to your hotel, and my uncle's home is close by as well."

"How *is* Dr. Uukkarnit?" asked Joan.

"His age has finally caught up with him—which is one of the reasons he was excited when he heard you were researching the mystery of the 1931 translation of Lemaître's paper. Seems you two have quite a good reputation in the science community, and Uncle Luke would like to see the story done right. But some days are better than others; he wasn't all that well earlier this morning. We'll just have to play it by ear."

"I'm curious," said Tim, "how you reconcile your faith with the facts of science, if you don't mind my asking."

"I don't mind at all," Daniel replied. "The two are complementary. Science is the exercise of human reason to understand the workings of Creation. It reveals the majesty of our Lord; anyone who has seen photographs of the galaxies and nebulae, such as you show in your documentaries, understands what the Psalmist meant when he wrote, *the heavens declare the glory of God.* But by itself, science cannot speak to *meaning;* that is the province of faith. Faith does not contradict science—it goes where science rightly fears to tread."

"But since you have some knowledge of science, you would surely agree that much in the Bible reflects the flawed understanding of mortal men, not the words of an omniscient God."

"Quite the contrary, I believe the Bible is the inerrant word of God—and that the Holy Spirit guides us to the understanding of His word."

Joan could see that Tim was rolling his eyes.

"And if his word is coming from the mouth of a donkey?"

"Of all the phenomena in the universe, Tim, is Balaam's ass really the one you find most perplexing?"

Tim Faber laughed in spite of himself.

"Perhaps not. But let me ask you this: you believe man to be the apex of God's creation, am I correct?"

"Indeed," answered Daniel. "Fallen though we may be, we were made in His image, crowned with glory and honor, made rulers over the works of His hands."

"How is it, then, that the earth—the only part of 'creation' over which we have any dominion at all—is such an insignificant speck in the vastness of the cosmos?"

"Why did God make the universe so impossibly large? *For as high as the heavens are above the earth, so great is His steadfast love for those who fear Him; as far as the east is from the west, so far does He remove our transgressions from us.*"

"My rapier seems rather blunt today," said Tim. "However, since you're a good sport, parry this thrust, if you will: The heaven revealed in your Scripture—life beyond death, reunited with loved ones we've lost, in a world without sin or sickness or strife—given that there's not the slightest evidence to support such a fantasy, doesn't Occam's razor suggest it to be mere wish fulfillment?"

"But our wishes *are* fulfilled, every day; in fact, the existence of desire suggests the reality of its object. We hunger, and yes, *food* exists; we yearn to drink, and water slakes our thirst. But our very deepest desire is for a perfect Father."

Joan at last broke her silence.

"Is it wish fulfillment, Tim," she said, "to imagine that we can't get away with doing as we like, that there are eternal consequences for our sins?"

"Et tu, Brutessa?" asked her lover, trying to mask his annoyance with humor. "You might think you've got me there, but in fact, that too is wish fulfillment, straight up. We don't *want* to get away with evil. We desire our own punishment most of all." Tim stopped, suddenly, embarrassed at what he was saying. Where had that nonsense come from?

Joan laughed, startled by the unexpected response, and immediately regretted her laughter, for she'd heard pain in her companion's voice.

Daniel glanced at Tim and gave him a warm smile.

"I think," he said to his guest, "you've just given voice to a deep truth of the heart."

But Tim seemed lost in thought and remained silent for the rest of the ride.

⤳

Sandwiched between a Mercedes and a Maserati, the dusty pickup eased its way to the main entrance of Babylon West. Just as Daniel was telling Joan and Tim that he'd call to let them know whether it would be possible to meet with Uncle Luke later in the day, a singularly distinctive man waved at him, prompting Daniel to wave back. He was an older fellow in a pearl-gray suit, carrying a walking stick with an elegantly carved silver handle on an ebony shaft. He wore large wrap-around sunglasses and his long gray hair was tied back in a ponytail.

"You know Oz Osman?" Tim exclaimed.

"Who?" asked Joan.

"We have some business we're working through," Daniel explained.

"I'm impressed," said Tim, and then, turning to Joan, added, "He's a legend in Vegas. Built this place, Temptation Island, and probably half a dozen other hotels. He started out in the Sixties as a cheesy lounge act—a magician and hypnotist—and ended up at the top of the heap."

"Perhaps not the best heap to be on top of," Daniel said softly, for Osman was approaching his truck.

"I see you have guests, Deacon Gold! Are they checking in?"

Daniel nodded and began to say, "There's no need for you to—" but Osman was paying no attention.

"Come, come, come. Mega VIP treatment for any friends of Friar Gold! Sergio!" A lackey materialized at Osman's side. "Have this chariot parked over there—" he motioned to a highly visible area normally reserved for guests with Bentleys and Lamborghinis. "Father Gold is, I'm sure, full of grace, but perhaps lacking in the social graces, for he hasn't yet made introductions."

"Meet Joan Reed and Tim Faber," said Daniel, "from Science Cable TV."

"A pleasure, Mr. Osman," said Joan, and she shook the impresario's hand.

"Please! Everyone in this town calls me Oz—excepting Monsignor Gold, of course, who is as formal as a Pharisee—and the two of you shall be no exception. You're here on business?" He addressed the question to Tim.

"We are, though we're planning on taking some time off as well."

"Excellent! Balance in all things!" He glanced at Joan and asked, with mock concern, "You're not afraid of heights, are you? No? Excellent. Sergio! Make sure my friends here are upgraded to Emperor quarters—our most luxurious," he added in an aside to the New Yorkers before turning back to his assistant—"as my personal guests."

Tim laughed with delight.

"Thank you, that's very generous, Oz."

"I can't resist asking," said Joan, who, though she wasn't entirely sure if Osman had been mocking or only teasing Daniel, had decided to give him the benefit of the doubt, "whether your Ozymandias exhibit is related to the poem by Shelly."

"Come, come, I'll show it to you myself!" exclaimed Osman. "You don't mind, do you, Vicar?" he asked Daniel.

"On the contrary, I'd like them to see your latest attraction."

Tim and Joan and Daniel followed Osman, who led them through a door flanked by two imposing guards, down a private passageway, and up a small elevator, until they emerged into a darkened room that looked onto the exhibit, *Ozymandias Unveiled.*

"One-way mirror?" Tim asked.

"Quite," Osman replied.

A crowd was gathered by a hundred-foot-tall statue, made to look as though it had been sculpted from ancient blocks of marble inlaid with rubies, sapphires, and jade. Around the statue's base, beautiful young men and women in flesh-colored bodysuits danced and writhed and occasionally performed impressive gymnastic feats. The ten-story figure looked something like an Egyptian pharaoh wearing a golden crown. Every few minutes its eyes blazed fire, and, in a basso profundo that was like a roll of thunder, it proclaimed these words:

"My name is Ozymandias, King of Kings,
Look on my Works ye Mighty, and despair!"

"Well, you've certainly captured the 'sneer of cold command,'" said Joan. "But it's supposed to be a ruin—aside from the head, only two 'trunkless legs' remain."

"A fine exhibit *that* would make!" replied Osman in mock dismay.

"Then I take it you don't feature the rest of the poem."

"Joan, dear, I find Shelly's romantic cynicism sophomoric and cheap. Don't you, really? How easy to mock greatness! I'll have none of it. You two are intellectuals—think of this as a post-modern reimagining of the Ozymandian myth."

"Is there a display of the king's 'works'?" asked Tim, who wasn't sure what to make of it all. "Or is that meant to be left to the viewer's imagination?"

"I leave as little as possible to the imagination," said Osman. "The works—they are all about us in the wonder that is Babylon West."

"Ah!" said Joan. "Oz and Ozymandias—you've created a self-portrait!"

"I'm flattered, Joan. But yes, the good fellow is an alter-ego of sorts. However, enough about me." Osman turned to Tim. "Science shows, you say?"

"Yes," said Tim, eager to shine before the Legend of Las Vegas, "we make—"

"I *love* science," said Osman. "It's the antidote for so much that is wrong with the world."

"Exactly! I'm passionate on just that—"

"In fact, I've got quite the subject for one of your documentaries." He smiled broadly, revealing gleaming white teeth.

"Really!" said Tim. "I'd love to hear more."

Osman looked over at Daniel. "Reverend?"

"You seem to have an eager audience, Mr. Osman. Carry on."

"Excellent!" He clapped his hands. "Come, come. To my office, posthaste!"

~

"I must say, this is impressive," said Joan, as she and Tim flipped through a set of blueprints. They were in the casino magnate's magnificent office, which looked out over the Strip from the fiftieth floor.

"Wait until you see the 3-D renderings," said Osman, fiddling with his computer. "I've had engineers, archeologists, and Biblical scholars working on this for years."

"If you paid those scholars by the hour, it couldn't have cost you much," said Daniel. "Aside from the mention of building with bricks and tar, there are no other details in Scripture about the Tower of Babel."

"Ah, you're such a literalist," said Osman. "I, by contrast, have a poet's soul."

"We did a documentary on the Babylonian ziggurats a few years ago," said Joan. "Mountains of brick and tile. The greatest of them, of course, being in Babylon itself; presumably the archetype of the Biblical Tower."

"Yes, bless your soul, Joan, the *Etemenanki*—only it was no archetype, but the Tower of Babel itself." With a few keystrokes, Osman brought a three-dimensional rendering of the massive edifice onto the six-foot television screen across from his desk. "Ninety meters by ninety meters at the base, and ninety meters tall—clawing its way for thirty stories into the sky. With a temple to their great god Marduk at the top." He turned to look at Daniel. "That must have annoyed your Jehovah no end."

"These plans—is the Tower of Babel the theme for your next hotel?" asked Tim.

Osman frowned. "No, of course not, what a vulgar idea. The Tower is a sacred thing, don't you see? It will be the centerpiece of Babylon West. Our guests will be allowed to gape respectfully at its magnificence. Only there's a wrinkle; Brother Gold's church stands precisely where I wish to build. I've already offered him more money than he and his flock could possibly know what to do with, and yet he spurns me." Osman turned to Daniel. "You're quite the negotiator, I'll give you that." He swiveled back to Joan and Tim. "I ask you, though, is that a proper thing for a man of the cloth?"

"I think we'll stay neutral and let the two of you duke it out, Oz," said Tim, feeling he needed to assert himself or lose face in front of Joan. "But your idea for a documentary—is the Etemenanki what you had in mind?"

"As Joan pointed out," replied Osman, "that sort of show has been done before. No, my vision is grander yet. I think of the Tower as the first round in the showdown between science and religion. In this corner, *science*, fighting for freedom with all the brilliant audacity of the mind of man; in the other, *religion*, seeking to chain us in ignorance as it champions the oppressive tyranny of God."

"Ah, that's just what's on my drawing board," said Tim. "But to do it justice will take more than one show; I'm thinking of a series in at least ten parts."

"Yes, certainly," said Osman. "One which I would be delighted to sponsor, assuming of course that it is in harmony with my ideas."

"I'm quite sure we think alike, Oz. No offense, Dan, but to me, while the Bible is a beautiful fantasy, it's the hard facts of science that will be the salvation of the human race."

"I'm not offended at all, Tim," said Daniel. "But I'm afraid you're mistaking our host for an atheist, when nothing could be further from the truth. You don't deny the Triune God of the Christian faith, do you Mr. Osman?"

Joan noticed that Osman's face reddened—but whether it was a flush of embarrassment or anger, she couldn't tell.

"I don't dispute the existence of the Almighty," he said after a moment. "Nor of the Son or Holy Ghost. I simply don't care for them. I reject their claims upon me and will feast upon the fruit of the Tree of

Knowledge for as long as I draw breath."

"I see," said Tim, who didn't at all. "Well, nonetheless, there's, uhm, no doubt common ground here to be explored."

"Of that I can assure you," said Osman. "Now, I've taken up enough of your time, and Bishop Gold's, but let me leave you with these—" he handed them both cards. "That is my private number. Anything I can do, please, you simply must let me know. And for your time off, may I provide you with one of my personal drivers, whose Rolls Royce will be at your beck and call?"

"Thank you!" said Tim. "Sounds like an offer we'd be fools to refuse."

~

It turned out that Luke was not well enough to meet with them that day. Joan had insisted that, at least for appearances, they should have separate rooms, and, after Tim went off "to try his luck at the tables," Joan sat on the edge of her bed for a long time, then took out Osman's card and dialed his number on her cell phone.

"Wonderful! I was hoping you would call me," he said after she'd identified herself. "You have a quick and independent mind, rare in woman or man. Now, I'm all ears—your wish is my command."

"I wouldn't have called if it weren't something terribly important to me," said Joan, "and which I suspect will be easy enough for you. It's my brother, Willie. William Reed. He's a good man, Mr. Osman—"

"Oz, please."

"Of course, Oz. He just needs a break. If there is any way you could find a job for him—anything at all—"

"No sooner said than done, Joan. Give me his number, and I'll put William to work."

"God bless—" she stopped herself. "Thank you, Oz. You won't regret this, I assure you."

After they wished each other good night, Joan called Willie to let him know what she'd done, then put the phone down, held her head in her hands, and wept.

Whether they were tears of relief or anxiety, she couldn't say for sure.

Chapter Eight
The Whispering Wind

The day after we learned that our money was gone, my mother rose well before dawn. There were no more tears; in her face was a grim determination to continue our quest, no matter the obstacles that mortals or gods might set in our path. We knew no one in Seattle but Chinook Ray, so we set off for the Trading Post, though it would be hours before it opened its doors.

"I could not stay another minute in that accursed place, Uukkarnit," she explained to me as we walked in the early morning darkness. "I would kill the McSorley woman, but in this unfamiliar land I would be hunted down like a lame caribou. Your father himself will help me slay Kathleen Byrne."

We sang to pass the time, sitting on the stairs outside the Trading Post. Soon enough a light came on in a window on the second floor, for this is where Ray lived with his family, and his wife had recognized our songs.

"Yura Noongwook!" Ray exclaimed as he opened the front door. "Come in, please. But if you're here for me to take you to the station, it's not until this afternoon."

"No," said Mother. "Everything has changed. I would be grateful if we could talk."

Ray introduced us to Asaaluk, his wife, a woman as joyful and plump as her husband was somber and lean. She hugged us to her ample bosom, bade us sit down at their kitchen table, and served cornbread and strong coffee as my mother told our tale.

"You will stay here with us!" said Asaaluk. "And fear not, Ray will make everything right." She looked meaningfully at her husband. Outside, the sky was brightening, and I allowed myself to feel a glimmer of hope.

"Well," said the Chinook, buying time by lighting up another of his hand-rolled cigarettes. "There is great demand for soapstone figurines. Nothing so special as what you brought to me; only simple things, I can provide the materials and explain to you what sells. Your share of the profits will be forty—" across the table, Asaaluk frowned—"or rather, fifty percent. I do not know how long it will take to make back what you lost, but I think this is the best plan. And I have often seen, when men like your husband fall in love with—"

"You speak of what you do not know," my mother interrupted. "Taliriktug loves only his son and me, but he is enchanted by Raven in the guise of the white whore."

"I understand all too well," said Ray. "Such dark magic rarely lasts for long. When your husband frees himself from Raven's grasp and starts the long journey home, he will pass through Seattle and we will hear of his coming, of that I am sure."

"So you see, Yura," said Asaaluk, "there is no better place for you and your son than here with Ray and me."

My mother thought it over.

"Thank you," she said at last. "I accept your offer, and will work hard—and Uukkarnit, too, for he is a wise child, whose mind races to where few can go. Only it is hard for me to wait, not knowing—while—" Mother could not bring herself to say more.

"Ray," said Asaaluk. "Your cousin in Wenatchee, whose husband works for the men in pink—perhaps he could find out something for Yura, to ease her mind."

"Or torment her yet more," said Ray.

"Anything I could learn of Taliriktug would be more precious to me than needles of ivory," Mother said. "Tell me of these men in pink."

"My cousin's husband works for the Pinkerton Detective Agency," said Ray. "But he does little other than see that union organizers and communists are beaten to within an inch of their lives." Asaaluk's eyes narrowed ominously as she looked at her husband. "However," he continued, "I will contact him and see what can be done. What information can I pass on?"

Mother reached into her bag and handed Ray a business card that my father's lover had left behind. Asaaluk showed us a small spare room that would serve as our new quarters, and Ray listened while my mother explained the tools and supplies she would need.

That night, as my mother lay sleeping, I looked at her face, lit by the moonlight coming through a small window. There were fine lines I had never seen before on her forehead and between her eyes. "You are more beautiful than Kathleen Byrne," I whispered. "When Father sees you, his heart will burst with joy, and he will take you in his arms. You will go back to Nenana together, and I, Uukkarnit Noongwook, I will kill the white whore."

⟜

Asaaluk persuaded my mother that I should attend the local school in the fall, but that was months away, so I helped Ray, at first by unloading boxes and running errands, and later by improving the way he kept track of his inventory and sales. But in the first days of our stay, when I had free time, I found myself wandering in the direction of McSorley's Roadhouse and Inn. Perhaps thinking that I'd be lured by the player piano, Mother had expressly forbid me to ever go back. Disobeying her filled me with guilt, but something urged me on. Sometimes, when the breeze rustled through the dogwood trees, I thought I could almost hear words telling me to go. The Angakkuq had said that Sila, god of the wind, soul of the world, was responsible for the nagging of conscience. Was that it, or was it just a boy's curiosity?

Another force was at work, but I did not know its name.

The sign on the front door of the Roadhouse said CLOSED. I walked to a side entrance and without much difficulty jimmied the lock. Inside, it was eerily silent. Someone had left sheet music on the piano in the dining hall: *It Ain't Gonna Rain No Mo'*. I stared at it for a few moments, and found myself wondering, was that a good thing—sunlight piercing through dark gray sodden skies? Or words to be dreaded, a prophecy of drought?

I walked down the hallways and poked my head into room after room. Empty, empty, every one; but I saved Miss McSorley's room for last, and stopped, my heart pounding, just before reaching her open door.

When I finally stepped forward, it was to see a ghastly sight: Miss

McSorley, still lying on the couch, her cheeks sunken, her face ashen white. There was no sign of life, no rising and falling of her chest. I'd seen the dead before; she was gone. I moved closer, and a loose floorboard creaked.

Her eyes shot open.

"Hugo?" Her voice was like the crackling of dry leaves.

I froze. My every instinct was to run, but whatever had led me this far told me to master my fear.

"No, Miss McSorley, I'm so sorry. It's me, Uukkarnit."

She squinted at me, trying to see without her glasses in the room's dim light.

"Who?"

"Yura's son, Uukkarnit. You can call me Luke."

"Where is Hugo?" She spoke in gasps, her tongue swollen, her lips dry and cracked. There was an empty pitcher and glass on the end table, and I went to fill it before answering.

"I don't think there is anyone here, Miss McSorley." I raised a glass of water to her lips. She swallowed with difficulty.

"Ah, Hugo, you've deserted me, too. Like Demas did Paul."

"I'm sorry," I said. "Is there something I can do?"

She reached out and touched my face.

"Seamus," she whispered. "Your forehead was so hot. Now all that heat is inside of me. Oh, how wonderful, to feel your skin so cool—and now your momma burns! Are these the flames of hell, boy? But what mother wouldn't welcome hell to save her son. Come closer, child."

She peered at me, confused.

"Who did you say you were?" she asked, and then her eyes lost focus and she fell into a troubled sleep.

~

"Where have you been?" Mother asked me when I arrived back at the Trading Post.

"I need your help," I said, even more scared than I'd been in Miss McSorley's room. Whatever had impelled me to disobey my mother was still urging me on.

"We cannot afford trouble—what is it you have done?"

"Please," I said "Just come."

She had never seen me like this before, and reluctantly followed me outside. Our destination became obvious soon enough.

"You have gone against my wishes, Uukkarnit." She stopped a block from the Roadhouse. "Whatever you have done, do not expect me to set foot inside that place."

I looked at her with tears in my eyes.

"Never have I asked you for anything you did not deem it wise to give. Now I ask your help, this one time."

I walked forward, and after a moment I could hear my mother following behind. We came at last to the room where Miss McSorley lay fitfully sleeping, her clothes soaked with sweat.

"Why have you brought me here?" my mother asked me. "It would be well for her to die."

"We don't know if Hugo was telling the truth," I protested. "We only know that Miss McSorley is in pain. I'm ashamed that I'm just a boy who does not know what should be done for her. But you do."

Perhaps a minute passed as my mother looked at me; then she turned and went into Miss McSorley's bathroom, where I could hear her opening cabinets and drawers. She emerged with washcloths, a basin of water, and a bottle of rubbing alcohol.

"Watch what I am doing," Mother told me. "Then stay here and do the same, every ten minutes or so, until I return."

Sometimes Miss McSorley would open her eyes and stare at me, but showed no sign of recognizing who I was, nor did she refer again to her son. My mother returned to the Trading Post and talked with Asaaluk, and eventually Ray drove up in his Model T and he and I moved the sick woman, wrapped in blankets, to his car. They had cleared out an area where boxes were stored at the back of the store; we put her on a cot there, and Mother and Asaaluk and I cared for Miss McSorley for the next several days, until her soul left this world.

The Whispering Wind

It was not long afterward that Ray came home from a trip to acquire new merchandise and told us that he'd heard from his cousin in Wenatchee. Her husband had been in touch with the Pinkerton office in New York; since we could not afford to pay them, they had only made a few phone calls, but had still found out quite a bit. Miss Kathleen Byrne was no longer with Hearst's New York Journal-American; indeed, it seemed she had left the city altogether, and no one had any idea where she had gone. However, of one thing the Pinkerton agents had been quite sure, because the gossip was all over New York: Mr. Victor Noongwook, the hero from the Far Northern Frontier, had left the beautiful young reporter, perhaps only a few weeks before. As with his former lover, though, his whereabouts were unknown.

"Taliriktug is coming back to us," my mother pronounced, calmly and confidently. "You must stay alert, Ray, for news of his approach."

"He will hear when your husband is within two hundred miles," said Asaaluk. "Ray will spread the word throughout the Chinook Nation, and to many white men besides." She looked proudly at her husband.

"Have no fear, Yura," said Ray. "We will find him when he comes close."

That night I could not sleep, for my imagination ran wild and my heart beat so loudly in my chest. My father was coming home!

But weeks went by, and then months, and years, and of my father we heard not a word.

Chapter Nine
Into the Wilderness: Leavenworth, Kansas, 1921

"Oh my goodness!" exclaimed Lucille Johnson, standing by the front gate of Leavenworth prison on a hot summer day. "Davey Gold!"

David, who had wended his way through the multitude gathered outside the prison's forty-foot red brick walls, gave Lucille a great bear hug.

"I was in Fort Worth when I read that Jack was getting out today," he said, "and I figured, nothing is going to keep me away!" He surveyed the scene around them, and added, "He always could attract a crowd."

In addition to the hundreds of people milling outside the prison, there were six motion-picture cameramen, a bevy of reporters, and two marching bands.

"It's been forever!" said Lucille.

"Almost seven years," said David, noticing that her clothes were no longer quite so stylish, and the diamond and ruby rings had all but disappeared from her hands.

"Do you know," said Lucille, "on the day he surrendered himself at this gate, we caught a cab to come here—but Jack told the cabbie to sit in the back. He drove himself to prison, Davey!"

David laughed. "Probably the only time he obeyed the speed limit, too."

"Here he comes!" someone shouted, and the crowd pressed closer around them.

"This is too crazy," said David. "You two don't need me here right now."

"Jack never had a better partner, Davey," Lucille whispered to him. "He'll want to see you, I know he will."

"I'm staying in town, at the Big L. You hug him for me, Lucille."

David turned and began the long walk back to his small room in a cheap hotel.

Into the Wilderness: Leavenworth, Kansas, 1921

~

Only a year after Jack Johnson and David Gold had parted ways, the champion had put his title on the line in a fight in Havana, Cuba against yet another Great White Hope. This time his foe was Jess Willard, a taller, stronger, younger man whom Johnson dominated for fully twenty rounds; but the aging champ couldn't put the lumbering Willard away, and his strength began to fail him in the blistering afternoon heat. At the end of the twenty-fifth round, knowing the end was near, Johnson whispered to his cornerman to take Lucille away, but she was still there at the start of the twenty-sixth as Willard slammed a left into her husband's body, and then a crushing right to his jaw. "Oh my God," she cried, as Jack Johnson went down for the count and Willard became the hero of his race.

Johnson survived on charisma and showmanship following the loss of his title. He spent the next three years in Spain, appearing as a strongman and fighting exhibition matches against the likes of Arthur Cravan, the alcoholic nephew of Oscar Wilde, who wrote Dadaist poetry and had claimed the French light heavyweight title when his opponent failed to show up. After that, it was more of the same in Mexico, until at long last the former heavyweight champion of the world decided to come home. It would cost him a thousand dollar fine and a year and a day in jail.

~

In November 1918, Germany signed the Armistice that brought the Great War to an end. David had been on the front lines for nearly the entire war. For four years, he'd had a purpose: fighting with and for his fellow warriors, the Moroccans and Algerians, the outcasts and misfits, *les etrangers* like himself. He'd taken risks that became the stuff of legends, putting his own life at risk to help his friends, much as he'd done for Georges Lemaître.

Then, suddenly, came the yawning emptiness of peace.

His encounter with the young Belgian haunted David's dreams. He had visited Georges in the field hospital whenever possible, and the two had read to each other from the Gospels, recited the Psalms, and talked of the beauty of Genesis, before each received orders and went their separate ways. For months, he'd felt a joyous faith; but the joy soon faded, and there was only the daily reality of the trenches, the moans of the wounded, the light fading from the eyes of dying friends.

What was wrong with him, he wondered—why couldn't he sustain the intensity of belief, or simply have Lemaître's calm certainty and trust in God? Perhaps he simply wasn't one of the *elect.* Had God created him for the express purpose of being damned?

No, surely that was a demonic notion! Lemaître had been right: God must be good, utterly, completely good, the Father David had yearned for as a boy. Of that he was sure, for God had become man, suffered, and died to rescue us from our sins. As Georges had reminded him, Christ was Emmanuel—*God with us.* But all the more it tore at David's heart that He seemed so far away.

When he came home, the only idea that made sense to him was returning to the ring; it was the closest thing to war.

~

After David walked back to the Big L, he lay down to take a nap, but it wasn't long before he was awakened by a blaring car horn and shouting voices from just outside the hotel.

"Gold! Hey! Come on out, boy, destiny calls!"

From his window, he could see Jack, in a straw hat, tailored suit, and bright polka dot tie, at the wheel of his pale green Haynes touring car, with Lucille leaning her head against his big right arm. David smiled and then laughed out loud. Whatever his shortcomings, there was no one who loved life more than Jack Johnson. He grabbed his suitcase and headed out the door.

The threesome drove to Kansas City, and after Lucille had gone to bed the two men found a booth in the hotel bar and talked long into the night.

"I'm forty-three, Dave," said Johnson. "But a man fights with his mind more than with his fists, and I can think circles around the cretins in the ring these days. Dempsey? I'm no more afraid of him than I was of the bulls in Barcelona and Madrid. Every boxer should do a turn as a matador."

"I figured you'd want back in the game, Jack. I'm doing okay, I win my share, but there are a lot of fighters out there. These past three years since I got back from France, feels like I've just been killing time."

"Of course, boy, you've been wandering in the wilderness ever since you left my side! Now look, you're strong and quick and good-looking, but it's all about putting on a show. What you need is an *angle.*" Johnson leaned his head forward and stared at the younger man with narrowed eyes, as though he were trying to see through to his soul. David laughed.

"I'm serious, son. Now let's see. Gold—golden boy—nah, it's been done. We need something unique." Johnson suddenly slammed his fist down on the table. "Well if it isn't just right there in front of us, Dave. Oh, sometimes I impress myself no end. All that Bible learning you did in Chicago—you still read the Good Book?"

"Yes, of course, but—"

"But nothing. You walked in here a refugee from Palookaville. You're walking out as David Gold, the Pummelin' Preacher, undercard to Jack Johnson, the once and future heavyweight champion of the world."

"I'm not a preacher, Jack."

"Don't give me that! You spent three years studying—St. Paul never went to Bible college, and you couldn't stop the man from preaching wherever he went!"

"Actually, he studied for many years, they just didn't call it Bible college back then."

"Okay, bad example. The fishermen, then, Peter and his crew."

"They spent three years learning at the feet of the Son of God."

"Dave, Dave, Dave. I've seen you when you were so tired, your eyes were propped open with toothpicks, and there you were, reading your Bible. Look, even *I've* preached in churches now and then. You want to be authentic, no problem, I can get you behind a pulpit wherever we go. You can write yourself a sermon or pick 'em out of a book, we'll get you all set up."

David sat there, wrestling with the idea, looking for reasons to say yes. Okay, it was corny, even half crazy, but what else did he have going on in his life? He'd bailed out on Johnson once before; now the aging fighter needed him. There wasn't going to be any match with Jack Dempsey. The Manassa Mauler was ruthless, brutal, a force of nature who had taken the title from Jess Willard in three rounds in 1919, breaking several of the taller man's ribs, fracturing his jaw, and knocking loose six of his teeth. But Jack could take on has-beens and still put on a show, entertaining the crowd. *I could earn my keep as a fighter,* David told himself, *and have the motivation to turn my mind to God, to make my moniker real.* He reached his hand out across the table.

"Well, someone's got to stick around and make sure you treat Lucille right, Jack. So shake hands with the Pummelin' Preacher."

Jack Johnson's face lit up with his biggest, happiest smile. The kid could be unpredictable, but he was starting to learn what real life was all about. From the moment Lucille had told her husband about their meeting at the prison gates, he'd been pretty sure that, this time, Dave would come along for the ride.

～

David toured the country with Jack Johnson off and on throughout the next nine years. But it seemed that he didn't have the power to make Johnson "treat his wife right;" the two divorced in 1924, after Lucille accused her husband of having had numerous affairs. In 1925, at a racing track in Aurora, Illinois, the fighter met a middle-aged woman named Irene, who divorced her husband and married Johnson later that year. Once again, white America was outraged; for the third time, the black boxer had married outside his race.

One day in 1930, David Gold sat at the small table of a hotel room in Oklahoma City, looking at the text of a sermon that D.L. Moody had written decades before. David had penciled in a few words here and there about "the good fight," and "knocking Satan down for the count," and he would deliver it on the coming Sunday, at a nearby church. Jack had been right; many of the parishioners, intrigued, would be sure to attend the Tuesday night bout.

"I'm thirty-eight years old, and I'm a fraud," he thought. At first, David had written his own sermons, for never a day passed when he failed to study Scripture and muse on its meaning; but he could hear the congregations muttering and shifting in their seats when he spoke honestly, admitting his confusions and doubts. He told himself, why shortchange people, give them first-class ideas, and it had been Moody's sermon every since. He'd stuck with Johnson, a man who loved women, gambling, strong drink, and fast cars, and rationalized that he was being a loyal friend; but David knew that if it were not for his association with the famous man, his career would have ended years ago.

He swept the pages of the sermon, long since memorized, onto the floor. David had asked God for guidance, but the heavens were silent. He was on his own.

"Ladies and Gentlemen," proclaimed the announcer that Tuesday evening, looking out at a packed house. "You've heard him in the pulpit, now see him in the ring. Introducing the Minister of Mayhem, the Vicar of Violence, the one and only Pummelin' Preacher, David Goooooooooold!"

"Blessed be the Lord, my Rock," David prayed silently, "who trains my hands for war, and my fingers for battle." He stepped through the ropes and shook off the priestly robes he wore for show, while a young pug who called himself the Philadelphia Fury glowered at him from across the ring. The ref brought the two fighters to the center, where they touched gloves; then the bell rang, and the fight was on.

~

"Mr. Preacher? Sir?" A boy, perhaps twelve or thirteen years old, was looking up at David as he left the arena and started to walk back to his hotel. "My folks take me to church every Sunday, Mr. Preacher, that's where I heard you. I just wanted to say, I'm sorry you lost."

David had had a chance to put the Fury away early in the second round, after he'd staggered him with a right hook to the jaw, but he didn't follow through. A local reporter scribbled in his notebook, *he's lost the killer instinct.* Was that it? David didn't understand it himself. But he'd lost a ten-round decision and had heard the jeers of the crowd.

He smiled, thanked the boy, then walked on.

"Do you think maybe you just didn't pray hard enough?" The lad was walking at his side, looking up at him.

"Maybe not, son. Maybe I needed to pray harder."

"Well, see, I was wondering, seeing how Jesus said, if two agree about anything they ask, it will be done for them by my father in heaven—well, 'anything' includes boxing, right? So you and I could pray together for you to win your next fight! Then there'd be no way you could lose!"

David turned away so the youth couldn't see the tears in his eyes.

"That's a nice thought, kid, but this is between me and God. Look, I'm sorry, it's late, you ought to go home."

He started walking faster, then broke into a run. After a couple of blocks, he stopped and leaned against the side of a building, his heart racing, his mind distraught. What was wrong with him? Why hadn't he knelt down and prayed with that boy, prayed for the youth to follow in the Lord Jesus Christ's every step? David turned and walked briskly back up the street.

"Hey! Kid! I'm sorry! Hey, kid!"

The boy was nowhere to be seen.

I'm wandering in the wilderness, he thought, feeling the darkness of a deep despair. A loveless man, far from God. Back in his hotel room, David got out his Bible, paged through the Psalms until he came to number 143, then got down on his knees and prayed.

> *Answer me quickly O Lord!*
> *My spirit fails!*
> *Hide not your face from me,*
> * lest I be like those who go down to the pit.*
> *Let me hear in the morning of your steadfast love,*
> * for in you I trust.*
> *Make me know the way I should go,*
> * for to you I lift up my soul.*

Into the Wilderness: Leavenworth, Kansas, 1921

He lowered his forehead onto the bed, and stayed like that for a very long time. Would God answer him? Would He send a sign?

But all he heard were sounds from the street below, drunken laughter, and angry voices quarreling; and, through the thin hotel wall, a woman in the next room, sobbing softly long into the night.

Chapter Ten
Between this World and the Next

"You know those giant stone heads on Easter Island?" Tim asked Daniel, who was driving him and Joan to his Uncle Luke's home, just a few miles from Babylon West.

"Sure do," Daniel replied.

"Well, to this day there are people who insist they could have only been set in place by space aliens, because they simply can't imagine how primitive people could have moved nearly a thousand stone statues, each weighing as much as eighty tons, for five or ten miles. But of course there's an explanation for how ordinary humans were able to pull off such a feat."

"And so you think religious faith is much the same thing, attributing seemingly inexplicable phenomena to a supernatural cause?"

"Can you really deny it?" asked Tim. "There are some forty-three hundred religions on this planet, each with its own explanation of the origin of the world and of man. Some myths are more charming than others, but each is utterly wrong."

"The Bible is not a science textbook," said Daniel. "My faith addresses matters that can't be resolved by the scientific method—at least, not until the heavens are rolled up like a scroll. But about Easter Island: you made the point that the space-alien theory underestimates human beings. That's true! However, the belief that there's no higher purpose to life, that we owe our existence entirely to the random collisions of atoms, reduces us to meaninglessness and utterly trivializes human life." Daniel pulled his pickup into the driveway of a modest Spanish-style ranch home, shut off the engine, and turned to Tim. "So tell me," he asked him. "Do you *feel* meaningless?"

Tim opened his mouth to answer, then apparently thought better of it.

"Much as I'd like to hear the answer to that," said Joan, "I'm too excited about meeting Dr. Noongwook—this story is the meaning of *my* life, right now. I've got a number of questions prepared, boss man, so I'll take the lead, okay?"

Tim nodded his assent, and they followed Daniel to the front door.

A housekeeper ushered the three into Luke's home and led them to a large room filled with bookshelves, where the old man lay propped up on pillows on a daybed.

"Hello, Uncle," said Daniel. "I've brought the folks who are so interested in Georges."

The first thing Joan noticed was Luke's hair, which was lit by the sun shining brightly through the library windows; still thick and long, it fell down around his shoulders, white as virgin snow. His brown face was deeply lined, and his eyes were such a dark mahogany they were nearly black, yet warm and kind. He had a gentle smile, and the thought came to her, *this is a holy man.*

Joan suddenly realized that she had been staring into the professor's eyes, and he was returning her gaze. How long had their eyes been locked? She felt herself redden.

"Julia?" said Luke. "Have you come for me at last? I've waited for nearly twice the years that the Hebrews trekked the desert waste; yet for you, darling girl, I would wait 'til the end of time." He paused, sat up straighter, and now seemed to be looking at something beyond Joan, beyond the room. "Do you remember, sweetheart? Yes, of course you remember—how the Pleiades were your necklace on the night of falling stars."

Joan felt torn; to eavesdrop on such intimate memories was indecent, but to interrupt him seemed even worse.

"Is he senile?" Tim whispered, and Joan thought to herself, that's it, whatever it costs me, I'm done with this man.

"Uncle," said Daniel. "I'd like to introduce you to Joan Reed and Tim Faber, the people from Science Cable T.V."

Luke turned slowly to look at his nephew, then smiled. "Of course, Danny. Please, have a seat, all of you. Elena!" he called out. "Please see that our guests have something to drink."

"Just some bottles of water, Elena," said Daniel. "Thank you."

"We are so honored to meet you, Dr. Noongwook," said Joan. "I've been immersing myself in the life and times of Georges Lemaître, and I want the world to know what an astonishing man he was. Can you tell us when the two of you first met?"

"The winter of nineteen thirty-three," said Luke. "It's been almost eighty years."

Joan glanced at Tim to see if he'd registered the significance of the date, which was just two years after the Belgian physicist's revolutionary paper had first appeared in English.

"I love Georges," Luke continued, "and feel closer to him than ever, though he's been gone for over forty years."

"Please tell us about him," said Joan. "If you'd care to."

Luke smiled. "There I was, at twenty-one, gaping up at a desert sky ablaze with stars. As a small boy, I was taught they were holes in the ceiling of the great ice-house—igloo, you'd call it—which allowed in light from Udlormiut, a place of warmth and food, of water and rest. That's not all wrong, I think, for the stars hint at greater things than themselves. And it was those greater things he taught me, Ms. Reed. *He determines the number of the stars, he gives to all of them their names.*"

"Lemaître had an encyclopedic knowledge of the heavens, you mean?"

"A verse from the Psalms, which speaks of God." Luke was silent for a few moments. "I owe Georges and Milt my life," he said softly. "But that's a story for another day."

"Do you mean Milt Humason, Dr. Noongwook?" she asked, her pulse quickening as she thought about the strange suspicion that had been reported to the FBI. "We'd love to hear your tale."

"Oh, it's David who could tell it best," said Luke. "He and Georges, they were blood brothers."

"My grandfather," explained Daniel. "But he's long since passed away."

"That reminds me," said Luke. "The keys to the Talbot are in my top left desk drawer. I want you to sell it, Danny, and use the money as you think best. Only, first, take me for one last ride." He grinned like a mischievous child.

"One last ride? That's a bit melodramatic, wouldn't you say?" said

Daniel. "You're not departing this vale of tears before you turn one hundred, at the very least. But thank you, Uncle Luke, that's quite a gift."

"Just get it cleaned and tuned and put in a full tank of gas. I'll let you know where we're going when the time is right." Luke turned to Joan and Tim. "I know what you want, Ms. Reed and Mr. Faber; the answer to the mystery of the missing language in the translation of the 1927 paper. The answer is in a letter Georges wrote, a copy of which is in my possession; I meant to have it ready for you, but my files seem to be a bit out of order."

"He's a pack rat," said Daniel. "I'll help you find it, Uncle; if I leave it to you, these poor folks will be waiting for weeks."

"That's very exciting, Dr. Noongwook," said Joan. "But I can't help asking, can you tell us anything about what it says?"

"I want you to read it," said Luke, "and see what you think, before I say a word."

"Ah. Very well. We'll wait with the proverbial bated breath."

They said their goodbyes, and Daniel drove Joan and Tim back to Babylon West.

"I know this is none of my business," said Tim. "But the Talbot your uncle mentioned—that's a vintage car from way back, if I'm not mistaken. It would be amazing to tool around in one of those."

Daniel chuckled.

"Yes, it's a model from 1929. It was my grandfather David's; a present from a prize fighter friend of his who'd once been heavyweight champion of the world. Grandfather was forced to sell it, actually, and it was Uncle Luke who was able to buy it back and restore it, years later."

"You're full of surprises," said Tim. "And an accomplished apologist to boot. I'd enjoy talking more, sometime, if you don't mind my raw edges."

"I'd like that," said Daniel. "Most people are entirely too smooth."

He doesn't wear a wedding ring, Joan noticed, eyeing the pastor's left hand. And then thought: What is wrong with me? I've not yet broken up with Tim and here I am, thinking indecent thoughts about a man of God.

She felt her face flush, and hoped neither man had noticed.

~~⟶

Alone in his library, Luke settled back into his pillows, half listening to a Mozart violin sonata that played softly in the background. *The barrier between this world and the next is thinning, Julia. You're so close, I can almost feel you, almost smell the sweetness of your breath. It won't be long now, darling.*

It won't be long.

Chapter Eleven
The Fallen Man

Mother and I stayed at the Trading Post until 1930, longer than I ever would have dreamed. It was for my benefit, I suppose; with Asaaluk's encouragement, Ray had arranged for me to go to the local high school, which was attended primarily by whites and provided an education far beyond what I would have received back home. I developed a love for math and science, excelling to the point that Principal Swenson accused me of cheating. He was magnanimous in helping a few children of the aboriginal race, but for an Eskimo kid to do better than whites in such subjects was unthinkable. I handed him my textbooks and dared him to ask me as many questions as he liked; if I missed a single answer, he could fail me and I'd leave in disgrace. But he gave me back my books after five minutes, saying he had no time for such nonsense and warning me against the sin of pride.

Beyond that, though, if we had gone back to Nenana, my father would once again have been impossibly far away; it would have been to admit defeat. And, though she rarely smiled, I could tell that my mother enjoyed her work, putting more into the figurines of polar bears and kayaking Eskimos than Ray asked of her. Her work sold well, and our share of the proceeds grew to be more than could be hidden under the loose floorboard in our room. I hollowed out the insides of old schoolbooks, filled them with cash, tightly rolled, and stored them under my bed.

I graduated at the top of my class in June. That day, Mother took me aside, put her hands on my shoulders, and said, "You've grown as tall and strong as your father, Uukkarnit, only more handsome. What would I have done, what would I do, without you? Life would be too bitter to bear."

I gazed at her with devotion and love, at a loss for words. The lines on her face had deepened, and she looked at me with warrior eyes.

"It's time," she said, simply. "We'll leave at dawn."

~>

At King Street Station, Asaaluk, who had grown yet more stout, enveloped me in her arms and wept a fountain of tears. Ray, taciturn as ever, shook my hand, but then clasped me close and gave me a parting gift: an antique hunting knife, its handle carved from walrus tusk. We said our final goodbyes and boarded the train.

We made many stops, transferring in Chicago for the last leg to New York. Everywhere, conversations were somber and muted; the stock market crash of '29, which to us had been just another headline in the papers, had ushered in a darkness over the land. I heard fear in people's voices, saw panic in their faces. What if my father could not find work, if he, too, were among the desperate men with hopeless eyes?

After three days of travel, we arrived at Pennsylvania Station in New York, put our suitcases in a storage locker, and hailed a cab. The Pinkerton agents had given us the last known residence of Kathleen Byrne: 20 West 59th Street, on the island of Manhattan. The cabbie, clearly disdainful, made us show him some cash before he would take us anywhere. When my mother read him the address, he laughed.

"Looks like I've some upscale injuns in my cab! Well, your money's green enough, so off we go."

He started the meter and meandered south before backtracking, bringing us at last to an elegant stone edifice just off Fifth Avenue. Across the street was a low stone wall that bordered Central Park.

A uniformed doorman looked askance at us as we approached the building's wrought-iron front doors.

"See here, be off with the likes of ya!" he said, though we were dressed respectably enough, and appropriately for the summer heat. The cabbie had been no fool; our brown faces were not welcome here.

"I have urgent business with Kathleen Byrne," my mother said. "She once lived at this address."

"Hah!" said the doorman, but I could see he was intrigued. "What sort of business would that be?"

My mother hesitated for a moment, then decided to risk the truth.

"She stole my husband. I've come to get him back."

He raised his eyebrows. "Mr. Victor?" She nodded and he smirked. "Lazy one—you're well rid of him, if you want my opinion. Out till all hours, came home at dawn and slept 'til afternoon."

"Watch your tongue," I said, with rising anger, "or you'll find it no longer in your mouth."

"Cheeky lad! I've a mind to box your ears."

"I apologize for my son's rudeness," said my mother, "but it is only natural for a boy to defend his father. Do you know the places my husband went at night, how he spent his time? I'll make this worth your while, if you can tell me where my husband or Kathleen Byrne might be."

The doorman palmed a five-dollar bill that my mother had proffered.

"Of Mr. Victor, I've not the foggiest, ma'am. But as to Miss Byrne— she was a bad sort, that one, and got what she deserved, you ask me."

"Speak plainly, please."

He smirked again and rubbed two fingers together. My mother showed a glimpse of another bill, then said, "First, tell me what you know."

The doorman lowered his voice to a stage whisper.

"Only that she was shipped off to where they keep the lepers. You can hardly blame her lover—sorry, your husband, ma'am—for leaving, for I've heard a leper's parts fall off one by one; today their nose, tomorrow their fingers or toes. Who'd want to wake up next to a horror like that?"

"Where is this place for lepers?" my mother asked.

"I've no idea," said the doorman. "Perhaps in hell."

"That's not good enough," said my mother, and turned to go.

"Hey! You owe me, you miserable squaw!" The doorman reached out to grab her shoulder, and then the ulu knife was flashing, cleanly slicing off the brass buttons of his coat. My mother held its blade a fraction of an inch from his jugular, and stared him in the eye.

"You're lucky I let you keep anything at all," she said at last. The doorman backed off slowly, sweat forming in beads on his forehead, and we turned and walked away.

~⟶

Over the years, I've often dreamed of the man my mother found in Central Park. We never learned his name; I know him only as the fallen man, though sometimes in my dreams he opens his sorrowful eyes and speaks.

Mother and I were resting on a park bench in the shade, trying to decide what to do next. I paid little attention to her ideas, for my mind was racing with troubled thoughts: had my father really descended to the level the doorman had described? As though she knew what I was thinking, Mother stopped in mid-sentence and said to me, "Hold close to your memories of Taliriktug, Uukkarnit. Though he has betrayed us, yet we will not betray him in our hearts. Many are there who would break your spirit because their own are shattered, and they have not the strength to set themselves right."

Finding Kathleen Byrne was our best hope of finding Father, and we decided to seek out a library where I'd learn everything I could about lepers, their strange disease, and the mysterious places where they are sent. Our throats were parched from the summer heat, so I went to buy us lemonades from a man hawking cool drinks and custard from his pushcart, a block away. I was gone for less than ten minutes; when I got back, my mother was nowhere to be seen.

Panic gripped me; how could I have left her side?

"Uukkarnit!"

It took me a few moments to find where her voice was coming from, but then I saw her, kneeling in the grass by some elm trees fifty yards away. Lying on the ground was a man, about my mother's age, who seemed more dead than alive. He had an intelligent face that seemed frozen in anguish, the face that yet haunts my dreams. Mother had taken a scarf from her handbag, cut it in half, and was using it to stem the bleeding from his wounds.

She had heard a shout for help and saw the man being attacked by robbers who beat him senseless and made off with all his valuables; there was nothing to show his name or where he lived. Only the slightest motion of his chest showed that he was still among the living.

My mother took one of the lemonades and put a few drops on the man's lips.

"I thought, Uukkarnit, of your father, alone in a land where people like us are despised. Who would be there for him, if he were to meet with misfortune, other than strangers, as we are to this man?"

My heart swelled with love for my mother, and I helped her to minister to the fallen man. When his bleeding was staunched, I went to find help and hailed a mounted policeman who was patrolling the park. After he'd assured us that the man would be cared for at a nearby hospital, and declined to accept mother's offer of money, I asked him where the closest library might be; it turned out there was one sixteen blocks south of us, less than a mile away.

Twenty minutes later we arrived at the most magnificent structure I had ever seen, a white marble palace guarded by two great stone lions. We climbed the broad stairs, walked past massive columns, and entered into a reading room that seemed impossibly large, the ceiling five stories high, covered with ornate carvings and murals of idyllic clouds in an azure sky. This was my introduction to the New York Public Library.

For five hours I explored, scouring the card catalogues and bookstacks. My mother and I paged through a large illustrated tome titled *Infectious Diseases*. Leprosy: attacks the peripheral nerves, skin, respiratory tract, eyes, and lining of the nose. Lack of ability to feel pain, resulting in repeated injury. Incipient blindness. We paged through a grotesque gallery of the afflicted, their faces disfigured by obscene growths, hands bent and twisted into claws.

"I would choose death over such a fate," said my mother, looking away from the book.

I read on: Hansen's Disease. Mycobacterium leprae. Leprologists. *National leprosarium.*

"Mother," I said. "There's only one place in the United States where lepers are sent: United States Marine Hospital Number Sixty-Six. It's in Carville, Louisiana."

"Is that far?" she asked.

I set off to find out and came back shortly with the answer.

"Fourteen hundred miles, or thereabouts. We'll walk back to Pennsylvania Station from here, then take a train to a city only sixty miles from Carville, called New Orleans."

My mother looked at me as though I were Magellan and Marco Polo rolled into one.

"How grateful I am for you, Uukkarnit!" she said, standing up and, in a gesture of unusual intimacy, running her hand through my hair. "Come, we have travelled this far, we'll not rest until we find your father and bring him home."

~

We arrived two days later at New Orleans Union Station, and I began asking whether anyone could help us get to Carville. One after another, the men I asked shrugged or scowled and turned away, until a skinny black man in overalls approached us.

"You da folks wan' go ta Carville?"

It took me a moment to understand what he had said, and when I nodded yes, he added "Quoi faire? Why you wan' go d'ere?"

"We have business at the Marine Hospital," I explained. "Can you help us?"

"D'at place give me the frissons!" he said, his body language telling us what he meant, but then smiled. "I am Gabriel. Sure, I take you ta Carville, no problem."

We introduced ourselves and negotiated the fare, which turned out to be the price of gasoline and any other automotive necessities, plus three dollars for Gabriel to take us there and back—though there might be a surcharge, he explained, if our conversation proved to be dull.

Before he began the elaborate process to start his Model A, Gabriel bowed his head in prayer.

"Cher Dieu, bless d'ese sojourners whom you have brought to me, 'n bless your servant Gabriel 'n his miserable voiture, may its wheels roll for one mo' day, par les mérites de Jésus Christ, mon Sauveur."

The sixty mile journey took four hours on the dusty roads, with frequent stops to make repairs. These would be accompanied by a blizzard of Cajun cursing, although Gabriel's good humor always returned as soon as he got back behind the wheel.

"Dem's da bald cypress," he said, telling us about the unfamiliar landscape, "which love da bayou, oh yeah. 'n dat d'ere's a sweetgum, wit' d'ose star-shaped leaves." He pointed out the slash pine, and the sweetbay magnolias with songbirds on every branch. We saw egrets, and a pelican, a creature so strange to us that my mother and I laughed, and Gabriel, pleased that his passengers were happy, joined in our merriment.

In turn, we told him of our snow-bound land; of the tundra, the herds of caribou, the spawning salmon, the blue glint of the glaciers, and the grizzlies who, when they stood and sniffed the wind, were ten feet tall.

"No, you are teasing me," he said, delighted at what he was hearing. "But, if d'at be true, I drive you d'ere, no charge!"

At last we reached a high iron gate that marked the entrance to Marine Hospital Sixty-Six, where we were stopped by a uniformed guard.

This I hadn't expected.

"Comment ça se roule?" asked Gabriel, flashing the man a big, gap-toothed grin.

The guard winked at him, but turned a stern face to mother and me.

"What's your business here?" he asked.

My mother nudged me. "We're here to see Miss Kathleen Byrne," I said. "We've important matters to discuss."

He told us that appointments had to be made in advance, and I explained that we'd travelled all the way from the Alaskan Territory just for this purpose.

The guard picked up the phone in his booth and briefly explained the situation to someone at the other end. "Yes, Sister Genevieve, just a woman, her son, and their driver, monsieur Gabriel." There was a pause. "Yes, him." He listened for a moment more, then thanked her and turned to us.

"You're in luck, the Sister Servant Superior will see you. You know the way, Gabriel."

"Indeed. Merci bien, mon ami."

We drove through what seemed a vast park, though one surrounded by a barbed-wire fence. Everywhere were live oaks, their ancient limbs draped with Spanish moss.

"Sister Genevieve, she da big boss," Gabriel told us. "Been here many, many years."

"Why do you and the white soldier both call her 'sister'?" mother asked.

He laughed. "Sister Superior, she head of da nuns who work here. D'ey all volunteers, Uncle Sam don't pay d'em a dime. No one else want ta take care of lepers, everyone scared but da sisters. Don't know d'at I would be so brave, myself."

"A nun," I explained to my mother, "is a woman who has devoted herself to the white man's God."

"Oh la la!" exclaimed Gabriel. "You t'ink d'is a suntan, you t'ink I roll in da mud of da Big River, 'n it come off in da bath? D'ere God is my God, you bet, and your God, too."

"I'm sorry," I said.

"Yeah, d'ats okay. Jésus Christ, He forgive sins every day, even mine."

We arrived at a grand ante-bellum mansion, with a graceful balcony from which one could reach out and touch the trees. Gabriel explained that this was the administration building; the lepers themselves lived in wooden cottages linked by boardwalks, spread out over the grounds.

"I am going to breathe in da fresh air, 'n sit in d'at little chapel over d'ere. You come for me when you're t'rough, no rush."

We had hardly gotten out of the Model A when Sister Genevieve came out to greet us, ushered us inside, and offered us iced tea.

"You told Sergeant Blanchard that you wish to speak to one of our patients, a Miss Kathleen Byrne?" she asked, once we'd been seated and had assured her that the journey from New Orleans had not been overly arduous.

"Yes, please," my mother replied.

"I regret to say, we have no one here by that name. But that is not surprising; it is common practice for our patients to come here under assumed names, such is the shame associated with their disease. Even some of those who work here change their names. So, what to do? I must respect the privacy of our patients, I cannot parade them by until you see your Miss Byrne."

Sister Genevieve could see the disappointment on our faces, and offered us a kind smile. "But do not lose hope. You have come a terribly long way, and I would like to help you. Tell me whatever you can of your story, and I will see what I can do."

And so my mother told our tale, from father's role in the Great Race of Mercy to the story we'd heard from the doorman two days before. When she finished, the Sister Superior stood up, came behind, and put her hands on us.

"Bless you, dear ones. You have suffered much. I need to think about what you have said, and there is a matter to which I must attend. You are welcome to wait here or take your drinks outdoors, where we've benches in the shade."

Mother said she'd enjoy the fresh air, so we thanked Sister Genevieve and seated ourselves outside with fresh glasses of iced tea.

"I no longer have the strength to kill, Uukkarnit," said my mother, once we were completely alone. "I am too tired, too filled with sadness. I only want your father back. Are you disappointed in me? Speak the truth."

"Never," I said. "Never in a thousand years."

~⇒

We must have both fallen asleep, for I awoke with a start, with my mother's head resting peacefully on my shoulder.

"Yura Noongwook?"

There was a nun standing in front of us; I looked up and found myself staring into the face of Kathleen Byrne.

Chapter Twelve
The Prayer Candles

Joan hadn't seen her brother in over twenty years, only talked on the phone a few times and written him brief notes with checks attached. She had parked her rental car outside his address on the outskirts of Las Vegas, and spent a while surveying the scene. Willie was living in an old single-wide trailer set in the midst of a large fenced-in yard, surrounded by heavy equipment that she recognized from her grandfather's construction business: excavators, trenchers, graders, backhoes, all looking like skeletons in a dinosaur graveyard. A hot wind blew eddies of dust around the yard. No one had used that equipment in years.

She leaned her forehead against the steering wheel. Willie had been working for a developer until the real-estate meltdown, putting in sewer laterals and underground lines. Then, all of a sudden, nobody was buying; whole subdivisions built on spec were just sitting there empty, and if some sucker came to look at one of the homes, his boss, Judson, paid him to pretend to be living in the house next door, grilling burgers on a backyard bar-b-q. On one of their phone calls, he'd described to Joan how he stood in front of a mirror and practiced his one line: "Hey, buddy, you'll love it here—when you move in, come on over and bring the kids!" But he couldn't concentrate, all the memories and regrets of his wasted life crowding into his mind; he just kept flipping those burgers until they were charred, and black smoke filled the air. Willie had persuaded Judson that his junkie girlfriend, Sugar, could pose as his wife, but she'd show up manic or depressive and in either case was bad news.

My baby brother, I should have taken care of him, she thought. He has a good heart, just never had a dad, no one to steer him right. After their father died, their mother, Star, had quickly remarried, and when Joan worked up the courage to say that her stepfather had been touching her, Star had sent her off to live with her grandparents. *Girls imagine things like that*, her mother had explained. *I got nothing without this man, can't let your fantasies ruin my life.* She'd been twelve, and Willie only four. He'd stayed with Star until the day she died, then went off alone into the world, fifteen years old.

A knock came on the car window, and Joan raised her head. It was Willie with his killer smile that charmed everyone, even in a face ruined by crystal meth.

"You okay?" he asked. "I was gettin' worried about ya."

He was so skinny! All Joan could do was hug her brother and cry.

"Ah geez, you're gettin' me all wet, come on in."

He led her into the trailer and introduced Joan to Bunny, his pet rabbit. She noticed that there were little Bunny turds everywhere.

"Are you still seeing Sugar?" Joan asked.

"Nah," said Willie, trying to look nonchalant, "that didn't work out."

Joan saw two faded black-and-white photographs that Willie had pinned to a corkboard: herself, in a ruffled dress she must have worn to a birthday party when she was maybe ten years old, and their father, still in his twenties, only a few years before he died. Look at him, she thought, in his white t-shirt and thick wavy hair; he could be my son. But I don't have a son, just this long-dead father, frozen in time. People like Willie and me don't have children, she thought. We're too broken inside.

"Tell me about him again," said Willie. "I can't hardly remember a thing from back then."

"He was gentle," said Joan, smiling at her brother. "Just like you. We'd kneel together at bedtime and pray. And giggle when I asked for silly things. I should have been praying for you, all these years; but after dad was gone, I never prayed. We should pray, Willie, we should both pray."

"Better you than me, sissie; don't think God wouldn't hardly listen to my prayers."

"I don't know," said Joan, wondering for a moment how God decided whether a prayer deserved his attention.

"I never understood how he died," said Willie. "Mom never gave me a straight answer."

"Story kept changing," Joan replied. "Motorcycle accident. No, a brain tumor. No, he drowned. Hey, maybe it was all three!"

"Yeah, tumor caused him to drive his hog right into the Truckee," said Willie, and they both tried to laugh. "Mom was fifty-one fifty, we both got the scars to prove it," he added, using street slang referring to the section of the California penal code which allowed for involuntary commitment to a mental ward.

"I hated her for sending me away," said Joan. "Still, I was jealous of you, getting to be with her. I wanted her to love me. I remember following mom around, I couldn't have been more than five, asking, 'do you love me?'"

It flashed through Joan's mind that she'd asked the same question of her husband before he'd left. Yes, of course I love you, babe. Just not enough.

"It wasn't no picnic," said Willie. "We moved outta Placerville, down to Fresno, a couple years after you left."

"That bastard she married, Lonnie, he'd left by then?"

"Yeah, he didn't last long. Fresno's where she got hooked on pinks, we'd go to Thrifty's and she'd load up on Preludin, then buy me that coconut pineapple ice cream. Man, I loved those cones! If she had a job, I'd get three scoops. We were living in rat-infested dumps, ya know, places without windows or running water, but if mom was doin' pinks she'd be in hyper overdrive, scrubbin' every square inch, they'd be the cleanest dumps you'd ever seen. Afterwards, she'd be in bed for days, I'd go out and scrounge through garbage cans lookin' for somethin' to eat."

"I know," said Joan. "I know it was tough."

"No, I don't think you do know," said Willie, just matter-of-fact, no anger in his voice as he absently stroked Bunny's ears. Even the rabbit looks skinny, Joan thought, and she looked around for a carrot or some sort of rabbit food, but there was nothing in sight.

"I was maybe eight when she met Lou," Willie continued. "He was a carpenter, worked framin' jobs—my kind'a guy, I mean, if I had a two-by-four I could pretend was a dozer and push around in the dirt, I was a happy boy, and Lou had plenty of those. He was a decent man and loved mom like nobody's business; she wasn't much past thirty, still had all her looks. But her brain was short-circuitin', sissie, sometimes I could almost see the sparks fly. She made him stop workin' in the wintertime 'cause she started thinkin' if he were out of her sight he'd be off with some other woman. Why only winters, I dunno, it was all crazy made-up stuff. We'd hunt for pecans that lay under the snow, put 'em in gunny sacks and sell 'em in town; those winters were lean times, man. At night, if I had to cough, I'd stifle it with a pillow, 'cause she thought coughs were some kind'a secret code, messages his girlfriends had given me to pass on. Lou hung in for five years, then he was gone, too. After they made Preludin illegal, mom was drinkin' Coca-Cola and Wild Turkey 101. You know the rest."

"Yeah, her farewell present to me," said Joan. "Gramma called to say mom had shown up, asked me to come over. I joined her and Grampa in the backyard, we were wondering what mom was up to and where you were, when we heard the shotgun go off. All three of us knew what that meant, there was never a doubt in our minds. I knew they couldn't handle it, Willie, that it'd be up to me. Well, I was all grown up, I went in and cleaned up the mess. Took some time, there were bits of her teeth and skull embedded in the bathroom wall."

Brother and sister were silent for a while, and there was only the sound of the wind, stirring up little tornados of dust in the yard outside.

"Judson's been lettin' me stay here, guard his crap," said Willie, deciding a change of subject was in order. "I told him he ought'a auction it off, but the crazy bastard thinks he's gonna get back in business some day."

"I don't know how you can stand living here," said Joan.

"I've lived in worse," said Willie, then gave her one of his irresistible smiles. "It's so great to see you, sissie, seems like forever and a day."

Joan felt her face flush, and thought, I've been ashamed of him all these years for being in and out of prison, no criminal mastermind, just a two-bit crook doing B&E's to support his appetite for crystal meth. I should have gotten over my shame. A memory came to her of stepping off the school bus and seeing Willie waiting for her in his poopy diapers. She'd been ashamed then, too.

"I was angry at you," she said. "Angry that you were doing hard time, because I'd imagine the worst was going on at Lacy and all the other places you got locked up."

"It was a bore, mostly," Willie replied. "But I don't do that stuff anymore."

"You're still using drugs, don't tell me you're not."

"What, I look like I'm tweakin' right now?" Willie gazed at her with his beautiful, sad eyes.

"Let's not argue," Joan said. "You look like you could use a meal— Denny's has always been your favorite, right? I noticed there's one half a mile down the road. We can bring back something for Bunny, too."

"That'd be nice," said Willie, and they headed out to Joan's car.

~

"Has someone from Babylon West gotten in touch with you?" asked Joan, as she watched her brother bite into a bacon double cheeseburger.

"Hell, yeah," said Willie. "I got a call from the Oz man himself. Figured you knew all about it. My sister, hob-nobbin' with Vegas royalty, never would 'a dreamed."

"Woah!" Joan had assumed Osman would just have some assistant follow through. "That's wonderful, did he say what he'd like you to do?"

"You really don't know? He wants me to work directly for him, doin'—well, all he said was, 'this and that.' But I start in the mornin'. Already set the alarm."

"You're kidding!" The astonishment in Joan's voice registered with Willie, who looked down, his face darkening.

"What, you thought he was gonna have me cleanin' toilets and moppin' floors?"

"No, I'm just so glad for you, is all." But that *was* pretty much what she had been thinking. Before going to bed the previous night, she had gotten down on her knees, just as she had so many years ago with her dad, and prayed for Willie to catch a break. She'd worried all the while that doubt was keeping her prayers earthbound, that God only listened to people with a deep, abiding faith.

"Ah, that's okay, Joanie," her brother said, his face relaxing into that charming smile. "It floored me, too. But I just figured, that big sister 'a mine can pretty much do anything. Ya know, last bar I got thrown out of, everyone's watchin' some hockey game and I kept tellin' the barkeep, turn the channel, man, my sister's show is on. Turn to channel one-thirty-seven, you morons, ya might actually learn somethin'. Didn't go over real well."

They both laughed.

"Hey, by the way," said Willie, "that Pastor Gold you mentioned picked you and your boss up when you flew in—was that Dan Gold?"

"Yes," said Joan. "How do you know him?"

"Aw hell, everyone knows Pastor Dan. He runs a soup kitchen out'a his church, I've eaten there many a night. Big dude, never needs any help keepin' the peace, folks know not to mess with the man."

"Do you know how he got those scars?" Joan asked, and she could tell the eagerness must have shown in her face, because Willie grinned at her.

"You like Big Dan, huh?"

At first she felt annoyed, but then Joan smiled back at her brother.

"Well, sure," she said, "who wouldn't?"

"What I heard," said Willie, "when he was a kid he was burned in a fire that killed his parents. But people say all kinds 'a crap, so who knows."

The two traded stories and reminisced for another two hours until Joan at last dropped Willie off at the trailer and drove back to Babylon West. That night, in her hotel room, she searched for old news stories about Daniel Gold, and finally found a clip of a TV broadcast from 1973.

Fire claimed the lives of local pastor Nathan Gold and wife Samantha late last night as they slept in their Las Vegas home...the prognosis is uncertain for their 13-year-old son, who suffered third-degree burns..."They always had prayer candles burning, lots of them," said a neighbor. Ironically, it might just have been one of those candles whose flames were spread by the gusting desert winds...

∼

Earlier that day, around the time Joan had taken off to meet Willie,

Tim had been in his room, trying to decide what to do. Daniel had given him his cell phone number and an open invitation to call any time, and he was tempted to do just that. His ego had been bruised by their conversations to date, and that morning he'd rehearsed several devastatingly powerful arguments for atheism while he showered and shaved. Tim laughed, imagining Daniel growing flustered, unable to counter his withering critique.

But something bothered him. He *liked* the man. He wanted Daniel to like him. Maybe they could get together for a beer and just talk, get to know one another, hash things out.

On the other hand, there were plenty of Daniels out there. This Oz character, however, who obviously wanted to curry favor with a hotshot producer like himself, no doubt with the hope of gaining some additional publicity for his wacky Tower of Babel scheme, *he* was another story. How many times would Tim have the opportunity to be chauffeured around Vegas in a Rolls Royce limousine?

That settled it. Today, he'd take Oz up on his offer; he could always follow up with the pastor tomorrow, or the day after that. After all, he and Joan would be at Babylon West all week, there was plenty of time.

Chapter Thirteen
Lazarus

"Mrs. Noongwook?" Kathleen Byrne repeated, and my mother stirred. "You must be Victor's son," she said to me. "I'm sorry, but I don't remember your name."

Though her hair was completely covered by the headpiece of her habit, and five years had passed, I knew instantly who she was; but I stayed silent. It was my mother's right to say the first words.

Mother opened her eyes, and the two women looked at each other for a moment that seemed without end.

"You knew me as Kath—"

"I know who you are," said my mother. "Can you tell me where my husband is?"

"No, I'm so sorry. But I would like to tell you everything I do know," said Kathleen. "Can we go to my room and talk?" She kneeled in front of us, on the ground. "I beg you, please."

"Very well," said my mother, and we followed her to a small room in the nuns' quarters, not far away.

$\sim$

"I seduced your husband, the father of your son, and lured him to New York, on a whim," said Kathleen Byrne. "It would be thrillingly shocking that I was living with this hero from a place people only read about in books, I'd be the talk of the town. Such was the depth of evil in my heart.

"But something happened that I didn't expect: I found myself falling in love with Victor—at least, I thought it was love. To go off and cover news stories, to be away from him, to wonder where he was and what he was doing, became agony, and I never gave a moment's thought that you were feeling such pain yourself. After a while, I quit my job so that we could be together all the time. That was the beginning of the end.

"I put the money I'd saved into shares of a trust that invested in

Florida real estate, so we could still afford the dinners out and parties at the Plaza hotel. The stock had tripled in the previous two years, but of course it turned out that '25 was the top; by 1926 I had not a dime left to my name. Hearst had been furious when I quit; it wasn't hard to believe the stories he spread that I was unreliable, damaged goods. My reporting career was over, no one would hire me.

"Victor wasn't happy about that—nothing was making him happy, it seemed. He'd been spending time at the 21 Club, a speakeasy only a few blocks from where we lived, and started drinking more and more. His contract to promote Listerine was soon cancelled, and nothing came along to take its place. Victor and the Great Race of Mercy were old news, all people wanted to hear about was Aimee McPherson, the faith healer who'd disappeared.

"The day came when Victor left and never came back. Only a year earlier, I had been at the top of the heap, the world adored me, and I could let money run through my fingers like sand. I had been loyal to no one, and now no one stuck by me. I was broke and alone. I didn't leave my apartment, I didn't get out of bed, I didn't eat.

"One day, I roused myself, it must have been the middle of the afternoon, made my way to the bathroom, and when I caught a glance of myself in the mirror, I screamed, for what I saw was a monster, a horror, a freak. I sank to my knees on the cold tile floor, and the only thing I could think to do was pray. All I had were memories of childhood trips to church, but I said what I could: Blessed Virgin Mary, I left you and Jesus, the fruit of your womb, so long ago; and now here I am, a prodigal daughter, calling out for you to save me, if there be any way that I might find my way home.

"I stayed like that for hours, murmuring prayers, until at last I fell asleep, and awoke sometime in the middle of the night in that darkened room. Yura, for the first time since my childhood I felt an inexplicably sweet peace, it was as though my adult life had been nothing but a bad dream. I didn't want to move, I didn't want to do anything to break that beautiful peace. And that is when I heard a voice so clearly not my own, asking, 'Do you love me, Kathleen?' The question terrified me, because I had turned from God and lived my own wicked way, yet it made me look within my heart and find what I hadn't known was there. 'Yes, I love you, Lord,' I replied. 'Therefore do not be afraid,' he said. 'Turn on the light and see yourself as you are, then go, and do what you know is right.'

"I stood up and turned on the electric light. My face was just as it had always been, but my hair had turned pure white. I puzzled over the Lord's words, until the answer came upon me like an avalanche. Only two years before, I had done a story on the Carville leprosarium, all ugliness and sensation to sell papers for Hearst. I'd mocked the nuns behind their backs. The image I'd seen in the mirror, that had sent me to my knees, had been a leper's face.

"Within the week, I travelled to Louisiana and asked to join the Sisters of Charity, and I've been here ever since. When I entered the novitiate, I became Sister Anna Lazarus. Kathleen Byrne is no more."

"You did this for your God?" my mother asked her.

"No, Yura, my God did this for me."

We sat in silence for a few minutes as mother thought over what had been said.

"But you did not do what would have been hardest of all," said my mother. "The thing this God would most have wanted you to do. You did not come and see Uukkarnit and me."

I saw the woman we had once known as Kathleen Byrne turn pale and drop her gaze to the ground.

"You are right," she said, raising her head at last. "I am sorry, from the bottom of my soul. I did what was easier; I was too ashamed to face you and your son."

My mother later told me that what happened next was as though a bolt of lightning had flashed through her mind. She realized that somehow she had been given a great power, something so much mightier than anything of which she had ever known, ever heard, ever dreamed.

She had the power to forgive.

She had no idea from whence this power came, she only knew it seemed, not an exhilarating thing, but a burden, impossibly heavy to lift. But something, or Someone, was telling her, Yura, only you can do this, and do it you must; whether it tears the sinews from your bones, you must lift this burden up.

"I forgive you, Sister Anna Lazarus," my mother said. "And I forgive Taliriktug. I forgive you both."

Then my mother realized that she'd been wrong, the burden was not in the saying of those words, but in having left them unsaid. She'd forgiven her husband and the woman who'd stolen her happiness, and what she felt now was lightness itself.

Sister Anna's face was wet with tears.

"Perhaps Taliriktug, also, is too ashamed to return," my mother mused.

"I have only one thought as to where he might be," said Sister Anna. "Your husband drank often with a man he admired, who boasted of the riches to be had out west and claimed to own silver mines somewhere in Nevada."

"Then we will go there next," Mother said. She rose, and I followed her to find Gabriel for the long drive back to New Orleans. This was the only time I believe we saw a leper; a figure, standing in the shadows, waiting until we were gone to step out into the light of day.

Chapter Fourteen
The Intersection of Grand and Lafayette

"All you're talking about is throwing a fight, not killing a man," said Jack Johnson to David Gold as the two of them had breakfast in their Oklahoma City hotel. "It ain't that big a deal. Over the years, I shelled out for a few chumps to take a fall, when it wasn't an important fight, just to keep things smooth—after all, you never know, anyone can land a lucky punch. So, from what you're telling me, you'll have one bout handed to you, and you'll hand some chowderhead another. Everyone does it. You don't have to look like you just sold your momma down the river, boy. Cheer up."

"Yeah, I know all that, Jack," said David. "I'm fine."

"If you're fine, I'm a member of the Ku Klux Klan. Look at you, hardly eaten a bite, eggs getting cold." Johnson reached over and helped himself to one of David's slices of toast. "No point letting good food go to waste."

"If I say I'm fine, I'm fine," replied David.

"Touchy! Okay, I'll go easy on you. Let's think happier thoughts. I got a surprise for you, how we're getting to Reno." The two men had fights scheduled in Reno over the next several weeks. David knew that Irene, Johnson's third wife, was meeting them there, and that his friend was anxious to show off the two new cars a Nevada dealer had waiting for him. "But first, got to go to the little boy's room," the champ added. "I'll be right back."

～

After thinking it over for days, David had decided to end his boxing career. He was thirty-eight; no one took him seriously anymore, though he could still eke out a living through the novelty of being the Pummelin' Preacher, hawking his fights on Sundays to parishioners who might show up that Tuesday or Friday night. The problem, he told himself, is that I can't seek after the Lord, nor expect Him to listen to me, when

I'm earning my bread by punching men's lights out. I'm living the life of a brute, and wondering why I feel far from God.

It seemed to him that his losses in the ring were a gift, a message. Isaac's son, Jacob—surely, David thought, a fellow no less lost then he—was wounded while wrestling with an angel of God, whom he asked for a blessing.

He saw now that the wound itself *was* God's blessing.

But what would he do next? The Depression was like a storm gathering strength as it spread over the land, and there was no telling what the morrow would bring. How would he earn his keep?

David had no savings; he'd lived off his share of the purse from each fight, and the proceeds had been meager the past few years. He could have received love offerings for his Sunday sermons, but he thought that asking for them would have made him seem weak, as though he wasn't a winner, raking it in in the ring. If he were only an also-ran, why would anyone come to hear him preach?

There were bucket loads of dirty money to be had in the boxing world. David had never taken any before, but the more he thought about his situation, the more he wondered whether he wasn't being just a tad Pharisaical; boxing was entertainment, after all, and entertainers are paid to perform a script. Would participating in a rigged fight really be any different?

That was how David Gold had ended up in his hotel room the previous night, waiting as a sequence of operators connected a long-distance call to New York. After half an hour, the final operator told him that the party he'd requested was on the line.

"Hello, Ben," he said, and identified himself to the man on the other end of the phone.

"Davey Gold!" said the man named Ben. "Ain't this a small world. Just the other night I was hearin' stories about your dad, I got a lot of respect for the man, I kid you not. He's still in Sing Sing, right? You want me to bring him something, give him your regards?"

"No need for that," David said.

"I heard stories about you, too, Davey, about the old days, heard you used to be my kinda guy, a real terror. Hell on wheels. Where was it you used to hang out?"

"Grand Street," said David.

"Yeah, that was it. Me, I cut my teeth 'round the corner, on Lafayette. Moe and I, we started a protection racket there, back when we were just punk kids. Dollar a week from each pushcart merchant or we'd torch his goods. Some days, tell you the truth, I'd pass on the greenbacks, preferred to watch the flames."

They're all like him, David thought, anyone I might deal with. But if I'm going to do this, at least my cousin Ben will make it worth my while, and I can count on him to come through.

The two men talked for twenty minutes. After his loss to the Philadelphia Fury, the Pummelin' Preacher would go in as an underdog against any decent fighter. Ben would score by paying off David's opponent and betting big on the Pastor, who would win with a dramatic KO in the middle rounds. But what really intrigued the New Yorker was the money he could make from the follow-up bout. Once the news spread that the Pummelin' Preacher was on the comeback trail, there'd be all sorts of coverage in the sporting news. They'd advertise a tune-up fight against some palooka, as preparation for David taking on one of the big names, like Schmeling or Sharkey. But of course, he'd never get beyond the tune-up; the palooka would win in a shocking upset when the Pastor took a dive in one of the early rounds. Ben would make money on both fights and pay David well for his trouble.

After that, he'd be done with the dirty business, and his life would be all about God.

A commotion at the other end of the restaurant stirred David from his musings, and he stood up to see what was going on. Of course, as he should have expected, Jack was in the middle of it. The champ was standing in front of three thuggish looking men, keeping them away from a young man and woman who were seated in one of the booths.

Then one of the men drew a gun and pointed it between Johnson's eyes.

Chapter Fifteen
A Free Spirit

At the New Orleans public library, I discovered that Reno was the largest city in Nevada, so, though there were silver mines scattered throughout the state, it seemed the best place to start. Gabriel said he'd love to drive us, but feared the Model A would never survive the journey and we'd all be stranded in some desolate desert place. He asked his God to bless our travels, and we said goodbye to him at the station. There was a train leaving for Oklahoma City in a few hours; we'd spend the night there and catch another line bound for Denver the next day, then make our final transfer in Salt Lake City.

⁓

The next morning, my mother was still musing over the events of the previous day.

"Those lepers," she said to me, as we ate breakfast in our hotel, "they are outcasts, despised, just as we are, just as the black man, and the red man, too. Who is there to care for the strangers, the sojourners, the exiles in this land? Not Sedna, not Tatqim, not even Sila, breath of the world. Although the white woman was too weak to come to us and set things right, still, there was something powerful at work that led her to a place where lepers dwell, to live among them and seek to ease their pain. Of herself, I do not believe she would have followed such a path."

My mother's words brought back a memory from Alki, when the voice in the wind that blew through the trees had led me back to the Roadhouse, where Miss McSorley lay dying. But my thoughts were abruptly interrupted; three men were approaching our table with leering looks and evil in their eyes.

"Robbin' the cradle, ain't ya, good lookin'?" said their leader.

"Didn't know they let squaws in here," said another. "Maybe we better take her outside."

My mother's eyes never left mine. I knew she had her right hand on the ulu knife, just as the ivory handle of the hunting knife Ray had given me was in mine. I was sure that these men were cowards, like all bullies, and we would quickly have them on the run; only at just that moment, from out of nowhere, a large black man stepped in the way.

"'Scuse me, 'scuse me," said this fellow, who seemed to be playing the part of a buffoon. "Sorry, but this dining establishment is reserved strictly for human beings. Y'all need to turn around and slither back into whatever hole you crawled out of."

I had to stifle my laughter, and that was the point when the third man pulled a gun.

"We got a nigger with a mouth on him," said the gunman. "What say we find us a rope and a tree?"

"I really don't want to have to hurt you boys," said the black man, sounding remarkably nonchalant.

"You're goin' ta find out what hurtin's all about, boy—" said one of the other men, and then someone else appeared behind them, a bigger man yet, with the broadest shoulders I had ever seen, and put two of them in chokeholds while the black man laid the gunman out cold with a single blow to the point of his jaw.

Such was our introduction to Jack Johnson and David Gold.

~

"No way you're taking the train to Reno," said Johnson. He had been so gracious and exuberant in asking us to join them that my mother had agreed, and the table was now piled high with omelets, ham steaks, and French toast. "That'll take forever, and railway food ain't fit to eat. No, you're coming with us, instead; won't cost you a dime and we'll be there in time for dinner at the Riverside Hotel."

"Just how *are* we getting to Reno?" David asked.

"Same way as the birds," said Jack, with a huge grin.

"Don't tell me you're the pilot," said David. "Because if so, I'm joining them on the train."

"I might just learn to fly, now that you mention it. But not today—'cause I happen to be a close friend of the best pilot in this whole wide world. In fact," Jack said, turning to my mother, "she's a woman, 'bout the same age as you."

My heart leapt in my chest—to fly in an airplane! I had never imagined such an adventure would be possible.

"Mother," I said, "it will save us at least a day of travel. We've *got* to go with them!"

My mother allowed herself a small smile.

"If I can trust Mr. Johnson that the pilot is a woman, I suppose so."

After feasting for another half hour, Jack arranged for a taxi to take us to an airfield just outside of town. As we were leaving the hotel, we were approached by an elderly black gentleman with the most extraordinary white hair and beard.

"Excuse me, but aren't you Jack Johnson?" he asked, his voice deep and gravelly, yet warm.

"The one and only," replied our host.

"Saw you take apart Jeffries, must be twenty years ago; it was a glorious thing, sir, a sight to behold."

"A sweet memory," said Jack, and shook his hand.

The old man turned to David, who, though polite, hadn't had much to say since the altercation earlier that morning.

"Now you, preacher man. You took a pummelin' yourself, Tuesday night, but I reckon I've seen men take worse. You just stay in the Word, son, and all will be well with you, win or lose. Walk the narrow path. You hear?"

David stared at the man, and it seemed to me his face grew pale.

"I hear you, sir," he said.

"All right, then. Good day to y'all." The gentleman ruffled my hair affectionately, winked at mother, and ambled on.

~

I could see from a mile away which airplane was waiting for us: it was blood red, a crimson bullet, sleek and smooth, its cantilevered wing mounted atop the fuselage. At Jack's request, the driver let us off on the runway not far from the plane. Standing next to it was a handsome woman in her early thirties, wearing a brown leather jacket and aviator hat, with goggles pushed up on her forehead, "Hello, champ," she said. "My God, but you're getting fat!"

"Say what? I'm just big-boned," Jack replied, and made a valiant effort to suck in his gut.

"I don't suppose you smoke cigarettes or chew gum, do you?" she asked. "Might help you shed a few pounds."

"I puff only on fine cigars, you know that," he responded. "And chewing gum, why, that's just rude."

"Too bad, I've got contracts with Lucky Strike and Beech-Nut, I could have kept you well supplied." She looked us over. "You've brought guests. I'm Amelia Earhart, pleased to meet you."

We all shook hands. After Mother had introduced herself, she began to say, "This is my son, Uukkar—"

"Just call me Luke," I said, and then blushed a color to match Miss Earhart's plane. My mother raised her eyebrows, but from then on, Luke was my name.

"You can fit us all, can't you?" Jack asked.

"The Lockheed seats six," Amelia replied. "But it's just as well there's only five of us, champ, considering your avoirdupois. Let's get a move on, I want to be well past the Rockies by mid-afternoon."

After feeling the thrill of my first take-off, I lost interest in gazing down at the Oklahoma countryside, and my mind drifted, as it did so often, to thoughts of my father. In the New Orleans library, I had paged through one story after another about silver mining in Nevada. I didn't share them with my mother, for they made me sick at heart. Hundreds had perished, hundreds more maimed. Some mines plunged thousands of feet below the surface, where underground hot springs drove the temperatures unbearably high. Men had been blown to bits by premature explosions, tumbled down shafts to their deaths, or been crushed by runaway ore cars; but most terrible in my mind were the cave-ins, burying men alive. What would a man's last thoughts be, trapped in the suffocating darkness? What thoughts would my father have?

A hot wave of anger brought tears to my eyes. Could any treasure be worth more than the love of one's wife and child? Could it really be pride that was keeping him from us—was my father too ashamed to return, a prisoner of his own regret? Did he not realize, if we but saw him from afar, taking the first halting steps toward home, that we would rush to meet him, throw our arms around him, and assure him of our love?

These musings were interrupted by a conversation between my mother and Miss Earhart, who had been intrigued to hear that we'd travelled all the way from the Alaska Territory, and encouraged mother to tell her tale. When she'd related the events of the past five years, however, Miss Earhart seemed displeased.

"No offense, Yura, but if that had happened to me, I wouldn't have chased after my husband; I'd have gone about my business, made a life for myself, and found comfort in another man's arms."

"Why marry at all, then?" my mother asked. "Or perhaps you intend to stay single."

"Oh, there's a fellow I may well marry," our pilot replied. "But we shall each be free; he may have his lovers, I'll have mine."

My mother thought about this for a while.

"What you call freedom," she said, "might it not only enslave you to desire?"

Miss Earhart busied herself with the instrument panel, explaining that there could be some turbulence as we approached the mountains, and gave my mother no reply.

~

Soon enough, we were passing over the southern end of the Rockies. We had seen great beauty in Alaska, but never a vista such as this: to the north, extending to the far horizon, craggy summits rose out of a sea of white mist and clawed the sky. I saw that Mother, too, was captivated by the spectacle, and felt sure that her mind was filled with the same questions as mine.

Whose hands, I wondered, had crafted the clouds, whose knife had sculpted these mountain peaks?

Chapter Sixteen
Dreams of the Dead

This is the way Daniel's dream always began: he was back in his old home on Hacienda Drive, in the TV room in their walk-out basement, and when he was done watching Mash *there was that moment when he'd have to turn out the lights and race up the stairs to escape from the terror of that perfect blackness...*

Dad was at the top of the stairs and caught him, swept Daniel up in his big arms. "You've been this way ever since seeing that dumb movie I warned you about. Are you going to listen to your old pops next time?"

Daniel hung his head and leaned against his father, who hugged him close and then set him back down. It was true, *The Exorcist* had freaked him out. "The other kids laugh and make vomit jokes, dad. But there *are* demons, you've said so yourself, it's in the Bible. So it's real."

"Come here with me," his father said, and they went to sit on the living room couch. "Yes, of course there are demons and evil spirits, and one story after another of Jesus casting them out. You are safe, Danny. Look here—" His father picked up one of the Bibles which were always at hand and turned to *Romans*. "*We are more than conquerors through him who loved us,*" he read. "*For I am sure that neither death nor life, nor angels nor rulers, nor things present nor things to come, nor powers, nor height nor depth, nor anything else in all creation, will be able to separate us from the love of God that is in Christ Jesus our Lord.*"

Daniel nestled against his father.

"Now I'm going to turn to the end of Ephesians, and I want you to read to me, son. Because this is how we stay safe, even when we feel all the forces of darkness arraigned against us."

"*Put on the whole armor of God,*" Daniel read, "*that you may be able to stand against the schemes of the devil. For we do not wrestle against flesh and blood, but against the rulers, against the authorities, against the cosmic powers over this dark world...*" At thirteen, his voice was changing, but he read well, after a few verses unconsciously imitating the cadence his father used when preaching in church. "*...Stand therefore, having fastened on the* *belt of truth, and having put on the breastplate of righteousness, and, as shoes for your feet, having put on the readiness given by the gospel of peace. In all circumstances take up the shield of faith, with which you can extinguish all the flaming darts of the evil one..."*

But one of those flaming darts must have gotten through that night. He was in his childhood bed, but somehow fully grown, a fifty-one-year-old man, and the first thing he noticed was the smell of smoke and something like burning rubber. Then it was the noises that absorbed his attention, all the light bulbs popping and the crackle and woosh that was above and below and on every side, and then the blistering, suffocating heat.

He started to stand up, but in the dream it was more like swimming through flames; Daniel swam higher and higher until he perched on the roof, and that's when he saw Him: Jesus, calmly walking toward him on a sea of fire, His hand outstretched, His lips mouthing the words, *Come to Me.*

Daniel stepped out on the tongues of flame, one step, a second, a third, his eyes on the Savior; then cries reached his ears and he looked down and saw the nightmare sight, his father and mother, writhing, their skin melting away and their bones dissolving in the maelstrom below. At once he sank below the surface of the crimson sea and drifted down.

Where was the hand to lift him up?

But here was the Lord, beside him as the fire burned him, as it burned them both; Christ Jesus, drifting down along with him, and whispering, *"I am with you, I am with you, even now..."*

Daniel awoke with a start, drenched in sweat, the clock by his bedside showing 4:13. A spasm of neuropathic pain passed through him, sending white-hot needles through familiar pathways in his face and arms and hands. *He has said to me, "My grace is sufficient for you..."* There'll be no more sleep this morning, he thought, not after the dream.

After a few minutes, he got out of bed to take a shower, and that's when the bottle of Johnny Walker on the dresser caught his eye. What was it doing there, mocking him, tempting him, what work of the devil was this?

Daniel flicked on the lights. No, it was only a vase he'd recently emptied of flowers. How long had it been since he'd tasted a drop? Over twenty-five years. Suddenly weary to the depths of his soul, he knelt by the side of his bed to pray. Dress me in your armor, Lord, he thought; the belt of truth, the breastplate of righteousness...

I looked down, and sank below the surface of the crimson sea.

Lord, I believe, prayed Daniel Gold; help Thou mine unbelief.

~

Where was Joan's mother? Last she'd seen her, mommy had been in the kitchen—look! there was her shadow, disappearing around the corner—and now she could hear the click of her heels walking down the hall.

"Mom? Mommy?"

There was something she wanted to ask her mother, something she needed to know, and Joan hurried to find her. But the hallways of her childhood home were suddenly unfamiliar; they'd become a web of interconnecting passageways, and the faint echoes of her mother's footsteps had faded into silence.

Something she needed to ask her...

Wait, here was a place she recognized, at last: little Willie's room. And, joy of joys, her father, kneeling by the side of her brother's crib, in prayer!

"Daddy?" Joan walked over and touched his shoulder, then noticed the crib was empty. And why did her father feel so hard and cold?

He was only a statue. Beneath her fingers, a network of cracks spread out, and the figure of her father began to fall apart, crumbling into sand. She backed away in horror and screamed.

Baaammm!

That sound—the unmistakable blast of a shotgun. Joan rushed out into the hallway, which had somehow telescoped into a passageway one hundred yards long, at the far end of which was a door.

The bathroom door.

Don't go there, she told her younger self, but, against her will, Joan started down the long tunnel that led to that awful door.

Why does it have to be you?

She broke into a run. *Okay, then, just get it over with.* But no matter how fast she ran, the door still seemed as far away; she was crying, gasping for breath, and then, abruptly, there it was, in front of her, and she turned the handle to find—

The desolation of an empty field. A warm wind gusted, making sad sounds in the telephone wires strung high above. What was this? A rabbit, hopping over to her. She bent down and scratched its ears and it nuzzled against her with its little pink nose.

"There you are, Bunny, I've been searching for you, everywhere."

It was Willie! Joan broke into tears of relief, then gasped in terror. A shadow of something huge and monstrous had fallen over her brother—

"Willie! Watch out!"

Hey, wake up, darling, you've been dreaming.

Joan opened her eyes.

It's okay, sweetheart, it's only a dream.

Ah, thank God! She was safe, cradled in the arms of her husband, Jesse, in the comfort of their bed in Dobbs Ferry, New York. Soon he'd be leaving to catch the train to his Wall Street job; she wished he would just quit, so they could be together all the time.

"Don't ever leave me, Jess," she whispered. "Don't ever leave."

Shhhh. He gently stroked her cheek. *Go back to sleep.*

Wait. Something was wrong, terribly, terribly wrong, he wasn't her husband at all...

Joan awoke in her hotel room, her heart pounding in her chest. She'd pulled the curtains closed over the windows and the room was completely dark, but the amber lights of the clock on her nightstand showed it was already morning, 5:28 AM. *Now, do it now.* She slipped out of bed and kneeled in prayer.

"Heavenly Father," Joan prayed. "Help me to find the faith of my youth. Show me the way I can help my brother, Willie, who is so desperately lost. Please, Father, draw him to you, let him feel your love; take anything from me, but give him that..."

Dreams of the Dead

She prayed until she found her eyelids closing and her thoughts becoming confused, then crawled back into bed and fell into a deep, restful sleep.

～

After a long, rainy winter, how good it was, Tim thought, to feel the warm, sweet, soft spring breeze. His wife Teresa was sitting out on the patio in her thin plaid bathrobe, drinking coffee. Sometimes her beauty made his stomach do flip-flops and his knees grow weak. Tim knelt, rested his head in her lap, and let her caress his face.

He could imagine no greater bliss.

"How is it you've gotten so old?" Teresa wondered out loud. "How did it happen so fast?"

"What do you mean?" he asked.

"I hardly recognize you anymore. What happened to all your beautiful black hair?"

What? Tim reached his hand up to his head, and indeed, all he could feel was a fringe. He reached for his sunglasses and turned them around to use as a mirror. It was as though someone had given him a tonsure! He was Friar Tuck!

Tim got to his feet and stumbled toward the house. His eyesight must be going as well, for he couldn't focus on anything, the world was a hazy blur. He groped his way to the kitchen and splashed cold water on his face. There, now he could see better. This must be a practical joke Teresa was playing on him. Tim smiled and walked back outside.

She wasn't there.

"Tress!" he called. "I don't get mad, I get even! Come on back!"

But the world was silent and still. Then, what had been a gentle breeze began to grow stronger, and soon the wind was howling and the patio furniture was sent flying, the pine trees were uprooted and the house behind him was ripped from its foundation by the force of the storm.

Finally, all was quiet and calm.

It was as though he'd been transported to some B-movie vision of heaven: he was walking on fluffy clouds and gradually became aware of others, no doubt angels, dressed in white gowns and sporting oversized wings. They'd glance at him and hastily look away, muttering among themselves.

"He's on the docket, his case is coming up soon."

"Oh yes, that one. Left the wife of his youth."

"He's in for it, then, poor devil."

Tim's sense of amusement at his surroundings vanished in an instant. Yes, somehow, incredibly, it was true, it was really, really true: he'd left Tress years ago, abandoned her for someone long forgotten, whose face was now a blank. He sank to his knees in despair.

Gone were the cheap special effects. He was in a vast, smoldering garbage heap; there were urchins picking through the trash, probably to salvage something worth a penny or two that they could use to buy food. Well, Tress, this will set things right, then, he thought. If this is Gehenna, if I'm in the Hell that believers speak of, that's what I want, let it be my fate.

Only what if it were to be worse, far worse than this?

Then appear before me, O Judge, and do your worst; for there is nothing you could inflict that would match the punishment I deserve!

Something was taking place in front of him, from out of a dark cloud something great and terrible was taking shape, and Tim thought, *yes, yes, show yourself, Ancient of Days, show yourself as the Old Testament reveals you, an angry god, a raging god, a veritable Moloch, come and devour me, for that is exactly what I want!*

From out of the blackness of a whirlwind, the face of God appeared to Tim Faber.

He was looking at himself.

Brrrriiiinnng....brrrriiinnnng....

The phone by the side of his bed woke Tim from his dream and he fumbled for the receiver.

"Yes?" he said, disoriented. Already the dream was starting to fade.

"Mr. Faber? This is Vicky, I'm your personal chauffeur. I was supposed to meet you at four this afternoon, are we still on?"

Tim glanced at the clock: 4:16. Oh, crap!

"Yes, yes, I laid down to rest and must have fallen asleep. Sorry, let me get myself together and I'll be down in five minutes, ten tops."

"No problem, Mr. Faber, I'm waiting out in front. You can't miss me, I'm in the big burgundy Rolls."

Tim set down the phone and ran his hands through his hair. He'd had some kind of bad dream, that was for sure, must have been all that spicy Asian food at the Babylon West buffet. Well, that was a mistake he wouldn't make again!

Tim changed into a fresh shirt, washed his face and gargled some mouthwash, then headed out for the elevators. If Vicky looked anything like she sounded, he thought, she'd be quite a sight. Of course—would Oz settle for anything less? He laughed, and clapped his hands. A night in Vegas with a hottie driving him in a burgundy Rolls!

Surely he was leading a charmed life!

Chapter Seventeen
Angels of the Lord

Eighty-one years earlier, David, too, had been dreaming. Unable to sleep, he'd gone to the local boxing club to work out; it was late at night, and the place was deserted, with not another soul in sight. He'd been working the heavy bag for about half an hour when, suddenly, floodlights came on over the ring. A man stood there, leaning against the ropes, clad in boxing shorts, his gloves already laced.

"Good evening," David called to him, but the newcomer only regarded him in stony silence. They locked eyes for a moment, and then the man motioned with his right arm for David to enter the ring.

"I'm just here tuning up for my fight tomorrow," said David, walking over next to the ropes, but before he knew it, he was being pulled in and the fellow was upon him, stunning him with a stinging left hook. Was he a madman? Regardless, there was no choice but to fight.

There was no referee, no breaks between rounds, just a slugfest that went on into the small hours of the night, the two men battling until the sky began to show the first faint signs of morning light. He was good, he was the best David had ever fought, but the Pummelin' Preacher was holding his own until the stranger struck him with a body blow that came from out of nowhere and shook him to his core, buckling his knees.

He's as fresh as when we started, David thought. *Any time he wanted to, he could have taken me down.* Still, he did not let his opponent prevail, but held on to him tightly, in a desperate clinch.

"Let me go," said the man, "for the dawn is breaking."

"I will not let you go unless you bless me," David replied, recalling the words that had been spoken over three thousand years before.

His opponent smiled for the first time, a knowing, gentle smile, though his grip was hard as steel, and asked him, "What is your name?"

David Gold awoke to morning sunlight streaming through the windows of his room at the Riverside Hotel. He'd been in Reno for the past three weeks awaiting the fights that his cousin Ben had set up, the first of which was set for later that day. Jack Johnson, who at the age of fifty-two was still attracting crowds to exhibitions at which he'd clown with sparring partners and sign autographs, had booked a suite of rooms, and his wife, Irene, had explained to Yura that they'd simply go to waste if she and her son didn't use them. Luke started out doing research at the Reno Public Library, but soon began haunting the largest of the assay offices in town. While no one there had heard of his father, he learned the locations of the largest mines, and Jack and Irene began driving Luke and Yura out into the Nevada desert, first to the Rochester mine, then to Virginia City, where they spent two long days talking to men working the Comstock Lode. But it had all been to no avail.

For David, these weeks had been a hellish time. He never went to the gym; the outcomes of the fights were preordained, so why bother? He'd open his Bible and find himself reading the same lines over and over; it was as though they were written in a strange language, with words that had familiar sounds but made no sense. He'd try to pray, but his prayers were leaden, however much he aimed them at heaven, they sank into the earth.

David sat up, thinking over his dream. *What is your name?* A sweatshirt with "Pummelin' Preacher" printed on it was draped over the back of a chair, mocking him. His life so far had been a waste, a fraud, and now he was sinking yet deeper into sin! And using God as his excuse, when in fact, he was refusing to trust in Him! In a fit of anger, David sprang from the bed, tore his sweatshirt in half, and flung it across the room.

He was suddenly aware that his whole body ached, as though he'd been mauled in the ring.

I can't go through with this fight, he thought. I've never taken dirty money before, and it's the devil's own doing that I agreed to it with Ben. But if I bow out now and there's no fight, then all bets are off and no one will have lost a dime. I'll cable my cousin and explain that I just can't do it; anyway, I'm sure he's got bigger fish to fry.

David sank to his knees and prayed from the Psalms he knew by heart.

Have mercy on me, O God,
  according to Your steadfast love,
  according to Your abundant mercy
  blot out my transgressions.
Wash me thoroughly from my iniquity,
  and cleanse me from my sin...
The sacrifices of God are a broken spirit;
  a broken and contrite heart, O God,
  You will not despise.

His dream had ended with a question: *What is your name?* Jacob's blessing had been a new name, David thought, one that set him in a different direction, on a better path. Well, he was ready, if only God would tell him which way to go!

He picked up his Bible and found that it opened to the ninth chapter of the Book of Acts. His eye fell on verse sixteen: *I will show you how much you must suffer for my sake.*

No, that can't be right, those were not the words God spoke! He blinked and looked again; this time the verse was as he remembered.

I will show him how much he must suffer for my sake.

You spoke to our forefathers, David thought. Speak to me. Don't hide yourself, Lord; answer the question I asked years ago: what do you want of me?

Again, he prayed from the Psalms.

Keep steady my steps according to your promise,
  and let no iniquity have dominion over me.

Silence. He could hear the ticking of the second hand of his watch from across the room. The minutes stretched into hours as he prayed, searching for a way out of what he saw as an aimless, worthless life.

You won't answer me, will You, he thought.

And that is the moment when someone knocked on the door to his room.

Slowly, his heart racing, David rose from his knees, walked over, and opened the hotel-room door. Standing before him was a young woman in stiletto heels and a cheap, revealing black dress, her face garishly made up. A call girl! Was this some kind of twisted joke?

"I'm sorry, you must have the wrong room," he said curtly, and closed the door in her face.

He felt as though someone had just thrown him into the Arctic sea! In anger and frustration, David slammed his fist into the wall, leaving a sizable hole. Were his prayers to be answered only by the devil's mockery?

He saw himself, a child throwing a tantrum, and his face burned with shame at his own anger and impatience. What right did he have to expect the Lord to answer his questions? What cross had he ever lifted to follow Him? Despair and self-loathing engulfed David Gold.

Was this what it felt like to be cut off from God?

PART TWO

THE CHURCH OF THE HEART SET FREE

Chapter Eighteen
The Passion of Justin James

For years, men had dreamed of taming the Colorado River. It wasn't the longest or widest river in the land, but it was the wildest, hands down. It might have taken a few million years for the Colorado to carve the Grand Canyon, but in mere hours it could transform itself from a smooth, placid stream to a raging torrent, obliterating landscapes in the process.

Over the centuries, the Colorado had periodically flooded California's Imperial Valley, providing it with a rich bed of fertile soil. As Americans settled the West, they realized that the valley could become a paradise for farmers—if only there were water to grow crops! One dreamer after another tried to solve the problem, with dollar signs in their eyes. In the early 1900s, an ambitious entrepreneur had dug canals, diverting water from the Colorado to the Imperial Valley, and for a few years the area thrived, attracting thousands, who built entire new towns. But the river was only playing them for suckers; in 1906 it roared through those canals, uncontrollable, sweeping away everything in its path and creating the thirty-five-mile-long Salton Sea.

It turned out, however, that there *was* a way to tame the river, but it would take the creation of nothing less than one of the wonders of the world. It would take a colossus.

During the 1920s, engineers developed plans for an enormous dam, twice as tall as any that had ever been built, not only to control the wild river and irrigate California farmland, but also to generate vast amounts of hydroelectric power to fuel the rapid growth of the western states. There was just one location that made sense: a stretch of the Colorado between Nevada and Arizona that ran through Black Canyon. It would be a daunting project under the best of conditions, but they'd have to construct the dam in a blistering desert, in the middle of nowhere.

Their only link to civilization would be a small town that had grown up around a railroad depot thirty miles from the dam site, called Las Vegas.

On the first Sunday after the murder of Pastor Justin James, no one at the Church of the Heart set Free knew quite what to expect.

The church was a modest brick building on the edge of what was known in Las Vegas as Block 16, a stretch of brothels and saloons not far from the train station, where men could gamble and carouse to their hearts' content. It was one of two blocks where liquor sales had been allowed when the city was founded in 1905, and Prohibition didn't slow down the drinking one bit. If the local police heard that the Feds were planning a raid, they'd tip off the bartenders—in return, of course, for a show of appreciation in hard cash.

Federal spending in Nevada nosedived in the years after the Great War ended; mines shut down, and the local railroad company went bankrupt. Block 16 still brought in some traffic, but, by the late 1920s, the prospects for Las Vegas looked increasingly bleak.

Then, like a thunderbolt, what most had assumed was only the most far-fetched of fantasies came true: in 1928, just before Christmas, President Coolidge signed an act of Congress authorizing the construction of a massive project in nearby Black Canyon. It was to be called Boulder Dam, and it promised salvation from certain ruin. A celebration that lasted for days ensued. Strangers hugged and toasted each other with bootleg liquor which flowed like water throughout the town.

By mid-1930, as the Depression deepened, the magnitude of the jackpot the city had won became increasingly clear. Throughout the land, factories and stores were closing and the ranks of the unemployed were swelling, but there in southern Nevada the Feds would be hiring thousands of men to build the dam! Oh, the business leaders of Las Vegas were licking their chops. All those hard-working fellows, living in the middle of a desert, with nowhere else to spend their cash! Up in Carson City, the state legislature was talking about legalizing gambling and reducing the waiting time for divorce; soon legit businesses throughout the city would be able to get their share of the workers' wages, not just those shady operators on Block 16. And who knew how much was to be made off the divorcees from California and New York!

The only problem was Pastor Justin James.

He was a slight, plain-looking man, but when he spoke, whether to a single listener or to an entire congregation, his presence and passion were electrifying. The wives of the mayor and the bank president persuaded their husbands to join them on Sunday mornings at the Church of the Heart Set Free. Soon, many of Las Vegas' leading lights followed suit, though they steered well clear of the drunks, busted gamblers, and prostitutes who filled some of the pews.

The trouble was, Pastor James wouldn't stick to preaching the Bible. The more the politicians schemed and folks made plans to fleece the workers who would soon be toiling in Black Canyon, the more he spoke out.

"Brothers and sisters," he said, one Sunday in August of that year. "I have eyes to see and ears to hear; I know the words that are on your lips in these heady days, but I ask you: what is in your hearts? Mr. Farnsworth," Pastor James called out to the town's banker, "would you open your Bible and read to us from the sixth chapter of Matthew, verses nineteen to twenty-one."

Farnsworth licked his index finger and took his time turning pages, then cleared his throat nervously and read.

"*Do not lay up for yourselves treasures on earth, where moth and rust destroy, and where thieves break in and steal, but lay up for yourselves treasures in heaven, where neither moth nor rust destroys and where thieves do not break in and steal. For where your treasure is, there will your heart be also.*"

"There will your heart be also," echoed Pastor James. "My friends, ask yourselves, where is my treasure, where is my heart? Oh, I know, out of the hearts of men proceed evil thoughts; but we have the Cross. We have the mind of Christ.

"The Lord warns us to be on our guard against all kinds of greed. Mr. Barlow," he called out to a wealthy grocer who had made no secret of his plans to open several casinos if the gambling bill should pass. "Would you read to us from Luke, chapter twelve, verses sixteen to twenty-one."

Barlow, an obese man whose wife constantly hectored him to take an evening constitutional and spread a bit less butter on his toast, shifted uncomfortably in his seat.

"Well, let's see, pastor. Ah. Here we are. *And he told them a parable, saying, 'The land of a rich man produced plentifully, and he thought to himself, 'What shall I do, for I have nowhere to store my crops?'*

"*And he said, 'I will do this: I will tear down my barns and build larger ones, and there I will store all my grain and my goods. And I will say to my soul, 'Soul, you have ample goods laid up for many years; relax, eat, drink, be merry.'*"

Barlow chuckled at this and winked at his wife before continuing to read.

"*But God said to him, 'Fool! This night your soul is required of you, and the things you have prepared, whose will they be?' So is the one who lays up treasure for himself and is not rich toward God.*"

Pastor James let the silence last for an uncomfortably long time, and Barlow put a handkerchief to his forehead to wipe away the drops of sweat.

"You will make decisions in the days ahead," said Pastor James. "Some of them may affect many, some perhaps only yourselves. But in everything you do, every decision you make, large or small, ask yourself, what would Christ Jesus have me do? Then act on it, else your faith is no faith at all.

"In our city, there are some tempted by riches; elsewhere, by fear of hard times to come. Is the answer to further the spread of gambling? Some say it is a harmless diversion, but you know better; you know well it lures men to destruction and despair. Is the answer to cut in half the waiting time for divorce? What God has joined together, spoke Jesus to the Pharisees, let no man separate.

"Whether tempted by greed, or driven by fear, I tell you: be still, and wait upon the Lord. God is faithful; he will not let you be tempted beyond what you can bear.

"Friends, a great opportunity does indeed lie before us. From all over this country, thousands are assembling in the desert, not far from here, and thousands more are on their way. I assure you, many are souls not yet saved. The harvest is indeed plentiful, but the workers are few! Before ascending to be at the right hand of the Father, Jesus commanded His disciples—not only those who walked the earth nineteen hundred years ago, but all of us who follow Him today—to go and make disciples of all nations. And behold—you need not travel to the ends of the earth, for, praise be to God, He has brought the nations to our door!

"Put aside thoughts of mere monetary gain, beloved, and, with joyful hearts, let us labor together in the fields of the Lord."

Accompanied by his daughter and a handful of others, Pastor James worked tirelessly to evangelize the job-seekers camped in Black Canyon, and the employees of Six Companies, Inc., the consortium that had been formed to build the dam. He walked the streets of Las Vegas and the hallways of the state capitol, talking truth to anyone who would lend him an ear.

Dark words came back to the mayor and the banker and others who sought to prosper from the dam: That moralizing meddler is causing trouble in Carson City and at Six Companies; he's upsetting the worthies of the town. *Do something about him—there's money to be made, but only by those who follow the rules.*

The intensity of the pastor's efforts increased, for he knew full well he was a marked man.

~

On a Friday morning in September 1930, Anne-Marie had gargled with mouthwash before heading to the Church of the Heart Set Free. She'd been meeting with Pastor James about her drinking problem—Anne-Marie had been drunk for much of the past twelve years—and wasn't quite sure if she wanted to admit that she'd had a wee nip already that morning. As she pushed open the door to the church, Anne-Marie decided that she'd wait to see if the pastor asked. Please God, she prayed, let me have the courage to tell the truth if he does!

What she found inside sent her running in tears out into the street.

At first, her friends around the corner in Block 16 thought she was having a drunken fit. But they followed her back, and found that what she had told them was true: Pastor James had been shot dead at close range and nailed to the church's rough-hewn cross.

The word spread in Las Vegas like fire through dry brush. That Sunday, when the time came for the ten AM service, the church was empty but for Anne-Marie and four others who loved the Lord and his servant, Justin James. They were the only ones who had attended his funeral the previous day, for the elders of the church had stayed away out of fear for their lives, and the pastor's daughter was nowhere to be found.

"Can it really be that no one else is going to show?" asked Anne-Marie.

"Damn Yankee cowards, ever' last one," said the southerner who called himself General Robert E. Lee. Whether or not he really had fought in the Civil War was a matter of some debate, but he certainly looked old enough for it to be true. "Y'all know I'd hunt down the murderin' dogs who did the deed, but seems it could've been anyone in this town."

"Vengeance is the Lord's," said Mr. Polwarth, who, if he stood on his toes, might have been five feet tall. Rumor had it that he'd worked on Wall Street before losing everything at the gambling tables of Block 16, though the only evidence for this was his habit of perpetually wearing the same tattered three-piece suit. "I suggest we carry on our worship as best we can," he added, "in honor of Pastor James."

"That's an excellent idea," said Isaiah Trueblood, who was half Apache and half black. He had a fearsome countenance, but was timid to the point of paralysis, something Pastor James had been helping him to overcome. "We were in Matthew, but maybe someone else sh-sh-should read."

"I can start us off with a hymn," said Lauren McBride. She was a tall, gawky girl barely out of her teens, who until recently had worked as a prostitute on the second floor of the Arizona Club, by far the swankiest saloon in town.

After Lauren sang Blessed Assurance in a sweet soprano, and Anne-Marie, General Lee, and Mr. Polwarth each read a chapter from the Gospel of Matthew, Isaiah unfolded a newspaper he'd been carrying and passed it around.

"We can't go on like this forever, we need us a pastor. Read it, Mr. Polwarth. Ain't this ju-ju-just the man for the job?"

Mr. Polwarth squinted at an article from the sports pages of the Las Vegas Evening Review and began to read.

"Boxing fans will be flocking to Reno this coming Saturday night to see up-and-coming heavyweight Carter Jackson go up against the Pummelin' Preacher, veteran David Gold. The Preacher, perhaps the only boxer whose resume includes a degree from the Moody Bible College, is known to appear in local pulpits prior to his bouts, but on this occasion, he may have chosen to spend his time preparing to defend against Jackson's fearsome left hook..."

"Well, by gum!" exclaimed General Lee. "A pummelin' preacher is *exactly* what we need!"

There was general consensus that Isaiah had had a stroke of pure genius, though Mr. Polwarth pointed out a potential glitch.

"He's a boxing star, and the members of our congregation who have two nickels to rub together have deserted like the proverbial rats. We'd be asking him to lead *us*—the ragtag riffraff of Las Vegas—with no promise of remuneration, our last pastor having been brutally slain by assailants unknown."

"We would, wouldn't we," said Anne-Marie. "But do you have a better plan?"

Mr. Polwarth was stumped.

"I'd go up ta Reno," said General Lee, "only mah arthritis is actin' up real bad."

"As would I," said Anne-Marie, "only I know I'd end up getting drunk."

Isaiah just shook his head. Everyone understood that his agoraphobia made travelling out of the question.

"I fear my diminutive stature might make conversation rather awkward," said Polwarth. "Staring up at the man, I mean, he's evidently quite tall."

All eyes turned to Lauren McBride.

"Me?"

"Th-th-there's no one else, Lauren," said Isaiah.

"Oh my," she said, and blushed a deep red. "What chance do *I* have? I'm no one at all!"

Lauren looked around her; by all rights Mr. Polwarth ought to go, but he was looking sheepishly at the floor, and the others were avoiding her gaze. They were asking her, the youngest, to do the hardest job! For shame! Well, with all her heart, she wanted a Pummelin' Preacher to do battle for them and guide them, and if that meant that she'd have to find the courage to go to Reno and ask this man, she'd answer the call!

"All right," said Lauren. "I'll do it."

There were cheers and sighs of relief, and each of them emptied their pockets to come up with the train fare to Reno. Mr. Polwarth suggested that the best plan would be for Lauren to travel there on Saturday and persuade Mr. Gold to accompany her back to Las Vegas after the fight. They all agreed this made sense, and, after praying and making plans to search for Pastor James' missing daughter, they parted company, their hearts still heavy, yet lightened by hope.

It didn't take Lauren long after arriving in Reno to find that the Pummelin' Preacher was staying at the Riverfront Hotel. She did the three-mile walk from the train station barefoot, carrying her best pair of dress shoes. Lauren's feelings had been hurt when Anne-Marie told her to make sure and not dress like a "cheap whore;" why, she could even smell the liquor on her friend's breath!

"Don't you worry, Anne-Marie, dear, just try and be sober when I bring the man back," she'd replied. Lauren hadn't meant to lose her temper, but, Jiminy Cricket, of course she'd only wear her finest things!

It was late afternoon by the time she arrived at the hotel. Looking at the well-heeled clientele milling about in the Riverfront's elegant lobby, it passed through Lauren's mind that she could earn an easy ten or twenty dollars by turning a few quick tricks. She gasped and struck herself on the forehead with the heel of her palm. "Stupid, sinful girl," she thought, and began repeating a phrase she'd invented, inspired by one of Pastor James' last sermons.

"Trust in the Lord, don't turn tricks; trust in the Lord, don't turn tricks..."

After using her wiles to find out Mr. Gold's room number from a wide-eyed valet, she made her way up the hotel staircase, muttering her mantra all the way.

Lauren paused outside of David's hotel room to compose herself, put on her shoes, and asked the Lord to help her find the right words. Then she knocked on the door. He won't be in, she thought, but before she knew it the door swung open and she found herself gaping up at the Pummelin' Preacher himself.

"I'm sorry, you must have the wrong room," he said angrily, and abruptly shut the door in her face.

This can't be happening, she thought. I didn't get to say one word. Please, God, don't do this to me! I can't go back to Las Vegas like this, a total failure! We need this man.

And then she did the one thing she had told herself never to do.

She started to cry.

Chapter Nineteen
Whom the Lord Came to Save

David's right hand, which he'd pounded like a sledgehammer into the wall, was pulsating with pain and already starting to swell. He winced and leaned his head against the wall in shame. Gradually, the sound of someone sobbing entered his consciousness, and he thought, well, that's perfect, perhaps the whole world is weeping right now.

What do you want of me, he had asked God. Direct my footsteps according to your word.

Wait a minute. Why is a call girl crying outside my room?

David flung open the door. Lauren was a pitiful sight: her dress was spattered with dirt from the three-mile trek, her mascara was running, and something awful was dripping from her nose. *I saw her as a Pharisee would have,* he thought. But God had revealed to him a human being, one who suffered no less than he, and a stab of pain ran through his heart.

"I'm so sorry," he said. "Can I help you?"

"I surely hope so," she replied, holding back tears.

"Please, come in." He stepped back, and Lauren stumbled as she stepped into the living room of his hotel suite

"Oh, gee!" She kicked off her six-inch stilettos. "What must you think of me, Pastor Gold! I just about never wear heels, but I wanted so bad to make a good impression."

"That doesn't matter one bit." *Pastor* Gold! David inwardly winced and tried not to think of himself as a fraud. He motioned for Lauren to sit on the sofa and seated himself on a chair across from her. "You know me, it seems, but I'm afraid I don't know who you are."

"Me? I'm Lauren McBride, from Las Vegas, which isn't nothing like Reno, just a little town four or five hundred miles from here. I've come about my church, the Church of the Heart Set Free."

This girl is so thin her ribs are showing, David thought. I thank you for leading her to me, Lord; grant me the wisdom to do Your will.

"I want to hear all about it," he said. "But when was the last time you had a decent meal?"

"I'm not sure—yesterday sometime. But I'm used to it, don't worry about me."

"Well, then you're tougher than I am, Lauren, because if I don't have dinner, I'm going to pass out."

"I could eat a horse, to be honest," she said, "but I only have fifteen cents to my name."

"It just so happens that I have cause to celebrate this evening," said David. "So dinner's on me. Tell me what you fancy; personally, I'm ordering a twenty-four-ounce porterhouse, medium rare."

"Just order two of those, sir, and thank you from the bottom of my—oh my gosh," Lauren exclaimed, "your poor hand!"

Indeed, David's right hand was throbbing and black and blue.

"I'm capable of great foolishness at times," he said, and asked her to wait while he found a bellhop to go for the steaks and a bucket of ice for his hand. Then a thought struck him: Jack was off signing autographs, leaving Yura and her son at the hotel that evening. Finding the Alaskan a few minutes later in Johnson's vast suite, he briefly explained the situation; soon, she came by and took Lauren under her wing, leading the grateful young woman back to her room for a hot bath while Yura cleaned her dress as best she could.

As David ran his hand under cold water, waiting for Lauren's return, something nagged at him, some task he needed to do. Of course, the fight that evening! Using the guest phone in the hotel lobby, he asked to be connected with the boxing arena and told them to scratch him from the card.

But there was still the matter of his cousin. Well, Ben wouldn't have arranged to pay Carter Jackson until after the match, David thought, so the no-show shouldn't cost him a dime. He thought for a few moments, then asked the concierge to arrange for a telegram that would be sent to a Benjamin Siegel in New York City:

BEN—COULD NOT FIGHT STOP RETIRING STOP WILL MAKE WHOLE ANY LOSS STOP—DAVID

~⁓

Lauren had barely made a dent in her porterhouse steak before she began to unburden herself to David Gold.

"Our pastor Justin James was gunned down ten days ago, and my heart's broke with missing him. What they're building in Black Canyon, I just know that's what's behind his murder, it's changing everything in Las Vegas. People say it's to be a great dam, so powerful it'll turn night into day and make the desert bloom. They'll be hiring thousands, and each day more men show up, coming from everywhere for the jobs. What Pastor James cared about, he didn't want them drinking and gambling and spending time with women like me—like I used to be, anyway, for I have sinned, sir, but don't ask me to confess to you, 'cause I'd rather lay down and die than talk to a man about my sins."

"Don't worry, there's no need for that," David said.

"Thank you. Anyway, Pastor James cared about those men's souls. He spoke the truth whether anyone wanted to hear it or not, and there are lots of folks in our town don't much care for the truth these days, not one bit. I guess they hated it enough to kill a good man, just so nothing got in the way of their dreams of getting rich.

"There must have been a hundred or so would attend most Sundays at the Heart Set Free, but after Pastor James was killed, people are too scared to show. Last week it was just Anne-Marie and the General and Isaiah and Mr. Polwarth and me, and it's not that we're so wonderful, it's more like we got nothing much to lose. But we do know where our treasure is, sir, it's the Lord, and it was the pastor who showed Him to us, not just on Sundays but every time we had a problem, whether it was about a verse in the Bible, or how we were gonna earn the money for food if we couldn't make it through sin.

"I loved him like a daughter ought to love her own father, like I never loved mine because he wasn't no good. And I can't believe Pastor James is gone."

Lauren stopped to wipe the tears from her eyes and blow her nose.

David felt a love for the slain pastor rising in his own heart: this was the sort of man he should have been, the kind of life he should have led. He knew what Lauren was going to ask him, yet it seemed impossible, a far greater honor than he deserved; or perhaps they only want me to put on an exhibition match, he mused, to raise money so their church can hire a real pastor to take the place of Justin James.

"I'm in awe of your pastor, Lauren, and I grieve for your loss. Tell me what I can do."

"Oh!" she exclaimed, flustered to realize that she hadn't even gotten to the reason for her trip. "You can lead us, sir, and take up where Pastor James left off. It's like my friend Isaiah said, Las Vegas is a hard town, we need a fighting man to pastor the Church of the Heart Set Free. We don't have nothing to pay you, though, 'least not right away." Lauren looked down, abashed, as the temerity of what she was asking for began to sink in. "Maybe it's a crazy idea, you being in the newspapers, for goodness sake, and us being nobody at all. But will you come and be our pastor, anyway?"

David felt a wave of doubt and shame passing through him. For years, I've been an imposter, he thought. Why wouldn't this be yet one more act of pretense?

And then he heard these unspoken words, soft but clear, as if someone were whispering them into his ear: *Because I will be with you. This is what is wanted of you, David Gold: to step into My armor, and live your faith in Me.*

He felt himself breaking into a cold sweat.

Now.

"Yes, Lauren," he said, and no greater reward could he have asked for than the sweet, joyous smile on her face. "With all my heart, yes."

The next day was Sunday, and Mr. Polwarth, General Lee, Isaiah Trueblood, and Anne-Marie were at the Church of the Heart Set Free, hoping that Lauren would return that day, a bearer of good news. They'd gone straight there after seeing her off at the train station Saturday morning, and had spent the night at the church praying for

119

the success of her mission until they curled up in blankets on the hard wooden pews to catch a few hours sleep. When dawn broke, they rose and prayed together, then sang their way through the hymnal and read Scripture and prayed some more. They'd decided to fast and remain in the church until Lauren's return.

At midday, Sheriff Stone and his cadaverous deputy, Drake, walked in while the foursome were singing *It is Well with My Soul*. Despite the Sheriff's loud throat-clearing, they sang through every one of the six verses before turning toward the two uniformed men.

"If y'all need hymnals, we got a passel of 'em," said General Lee.

"We could use your low tones, Stone," said Mr. Polwarth, eying the Sheriff's ample girth. "Though I'm guessing your boy Drake might be more of a countertenor."

"Clam up, all of you," said the Sheriff. "Hope you been enjoyin' your sorry selves, 'cause this is your last service. I'm giving you a warning as a favor, it's not like I don't got plenty else to do. Come morning, this building's being repossessed."

"What are you talking about?" asked Anne-Marie.

His deputy snickered.

"Oh, I got your attention now, don't I," said Sheriff Stone. "James borrowed from the bank to build this place, and the loan's due and payable now he's passed on. But that's more'n you need to know. Not meaning any offense to the four of you upstandin' cit'zens, but face reality. You got no pastor and no congregation and a bill you couldn't pay in your wildest dreams. So sing yourselves a last song and skedaddle or it'll be the Blue Room for you, every last one." Sheriff Stone turned on his heel and walked out with his deputy in tow.

The four friends looked at each other for a while in somber silence.

"Do you think all that's for tr-tr-true?" asked Isaiah.

"It doesn't much matter," said Mr. Polwarth. "Truth or lies, they'll remove us by force of arms."

"Well, I ain't never surrendered yet," said General Lee. "Train from Reno arrives at five. But any way ya look at it, we're goin' ta need reinforcements. Anne-Marie, you 'n Isaiah go round the corner and rattle all the cages 'a Block Sixteen, see if you can't round up some 'a them lily-livered losers used to sit in these pews."

"I don't know if that's wise, sending Anne-Marie," said Mr. Polwarth. "What with all the temptation to drink, I mean."

"Well, if she's up for it, she's goin'—'cause you ain't 'xactly the most popular man in town, Polwarth, you're stayin' here with me, mannin' the barricades."

"Come on, Isaiah," said Anne-Marie. "You'll be my moral support."

The two left Mr. Polwarth and the General in the church, where they fell into fervent prayer.

A trickle of men and women began arriving at the church as the afternoon wore on. It was only a few blocks from the railroad depot at Main and Fremont, and they could all hear the whistle of the five o'clock train as it rolled into town. But the minutes ticked by, and it was five-thirty, then six, and there was no sign of the Pummelin' Preacher or Lauren McBride.

"Where'd y'all leave your backbones?" asked the General, as he observed the gloomy faces all about him. "I have not yet begun to fight!"

"Let's raise a joyful noise up unto the Lord," suggested Anne-Marie, and, much to everyone's surprise, Isaiah Trueblood began singing *'Tis So Sweet to Trust in Jesus* in a wavering tenor that gained in strength verse by verse.

Word spread that something akin to the Alamo was taking place at the Church of the Heart Set Free. All that evening, more and more drunks and busted gamblers and women of the night filled its pews, until what had started as a trickle became a mighty stream. Mr. Polwarth discovered an extra box of hymnals no one had noticed before, and he and Isaiah started handing them out while Anne-Marie sang louder and more joyously than she ever had before.

The sound of many voices singing God's praises brought more to the church until there was no room left, and a small crowd stood outside its doors, uncertain what was happening, yet filled with awe.

∼

Early Monday morning, Sheriff Stone and his deputy returned, parked a Black Maria outside the church, and surveyed the scene. People were still milling about on the street; inside, some were praying, some singing, some snoring where they sat in the pews or lay on the floor.

"Polwarth!" the Sheriff thundered, spotting his diminutive nemesis snoozing nearby. "I gave you fair warning. Now clear the premises pronto, or you and your pals will rue the day you were born, so help me God."

Mr. Polwarth rubbed his eyes.

"I'm pleased you know you need God's help, Stone, because—" he broke off suddenly, his eyes growing wide.

"You worthless runt," said the Sheriff. "What are you doing in a house of worship, anyway, you and your crowd, you're the sorriest sinning scum of the earth."

"Well isn't that something," said a voice behind him. "Just the folks our Lord Christ Jesus came to save."

It was then that the first rays of the sun came beaming in through the east-facing windows, projecting Sheriff Stone's shadow on the far wall. The hairs stood up on the back of his neck; another shadow now covered his, the shadow of a tall man with the broadest shoulders he had ever seen.

The Sheriff, who was no coward, turned around slowly and looked up into the eyes of the stranger who'd come up behind him.

"And just who might you be?" he asked coolly.

"Pastor David Gold," the man replied, "of the Church of the Heart Set Free."

Chapter Twenty
To Walk in the Newness of Life

Our airplane voyage from Oklahoma to Nevada had been exhilarating, yet dismaying: we'd looked down in wonder on the harsh beauty of the land, but where, in all its vastness, could we find one man?

Often during our time in Reno, I woke in the stillness of the night, and hours would pass before I finally fell back asleep. Had I somehow failed my father, was I not deserving of his love? Or had he never really loved me or my mother and only been an imposter for all those years? I had always thought of him as my hero, the man I wanted to be. But how was I to think of him now—as a coward, who after leaving his lover did not have the courage to stand before his wife and son?

His image was hazy in my mind. There were times when I couldn't remember the details of his face, and to refresh my memory I'd look at the pictures of him that we showed to the miners. Some days I stared at those pictures for a very long time. Have you seen this man?

Others my age were going to college, or looking for jobs, beginning their lives. Angry thoughts would rage through my mind, and I had no outlet, no one to whom I could talk.

Until the day we left Reno, I'd avoided David Gold. He was taciturn, brooding, a mystery to me, while Jack Johnson was such a happy extrovert, so utterly self-confident, that it lifted my heart and raised my hopes just to see his smiling countenance. And yet each trip into the desert with Jack and Irene had ended in failure, with no trace of my father to be found.

On the evening before our journey to Las Vegas, Irene and Mother and I were listening to Jack play Bach on his bass viol when David entered, bringing Lauren with him, his eyes filled with light. He introduced us to Lauren and asked her to explain why she had come.

"We're catching the morning train to Las Vegas," he said when she had finished her tale. "Yura, I think you and Luke should come with us. Everywhere I've been, men are losing their jobs, but that dam that's being built on the Colorado is hiring thousands. Seems to me a better chance of finding your husband there than anywhere else."

It was almost as though the dam were a trap that had been baited, and all we'd have to do was lie in wait. My mother turned to me, and I nodded.

"What do you think, Mr. Johnson?" she asked Jack.

"Sounds plenty smart," he said, and then looked at David. "But you ain't taking that train."

"Jack, I love you, but I've got to do this, and do it now," his friend replied. "This is what God wants of me, I can feel it in my bones."

"Oh, I got that," said Jack Johnson. "I just want you to get where you're going in *style*—I mean, you do reflect on me, brother, having been my boon companion these past nine years. See, I've decided to keep my Duesenberg, so I'm giving you the Talbot. It's a sweet ride, Davey, and it'll seat the four of you just fine." Jack tossed him a set of keys. "Now go to this Las Vegas of yours, with my blessings." He hugged David and then added, "You stay tough, now. Preach love and breathe fire."

~

A few wispy clouds tinged with pink were floating in an indigo sky as we left Reno Sunday morning at first light. Tonopah, site of the largest gold and silver mines where we'd not yet searched for my father, was halfway to Las Vegas, and we hoped to arrive there by noon. The farther we drove into the desert, the hotter the wind blew through the Talbot's open windows, and it wasn't long before we stopped to stretch our legs near a stand of cottonwood trees growing by one of the few streams we came across that day.

"Luke," said Lauren, joining me in the shade. "There must be a lot that's wonderful about your father, for you and your mom to be searching for him for so long."

Her words startled me, and I felt tears stinging my eyes. "Well, he's ours, anyway," I said, with pretended nonchalance. "He belongs with us."

"My dad put me through such hell, I used to wish he would die," she said. "Even prayed for it. Do you think that's terrible?"

I looked down, not sure what to say. This young woman was not much older than me, but she was braver, unafraid to speak the truth.

After a few moments, she started to turn away.

"Wait," I whispered. "I don't know if that's terrible, but there're times when I feel the same way. When I wish that we'd find out my father had died, so we could just give up and go home and I could start living my life. But as soon as I think that, I feel sick, because I love him, Lauren, with all my heart. Does that sound crazy to you?"

"Not one bit," she said. "You feel all alone, don't you, even though I can tell you're close to your mom. I'm so glad we're on this trip together, Luke. You're not alone; you and me, we're brother and sister in Christ."

"But I'm not a Christian," I said. "I'm not anything, really."

Her eyes widened.

"You don't know the Lord?"

I shook my head.

"Come on, you two," we heard David call out. "Let's get back on the road."

"Don't worry," she whispered to me. "You will."

❧

Tonopah turned out to be a small city at the foot of a bleak mountain range. As usual, I started out at the assay office, showing my father's picture and asking questions to anyone willing to talk.

"Don't recognize the fella," said one, "but I was you, son, I'd head on up to the Belmont, they're the only one been hirin' for some time. I know they got folks from all over workin' that mine."

It was too far to walk, so over lunch we decided that David and I would drive to the mine while mother and Lauren continued to talk to people in town, and we'd meet back at some benches in the town square when we were done. But when we arrived at the Belmont it was like nothing I had ever seen: men were stretched out on the ground, black with dust and grime, some with blood-stained bandages, shock in their eyes. Others lay in the stillness of death.

"You folks sawbones or volunteers?" asked a weary-looking man.

"They're tourists, Jake, drivin' that fancy car," said another, who was chomping on an unlit cigar. "Get 'em outta here."

"Tell me what you need," David replied, getting out of the Talbot. "I'll help if I can."

"Woah, Lenny," said Jake. "We can use someone with some muscle right now."

Lenny took the cigar out of his mouth, came closer, and squinted up at David. "You just musclebound, or can you work, and work fast?"

"Fast as any man."

"All right," said Lenny, "follow me."

I tagged along as he led us close to the mine entrance, where a large diagram was spread out on a folding table.

"We've had a roof-fall and a fire, our lucky day. Got four men still trapped in this stope here—" he tapped the diagram, "behind rocks and fallen beams, and my boys are exhausted, overcome by the damn smoke. Fire got started at the bottom of this winze—" he indicated a smaller shaft extending down from a horizontal passageway that led to the area he'd called the 'stope'—"where we'd piled some mine timber. We rigged a brattice in the drift and I got all my men who ain't trapped, hurtin', or dead putting out that fire, else no one's gonna survive the smoke, but it ain't quite out yet. I'll send Jake along to get you to the stope and help you clear debris. Anyone you boys manage to get free, we'll haul 'em back up in the cage. When you can't go on no more, we'll haul you back up, too. You game?"

"Let's go," said David.

"I'm coming," I said. As soon as I understood what had happened at the Belmont, I was seized with the conviction that my father was down there, trapped in the mine. And in that moment, I knew that I loved him and had never really wanted him to die.

"No." David put his right hand on my shoulder, and then, speaking quickly, whispered in my ear. "You're brave, Luke, and your father would be proud of you. But I need you to stay here." For a second, his grip was like iron; then he relaxed it, stepped into the cage with Jake, and was gone.

"Kid!" Lenny had the cigar back in his mouth. "You want to make yourself useful, go help Doc." He pointed me to a man in a porkpie hat who was bent over one of the miners stretched out on the ground.

I ran over, and Doc peered up at me with sad, red-rimmed eyes. My attention was captured, however, by the pale white face of the miner, who looked no older than me; I had the eerie feeling that I was looking at myself.

"You seen dead men before?" Doc asked me, getting up and throwing a tarp over the lifeless body.

"Yes sir."

"Well, you'll be seeing some more. Listen up, I'm gonna school ya on what I want ya to do for the living while I get me some shut-eye. Damn hands are shaking, I'm so tired."

Doc explained a few simple things he wanted done for the wounded men, showed me where to get water to quench their thirst, and told me to wake him if any miners were brought up alive. Then he laid down, pulled his hat over his eyes and fell fast asleep.

~⟶

It was the ninth man I attended to who stopped me in my tracks. Though his hair and beard were less wild than in my memory, and he looked ages older, I knew him nonetheless.

"Mr. Slade!" I exclaimed, and offered him water, which he eagerly slurped up.

"I know ya?" he asked, after wiping his mouth with the back of his hand and peering up at me.

"I'm Luke—we were on the boat together from Skagway to Seattle. But that was four years ago, and we only talked once; my brain just stores things away, somehow. I'm so glad you made it out of the mine."

"Only four years ago, was it? Seems ages since I been up at the top 'a the world." His voice was hoarse and pitifully weak. "Like some kind 'a dream."

"You told me about how you panned for placer gold," I said, thinking to cheer him up, "and rafted into town and stayed at the most splendid hotel."

A spark of recognition gleamed in Sourdough's eye. "Yeah, you're the boy with the good-lookin' momma. How 'bout that. Well, don't listen to what old fools got ta say, son; ain't hardly no one left in Dawson City. And the Fairview, she's nothin' now but the wind howlin' through open windows in empty rooms."

He started coughing and I helped him to turn onto his side. His spit came out thick and black.

"Can I do anything for you, Mr. Slade? Do you need to see Doc?"

"Hell no, let him be." He took a deep gasp of breath and then spoke to me in a whisper. "I was the crew chief, Luke. I saw them beady-eyed rats start to scurry, I knew I had ta get the men out, but everything started fallin' 'fore we could clear the stope. Men dyin' like that, what sense does it make, boy? Old-timer like me hardly matters, but the young ones? No sense at all."

"You better rest, Mr. Slade," I said, seeing how hard it was for him to breathe. "But keep your hopes up, the man I'm travelling with, Pastor Gold, he's the strongest fellow you've ever seen, and he's gone down to get your men out."

Sourdough managed a smile.

"You got a pastor workin' rescue, kid? Well, ain't that the damndest thing. Bring him by, I ain't been to church in, well, never, but maybe he can give me a blessin' or somethin', put in a good word for ol' Sourdough Slade."

"I'll bring him over, Mr. Slade. You rest up. I'm going to make the rounds now, I'll check on you in a bit, okay?"

He nodded and closed his eyes. I attended to several more men and was beginning to work my way back through the first ones I'd seen when I heard voices shouting and the clanging of the cage arriving at the top of the mine shaft. Jake was with three men, bloodied and blackened from their ordeal.

"Doc!" I shook the company physician awake, and he snorted and looked at me with startled eyes. "There's three men just came up, and Jake might need help, too."

Lenny and I helped the men out of the cage while Jake bent over, shaking with dry heaves. Moments later, a flatbed truck carrying half a dozen men pulled up with a screech of brakes.

"'bout time you guys showed," said Lenny, then turned back to Jake. "Pull yourself together and tell me what's going on."

"Big guy's still trying to get the last man free," Jake gasped. "I couldn't hardly breathe no more, I'm done."

Lenny threw away his cigar and waved to the man who'd been driving the flatbed.

"Bring your two best men with you and get in the cage with me," he shouted, and a minute later the four descended into the darkness of the mine.

I tried to keep up with Doc and figure out as quickly as I could what he was asking for as he tended to the three men, but all the time my mind was distracted with thoughts I couldn't push away: was the last man my father? If I had the chance to talk to him, and he hadn't long to live, what would I say?

I love you. I forgive you. No other words would matter.

"Quit your day-dreamin' boy, and get me water," Doc snapped at me, and I went to refill the bucket.

When the cage came back up, Lenny and one of his reinforcements were supporting David and another man, young enough to be my elder brother, his left arm dangling uselessly from his shoulder, teeth gritted in pain.

David dropped to his knees near me.

"I'm going to rest for a bit," he said in a voice that was hardly more than a mumble. "Then we'll get back to town before your mom and Lauren—" he leaned against my chest— "start to worry."

His eyes closed, and he began to snore. I lowered him as gently as I could to the ground and put some towels under his head. Doc came over and listened to his heart and lungs.

"That's one strong sumbitch," he said. "Just let him sleep."

"We owe your dad, kid." Lenny was squatting beside us, chewing on a new cigar. "I didn't yet have a chance to learn his name. Or yours, either."

For a moment I was confused, then realized whom Lenny meant.

"I'm Luke, and this is Pastor David Gold, my mother and I are travelling with him and a friend."

"You're kiddin' me, right? No? Well, we got some souls could use prayin' over, that's for sure."

I took out the picture of my father and handed it to Lenny with a quick explanation. He stared at it, then showed it to Jake before handing it back to me and shaking his head.

The conviction that my father had been one of the men trapped in the mine, which had seized me not long before, now seemed absurd. And if the father I sought, whom I once thought so brave and loving and true, wasn't any of those things after all, did the man I loved even exist? Perhaps I was only chasing a phantom.

My mother and Lauren arrived long before David woke up, having hitched a ride to the mine to see why we were so late, and I filled them in on the afternoon's events. We sat in the Talbot and closed our eyes, and the sun was setting by the time David woke up.

Lenny invited us to share their dinner by an outdoor fire and called the men together so that David could lead them in prayer. Shortly after, the fourth man who'd been rescued came up to him, his arm in a makeshift sling. He said he'd been to church as a child and still read his Bible, but he'd never been baptized, it was something he hadn't thought about until the roof-fall, until he could feel the cold breath of death in his face, could David baptize him that night, right then and there?

The two walked off together and talked for a while before David led him back and asked me to bring the bucket of water.

"Sam has asked to make a public confession of his commitment to God; the words he'll say mean that his old life is dead and gone, and he lives a new life in Christ."

I set the bucket at his feet and listened as he spoke and the wounded man echoed his words.

I believe that Jesus is the Christ, Son of the Living God, my Lord and my Savior...

Beautiful words, rich in mysteries just beyond my understanding.

...that I have been buried in the likeness of His death and raised in the likeness of His resurrection...

The fire danced and shadows played on the faces of men grown suddenly solemn.

...to walk in the newness of life.

Sparks flew up toward a darkening sky that was beginning to fill with stars.

I baptize you in the name of the Father, and of the Son, and of the Holy Spirit.

Water poured over the young man's hair and down his face, washing away soot and grime, his skin suddenly white where the water flowed.

Thank you, Father, for leading Sam Greeley to profess his faith; guide him in the narrow path, and help him to be a witness who will draw others to You...

Diamonds of light exploded in the droplets that scattered as Sam shook his head and laughed.

Amen.

David wrapped his arms around him, the miners clapped and cheered, and a moment later things returned to the way they had been, with jokes and oaths and the clatter of dishes and gulping of beer. But I was still on the other side of the looking glass.

Buried...raised...new life.

Sam stood a few steps apart from the others, looking into the fire and running his one good hand through his hair. I approached him, filled with a hunger to know more.

"Mr. Greeley," I said. "What does it mean, to be living a new life?"

He looked at me for a while before answering.

"That I don't have to be afraid, 'cause the Lord Himself lives in me. I mean, I reckon I'll still be fearful a' times, but least I'll know it's pure foolishness to feel that way."

I had a hundred questions I wanted to ask, but didn't know where to begin.

Father, Son, and Holy Spirit.

Then I remembered what I'd promised Sourdough Slade.

"Pastor Gold," I said, "There's a man here I know, Mr. Slade, I met him on the boat from Alaska. He'd like to meet you. It was his men trapped in the mine, and he was pretty badly hurt himself."

"I'm sorry, Luke," said Lenny, "but Sourdough didn't make it. Just an hour ago, Doc told me he passed."

I felt a dull ache in my gut. Was there something I wanted, he'd asked me, more than anything the world had to offer? No, that wasn't it, those weren't the words he'd used...

"He never knew his father," I said to Lenny and David. "Never knew him at all."

~

"I'm a poor excuse for a pastor," said David, as though thinking to himself out loud. Since he was well rested, we had decided to push on toward Las Vegas and had just set out. "I've known you two for nearly a month," he said, his eyes seeking my mother's and mine in the rear-view mirror, "but we've never talked, not of anything that matters. Yura, you've been searching for your husband, and your son for his father, and I can only imagine your pain. You said something a little while ago, Luke, about the fellow who died, Mr. Slade, that he never knew his father. But Luke, Yura, do you know your Heavenly Father? For you have one, if you want Him—a perfect, loving Father, the living God."

"Those are just words," my mother replied. "I don't know what they mean."

"I'd like to know what they mean," I said.

"Is there a god you worship?" David asked.

"We don't worship anything," said my mother. "We fear much. Ours are not living gods, for I am a sculptress by trade, and I carve them out of soapstone, walrus ivory, and wood.

"Look," she said, pointing to the stars in Orion, "we say that those are steps in the snow, the stairway to the sky. But I would not care to climb it, for there is no comfort there. Our gods are as harsh as the world around us, they offer no relief. Tatqim, moon god, lusts after his sister, Seqinek, the sun, and gives her endless chase; their story is an ugliness that mars the beauty of the night. And your god, where is he? Can he, too, be found among the stars?"

"No," said David. "He is the *creator* of the stars, of the earth, sun, and moon, of all things. It is thanks to Him we have our being, that we draw each breath, and in our darkest moments know that He is with us, and loves us, and has promised us eternal life, eternal joy. He is your Father, and Luke's, and I'll tell you His story if you'd care to hear."

My mother looked at me with the trace of a smile and stroked my hair.

"Please," she said to David, "tell us more."

Chapter Twenty-One
The Call

David told us of our Heavenly Father, who spoke the world into being, and I imagined a universe suddenly ablaze with light, and the earth, newly formed, with its roiling, wine-dark seas. I saw mountains heaving up from the deep, shoots breaking through the planet's crust and spreading into emerald canopies, and then the swarming, teeming, roaring, bleating panoply of animal life.

Lastly, He made man, meant to have dominion over a good creation, living in innocence, harmony, purity, and peace.

Sometimes, in the twilight between wakefulness and sleep, I remember a time when I was young, so young, and my father was carrying me along a sweet-smelling forest trail, holding me close against his chest; I felt his strength and warmth and heard the beating of his heart...

Made in the image of God, man had been given the gift of free will. If we chose to live in obedience to Him, joy everlasting would be ours. But alas, we did not so choose!

There must have been a time when my father could have stayed true to us: a moment when Kathleen was standing next to him, her shoulder touching his, in his mind the keen awareness that he was breathing in her scent; a moment when he could have walked away...

And so, we inhabit a fallen world. I imagined the perfection of creation, crumbling into dust: Gone was the idyllic garden! Now blizzards rage across a barren tundra, wolves rip the flesh of caribou, and everywhere we see the face of death.

"Why give us free will, then?" asked my mother bitterly. "Look how it ruins lives, spreads havoc across the earth. Rather than a gift, it seems a curse."

"Because God made us capable of love," David replied, "and love is freely given."

"But if the world is good no longer," said my mother, "if we live in a land where the rebel angel who lured man into sin holds sway, what hope remains?"

"All the hope you could ever wish for," David answered, and he talked while the stars wheeled across the heavens, and the moon, born huge and golden, floated upward until it became a small white disk at the top of the sky. He told us of wondrous and terrible things; of Jesus Christ—Son of Man, Son of God!—and the Spirit burned the words he spoke forever into my heart.

~

"Imagine a man walking through a desert much like this one, long ago, in a distant land. This was a time when almost everyone worshipped idols like the ones Yura carves, and he did as well, until the one true God entered into his life. Now, at the Lord's command, this man, Abraham, has set off on a strange voyage. He's taken his wife, nephew, and servants, loaded his possessions on the backs of camels, but as for the rest—father, friends, neighbors, the world he knows—he's left it all behind.

"Where is he heading? He's not sure. Into the unknown.

"Why did he agree to what must have seemed like madness to everyone else? God promised to make his name great, that he would become a great nation, but most important, He told Abraham that all the people of the world would be blessed through him. Such a promise could only have come from a righteous God, a Lord of love and light, in whom there is no darkness at all. A God Abraham would believe in, have faith in, and obey, no matter the cost.

"As the years went by, Abraham's descendants multiplied and became the land of Israel, at times a mighty nation, but not yet great, not yet a blessing to the world. Sometimes they were noble and brave, but too often they were just like us—foolish, greedy, and prideful—for they lived in a fallen world, and were forever repeating Adam's sin of faithlessness to God.

"Yet though every man be false, still God is true, steadfast in His unfailing love. And in his faithfulness, He afflicts us; those He loves he disciplines. Time and again, Israel was defeated, humiliated, put under the thumb of rulers from foreign lands. But even in the depths of

135

their despair, the children of Abraham knew that they could count on the promises God had made. One day, He would send them a savior, of whom their prophets spoke—a messiah, a Christ, a King who would see that justice was done and the wrongs of the world set right."

David paused and drank from his canteen. The desert was lit by a bone-white moon and filled with strange shadows. I felt like one of the errant children of Abraham, waiting impatiently for the righting of wrongs, for the restoration of a long-lost past.

"Now, imagine another man, about thirty years old, walking by the side of a sea in that same desert land, two thousand years after Abraham. Look, here are two brothers, Peter and Andrew, fishermen casting their nets. 'Come, follow me,' the man says, and they leave their nets and follow him. And there, two more fishermen, brothers James and John, and he calls them as well, and they leave their father and boat behind. Where are they going? Like their forefather, into the unknown. But of this they're sure: the man they follow is unspeakably good, a worker of wonders, pronouncing good news of the kingdom of God.

"From now on, they'll be fishers of men.

"Who was this man? He lived nineteen hundred years ago, born of a woman descended from Abraham. But He had no earthly father, for He was the very Son of God. And now I'll tell you a great mystery: this man, Jesus, *was* God. You see, God is Love itself; before creation, before there was anything else to love, God loved, for He is three persons, each fully God: Father, Son, and Holy Spirit, in an eternal embrace of love, since before the beginning of time.

"So, the Creator of the universe left the throne of heaven and became one of us—for Jesus, though fully God, was fully man. He hungered and thirsted as we do; He suffered, bled, wept bitter tears, was tempted, yet lived a perfect, sinless life. Only in this way could He rescue our fallen world.

"And how the people of Israel longed for rescue! But they didn't understand the sort of rescue they needed. They chafed under the iron fist of Rome; surely the Messiah, their Savior, would be a conquering king who would gather them into an army and rid them of foreign rule!

"Well, Jesus was a king, all right—the King of kings!—but not the sort they had in mind. His people hoped he would lead them to storm the gates of power; instead, He proclaimed that the meek would inherit the earth, mourners be comforted, the merciful shown mercy, and peacemakers would be called children of God. He called on us to love our enemies, pray for those who persecute us, and forgive every offense, that we in turn may be forgiven. From His presence demons fled; at his touch, the lame walked, the blind saw, the sick were healed.

"Yes, He came to be our Savior, but He would rescue us from nothing less than sin and death. Now, I will tell you something amazing: to be saved, we must be reborn from above, transformed from within. The Son of God became like us that we might become like Him, the perfect likeness of His Father, and live as He lived, with one thought, one goal: to do His Father's will. But to accomplish our salvation, Father and Son would pay a terrible price.

"Hundreds of years before, a great prophet had foretold the coming of our Savior, and described just what Jesus would be like, though the people of Israel chose not to understand. He had written that the Christ would be a man of suffering, despised and rejected by men. And so he was!

"There was more that the prophet had written, words that chill me to the bone: He would be pierced for our transgressions, crushed for our sins; yet, the punishments that He would endure would bring us peace, and by his wounds we would be healed."

"I understand a parent suffering because of his children's sins," said my mother. "But this—it sounds as though you are saying that the Son of God suffered in our place; and that somehow, in this way, we would be saved."

"Oh, yes, Yura, but there's so much more!" Lauren exclaimed, and I saw that her eyes were shining with tears. "I'm sorry," she said to David, "but I just can't wait for them to hear the good news. I feel like Mary on Friday evening, and I want it to be Sunday morning so we can all run to the empty tomb!" Then she clamped her hand over her mouth and her fair skin turned crimson red.

"Dear Lauren," said David, and his smile warmed us against the chill of the desert night, "don't ever silence the promptings of your heart! They do me good.

"I'm eager to catch up with Lauren," he said to us, "But I'm first going to take you back to Abraham. Late in his life, God blessed him with a son, Isaac, whom he loved beyond all measure. Then one day, years later, as a test of his faith, the Lord asked Abraham to sacrifice his boy to Him. So great was Abraham's trust in God and His goodness, that he was ready to slay his beloved son, and only when his knife was raised did the Lord stay his hand.

"But what the Lord did not demand of Abraham, he gave of Himself, out of love for us, for His Creation, ruined by the Fall. Jesus was betrayed by one of his own, and given over into Roman hands; abandoned by those closest to Him, mercilessly scourged and beaten, and put to death in the most savage way known to man, death on a cross, nailed by the feet and hands. Yet that pain paled before what He suffered most. Listen to me, Luke and Yura: the Father sent His Son to take our sins upon Himself! To bear the sins of the world--I can hardly imagine the agony and desperate anguish. But only in this way could the chains that bind us to sin and death be broken.

"Do you see the faithfulness of God, at any cost?

"Jesus died on that Cross, and was buried, and those who loved Him were heart-sick with grief. But He died so that Death itself would be defeated; and on the third day, the Father raised Him up to life. Now you understand the empty tomb that Lauren spoke of, for on a Sunday morning, surely the gladdest day that ever saw a dawn, He appeared to those who knew Him, and in the weeks that followed to hundreds more. Jesus died as a man and was raised as a man, but a new sort of man, imperishable. He died as one of us so that we can die like Him, die to our old ways of living and thinking, and be raised like Him, reborn from above, rescued from sin and death, free to walk in the newness of life.

"These are the words of the disciple who knew Him best; I pray you'll write them on your heart: *For God so loved the world, that He gave his only Son, that whoever believes in Him shall not perish but have eternal life.*

"When Jesus returned to His Father, He sent the Holy Spirit to lead us to Him, so that when we put our faith in Him, the Spirit will reside forever in our hearts, our Counselor and Comforter, guiding us toward all truth. And Christ Jesus has promised us that the day will come when He will return in power and glory, to set all wrongs right; then justice will roll down like waters, righteousness like an ever-flowing stream.

"He will wipe every tear from our eyes. Luke, Yura, you can be sure of this: the suffering you've endured will be as nothing compared to the wonders He'll reveal in the new heavens and new earth, where there will be no more death or mourning or crying or pain, for this fallen world will have passed away."

David paused again to drink from his canteen. Lauren looked at him, her eyes glowing, and I could see that my mother was mulling over his words, though what she thought of them, I could not tell. But as for me, I felt electric, intensely alive, hungry to know this man Christ Jesus.

"Remember the promise that God made to Abraham?" David asked us. "The blessing that his offspring would bring to the ends of the earth was the Gospel, the good news that through the death and resurrection of Jesus, salvation can be ours. Here you are, four thousand years later, mother and son from a place Abraham never imagined, a land of snow and ice on the far side of the world, and look!—that blessing has come to you, praise God.

"And now it's up to you. How will you answer the call of God? Consider what I've said, read the Scriptures for yourselves, ask about whatever troubles or puzzles you. Take the time you need, only don't delay, because to turn from God is the way of sin and death, but to give ourselves to Christ is to gain eternal life."

David fell silent. Lauren looked at me and must have seen something in my smile, for she mouthed the words, *"I told you."* For a while no one said a word; we sped through the night, the only car on a lonely road, in a world enfolded in darkness. Was the God of Abraham, of love and light, keeping watch over us? The God who died, and rose again, defeating death? With all my heart, I hoped it true.

It *must* be true.

"Thank you," said my mother, her words suddenly breaking the silence. "I trust you'll understand if, for the moment, I've nothing to say. I think slowly; but, I hope, not badly."

"Of course," said David.

"My son, though—" my mother added, and again I felt the rare touch of her hand resting on my shoulder, "he is his own man."

The wind that had whispered through the dogwood trees four years before, leading me to where Miss McSorely lay dying, my mother's ministering to the man left for dead in Central Park, the transformation of Kathleen Byrne, surely these things were the Spirit at work in the world...

"I believe, Pastor Gold," I said, the beating of my heart so loud that I could hardly hear my own words. "I want to give myself to Christ."

"Ah, Luke," said David, "Praise God, praise God. That makes me a happy man."

Lauren clapped her hands, delighted, and leaned over into the back seat to kiss my forehead. David's eyes met mine in the rear-view mirror, and then something happened which I cannot explain. I left the car and was running through the open desert, in the heat of the day. Before me was a man, elegantly dressed, but reeking of evil; and behind him, a giant, towering over David and another who lay prostrate on the ground.

Abruptly, all was as it had been before, and David was just finishing a prayer for my mother and me.

"Are you all right, Luke?" Lauren asked.

"Oh yes," I replied, but for a moment, I had been shivering with cold.

The other figure in my vision had been that of a lifeless girl.

Chapter Twenty-Two
Nobody Messes with Pastor Dan

"Ya know," said Willie, "I was kinda hopin' Oz would make me a pit boss or somethin'. Funny, huh."

He and his sister were sitting at one of several long wooden tables in an annex that served as the soup kitchen of the Church of the Heart Set Free.

"You'd cut a handsome figure in a tuxedo," said Joan. "So what *has* he got you doing?"

"Mostly, I listen to him talk."

"To whom?" Joan asked.

"Me. Well, himself, really, I s'pose," Willie replied. "He laughs a lot at his own jokes. Sometimes he shows me magic tricks—corny stuff, ya know, like doves he makes appear and disappear."

"Must be from his old lounge act," said Joan. "What a character!"

"I guess. Anyway, part of my job, I feed the doves and clean out their cages. Which I'd like, tell ya the truth, 'cept for where he keeps 'em. Oz's got all these windowless rooms back of his office, really creeps me out. One of 'em's got this big bronze bull I'm supposed to polish, I'm guessin' he's gonna use it in one of his shows. Told me not to tell anyone about it, keep it between me and him, but nobody who really wants to keep a secret talks like that, so I figger he knows I'd tell ya 'bout it." Willie laughed. "Didn't think I'd end up rubbin' a bull's butt with a shammy, did ya?"

"Are you sorry you took the job?" Joan asked. "I hope you're not mad at me for getting you involved with him, if he's taking advantage of you, just quit."

"Oh hell, no, Joanie. Oz pays me better'n Judson. Like, forty bucks an hour."

"Are you going to save up some money?" she asked him, shocked at the amount he was making. "Don't just blow it on meth, or whatever you're getting high on these days." Joan cringed inwardly; no sooner were the words out of her mouth than she regretted them. Why couldn't she simply be glad for him?

Willie frowned and looked down. "You don't think much 'a me, huh."

"You're telling me you're not using? Don't lie to me in a house of God."

"Well, then maybe we ought'a step outside," Joan's brother replied, and shot her one of his killer smiles. "Though, come to think of it, is there anywhere God ain't?"

I deserved that, she thought to herself. Could I be any more sanctimonious?

"Touché. Ah, Willie, I think the world of you, honest. I just flip out, thinking of you OD'ing some day, throwing away your life. Here, I'll tell you what." She stubbed out the cigarette she'd been sucking on, then took the Camels pack out of her handbag and dunked it in her water glass. "I'm giving up smokes. That's how much I want you to get clean."

"Woah!" Willie's eyes widened. "Slow down, sis. You gotta be smokin', what, three packs a day?"

"At least. Since I was eighteen years old."

"Ever try to quit before? Nicotine sinks hooks into your brain deeper than ice or smack."

"A few times." Joan looked her brother in the eye and tried to appear confident. Why did words keep coming out of her mouth before she'd thought them through? Still, giving up smokes for Willie felt right. "Yeah, I never made it more than a few weeks. But this time's different. If I can do it, wuss that I am, so can you."

"This being a soup kitchen," said Daniel Gold, appearing suddenly at their table, carrying a tray with three bowls, "I come bearing soup." He sat down next to Willie and handed each a bowl and a package of oyster crackers. "As your brother can attest, my cream of mushroom soup is infamous in these parts; one spoonful and you won't be able to stop."

"That's no lie, Joanie," Willie said.

"Thanks, Daniel. I'm not really hungry, but, if you insist—" Joan swallowed a small amount, then found herself joining the other two and slurping down her entire bowl.

"Campbell's, plus an extra crate or two of mushrooms and half a vat of half and half," Daniel explained.

"Aha. I might have to try my hand at this on a smaller scale," Joan remarked. "And we were just discussing matters of temptation!"

"You're neither of you on a diet, I hope," said Daniel.

"Not hardly," said Willie. "We were talkin' 'bout cigs—" he looked at his sister—"and crank."

That's a confession of sorts, thought Joan, feeling hopeful. Still, she already had the hunger to light up, and looked sorrowfully at the sodden pack in her water glass.

"I just quit," she said, and scooped up the Camels pack into a napkin before depositing it in the trash. "Throw in a prayer that I can keep away from them, if you think of it."

"Let's pray right now," Daniel replied, and grasped Joan's and Willie's hands. "Heavenly Father, through your Son we can do all things; we beseech you to grant my friend, Willie's dear sister Joan, the strength that she may never smoke again; through your grace, remove every trace of her desire for cigarettes, that nothing but your will shall be the master of her life. In Jesus' name we pray, Amen."

"I dunno," said Willie. "I just feel bad for Joanie, doin' somethin' like this to help her crack-head brother. Look, half the bozos in here are suckin' down smoke. Temptation? We're surrounded by it. Well, I surrender, I'm comin' out with my hands up. Deck's stacked against us, it's one big trap out there. How's Joan supposed to deal with that?"

"Indeed," said Daniel. "We live in enemy territory; without Christ, we haven't a chance, we're sitting ducks. Utter the Lord's prayer; in about thirty seconds, you've asked for everything you need, ending with a cry from the heart that knows its own weakness, and knows the world for what it is: *Lead us not into temptation, but deliver us from evil.*"

"I know Jesus was led into the desert to be tempted by Satan," said Joan, eager to get the attention off herself, "but the scene always seems to me like Lex Luther shooting bullets at Superman; they just bounce off his chest."

"So if we were like Jesus," said Willie, "we wouldn't even feel temptation, huh."

"Ah, there you've both got it wrong," said Daniel. "And this is good news. The writer of the letter to the Hebrews put it like this: *For we do not have a high priest—that's Jesus—who is unable to sympathize with our weaknesses, but one who in every respect has been tempted as we are—yet without sin.*"

"In *every* way," Willie repeated. "Heavy. But I doubt they had crank back then."

Daniel pretended to box Willie's ears.

"There is *nothing* new under the sun, my man, just variations on Satan's same sad tune. Here, try this on for size: near the beginning of a notebook that Uncle Luke shared with me, my grandfather David made a note about the Greek word translated 'temptation' in the Lord's prayer. It's built from a word that means to *pierce through, as with a spear.* Do you get it? Do you see how much Jesus understands exactly what temptation means?"

"This is personal for you, isn't it," said Joan, feeling the intensity of Daniel's speech.

"Isn't a day goes by I don't think about booze," Daniel replied, his voice soft, matter-of-fact, no trace of self-pity in his words. *He'd awakened that morning to see the bottle of Blue on his dresser once more, Johnny Walker, like a sweet dream, like a vision from Hell, and he'd walked over, the thirst for it alive in his throat; inches away, and it was still there, this time no mere trick of shadows and light. Not until he reached out to touch it did the bottle vanish, leaving his hand clutching the air. It was only to see if the bottle were real, he thought, but the truth pierced him like a spear...*

"Without Christ, we're lost," he continued, "swallowed up in the Outer Darkness while yet alive. But you know, He always gives us a way out, a means of escape."

"Maybe death, huh," said Willie. "Ain't that the ultimate escape?"

"If you mean by taking your own life," said Daniel, "no, that's the last temptation, the devil's lure. But yes, when nothing else avails, I think the Father rescues us through death. For there are worse things than dying; and in Christ, we die into life, abundant life."

"And for the poor bastards who ain't in Christ?" asked Willie.

"Whether they've a chance to find their way home from hell, I'm not sure, my business being the leading of souls to the Lord in this life; but one can hope."

"Speaking of worse things than dying," said Joan, "I've wondered, since we're told to turn the other cheek, how does that square with war?"

"I can't believe we're s'posed to be passy-fists," said Willie. "Just a few weeks from now'll be ten years since 9/11, and I'm glad we bombed those SOBs."

"We need not be pacifists to follow Christ," said Daniel. "There are righteous wars, times when I must kill the enemy that I'm nonetheless required to love, especially when there is no other way to save the innocent. But never out of a desire for revenge; for 'vengeance is mine, saith the Lord.' The day will come when all matters will be set right, Willie, you can count on it."

"So it's not hypocritical for me to follow Christ and still study Krav Maga," said Joan, who had in fact been wondering about how learning the art of self-defense jived with the Sermon on the Mount. "Throwing muggers over my shoulder and whatnot."

"As long as it's not what you put your trust in. Remember this: when you meet hatred with love, the Holy Spirit shines in you with a blazing light. There is nothing in all the universe mightier than the Cross, nothing that can match the power of self-sacrificial love."

Just as Daniel spoke those words, an argument that had been going on between two homeless men halfway across the room escalated into a shoving match. The pastor rose slowly and took a few steps toward the men, who, noticing him, mumbled apologies to each other and sat back down.

But what had gained that reaction, Joan wondered: was it the breadth of his shoulders and the power of his arms, or the gentleness of Daniel's smile and the kind light in his eyes?

"Told ya." Willie laughed wryly. "Nobody messes with Pastor Dan."

Chapter Twenty-Three
Wounds

When we arrived in Las Vegas early Monday morning, Lauren guided David to the Church of the Heart Set Free, though he decided to park some distance away when he saw the crowd milling about on the sidewalk and the police wagon stationed directly in front. The sky, which only an hour ago had been dark sapphire, had turned a pale blue. The sun had not yet risen, so the air was still only pleasantly warm, and it felt glorious to get out and stretch our legs. David looked up, raised his arms, thanked God for our safe arrival, and prayed from the Psalms he knew so well.

Bless the Lord, O my soul!

O Lord my God, You are very great!

You are clothed with splendor and majesty, covering yourself with light as with a garment, stretching out the heavens like a tent.

He lays the beams of his chambers on the waters; he makes the clouds his chariot; he rides on the wings of the wind...

As we approached the church, Lauren began greeting people she knew and asking them what was going on.

"That what we *all* wanna know," said one weather-beaten old codger. "Dem inside been singin' all night ta raise the dead, 'n now the coppers just showed up lookin' like they had bad eggs fer breakfast."

"I think everyone's waiting for *you*," Lauren said to David, and the crowd began to part to let us through.

"Who's the big man?" someone called out.

"He the new pastor? Hallelujah!"

"That's the Prophet Elijah, you fool!"

"Prophet Elijah's our new pastor, hallelujah!"

Moments later we were inside, and in the golden light of dawn, David introduced himself to the men I came to know as Sheriff Stone and Deputy Drake.

"He ain't for real," the deputy sneered. "I recognize him from the papers—he's that pug calls himself the Pummelin' Pastor, was a no-show just the other night up Reno way. They say he can't hack it in the ring no more."

"You just let me handle this, Drake," the sheriff said quietly, before turning back to David. "You're showin' up a day late and more than a few dollars short, Pastor Gold. This building is being foreclosed on, there's an eight-hunnert-dollar mortgage that's way overdue. Now, I'm sure you're an upstandin' citizen, bein' a pastor and all, so why don't you help us clear the place peacefully? That way this fine congregation of yours don't get their butts dragged off to the Blue Room for trespassin'."

"One night in the Blue Room, he'll vamoose," said Drake.

The sheriff ignored his deputy's comment and kept his gaze steadily on David's eyes.

"I don't see a foreclosure notice posted, Sheriff," David replied. "and I'm sure you'd agree the church has the right to make good on its debts."

"You want a notice posted, that can happen in about three minutes," said the sheriff. "But if you're under some illusion there's money in the coffers here, lemme set you straight: there ain't." He lowered his voice to a whisper. "You came here lookin' for a quick buck, you came to the wrong place."

"Let me put your mind at ease, Sheriff; I've got title to a vehicle I can put up as collateral which is worth four or five times what's owed. It's a '29 Talbot that's parked around the corner on Ogden; I'm sure you won't let anything happen to it, being an officer of the law, but—" He turned to Lauren, who was standing by my side. "Miss McBride, to minimize the burden on our police force, would you please round up a few volunteers to keep an eye on the car?"

Lauren cheerfully ran back outside. After she left, I realized that, in the press of the crowd, her bare arm had been resting against mine; it had been a delightful feeling, and my arm was still tingling long after she was gone.

"Loan still has to get paid, Gold," said the Sheriff. "I dunno, we might have to take possession of that Talbot of yours for safekeeping, I'll look into it. Meanwhile, though, Pastor, seems a shame if you didn't deliver a sermon to this crowd, maybe teach us a thing or two."

"Gladly, Sheriff," said David. "I'd like to address the congregation."

"Let's hear what ya got, pug," muttered Drake.

A diminutive man in a frayed business suit who had been standing on the front pew jumped up and waved his arms.

"Pastor Gold! Polwarth's the name, at your service! I take it you have accepted our offer to shepherd the Heart Set Free?"

"Indeed, if you'll have me," David replied, and a great happy roar went up from the congregation.

My mother and I managed to find a place in back where we could lean against the wall. David walked to the pulpit and stood there for a while, looking down, as though collecting his thoughts.

"Brothers and sisters," he began, but there was something odd about his speech; it sounded stilted, mechanical, as though the words were not his own, and after a short while he stopped in mid-sentence and looked back down. In the long silence that followed, I heard Drake snickering and the sounds of people stirring uncomfortably in their pews.

Then David raised his head and began to speak.

"Up until just the other day, I was a pug. A boxer. I was boxing in France back in 1914, and when the Great War began, I volunteered in the French army, and soldiered over there for four years. I wasn't trying to save the world, or make it safe for democracy, or anything like that; I just liked mixing it up. I wanted in on the biggest fight around." He paused and looked about the room. "I'm guessing there's more than a few here who've worn a uniform."

"Hell, yes," one man called out. "Wyatt Swift, United States Navy, boatswain's mate, Santiago de Cuba, '98. Everyone talks 'bout them Rough Riders, but it was us sunk that Spanish fleet."

"U.S. Army, Second Division, field artillery, Pastor," said another, whose right arm was missing below the elbow. "I was a gunner, saw action at Belleau Wood."

"Thirty-third, we fought alongside the Aussies at Hamel."

"Hundred-seventh infantry, and ain't that Black Jack Pershing a son-of-a-bitch."

Perhaps a dozen other men who'd served in the Great War spoke up.

"Anne-Marie, Pastor," said a woman. "I was a YMCA girl, most of these doughboys probably cried on my shoulder one time or another."

"General Robert E. Lee, Pastor Gold, pleased as punch to make your acquaintance," said a grizzled old-timer, eliciting laughter from the congregation.

"The feeling is mutual, General," said David.

He let ten or fifteen seconds go by, and the room became very quiet.

"I saw things during the war that I thought would drive me mad: friends I'd been laughing with a moment before, their lives snuffed out in an instant; parents carrying the broken bodies of their children from the rubble of their home. I saw some, untouched by war, who showed the coldest cruelty to those thirsting for kindness, and I saw brave men shunned while cowards had medals draped around their necks. The land was savaged, and millions died, and all for *nothing*, for no reason at all. For a long time, I doubted the goodness of God. I looked inside myself for faith and came up empty. I wondered if He was even there at all."

"Don't sound like no preacher to me," Drake sneered, but David either didn't hear him or else paid him no mind.

"It isn't just soldiers who bear these sorts of scars; I doubt there's anyone in this room who hasn't been wounded in some way. Sometimes we're hurt by others, but for me, nothing's been more painful than seeing the evil in my own heart."

There was an awkward silence, and then Lauren, who had returned only a few minutes before, spoke out.

"I lost track how many times my dad beat me," she said. "And he did worse than that. It made me angry, filled me with hate. I need a whole lot of help from Jesus to learn how to forgive."

Her words opened up a floodgate from the rest of the congregation, and they called out their stories one by one. Some named the ones who'd hurt them: vicious pimps, alcoholic husbands, runaway wives. Others told of bringing hell down on their own heads: a gambler who'd robbed his children to place a bet; a morphine junkie, stunned by the ruin of her life.

Wounds

"These wounds we bear," said David, after the last story was spoken, "these wretched memories, what meaning do they have in our lives? They can torment us, I know that well enough; race through our minds when we're trying to escape into sleep, come back to us in dark dreams, sit like a weight on our chest the moment we awake. And here's the heart of the matter: they'll lead us to God or to the Devil. It's up to us. It's our choice.

"When I signed up to fight the Germans, I only knew a few words of French. But I found several that are pretty much the same as in English, like some action words, where if you add an 'ay' sound at the end, voila, you're speaking French. So, if I wanted to ask a girl to dance, I'd screw up my courage to go over and ask, 'Dancer?'

"Early on, when I wanted to say a blessing over the hardtack and watery stew they served us in the trenches, I took a chance and announced that I wanted to 'blesser' our grub. That got a big laugh from the troops around me, because it turned out that in French, *blesser* means *to wound*.

"I was young then, and full of myself, and it was only years later that I realized what seemed a mistake, an accident of language, in fact revealed a great truth: *in our wounds we find the blessings of God.*

"What are they, these wounds of ours? Punishments, at times; and thanks be to God that he lets us suffer the consequences of our foolishness, our evil, for too often suffering is all that turns us to Him and keeps us from burying ourselves in the depths of Hell. The Devil will dole out much that we ask for in our blindness, but God will give us what we need. And sometimes we need to lose, to be the boxer battered down to the canvas and hearing the jeers of the crowd, the gambler rolling snake eyes time and again. We need to lose home, lose love, lose anything and everything we used to point to with pride. Because what we need is God Himself.

"What, then, are we to think when we're wounded through no misdeeds of our own? Where's the meaning, where's the blessing in those wounds?

"Never forget that the Lord has felt every pain we feel. He did not come to save us from suffering, but so that our suffering might be like His. He came so that we could learn to die as he died—to our own desires, our own will. Close your eyes for a moment and picture Jesus, our Elder Brother, in the Garden of Gethsemane, kneeling in prayer, fully God and yet fully man. Facing agony unspeakable, he asks, *Father, if You are willing, take this cup from Me,* His sweat falling like drops of blood to the ground. And then He speaks these words: *yet not My will, but Yours be done.* When, in our darkest moments, we can whisper those words to God, to Him who is always with us and will never leave us, then we are one with Him and truly blessed.

"This is why Jesus said it was so difficult for a rich man to enter the Kingdom of Heaven. By *riches* He meant not merely money, but *anything* that tempts us to feel self-sufficient: a multitude of friends; robust health; skills, and savvy, and splendid common sense. Anything that tempts us to believe the lie that *our* will matters, that we can trust in ourselves to get through whatever might come along. Because we can't. Without God, we're utterly lost.

"Nineteen hundred years ago, our Savior, the Son of God and Son of Man, spoke from a hillside to an assembly of men and women much like us. He told them then, as he tells us still today, that blessed are the poor in spirit—those who know that riches, of any sort, will not suffice. Blessed are the meek, blessed are those who mourn; for they will be comforted, and all the earth, and the Kingdom of Heaven, will be theirs.

"I find this awesome and amazing: that by suffering with Him, by *dying* with Him, dying to anything but the doing of His Father's will, we will be *raised* with Him—raised into His glory, into eternal life!

"Jesus had more to say on that hillside: he told us how we can be so blessed as to become the children of God and see Him face to face. We're to hunger and thirst after righteousness; be peacemakers in an angry, warring world; merciful amid the callous and unsparing; pure in heart when so much that surrounds us is desperately corrupt.

"As a younger man, when I read this in the fifth chapter of Matthew, the Sermon on the Mount, His words only brought me to despair. Me, a peacemaker, pure in heart? How on earth could I accomplish *any* of these things? Because of myself it would surely be a hopeless quest, a futile dream.

"But in Him all things are possible.

"I told you that during the Great War, many times I looked inside myself for faith and found nothing there. Well, of course not! It's only by looking to Jesus Christ that anyone finds faith."

David fell silent, and after a few moments someone called out, "We need you, Pummelin' Pastor!"

"There's no such man, I'm afraid," David replied. "Or rather, when I played that role, I was a fraud. I don't *feel* worthy to lead you, but that the workings of the Holy Spirit have brought us together, I have no doubt.

"Truly, if you want me as your pastor, all I have to give you is in these words from the Letter to the Hebrews: *let us also lay aside every weight, and sin which clings so closely, and let us run with endurance the race that is set before us, looking to Jesus, the founder and perfecter of our faith.* I'll stand up here for one reason, with one goal: to inspire you, goad you, cajole you, implore you, beg you if need be, to keep your eyes fixed on Jesus Christ."

David paused and thumbed through the pages of his Bible.

"Ever since the War, I've prayed from the Psalms, and I'm going to pray for us from the first verses of Psalm 103."

He bowed his head.

"Bless the Lord, O my soul;
And all that is within me, bless His holy name!
Bless the Lord, O my soul,
And forget not all His benefits:
Who forgives all our sins,
Who heals all our diseases,
Who redeems our life from destruction,
Who crowns us with lovingkindness and tender mercies,
Who satisfies our desires with good things,
So that our youth is renewed like the eagle's."

With those words, David was done. The small man, Polwarth, went up to him, and the woman named Ann-Marie, along with Lauren and a few others, and the old fellow who'd called himself General Lee.

I turned to look for Stone and Drake, but they were nowhere to be seen.

Chapter Twenty-Four
The Wings of a Dove

"I still can't get over it," said Isaiah Trueblood, "Ed, showing up all hangdog-like, cozying up to Pastor Gold."

He and Lauren and I were sitting in a small back room at the Church of the Heart Set Free a few days after our arrival in Las Vegas. When I first met Isaiah, he reminded me of certain young men in Nenana who walked the streets casting looks dark with menace, but in the next instant his face relaxed into a shy smile, and when he shook my hand his grip was as gentle as it was firm. His skin was a deeper brown than mine, and his cheekbones seemed as though they'd been carved from rich, warm wood by the sharp strokes of my mother's knife.

I could tell that he and Lauren were good friends; they were comfortable together in silence in a way that comes only from a special closeness.

"I didn't see him Monday morning," said Lauren, "so I guess Edward was waiting to see how things went."

Ed Grimm, I discovered, had shown a talent for evangelizing to the men who were beginning to assemble in Black Canyon.

"The General and I were talking to Pastor when he walked in," said Isaiah. "Lee said he was surprised Grimm had the guts to show his face after he and the others had run off like yellow-bellies. But Pastor Gold shook Ed's hand and told the General that what Jesus said about forgiveness seems easy enough until you actually have to d-d-do it."

Lauren laughed, but then her face darkened.

"None of the other elders has come back to the church. You don't think Edward's going to be made one, do you?"

"Not right away, at least," Isaiah replied. "Pastor said he wasn't ready to make any decisions 'bout that."

"I read we're to forgive someone even if he asks seven times in one day," I said, having been intrigued when I'd read Luke 17:4 the previous night. David had given me a Bible and told me to read the first four

154

books of the New Testament, and I hadn't been able to resist starting with the one that bore my English name. "But I suppose seven was just a 'for example.'"

"I remember Pastor James reading from Matthew that Jesus said seven times seventy times," said Isaiah.

"I haven't read that one yet," I admitted. "Four-hundred ninety times! So, He must have meant that we're to never stop forgiving, as long as they *repent* each time."

"Jesus can't have meant letting people hurt us over and over," said Lauren. "Even if they really mean it when they say they repent. But what's scary is, why else would you have to forgive someone so many times?"

"Well, if I forgive someone, that don't mean I have to let him take advantage of me," said Isaiah. "I just f-f-forgive him, is all."

"Seems like it depends on what Jesus meant by *forgive*," I said.

"I think it means I stop wishing my father would be torn to pieces by hungry wolves," said Lauren. "That my heart won't ache for revenge. But if he wants to see me again...I don't want it to mean I have to do that."

I conjured up an image of the Bible in my mind and flipped through the pages I'd read in Luke.

"Do you know the story Jesus tells about a man with two sons, where one of them gets his father to give him his inheritance even before he dies, then goes off and wastes it all?"

Isaiah nodded, and Lauren said, "Oh yes! The prodigal son."

"Well, I'm just thinking, didn't the son take advantage of his father—he must have hurt him terribly!—and yet, his father didn't just forgive him from a distance, he ran to meet him the moment his son turned for home. It seems to me like he welcomed him right back in and wiped the slate clean. So wouldn't that mean giving his son a chance to hurt him all over again?"

My friends considered this for a bit.

"But the father in that story, I thought he's supposed to be God," said Isaiah. "So he would know the prodigal really did repent."

"What would the point of the story be, though, if we weren't supposed to imitate the father?" I asked. "*We* can't look inside people's hearts like God."

"Well," Isaiah responded, "point could be the prodigal was blessed by the wounds that came from his sin, like Pastor Gold was saying—otherwise he'd 'a never turned for home."

"That's true, but, awful as it seems to me, Luke might be right, too," said Lauren. "It's like Jesus is telling us we can't play it safe. When He says to turn the other cheek, that's like forgiving, isn't it? And then we might get slapped again."

"I know I've got three more Gospels to read," I said, "and it looks like another thousand pages besides, but maybe we're not supposed to be worried about other people taking advantage of us. Maybe it only matters that we don't take advantage of *them*."

"That goes down hard, though," said Isaiah. "Still, you and Lauren got me thinking. This might sound like a fool thing to say, but do you think sinning is like slapping God in the face? Then, when I repent 'n ask God for forgiveness, it's as though He turns me the other cheek? So, if—okay, *when*—I go and sin again, it's like I'm striking Him again, ain't it."

Lauren and I somberly nodded our agreement.

"Seems like we take advantage of God over and over," said Isaiah. "Must break His heart."

"If we're supposed to forgive people pretty much forever, is that the way God forgives us?" I asked.

"Yes, 'cause Christ died so we'd be forgiven for all our sins—even the ones we haven't gotten around to yet, is how Pastor James put it," said Lauren. "But we're only forgiven if we believe in Him."

Something ominous began to cross my mind.

"Is it ever too late to believe? I mean, if the prodigal wasn't sure what to do, or was too scared to head for home, and kept thinking and thinking about it and trying to get up his nerve, would there have been a point at which his father would have given up watching for him and just turned away in disgust?"

"I always thought we've got to believe before we die," said Lauren.

"But that don't seem fair," said Isaiah, "seeing some folk live a lot longer than others. Seems like God would give everyone the same chance."

My mind was racing with dark thoughts. What if something happened to my father—or my mother!—before they had faith in Christ? "Suppose a person believes a little bit," I said, "how would he know if he believed enough? Or what if he believed most of the time but then got confused by doubts and died before he worked it all out?"

"See," said Isaiah, "that's why I think there got to be some chance for folk on the Other Side. Maybe all the way up to Judgment Day, even."

"I don't know," said Lauren. "Remember how Pastor James warned us we could get so comfortable with sin that our hearts would grow hard against the Lord?" She turned to me and put her hand on my shoulder. "Luke, here's what I tell myself when my mind starts spinning like maybe yours is right now: God is good, through and through, He's nothing but good. Just trust Him, that's all. Take a leap of faith, right into His arms."

I'd heard the phrase 'leap of faith' to describe the decision to believe in God, but this was something else, this trusting in His *goodness* when my mind demanded understanding and sought the answers to every question. I nodded, trying to still my thoughts and focus on the goodness of God.

"Are you going to get baptized?" Lauren asked me.

For a moment, the words didn't register; once again, I became aware of her touch only in its absence, felt the pressure of her fingertips only as she drew back her hand. She was looking at me, her eyes a pale liquid blue.

"Soon, I hope. Pastor Gold wants to make sure I understand what it means to be a disciple of Jesus Christ. He says he's only just figuring that out himself."

"You thinking wh-wh-what I'm thinking?" Isaiah asked, looking at Lauren. She looked down for a moment and then smiled at him.

"Of course," she said softly. "It would be so wonderful if Luke could be baptized in the desert like the rest of us. We just need Julia to let us know when."

"I miss her something terrible," said Isaiah, and, evidently overcome by emotion, he turned away.

"Who's Julia?" I asked, and instantly felt like I'd intruded on something intensely personal out of mere curiosity. "Unless that's none of my business, I mean."

"We're talking about Miss James, Luke," said Lauren. "Pastor James' daughter. Isaiah and I, we're her best friends."

"She been missing since the Pastor was killed," the big man added.

"Was she the one who planned the baptisms?" I asked.

"No," said Isaiah, "more like the Lord lets Miss James know what *He* has in mind. See, she knows when the rivers'll show up in the desert—when the flash floods'll come and fill some arroyo to the brim. Ain't no black magic, Luke, she says it's the Holy Spirit coming on her, feels like a river's running right through her, and then she knows the time and place."

"Pastor James would gather us together," said Lauren, "and Julia led the way. By the time we'd get there, the water would be flowing calmly, and the sky starting to clear. It filled me with wonder, the light breaking through the clouds and shining down on a river in that desert dry as bones. I got baptized like that, and Isaiah, too."

"Let's pray for her," said Isaiah.

We prayed, and afterwards I listened as the two talked of Julia James. Her mother had died in childbirth; she'd been raised by her father and had never set foot in a classroom until she was accepted to Stanford on a scholarship three years before, at the age of sixteen. Julia had learned to hop freight cars so she could come home more often, and had thrilled her friends with tales of hitchhiking from Palo Alto to Barstow before riding the rails to Las Vegas. She'd dropped out after her second year, when it became clear that the dam in Black Canyon would bring thousands of souls to the desert, despite her father's pleas for her to remain in school. But it was obvious to all that he and his daughter delighted in working together.

So perhaps she'd gone back to Stanford; but why would she have left without a word?

"God can't let this stand," said Isaiah. "Pastor James slain like he was, and Julia only He knows where."

"Have you heard if the police have any leads on the killer?" I asked.

"Stone and Drake, they're worthless, don't give a damn," he responded with disgust. "People smell money, more'n they ever dreamed of, 'n all they could see was Pastor James didn't want them to have it. General's right when he says could be m-m-most anyone in this town."

"True, but Pastor made it real personal," said Lauren. "I've wondered, the way he called on Farnsworth and Barlow, in front of everyone at church..."

"I loved those 'ol boys getting a heaping 'a humiliation," said Isaiah.

"Me too," said Lauren, "but I wonder if it was right."

"Jesus gave the Pharisees a tongue-lashing that made my hair stand on end," I pointed out, chapter eleven of Luke's Gospel playing vividly in my mind. "And then when one of them complained that Jesus was being insulting, He laid it on even thicker."

"But Luke," Lauren replied, "if it cost Pastor James his life, with all the good he was doing, was it worth it?"

"Cost Jesus His life, too," Isaiah observed.

"That was different," said Lauren. "His death brought life to the whole world."

"Yeah but God'll somehow bring good out 'a this like He does with every evil," Isaiah insisted. "Maybe through us, even. Maybe now He means for us to fight harder."

"You know I will," said Lauren.

"If there's fighting to be done, count me in," I said, and unsheathed my hunting knife so that they could see I wouldn't be coming unarmed.

"I don't think that's the kind of fighting we'll need to do," said Lauren, smiling.

"Are you sure?" I asked. "At the end, when Jesus was having the Passover meal with His disciples, he told them, if you don't already have a sword, buy one, even if you've got to sell the clothes off your back."

Lauren appeared dubious, but Isaiah came over and put his arm around me.

The Wings of a Dove

"I got to leave for work now, sister," he said to Lauren. It was evening, and Isaiah worked a graveyard shift, sweeping and cleaning up at several establishments in Block 16. "But I'll tell you this: I like our new friend, here, yes indeed! And it's a sweet thing to me that he's got himself a sword."

"You don't have to worry," I said to Lauren, who seemed preoccupied as we walked home. She lived not far from where David and my mother and I had rented rooms, close by the church. "I've used knives my whole life, hunting with my father."

"That's not it," she said, and then stopped suddenly and turned to me. "There's something I kept from Isaiah. She must have placed it in my mail slot overnight." Lauren pulled a folded piece of paper from her pocket and handed it to me. Written in a neat hand was this message:

Dearest L,

Oh that I had the wings of a dove!

J.

"So she's alive," I said, "and somewhere nearby. But wishing for the wings of a dove, what does that mean?"

"I don't know. Maybe it's nothing more than letting me know she's all right, she had a strange way of talking sometimes. But I didn't tell Isaiah, because I knew right away when I saw him that he hadn't heard from her. I thought it would break his heart if he found out Julia had only written to me, because he's—well, I'm pretty sure he loves her terribly much. And I meant to tell him despite that, but the longer I waited the harder it became to tell the truth."

"Lauren, if she's been hiding since her father's murder, what if Julia only had time to get this one note to you? Isaiah's worried sick about her, you've *got* to tell him."

"I know, I know. It was the wrong thing to do. I'll tell him, and the others as well."

We'd reached the building where she shared an apartment with several other young women, some of whom still worked in Block 16.

Lauren leaned forward, whispered "Goodnight," and kissed me on the forehead.

Before going to the rooms my mother and I shared, I stopped at David's door; the thought had come to me to ask him what Julia's strange phrase might mean, but I hesitated, not knowing how I'd handle any questions he might ask. I had just decided to turn away when the door opened, and David nearly ran into me as he came out.

"Luke, were you looking for me?"

"I finished reading Luke's Gospel and was wondering which one you thought I ought to read next," I said lamely.

"Hmm. Well, go ahead and read John and then loop back around to Matthew and Mark. Then on to the Book of Acts. Look for me tomorrow so we can talk about what you've read so far."

"I'll do that, Pastor Gold. And oh, one other thing," I said in as nonchalant a voice as I could muster. "If you heard a person wish for the wings of a dove, what would you think she meant? Or he meant. Whoever said it, that is."

David laughed.

"I'll tell you this: that's the language of the Psalms, which are poems, songs really, many of them written by my namesake, King David; we'll get around to his story soon enough. They're in the Old Testament— open your Bible a little less than half way and you'll find them between Job and Proverbs. When someone quotes from a Psalm, though, you need to read the whole thing to get the context and see what she—or he—or whoever—might mean. There's only a hundred fifty of them, so read a few each night and you'll likely find your quarry in the next month or two. Might just find yourself praying them, like I do."

With that, he walked off into the night.

~

As soon as I entered our apartment I could tell something was amiss; my mother was sitting at our small dining table and avoiding my eyes.

"Mother? Is anything wrong?"

After a moment, she looked at me.

"Where have you been all these hours?"

"With Lauren and a man named Isaiah Trueblood, talking. I'm seeing how everything Jesus said bears on our—"

"There was no man you were walking with just now, only the girl. How much of this new religion of yours is about believing in the Christian God, and how much is about her?"

I felt my face flush and anger race through my blood, but was at a loss for words, so I walked straight into my room and closed the door.

Chapter Twenty-Five
Mene, Mene, Tekel, Upharsin

"I used to pray with my father when I was a child," Joan said to Daniel after Willie had excused himself and headed off to an appointment at Babylon West. "I've only just begun to pray again, and it's awkward now; I'm so aware of myself, when it used to be natural, like play."

"The awareness inhibits your prayer," said Daniel, "so you're thinking of it as something bad. But what if you could learn from it?"

"Hmm. Mostly I seem to be learning, to my shame, how easily I doubt."

"That you doubt what? The existence of God?"

"No, not that. I question the point of prayer. The other day, when I told Willie we ought to be praying, he said he didn't think God would listen to his prayers, and I find myself wondering, why should He bother answering mine."

"God listens to and answers every one of His children's prayers. But I take it's His *granting* of your prayers you doubt."

"Well, right, and I suppose you're going to say that He only grants those prayers which are in accord with His will. But if something is His will, surely it will be done anyway, whether I pray or not."

"Indeed. And yet, we're told to bring *everything* to God, to devote ourselves to prayer, to pray continually, to always pray and not lose heart. Why do you suppose?"

"It's good for me, I'm told," said Joan. "And yet, He knows what's needed, while I reel in confusion, with prayers that seem only a babbling of confused and halting words."

"But what if what you need most of all is *Him?* Your childhood memories of prayer are sweet because you had your father by your side; but God is no distant ruler of the cosmos, ordering matters by remote control. He's your own Heavenly Father, who wants you babbling in His ear and trusting Him."

"Well—I *want* it to be that way." Joan looked down at the table. "The hardest thing is the silence that follows prayer. It's overwhelming at times, God's silence."

There had been a time when she sought quiet, the sanctuary of hushed places, but now that was something that filled Joan with dread. The deathly stillness of home after Jesse left was a void, a silent darkness at the center of her life. Sometimes she cried out; at least then she could hear her own voice. So she filled the silence with whatever was at hand: television in her bedroom, radio in her car, a lover at work.

"You're not alone," said Daniel. "It was the silence of God that led to King David's lament:

My God, my God, why have You forsaken me?
   Why are You so far from saving me,
   from the words of my groaning?
O my God, I cry by day, but You do not answer;
   and by night, but I have no rest.

"And Jesus faced that silence on the Cross when he echoed David's words; it was the cup His Father would not let pass. But here I am, talking as though I were leading a Bible study, and you're in pain."

Joan realized with a start that her eyes were burning with tears.

"My husband left me for another woman in the spring of last year, and I fell into an affair with a man—" *Listen to me, she thought, talking as though I'd slipped on an icy sidewalk, rather than made a conscious decision to sleep with Tim* "—and now it's the strangest thing, I feel like I'm cheating on Jess. My husband—my ex, I mean. He divorced me, after all."

"That's a legal matter," said Daniel. "The heart makes its own claims, obeys its own laws."

"Yes. He's still a part of me, and I don't want that to change. I don't think it *should* change." She surprised herself with these words; this was far from the conversation Joan had imagined she and Daniel might have. "I can't believe that I'm not still a part of him, that we're not connected, even now, by nerves and sinews and veins. But my friends say I'd be a fool, an enabler, if I ever took him back. Not that he's coming back, of course."

"Do you think they're right?"

"I'm not sure it matters if they're right." She paused and the pastor waited, letting Joan collect her thoughts.

"I knew him too well," she said at last. "Reflected him back to himself too clearly. What should have made us closer, instead drove us apart."

"That rings true," said Daniel. "There are men who fall in love with nothing so much as the way they imagine they look in their lover's eyes. Their Scheherazade has no need to spin a tale, only to pretend she still sees her lover as he wants to be seen. But to reject the truth and choose to chase after lies is to burrow one's way into hell."

"That's a terrifying thought," said Joan. "I'll pray for Jess and Willie, both. And for myself."

"And I for the three of you. You know, prayer is a wonderful antidote to self-deceit—at least, if we listen to our own babblings, and babble from the heart. For we reveal our dreams and desires and foolishness and fears, not only to God but to ourselves. Don't be concerned how your words come out; there's no one who knows just the right words. That's why Jesus sent the Helper, the Holy Spirit, whose wordless groanings deep inside of us are the prayers we know not how to pray. And if we nourish ourselves with God's word, then, in His silence, the Spirit makes known to us the mind of Christ."

"Which is all the answer to prayer I could hope for," said Joan. "It's been years and years since I've read the Bible, though, to tell you the truth. I found the Gideon in my hotel room last night, opened it, and just sat there, wondering where to start. And don't say, at the beginning, or I fear the journey will seem impossibly long."

"Uncle Luke once told me he started with what he called 'his own' Gospel," said Daniel, smiling, "and finds himself returning to it more than ever in his old age. Perhaps because so many of Jesus' parables are found only in Luke, not least of which is the Prodigal Son."

"I was quite taken with your uncle; when we met, I wanted him to bless me, isn't that odd? Well, I'll follow his lead. The Prodigal Son— the Bible is all about fathers and sons, isn't it. And mothers and sons, I guess. But mothers and daughters, what about them?"

"There aren't many stories of mothers and daughters in Scripture, that's true," said Daniel, "though the Canaanite woman in Matthew Fifteen comes to mind; she's one of my heroes. This mother's heart is rent by the suffering of her demon-possessed daughter, and such is her love that, though not a Jew, she dares to throw herself on the mercy of Jesus, knowing He's her only hope. The extraordinary thing is, it appears that He rejects her, that He won't help after all. But she won't take no for an answer; she debates with the Son of God! And for showing such faith, her daughter is healed."

"I wonder," Joan mused, "if a daughter ever asked for her *mother's* demons to be cast out. My mom was afflicted in her mind, though it was Willie who bore the brunt of her madness; I was raised by my grandparents from the age of twelve. When I was small, I used to follow my mom around, asking 'Do you love me?' Are there demons that hollow out a woman, empty her of all care and affection?"

The two talked for a while of Joan and Willie's youth, and of the spirits which haunt the mind and cast long shadows on the soul.

"Las Vegas is an awfully strange place to find one's hunger for God reawakened," said Joan, as Daniel explained he'd have to be going. "But there it is. I'm grateful for the time you've spent with me."

"Not so strange, really," he replied. "It's in the desert where one most desperately feels thirst. You know, what you felt compelled to ask your mother—it's the same question God asks us. Though, as John wrote, He loved us first; we can only give back to him a pale reflection of the love He gives us.

"I'm thinking of the twenty-first chapter of John's Gospel," Daniel continued. "The disciples are greeted by the risen Christ, and after they've eaten together, He asks Peter, 'Do you love me?' three times; one for each time Peter had denied Him, after having sworn he would lay down his life for the Lord. But Jesus' questions, giving Peter the chance to affirm his love, are words of forgiveness, of reconciliation. Of grace. It's a powerful scene, and it brings me peace; you might meditate on it when the memory of your young self, toddling after your mother, comes into your mind. For in our own answer back to God, in responding to His gift of grace, all our wounds can be healed."

Back in her hotel room, Joan turned eagerly to the last chapter in

John and read it several times, then put the Bible down, closed her eyes, and visualized the scene, imagined blocking it, deciding on the camera angles and lighting. The disciples, on the Sea of Galilee, bone tired, with only an empty net to show for their efforts. The dark sky growing lighter, the coolness of the early morning air, the sound of water lapping the side of their boat. A hundred yards off, a stranger on the shore calls out: *Friends, haven't you any fish?* Well, now that you mention it, we've none, thank you very much, not one. *Cast your net to the right, then, you'll find some there.* And ah, the miraculous catch, the net too heavy to haul in! The beloved disciple clapping Peter on the back, pointing, shouting, *It is the Lord!* Cephas, like an eager child, diving into the water and swimming the length of a football field to shore. The warmth of the fire Jesus has prepared feels especially pleasing in the predawn chill, and they're famished, they feast on the bread and fish He's set on the burning coals...

Her mind wandered. If my father and I had prayed for the casting out of my mother's demons, would our faith have been strong enough? But, then, wouldn't the Holy Spirit have been praying, wordlessly, silently, deep within?

The silence of Joan's hotel room suddenly oppressed her. Do you love me, Jesse? she'd asked her husband. She missed the way he filled the silence, the comforting sound of his breathing, the rustling of the bed sheets when he turned over. Or the sound of Jess typing on his laptop while she lay next to him, reading, sometimes putting down her book, comfortably drowsy, listening, half in a dream, wondering if he would wake her with kisses, make love to her, so she could fall back to sleep cradled in his arms...

But it was all a lie! She came out of her reverie with a start, her feeling of peace replaced by the hard, cold ache of remembered betrayal: those must have been emails to his lover he was typing, she thought, as I lay beside him.

All our wounds can be healed, Daniel had said.

She tried to bring her mind back to the shore by the Sea of Galilee. Where had she left off? Ah yes, the fire Jesus had prepared, she could taste the bread and fish, smell the burning coals...the burning...

She looked down; in her hand was a cigarette, already half-smoked. There'd been an open pack on her nightstand, and she'd taken one out, lit up, and puffed away, unaware. She hadn't even made it twenty-four hours! A stab of self-loathing went through her—like a spear!—and Joan stubbed the cigarette out, only to light up another, thinking, I can't do this, I can't. Can't even overcome my *own* demons. Poor Willie! What hope was there for him?

She had questioned Daniel about the miracles Jesus worked, whether they were all a matter of physical healing of things which the ancients, in their ignorance, ascribed to evil spirits and ghosts. Are you talking in metaphors, she'd asked, in the poetry of faith, or are such things for real? He'd grimly assured her that demons were a fact, were the deeper reality beneath the surface of things. And he'd quoted Paul: *For we wrestle not against flesh and blood, but against principalities, against powers, against the rulers of the darkness of this world.*

Well, then: how was she supposed to fight against *that*?

~

At first, when Tim stepped outside the lobby of Babylon West, he thought his eyes were playing tricks on him. Perhaps it was the fierceness of the summer sun beating down, even though it was late afternoon, perhaps the suddenness with which he'd risen from his nap; but there, the girl by the burgundy Rolls, who must surely be Vicki, she looked just as he'd imagined after hearing her voice: slender but large-breasted; her lustrous black hair, worn shoulder length; long-legged, but still a few inches shorter than him.

Their eyes met; she waved at Tim and smiled. The only thing that bothered him was her teeth, which seemed just a bit too large, and impossibly white. But it troubled him only for the briefest moment. She introduced herself, they shook hands, he entered the dark, cool comfort of the limousine, and they were off.

"What do you do, Mr. Faber, if you don't mind my asking." Her eyes, behind mirrored glasses, sought his in the rear-view mirror.

"I'm the executive producer for Science Cable TV," Tim replied.

"Channel 137 in these parts. Documentaries and interviews, mostly, pretty dry stuff."

"No! I watch your shows all the time! I graduated from UCLA with a bachelor's in archeology last year, that's how I met Mr. Osman. I'm in the research department at BW—I only drive for him to make a few extra bucks."

"Well, how great is that! We do quite a bit in your field—I'm quite pleased you enjoy what we do. In fact, just the other day we aired one you might have seen—"

"Yes, yes, on excavations going on in the Mideast! The narrator said something which struck me as so profound I committed it to memory: 'When we brush away the dirt and debris of fables, myths, and legend, we unveil the truth hidden in antiquity. And it's the truth that sets us free, indeed.'"

"You know, those are actually *my* words, I added them after reading the first draft of the narrative script."

"That's extraordinary, Mr. Faber. There's so much I'd like to ask you—but this is your vacation, I should restrain myself."

"Oh, no, there's nothing I'd enjoy more, ask away. And please, Vicki, call me Tim."

She plied him with questions about his work, and it was quickly decided that conversation would be easier if Tim moved to the front passenger seat. They drove past all the familiar sights, used a special pass to watch part of the rehearsal for one of Cirque de Soleil's more risqué shows, and were whisked in to a wine-tasting at a private art exhibition in a cordoned-off room at the Strip's newest and most elegant hotel.

Back at Babylon West the two lingered for a while, talking in the front seat of the burgundy Rolls.

"I wish I didn't have to be going," said Vicki. "But I do. I've got something for you, though—" She leaned over across his legs, unlocked the glove compartment, took out a small envelope, and slipped it into the breast pocket of his shirt. "In case you want to have a little fun tonight. It's a bonus card you can use in the Chaldean Club; that's for the high-rollers, all the way in back, overlooking the pool."

"Well, I'm not exactly a high roller," said Tim. "I mean, I could be, if I wanted to, it's just that I, uhm, choose to use my money in other ways."

"You're smart about that, of course. But this card turns every one of your dollars into ten, it's free money, really. Anyway, they'll kill me if I don't get the limo back on time. This has been so great—I can't believe I got to meet you, Tim Faber."

"Thanks, Vicki, I've enjoyed myself more than you know. And here—" he extracted a business card from his wallet, along with a hundred-dollar bill. "In case you're in New York, or if you ever want to explore a career in cable TV..."

"That's sweet of you, Tim, but Oz doesn't allow us to accept tips." She took his card but put the folded bill into his breast pocket next to the envelope. "You can turn this into a thousand at the Chaldean Club; bet it and think of me for good luck."

"All right, then," he said, laughing, and they wished each other good night.

In the high-rollers room, Tim asked if it would be possible to convert the hundred dollars into a thousand and then leave to gamble at the lower limits he preferred, but it turned out the magic of a ten-fold increase only applied right there. Very well, then; he felt a happy buzz from the wine he'd been sipping in the limo, and more so from the conversation with Vicki, who was, he thought, an amazing young gal.

He looked around. The minimum bet in the Chaldean Club was $100, and Tim decided he'd feel foolish showing up at the blackjack or craps tables, where other players seemed to have tens of thousands in chips piled in front of them. Just to his left was a slot machine with a large, garish digital display that showed a steadily increasing total:

BABYLONIAN MADNESS!!!
PROGRESSIVE JACKPOT: $9,327,416.29

He scanned the rules: to win the jackpot required an investment of three hundred dollars. Very well, then, he'd have three chances at a fortune, and worst case end up with his original $100 intact. Tim watched for a while as a wizened retiree pulled the handle time after time in vain, easily running through several thousand dollars in just a few minutes. He studied the four spinning wheels, which featured images of grotesque animals with human heads, a winged bull, a lion, a bearded figure he took to be Marduk, a sultry goddess who he guessed must be Ishtar, some words that looked vaguely familiar but meant nothing to him, and an eight-pointed star. Four Marduks had to line up to win the nine million; there were numerous lesser prizes, of course, but the poor old fellow who'd been trying his luck gave up without getting back a red cent. There must be about twenty images on each wheel, Tim estimated. So, let's see, the odds of winning would be one over twenty to the fourth power; assuming one Marduk per wheel, you'd hit the jackpot once every 160,000 pulls, after an investment of forty-eight million dollars. Hah, no wonder Oz was rolling in dough! But I'm free-rolling with the magnate's own money, he thought gleefully, with nothing to lose.

The sudden thought came to him: what if Joan or Daniel saw him there, playing a three-hundred-dollar-a-pull slot? He looked around surreptitiously, then chided himself for being so foolish. Who would they be to judge him for having a little fun on his time off?

The machine eagerly gobbled up his hundred-dollar bill, then showed he had one thousand dollars to play after he inserted the bonus card. Okay, then! Tim tugged on the handle; it was curiously resistant, hard to pull. But how could that be, when a feeble old geezer had just been working that one-armed bandit like there was no tomorrow? He looked around again. No one was watching him, so he grasped the handle with both arms and pulled with all his might.

The wheels spun. Lion, Star, Grotesque Creature, Ishtar. He waited a moment, but evidently that combination was worthless. He breathed in deeply, grasped the recalcitrant handle and exhaled as he gave a powerful pull. Grotesque Creature, Marduk, Lion, and the word Tekel, whatever that meant. Worthless once again!

All right, one last chance remained. Tim braced himself for the strain of pulling the handle, but this time it gave him no resistance at all, and his excessive effort sent him tumbling to the floor. An elderly woman with a four-pronged cane in each hand came over and asked him if he needed help.

Mene, Mene, Tekel, Upharsin

"No, no, I'm fine," he said irritably. "Just tripped. New shoes."

As he slowly rose to his feet, he could hear the wheels spinning and the little click as each one came to a stop.

Mene

Mene

Tekel

Upharsin

Bells began sounding and lights started to flash.

"You've won the small progressive, you bastard," the old woman said peevishly. "Won't hardly be worth playing again for the rest of the week!"

Tim looked at the payout table on the slot machine: Mene Mene Tekel Upharsin was indeed the so-called small progressive. He gazed up at the electronic display:

Small Progressive: $149,264.18

As executive producer of a minor cable channel, he was decently paid, but my God, Tim thought, this is a small fortune. A crowd was gathering around. To a high roller, he wondered, would a hundred-forty-nine thou be a meaningful amount? He decided the best thing would be to play it cool.

"Ah well, I'd been hoping for the four Marduks, but this'll have to do."

A casino host came over, shook Tim's hand, and asked him if $144,000 in casino credit plus five thousand or so in cash would be acceptable. It was.

"We have a tradition," said the host, "of jackpot winners buying drinks in the Inner Sanctum." He pointed to two mirrored doors at the far end of the Chaldean Club. "Of course, it's entirely up to you."

"Far be it from me to disrupt tradition," said Tim graciously, as the host counted out stacks of hundred dollar bills. He handed the fellow two bills, but the slightest hint of a frown remained on the man's face until Tim had parted with five hundred.

The Inner Sanctum was dimly lit and furnished in high style, the ceiling and walls all shifting shades of blue, the bar a long, curved sweep of burnished steel. This is a Wall Street and Hollywood crowd, Tim decided; it was packed with men in Zegna sports coats, smoking large, expensive cigars, while the women he took for eye candy, all tanned, bare shouldered, gorgeous young flesh.

"Mene, Mene, Tekel, Upharsin!" someone shouted, and the bar burst into applause. I'm already a star here, he thought, for something as trivial as a lucky pull on a handle. Likely think I'm a mere money-grubber; they've no idea how accomplished I am! But he could hold his own with this sort, of that he was sure.

"Drinks are on Tim Faber!" he called out gallantly, and a blizzard of orders ensued, glasses and goblets were proffered on silver trays, and it was all rare bottles of MacAllen Old Sherry, Glenfiddich whiskey, Belvedere vodka, and Dom Perignon champagne. Men clapped him on the shoulder; women glanced at him and looked away and then looked back again. He was getting tipsy; when one femme fatale, who, Tim thought, looked a bit like Charlize Theron on a very good day, held that second glance for an extra two seconds, he broke off his conversation with a group of investment bankers who'd been pitching a Science Cable TV IPO, and went over to introduce himself.

~

Back in his hotel room, Tim ignored the blinking red light on his bedside phone, divested his pockets of wads of hundred-dollar bills, gathered them into a great pile on his bed and dove into it as though he were a boy playing with fallen autumn leaves. He lay on his back for a while, his head spinning and heart pounding. There'd been too many shots of Grey Goose amid much flirting; then a retreat to an even more dimly lit back room, where he'd done lines of cocaine with three young ladies who looked barely out of their high-school years. Too much craziness! Tim found the bar bill in his breast pocket; squinting at it, the blurry number gradually resolved into a figure that was more than his monthly salary. Well, it was all Oz's money, anyway, if you can't have a blow-out night now and then, what's the point? Still, he felt frustrated and annoyed; none of the flirtations had been consummated, and he was troubled by a deepening emptiness, a lack of—well, *realness* in himself. The jackpot had briefly been a thrill, but money wasn't his thing, and the people with whom he'd been partying at the Inner Sanctum weren't interested in *him*, in who he was.

Tim's unhappy reverie was interrupted by the ringing of his cell phone. It was a call from the Las Vegas area code; had he given his number to anyone that evening?

"Yes?" he said.

"Tim? It's Vicki. I know it's late, I hope it's okay I'm calling you. I left a message in your room."

"Yes, of course it's okay."

"I'm not even sure what to say—I could get in trouble for this, because I'm not supposed to fraternize with the guests. Maybe this was a dumb idea."

"No, relax. You can trust me." He sat up, feeling a jolt of energy at hearing Vicki's voice, and leaned back against the headboard.

"Can I? I hope so. I'd really like to see you again. I don't know, maybe you think this is really tacky or desperate or something, me calling you like this."

"Don't be silly, I'm delighted." The edginess in her voice excited him. "Do you want to get together right now?"

"No, I can't, not now. Look, maybe this was a bad idea."

"Tomorrow evening then." She's a super smart young woman, Tim thought, but something is troubling her; given the interests they shared, how natural that she would be attracted to his maturity and calm wisdom. "I want to see you again, too."

"That's really good to hear," she said, her voice barely more than a whisper. "Okay. I'll pick you up in front of BW, then, same time, same place, only I'll be driving my Porsche."

"Okay," said Tim. "And Vicki, you won't believe what happened this—"

But she had already hung up the phone.

He got out of bed. Sleep was going to be hard now! Perhaps he'd do a little more gambling, then hit the sack at dawn, sleep through the day, and wake up fresh for whatever tomorrow evening might bring. Tim went into the bathroom, turned on the shower, stripped off his clothes, and regarded himself in the mirror. He was really in pretty good shape, and that bald spot was hardly noticeable at all!

Before heading back out to the casino, he stopped by the bedside table, opened the drawer, and took out the Bible. I can turn to any page, any line, he thought, and use it to demonstrate the idiocy of religious dogma! He juggled the Bible between his hands for a moment, then opened it, closed his eyes, and put his index finger down on the page. It had opened to the Psalms, and he'd singled out the eighth verse of Psalm 139:

If I ascend up into heaven, thou art there; if I make my bed in hell, behold, thou art there.

Well, of course, Tim thought scornfully. A figment of one's imagination can be found anywhere at all!

Chapter Twenty-Six
Bountiful Harvest

It didn't take long after the success of David Gold's Monday morning sermon for things to start going wrong.

"I deeply regret to inform you," said General Lee the next day, "that the constabulary seized your vehicle by brute 'n overwhelmin' force 'a arms. Don't know what to say, Pastor, I'd fall on mah sword, if I had one."

The General's expression was sorrowful, but his head was unbowed and his voice forthright.

"Was anyone hurt?" asked David.

"We incurred a few glancing blows from Detective Drake's cudgel, resultin' in a few abrasions, a contusion or two, and much injured pride."

"Praise God that's all," said David. "Don't let this trouble you, General. It's only an automobile, one I was probably foolish to bring to what is, after all, a war zone of sorts."

"Thank you mightily, sir. There anythin' else I can do for you?"

"Nothing right now," David replied, and the General slowly made his way to the door. "Well, there is one thing, come to think of it. I'd like to know your name."

The old man paused but didn't turn around.

"Why, it's General Robert E. Lee, just like I tol' you the other day."

"All right," said David. "I'll remember that."

It may have been "only an automobile," but David worried nonetheless, for it seemed his best hope for paying off the church's debt, helping the poorest members of his congregation, and supporting himself. The Talbot had supposedly been seized as collateral for the loan, so he asked repeatedly for an appointment with the president of the bank which held the mortgage, but it seemed that Mr. Farnsworth was an exceedingly busy man.

More irksome than the impounding of the Talbot, however, was the melting away of the congregation which had filled the church to overflowing for David's inaugural sermon. As he looked out from the pulpit, David saw the Church of the Heart Set Free grow emptier with each passing week! All the wasted years and the half-hearted sermons delivered to promote his fights—had they ruined whatever talent he once had? What had made him think that he could ever be a compelling mouthpiece for God?

Justin James had decried the money lust that had descended on Las Vegas like a virulent plague, and fought with all his strength against the legalization of gambling that would be put to a vote early the next year. David felt a keen desire to follow boldly in his footsteps, no matter the risk, and buttonholed everyone he could find to lobby against the proposed new law.

"I think you're making a mistake," said Edward Grimm to him one day.

"Why is that, Mr. Grimm?"

He tried to mask his dislike for the man, whose dour countenance and monotonous voice grated on his nerves. How Grimm could possibly be an effective evangelist was more than David could imagine.

"It's a lost cause. And I don't see our proper role as dabbling in politics at all. It only takes time away from the real work that needs to be done."

"I see. So what would you propose?"

"I'd put all our efforts into the dam, Pastor Gold. That is where they'll be the most souls to save. Management has set up a perimeter and shut off access to anyone but authorized workers; I'd lobby them for access, if I were you. And the makings of a tent city are going up on the outskirts of the dam site, people arriving with not much more than the shirts on their backs."

"We should reach out to them, of course, Mr. Grimm, I'll join you there as soon as I can. And thank you for your advice." It was hard to know which way to turn sometimes; there was need everywhere David looked. The dam was important, of course, but work had barely begun, and few people had yet been hired. Why was the man so eager for him to abandon the work that Justin James had pursued with such passion?

There was at least one way in which Grimm was right, David realized; the real battle was for the hearts of men, regardless of the laws of the land. He pored over Scripture in his room late at night, looking for inspiration. Yes, much good could come from Boulder Dam, but nothing that could compare to the power of God to transform lives! He copied out verses from the prophet Isaiah and thought about how to weave them into his sermons.

"You can profit from the men who come to toil in Black Canyon," David spoke from the pulpit; "the dam can provide electric light to far-away cities, can allow crops to grow in arid lands; but it can't quench the thirst deep within you, it can't provide the living water, the bread of life.

"Listen to the words of the Lord:

"*I will turn the desert into pools of water, and the parched ground into springs.*

"*For waters break forth in the wilderness, and streams in the desert.*

"*The wilderness and the dry land shall be glad; the desert will rejoice and blossom.*

"The wilderness and the dry land—they are our own souls."

The following Sunday there were only half as many who came to take communion and listen to David preach.

~⁀⁀⁀

"You came to the wrong place, Gold."

David found himself flat on his back, looking up into the face of Sheriff Stone.

"It's the Blue Room for him," said Deputy Drake, and the next thing the pastor knew, the two lawmen were in the Talbot, heading directly for him at a terrible speed. David scrambled to his feet and took off, running desperately for cover. Only there was no cover, just the empty desert and the bleached bones of some long-dead beast.

But what was this directly ahead—a vast lake, perhaps even an inland sea! With a last burst of energy, he reached it and dove in, hearing the screeching of brakes as the Talbott stopped at the water's edge just moments before it would have smashed the life from his body.

"Pastor Gold! Over here!"

It was Lauren, with Anne, Isaiah, the General, and Mr. Polwarth, in a small boat perhaps twenty yards away. He swam toward them and they hauled him in before setting sail for the far shore. Exhausted, he closed his eyes and fell asleep.

"Pastor Gold! Help! Do something!"

David awoke to find that the once calm waters were seething, roiled by a fierce, howling wind. The small craft ascended the sheer wall of a twenty-foot wave, then careened down the other side.

"Save us! Pastor Gold!"

But I don't know how to sail, thought David. This isn't my boat! Why are they looking to me? He felt a rising sense of panic, clinging to the gunwale and fighting to keep himself from joining the others in their terrified screams.

And then another voice was heard.

Why are ye fearful, O ye of little faith!

David awoke in his room, soaking wet as though from the spray of a storm-tossed sea, the last words still echoing in his ears. It's only sweat, he thought, and sat up, put his feet on the floor and breathed deeply. Only a dream.

He began to stand up, but dropped back to the bed when he saw the man across the room, staring steadily at him, arms folded across his chest, hands taped as though for a fight. There was no mistaking who he was: the boxer with hands of iron, the angelic opponent of his dream in Reno.

The man smiled his strangely gentle, knowing smile, and began to sing in a rich tenor voice.

"Paul and Silas, bound in jail, got no money for their bail.

"Keep your eyes on the prize, Hold on.

"It's a fine song, don't you think, David Gold?"

And then he was gone.

⟿

"I've completed my research and can report with considerable confidence on the cause of our vacant pews," said Mr. Polwarth when he met with David later that day. "It's a new house of worship, a church called Bountiful Harvest. The gist of the sermon I heard there on Sunday is that God rewards our faith with health and wealth, and the more faith we can muster, the more such blessings He'll shower upon us. Their pastor let loose of a blizzard of verses to make these points, faster than I could take notes."

"2 Corinthians 8:9, I would guess?" asked David. *"For you know the grace of our Lord Jesus Christ, that though he was rich, yet for your sakes became poor, so that you by His poverty might become rich."*

"Yes, that was one of the first! And Malachi 3:10, which suggests that tithing might be a most profitable investment indeed."

"Philippians 4:19 as well, I'd wager: *My God will supply every need of yours, according to His riches in glory in Christ Jesus.*"

"That, too, and many more like it."

"No doubt," said David, and he paused to refill their glasses with water. "So, what do you think of their gospel, Mr. Polwarth?"

The little man in the tattered suit took a long drink before he answered.

"You know, I was a stockbroker once, a man who rode the Long Island Railroad early each morning to Grand Central Station and took a taxi to my job on Broad Street, then travelled back to Great Neck late each night. I still ride that train in my dreams. Three years ago, in the fall of '27, I stole money from my clients and gambled it away. I lost my job, my wife, my children, and my erstwhile friends. So, as to this new church: I've already spent too much of my life serving the wrong master to be so easily led astray. There's many in this town who'd like to believe Bountiful Harvest's Good News; I'm not one of them, Pastor Gold."

"I grew up not far from Broad Street, myself," said David. "Here's to you and me, Mr. Polwarth—" the two men clinked glasses—"who once were lost, and now are found. What you told me about Bountiful Harvest—I should have guessed as much. We won a small skirmish the other day, and now the enemy's regrouped. We're in for a fight."

"Do you mind if I ask a few questions?" asked Mr. Polwarth.

"No, of course not, ask away."

"About the mortgage—is there any way we can avoid foreclosure? The others are rather fond of the church, humble as it may be. And, well, so am I."

"Only if I can get my hands on the Talbot and sell it for a fair price."

"What do you think the chances of that are?"

"I'm afraid I haven't a clue."

"Ah, well, we can always worship under the stars," said Mr. Polwarth. "So, then, how are things going with bringing the Gospel to the workers at the dam?"

"Mr. Grimm tells me the site is now off limits to anyone who doesn't have a work pass," replied David. "So, for the moment, we're shut out."

"I don't suppose you've heard anything about the investigation of Pastor James' murder—assuming there *is* an investigation, which I doubt."

"I'm afraid I share your misgivings. There's been not a word."

"The legalization of gambling—it's inevitable, I assume?"

"Short of divine intervention, it would appear so."

"Hmmm, things do look just a bit bleak," said Mr. Polwarth. "What do you think we ought to do?"

"Trust in the Lord with all our hearts," said David Gold. "For He is the Everlasting God, Creator of the ends of the Earth. He will not grow tired or weary! And we who hope in the Lord will renew our strength, Mr. Polwarth. We will soar on eagles' wings."

"Well," said the man who once fancied himself the Baron of Broad Street, "as plans go, I've heard none better. Count me in!"

Chapter Twenty-Seven
Secrets and Lies

Early the morning after David told me that "wings of a dove" was the sort of language found in the Psalms, Lauren and I took our Bibles, some bread rolls, and a thermos of coffee to the park by the railroad depot on Fremont Street. David had suggested reading a few each day, but we resolved to keep reading until we found the words Julia had written.

"Pastor Gold told me that these are songs," I said after we'd finished reading the first Psalm. "Do you have any idea what they sounded like?"

"I suppose like the hymns we sing at church," Lauren replied, and tried to sing the first verse to the melody of *Blessed Assurance*, but quickly broke off. "I wish we knew the tune!"

Reading the end of the Psalm, my spirit was dampened by the thought that my father might be numbered among the wicked and fated to be like the "chaff that the wind blows away." But I pushed the thought from my mind, and we forged ahead.

The third Psalm made me gasp.

"Look, Lauren! It says this one was written when King David was 'fleeing from his son!' That reminds me so much of my father. Do you think he left home for a woman, like mine did?"

Lauren had heard the story of David and Bathsheba, but wasn't sure if that had anything to do with Absalom, and said she didn't know.

When we reached the end of the Psalm, I was stunned again when the Psalmist implored God to "strike all my enemies on the jaw; break the teeth of the wicked."

"No wonder he loves these songs! It makes God sound like a heavyweight champ! Do you think Pastor Gold was named after the King?"

"Likely so," said Lauren.

"Seems like King David was in terrible trouble," I observed after we'd read the next several Psalms without finding Julia's mysterious words. "'Hear my cry for help...save me...deliver me from all who pursue me, or they will tear me apart like a lion and rip me to pieces!' It's the same thing just about every song!"

"Well, I only know a few stories about him," Lauren said. "I know that even though he wasn't a big man like Pastor Gold, he could take care of himself pretty well. I think when he was younger than me—your age, maybe—he killed a lion and a bear and a man named Goliath who had everyone else scared to death. Killed them all on his own." Lauren went on to tell me the story of David slaying the giant Philistine.

"I went bear hunting, once, back home, with my father and his friends," I said. "You can hardly imagine how large they are, standing on their hind legs. We had rifles, big ones, but I wish I'd known about slings!" I began to think through how I might go about building a sling like the one David might have used.

"Hey!" Lauren roused me from my daydream with a well-aimed punch to the shoulder. "There's a hundred forty three Psalms to go!"

We read on, until the beginning of the ninth Psalm caused my heart to skip a beat.

"Lauren, this one says it's to be sung to the tune of 'Death of the Son.' I've never heard that song, do you know how it goes?"

She chewed on her lip and thought for a bit before shaking her head.

"I don't know it, either. But the title gives me goosebumps, Luke. Jesus was the Son of God, and he died to save us, right? And he was King David's great-great-great-great grandson or nephew or cousin. So, I wonder if somehow this was a song about the Cross—even though it's in the Old Testament, which came way before the New. Before Jesus was even born."

It took a moment before Lauren's words sank in, but we agreed this was an eerie mystery, or maybe a prophecy, or both, and worthy of bringing to Pastor Gold.

On and on we read as the sun arced high into the October sky. We washed out the thermos and filled it with cold water, rationed out some of the bread and munched it, our backs against the trunk of one of the canyon oaks that lined Fremont.

"It's a rollercoaster ride with King David," I observed. "One minute,

God is his rock and fortress, and the next moment He's nowhere to be found."

"Life's like that, if you haven't noticed," said Lauren, and I sagely agreed.

The twenty-second Psalm stopped us once again, dead in our tracks. Neither of us had heard the tune it was meant to be sung to, *The Doe of the Morning*. But when I read the very first words of the first verse, Lauren punched me in the shoulder again, this time yet harder.

"Hey!" I cried out, startled.

"Luke! *My God, my God, why have you forsaken me?* Don't you recognize those words?"

I didn't, having only read the third Gospel.

"Those are the words of our Lord as he hung on the Cross! This is amazing! I mean, of course, I guess he knew King David's song. But still..."

We took turns reading, sobered by the Psalm's dark tone, and Lauren pointed out to me that the sixteenth and eighteenth verses seemed to describe what befell Jesus on that terrible Friday long ago. But in the next lines we saw the mood begin to change; it seemed to us like the dawn breaking after a long, dark night, and we couldn't help smiling with relief as King David sang that God has listened to his cry for help. We raised our voices as he proclaimed *all the ends of the earth shall remember and turn to the Lord,* and we shouted out the closing words, *it shall be told of the Lord to the coming generation; they shall come and proclaim His righteousness to a people yet unborn, that He has done it!*

"That's us he's talking about, Luke! Only we're born now, thanks be to Him!"

We read Psalm after Psalm, closed our eyes and snoozed, eyed the few crumbs remaining of our bread rolls and decided to hold off eating them until we at least reached the halfway point.

And then we reached Psalm Fifty-Five.

It began like so many others, with David assailed by enemies and calling for help from God. But the words became desperately grim:

My heart is in anguish within me;
the terrors of death have fallen upon me.

Fear and trembling come upon me;
    and horror overwhelms me.

With the next verse, we found what we were looking for, and our voices dropped to a whisper as we read these words:

And I say, "Oh, that I had the wings of a dove!
    I would fly away and be at rest;
Yes, I would wander far away;
    I would lodge in the wilderness;
I would hurry to find a shelter
    from the raging wind and tempest."

"David—Pastor Gold, I mean—was right! Did Julia have a place of shelter in the desert, Lauren?"

"She knew the desert better than any of us," my friend replied. "But I've no idea where her place of shelter might be. Luke, this is awful—I can't help but think of her, overwhelmed by the horror of her father's murder and in terror for her own life. I love her and I'm so angry at her! Why won't she let us help her?"

"I don't know. Pastor Gold said that we have to read the entire Psalm to understand what King David meant. We better continue, maybe there'll be a clue."

A few moments later, Lauren read these lines aloud:

Destructive forces are at work in the city;
    threats and lies never leave its streets.
For it is not an enemy who taunts me—
    then I could bear it;
it is not an adversary who deals insolently with me—
    then I could hide from him.
But it is you, a man my equal,
    my companion, my familiar friend.
We used to take sweet counsel together;
    Within God's house we walked in the throng.

Her voice trailed off.

"Are you thinking what I'm thinking?" I asked her.

"Yes, and it's more terrible yet. She's telling us that her father was betrayed, isn't she! Do you think—is that why she didn't leave a note for

Isaiah? But that can't be!"

I wasn't sure what to think, but I agreed that Isaiah couldn't possibly be complicit in the murder of Justin James.

"Polwarth," said Lauren, after thinking for a while. "He was supposed to have been a rich man, once. Could he have betrayed Pastor James for money? He even tried to discourage us from approaching Pastor Gold when Isaiah first brought up the idea."

"Really?" I exclaimed. "That *is* awfully strange. But still, I wouldn't have thought...Mr. Polwarth doesn't seem..."

Where once the Psalms had thrilled us, made our blood race and our imaginations soar, now we sat, dispirited and silent, pondering the mystery of Psalm Fifty-Five.

"Don't you think we ought to tell Pastor Gold about Julia's message and what we've discovered in the Psalm?" I asked Lauren.

"I couldn't do that without her permission, Luke. But you were right about my sharing it with Isaiah, the three of us were the best of friends."

"Why did you share it with *me?*" I asked, but Lauren only blushed and stammered and looked away. "That's all right," I said, and punched her lightly on the shoulder. "I'm glad you did. But wasn't she close to any of the others, too?"

"Yes, to the General and Mr. Polwarth and Anne, Julia called us the six musketeers. I think that's French for inseparable pals. Though we argued enough, most days."

"Well," I said excitedly, "I think I have a fairly brilliant idea! It's only right to share the message with Julia's circle of friends. And, when we tell them the secret of Psalm Fifty-Five, if one of them is the traitor, there will surely be something in their expression that will give them away, even if it's just the slightest twitch of an eye. I learned about this from the Angakkuq in my village—he's a sort of pastor himself, and wonderfully wise."

Lauren considered this for a moment, then agreed that it was a splendid plan which we should put into action right away.

But we could not have imagined the consequences my suggestion would bring.

It seemed that the Angakkuq's skill was considerably greater than ours, for each of our friends' faces were animated by surprise and dismay when they heard what we had to say. Perhaps they were all miserable traitors, or none of them; no one stood out from the rest, nor, as I had secretly hoped, broke down and confessed when confronted with King David's anguished Psalm. But whispered conversations soon followed. Mr. Polwarth muttered that he had always wondered about Anne-Marie, for it was she who had discovered the body of Pastor James. She'd made the early morning appointment with him; tempted by cases of gin, her conscience weakened by liquor, might she have set it up at the killer's request?

Lauren, in turn, had her doubts about Mr. Polwarth, while Isaiah was fingered by Anne-Marie. After all, the half-breed had been in love with the pastor's daughter; if her father had found out and forbidden the match—well, for all his timidity, Trueblood was a powerful man, and his aggression had been bottled up for years.

Isaiah thought it was perfectly clear that the traitor was Edward Grimm. Only the General abstained from speculating, while of course Grimm had been left in the dark, not having been one of the musketeers, and went his own way, evangelizing to anyone he could find in the proximity of the dam.

The next day, Lauren and I met again in the park to continue reading the Psalms and to see if we could use them for prayer the way David did. Please, God, we prayed, keep Julia safe, deliver justice to the killer and to whomever might have betrayed Pastor James! We lay on a frayed blanket, a single Bible open between us, and when our shoulders brushed together neither of us moved them apart.

But there would only be a few hours of bliss.

"Oh, I've got something to show you," Lauren said to me as we took a break to stretch our legs. "It's the only picture I have of Julia."

She handed me a grainy black and white snapshot, and I gazed at it, enthralled. Julia was tall for a girl, perhaps my height, slender, with dark hair framing a handsome, pale white face. But it was her eyes that captivated me; she wasn't looking at the camera, but gazing at something in the middle distance, and in her gaze was such an intensity and passion that I longed to know what she was looking at, what she was thinking. I wanted her expression, so serious and solemn, to soften into a smile.

I wanted her to look at me.

"Hey!" This time Lauren's punch seemed harder than usual. "I didn't give it to you to *keep.*"

I blushed and returned the picture. We returned to reading, but our shoulders no longer touched, and we quit for the day after the seventy-eighth Psalm. After that, I often daydreamed about the girl in the photograph. Julia running alongside freight trains, grabbing a handhold and pulling herself on board. Then it was the two of us running together, swift as the wind. Once, half asleep in the early morning hours, I imagined us meeting a hobo in a freight car, a man dressed in rags. It would turn out to be my father, and I'd forgive him, and we'd trim his long hair and shave off his wild beard, and tell him of the God who is love and whose son is Jesus, the Christ, and he would cry and hug me close. Julia would lead us to water, and we'd be baptized together by David Gold.

How I wanted to be with her when sudden rivers rushed through the desert and drenched the parched earth!

~

I spent time with David almost every day, learning more and more about the Bible and what it means to make Jesus the center of my life. I peppered him with questions, and often he told me that it would be pointless for him to answer until I had spent time obeying the Lord.

"A good understanding have all those who do His commandments," David

quoted from the Psalms. "You've read John's Gospel; read me the thirty-first and thirty-second verses of the eighth chapter, which are the Lord's own words, and then write them on your heart."

"*If you abide in my word,*" I read, "*you are truly my disciples, and you will know the truth, and the truth will set you free.* Free from what exactly, Pastor Gold?"

He laughed. "There you go, asking before obeying. To abide in the word of Jesus means many things, but not least is to *do* the things he says. Obey, and then tell me the answer yourself. What have you done this day because Jesus asked you to do it? Put aside your worries about tomorrow? Tried to love an enemy? Prayed the Lord's prayer?"

I was stymied for the moment and turned red.

"I'm not much of a disciple," I confessed. "Not yet, anyway. But it's not yet nine in the morning, so I've still some time to redeem myself, I hope. And oh—when Jesus speaks of *the truth*, it reminds me of a question I've been meaning to ask you. If a person has a secret, and doesn't reveal something to someone—that's different than lying to the person, wouldn't you say?"

The tensions between the musketeers had been growing ever since Lauren and I had shown them how Julia's note led us to the dark passage of betrayal in Psalm Fifty-Five, and it seemed to me something David should know about. But it wasn't my decision, was it? Didn't the right to share the message belong only to Julia and Lauren?

David looked me in the eye.

"It depends on the circumstances, Luke. But in asking that question, and knowing the circumstances, don't you already know the answer?"

I looked down.

"It's a just-suppose sort of thing," I said, ashamed of myself but unable to do what I knew was right.

"I want you to remember some other words of Jesus, words you've read before: *there is nothing hidden that will not be revealed.*"

"I'll remember," I said, and felt more miserable yet.

When I returned home, my mother asked me if I'd been with Mr. Gold yet again.

"Pastor Gold. Yes, of course."

"He's not your father, you know. It is wrong for you to be so close to him."

For a moment, I saw red.

"That's right, he's not my father—he spends time with me, he teaches me, he cares about me; he's not like my father at all!"

A terrible look of anger came over my mother, and she rose from her chair and slapped me hard across the face. She'd never struck me before, never in my life. I turned and ran, not wanting her to see the tears that were in my eyes.

~

Weeks passed and the days grew cooler. Fewer people were attending the Church of the Heart Set Free, and Mr. Polwarth told me about the false gospel that was luring so many to Bountiful Harvest. I had never cared for money, other than to keep our stomachs full and to have a place to sleep, and I wondered whether these people were worshipping the demon god who had lured my father from his home. After all, it seemed his lust for riches had been far stronger than his desire for either my mother or Kathleen Byrne.

I was walking on the outskirts of town one afternoon, thinking of how I might learn more about the desert surrounding Las Vegas and mount a search for Julia James, when I noticed Anne-Marie. She appeared to be wandering aimlessly, sometimes singing off-key, head bowed, a small flask in one hand.

"*It's time for ev'ry boy to be a soldier,*

"*To put his strength and courage to the test.*

"*It's time to place a musket on his shoulder,*

"*And wrap the Stars and Stripes around his breast.*"

"Can I walk with you, Anne-Marie?" I asked her, after I'd already been accompanying her for fifty yards without her seeming to notice.

She stopped and looked at me.

"I was a YMCA girl, did you know that?"

I thought for a moment; my brain stored everything I heard or saw, it was just a question of calling it back up.

"Yes, when we first arrived, you said that during Pastor Gold's sermon, but I don't know what it means. You mentioned doughboys crying on your shoulder, so I know it must have something to do with the Great War."

"It must," she murmured. "It must indeed. Tell me, Luke, tell me, boy with the strange last name, why do you want to walk with me, with sodden old Anne-Marie?"

"Because you seem sad and lonely," I said. "And if I felt that way, I'd want a friend."

She looked away and began walking.

"Sad, sad, sad, and lonely. Once I might have thought you a rude young man. But come along, come along for the ride. I trained cigarette dogs, did you know that? No, how could you. The four-legged heroes of the War to End All Wars.

"*Quarters kids us it's the rations,*
"*And the dinners as we gets,*
"*But I know what keeps us smiling,*
"*It's the Woodbine cigarettes.*

"Woodbine Willie, now there was a pastor for you. Who wouldn't believe in Jesus for a decent smoke!"

Anne-Marie fell silent, and we walked together for another hundred yards before she talked again.

"All those beautiful, doomed young men." She looked at me again. "Your age, I'd guess. Just as handsome as you, some more, some less. I lay with so many of them. That's the way the Bible puts it, anyway. Am I making you blush?"

"No, I know what you mean. I'm not a child."

"Indeed, I'd say not." Anne-Marie laughed. "So, you know of love. Have you seen death?"

"More than once," I replied. "But not so much as you have, I'm sure."

She was quiet again for a while.

"Do you look down on me for this?" She held up the hip flask. "On a toot with barrel-house hooch! A little drink-ee just to quiet the demons in my mind. You think me a disgrace before the living God, don't you. You're not a child? Have the guts to speak the truth."

"I only know that the men in my village who took up the bottle *all* became lonely and sad," I replied. "But it's what I've heard about my father that troubles me most. He left us nearly six years ago, and we've heard he's taken to drink. Now I can't help but worry that he's lost, Anne-Marie, I mean, that he's too far from God, that he'll be like the chaff the wind blows away."

"I'd heard your father was a louse, but I don't know the story. No offense meant; men are louses, that's all. You might be the lone exception. You and the odd pastor here and there."

I told her my story as we walked side by side. She was silent for a while, then stopped, gripped my shoulder with her free hand, and looked me in the eye.

"Let's pray for your father, Luke!" Her breath was powerfully strong with alcohol, but I didn't move away. "Let's get down on our knees right here and pray."

We got on our knees.

"But maybe God doesn't want to hear a drunken woman's prayers," she said, her voice desperately weary. "Perhaps they're an insult to heaven."

"The Son of God gave up his throne to save us from our sins, that's what I've learned. So then, wouldn't he yearn to hear a sinner's prayers? At least, that's what I hope, anyway, or he'll turn a deaf ear to my prayers as well as yours."

"First, tell me something, Luke," said Anne-Marie. "Tell me if you think I had something to do with the death of Pastor James."

A stab of pain pierced my heart.

"No. I know that couldn't be true."

She leaned her head against my chest for a few moments and then simply said, "Let's pray."

And so we prayed for my father, and for Anne-Marie to have the fortitude to give up drinking, and for me to have the courage to tell the truth.

She didn't ask me what truth I needed to tell, but when we said goodbye, I set out to find David and tell him everything I knew about Julia and the mystery of Psalm Fifty-Five.

Chapter Twenty-Eight
The Way of the Cross

A few days before Luke's walk with Anne, David finally received word that Mr. Farnsworth, president of the Las Vegas Bank & Trust, would meet with him at ten o'clock the next morning.

"Pastor Gold, it's a great pleasure, sir," said Farnsworth in what seemed to David an oddly obsequious voice. "Do make yourself comfortable. Would you care for coffee or tea? Or do you abstain from all stimulants?"

"No thank you, Mr. Farnsworth." David avoided the plush couch that the banker had pointed to and sat in a hard-backed chair opposite the president's desk.

"You are, I believe, more versed in the ways of the world than the typical man of the cloth," said Farnsworth, pausing to clear his throat. "So I'll speak frankly to you. We're quite concerned about the loan to the church. First, there was your predecessor's tragic demise; second, I understand that lately there has been a steep decline in attendance, and what parishioners remain are not among the well-heeled. Which does not bode well for your ability to service the debt, as we bankers say."

"I understand you used to be a regular member of the congregation," said David. "I'm sorry we haven't seen you there."

"I now attend Bountiful Harvest, if you must know. Pastor Holstein is a remarkable man, brings the Bible right smack up to date and in tune with these modern scientific times. Nothing morose, nothing gloomy about his sermons, no sir. We're not to hide our light under a bushel, you know, and I'm not about to bury my talents when I can multiply them tenfold. God is blessing Las Vegas abundantly with this dam, and it is our sacred responsibility to make the most of it."

"I see," said David. "Look, I'll come to the point. You're holding my automobile as collateral for the loan to the Church of the Heart Set Free. I'm eager to pay off the debt by selling the Talbot, which is worth considerably more than the church owes. It would seem simple enough to resolve this to our mutual satisfaction."

"Ah. Hmm," muttered Farnsworth. "Well, as it happens, I've asked you here to discuss a quite different proposition. One that should be much to your liking, I suspect. First, let me say that the loan no longer belongs to Las Vegas Bank & Trust; it was purchased by none other than Sebastian Bale. He has authorized me to release the vehicle to you, with a full tank of gas, the engine tuned, the body washed and given a hot-wax shine. And all you need do is drive it out of town and not return. Look here—" he set what appeared to be the deed of trust on his desk — "I'm ready to mark this 'paid in full' the moment you sign a letter agreeing to the terms I've just set forth."

David wasn't sure whether to laugh or lean across the desk and box the banker's ears, but decided to sit still and consider the best response. They could have destroyed the Talbot and then proceeded with foreclosure, or tried to kill him, just as they killed Justin James, but how much greater the victory if they could reveal David Gold as a phony, a fraud who left Las Vegas in disgrace just to retain a prestigious car! Lauren and her friends would become a laughingstock, and the church would wither away. However, as soon as he turned down their offer, all bets would be off, he reasoned; the auto's days would be numbered, and perhaps his own.

"Let me review the loan document," he said to Farnsworth, and took a few minutes to read it through. "I see that it can be paid off at any time, at the church's option. So, let me propose a deal to *you*, the likes of which you won't see again in your lifetime. The Talbot is one of the finest cars in the world, a work of art, and I'm willing to sell it to you for no more than the amount owed on the mortgage. You and I both know that's a fraction of the vehicle's worth, Mr. Farnsworth. If you act quickly, this is your lucky day. But my offer is good right now, and only now. So: do you want the Talbot, yes or no? If not, we can wish each other good day."

Farnsworth, stunned, sat back in his chair. To do anything without Mr. Bale's input was risky, perhaps very risky; but against that, the vision of himself, driving such a fine automobile...what a figure he'd cut, what a testimony to the power of his faith! Surely, seeing him driving a Talbot, Pastor Holstein would make him an elder, hold him up as an example to the rest of the congregation! And he'd have salvaged something of value for Mr. Bale, seeing that Gold had rejected their offer; he'd at least have extinguished a risky debt.

"All right," said the banker, his voice shaking just a bit. "All right. Wait here, I'll have my notary come in, then I'll write you a check which can be signed over to pay off the loan."

"Wise decision," said David, and he hoped Farnsworth hadn't noticed the drop of sweat that had just dripped from his brow.

~

Later that day, Sheriff Stone paid David a visit at the Church of the Heart Set Free.

"Congratulations, pastor, I heard about your paying off the mortgage," said the sheriff.

"Thanks," David replied. "I take it you've released the vehicle to its new owner."

"Oh yes, Mr. Farnsworth has already circumnavigated Las Vegas in the Talbot multiple times this afternoon. But that's not why I'm here." Stone fixed his eyes intently on David Gold. "Is there anything you can tell me about the whereabouts of the late pastor's daughter, Julia James? Anything at all."

David felt his heart skip a beat. What happened to him was one thing, but the thought of these men getting hold of an innocent girl chilled his soul.

"I've heard nothing," he said, glad that for the moment he didn't have to decide whether to lie.

"Well, if you hear anything, let me know at once. I have reason to think her life may be in danger; it would be better if I found her before someone else." He let his gaze linger on David's face for another moment, then turned to go.

"Wait a moment, sheriff, there's something I'd like to ask you. What can you tell me about Sebastian Bale?"

"You *are* new to this town," said Stone. "Bale owns half the gambling joints on Block 16. He's got big plans to expand when the state Legislature gets around to legalizing gambling in a few months. Assuming you don't talk them out of it, that is," he added, with the trace of a smile.

"Are you considering Mr. Bale as a suspect in the murder of Justin James?" David asked point blank.

The sheriff squinted at him and scowled.

"I'd watch what I say, I were you, Gold. Calling yourself a pastor's no protection against being prosecuted for libel and slander."

"I only asked you a question, there's no law against that."

"I've been hard at work on the case," said Stone, "whatever you might think. In fact, I'm going out of town in the morning, following a lead, be back in a few days. I'll keep you posted if anything breaks. You just make sure and let me know if something should surface about Julia James."

David nodded and watched the sheriff walk briskly out of the church.

~~≈~~

Early the next morning, David was awakened by the sound of pounding on his door. He answered it to find four large men outside, one of whom made sure he noticed the Colt 45 tucked into his belt

"Mr. Bale wants to see you. *Now.*"

"That's just fine," said David. "I've been looking forward to making his acquaintance."

They hustled the pastor into a Ford Model A, two of the thugs riding in front and two on either side of him in the back, and drove for fifteen minutes to a gated mansion on the edge of town.

"Wait here," said the gun-toting goon after they'd led David down several long hallways to an elegant library paneled in dark, burnished wood. "And keep your mitts off the books, Mr. Bale is particular that way."

Alone in the room, David decided to peruse the titles of the volumes that filled the shelves from floor to ceiling. It was an impressive and eclectic collection: he noted leather-bound tomes of ancient philosophy, an original edition of Calvin's Institutes, a treatise on alchemy, the writings of Abelard, and a manual penned by Franz Mesmer.

"Feel free to borrow any volumes that interest you, Pastor Gold."

David was startled; the man must have entered silently. But he remained looking at the bookshelf for a short while before turning around.

"What is the meaning of bringing me here at gunpoint, Mr. Bale?"

Sebastian Bale was standing with his back to an imposing fireplace. His appearance reminded David of some of the more curious characters he'd come across during his time in Europe: the man sported an artist's goatee, wore his long black hair pulled back in a pony tail, and affected the sort of sunglasses with round lenses that movie stars and wealthy women had become so fond of during the previous decade.

"Are you serious?" asked Bale. "My orders were that my men treat you with the utmost respect. If it would mend things between us, I'll have them dismissed at once."

"There's no need," said David. "But you can satisfy my curiosity: I'm thinking it was you who chose the verses that would be preached at the church you've paid for—at Bountiful Harvest. Am I right?"

Bale laughed.

"I'm really delighted at your perspicacity, I am! Not even that fool Farnsworth knows my connection to Bountiful. But in all modesty, I only provided Holstein with three or four choice selections, and let him mine the Holy Scriptures for the rest. Now please, let's sit down and get to know one another."

"I've a great deal to do, Mr. Bale. What is it you want from me?"

"Ah, perhaps the offer I made through Farnsworth offended you. Accept my apologies, please; it was merely a test. I had to know the sort of man I was dealing with, what you were made of. And I learned a great deal."

Sebastian Bale walked over to a table where a lantern slide projector—a 'magic lantern'—had been set up.

"What Holstein preaches at Bountiful Harvest," he continued, "it's all perfect rubbish, of course. But it sells like the proverbial hotcakes, wouldn't you say?"

"I don't get you," said David. "You prey on human weakness with your casinos and brothels and booze, you seduce with a false gospel, then talk as though you expect us to be friends. No, there's nothing on these shelves I care to borrow. We're wasting each other's time."

"Oh, don't be so hasty," said Sebastian Bale. "Let patience do its perfect work. I've another proposition to make you, one I think you'll find rather more to your liking." He flicked off the lights and the lantern projected a large image on the far wall.

It was a photograph of Justin James preaching at the Church of the Heart Set Free.

David sat down in an upholstered wing-back chair and stared grimly at the picture on the wall.

"First, I can assure you that I had nothing to do with your predecessor's murder. That's not my style, not at all. Too messy, really, and made a martyr of the man; it's so much more elegant to simply starve a church of its parishioners and thereby make its pastor irrelevant. No, that was the work of some unstable element whom I would just as soon see expunged from the face of the earth.

"I do hope that clears the air a bit, because what I have to say is well worth your time. When the government approved construction of a dam in Black Canyon, I asked the finest minds at Stanford, Princeton, and Harvard Universities this question: considering trends in scientific progress and in the mores of human society, if the State of Nevada were to legalize gambling and the Great Dam is successfully completed, what will the city of Las Vegas be like at the turn of this century, in the year 2000. And now I will show you the result of their efforts."

The magic lantern clicked and whirred and the image of Justin James faded from view, to be replaced by something which at first David could not make out. When he finally understood what he was looking at, he gasped.

Covering the wall was the image of a building, monstrously large, perhaps occupying an entire city block, with countless more such buildings to its left and right. This was a night scene, and each enormous structure was ablaze with electric light, garish and impossibly bright.

New images followed, changing so quickly that it was almost as though he were watching a motion picture show. Crowds flocked inside these structures, which seemed to be great gambling halls, complete with stages on which men and women, all but naked, performed before thousands. This was Sodom and Gomorrah, but on a massive scale, and most shocking of all, parents were bringing their children to these temples of sin. Airships, two or three times larger than any David had ever seen, were landing one after another on a vast field located in the middle of the city, disgorging passengers from all over the world. A sea of humanity flocked to this nightmarish metropolis, offering sacrifices of money, of decency, of honor, of the truth itself, to a panoply of false gods.

David Gold felt a chill run down his spine; no painting, no drawing, could possibly be as realistic as what he was seeing. These were photographs of a world that did not yet exist.

"I don't need to see any more of this," he said. "Turn it off."

Bale complied and the room went dark.

"Who are you?" David asked.

"I understand your distress," said Sebastian Bale, who was now cloaked in darkness. "But listen to me: you have seen a future that need never be. Your efforts, and those of Pastor James, to prevent the legalization of gambling have been laughable; but I assure you, it *can* be stopped. I make it my business to know the secrets of powerful men. One of the state's leading legislators is engaged in a clandestine affair, another is stealing money from the public as we speak. A few words from me and they will make sure the gambling bill is never passed.

"But that would only be the beginning! Just as I opened Bountiful Harvest, I can shut it down. And more than that: watch. I want to show you a very different picture of what Las Vegas could become."

The magic lantern whirred to life.

David saw before him a great city of wide boulevards and peaceful tree-lined streets. Once more, the changing images blended one into the next: mothers and fathers raised their children in safety and comfort, neighbor helped neighbor, schools and libraries and hospitals were open to all. Shops were shuttered on Sundays, and families walked to churches large and small that welcomed them with bells that pealed from steeples throughout Las Vegas. And there, at the very center, humble but shining bright as the noonday sun, was the Church of the Heart Set Free.

The whirring stopped, the image faded, and Sebastian Bale flicked on the lights.

"That is the future that can yet come to pass, David Gold. It's up to you."

"Assuming I believe that you could make either of these visions come true," David said. "What is it you would want from me?"

"Hardly anything at all, really," said Bale. "Only the recognition that you work for me. Not a public acknowledgment, mind you; it can be our secret. And you will be your own man; I'm strictly hands-off. I assure you, Las Vegas would be yours to guide on a righteous path."

David's mind was spinning. Even if the fantastical images were mere phantasms, still, if Bale could divert the city from its path of destruction—if the man's influence could help him to bring God into the hearts and minds of thousands, far, far faster than would otherwise be the case—

Faster than would otherwise...

David slowed his racing thoughts, and, from somewhere, there came a still, small voice.

My way is the long, lonely way of the Cross.

"I worship the Lord my God," said David Gold, "and serve Him only. Between you and me there can be no deal."

Sebastian Bale stared at David silently for a full thirty seconds.

"I advise you to think very carefully about what you are giving up, Pastor. And the bleak fate that will befall so many if the darker future comes to be."

"There's nothing more for us to talk about." David stood up and began to walk to the door. "I'll find my own way home. Good day."

"If you walk out of this room without agreeing to my terms," said Bale, "I warn you: all hell will be set loose upon your head."

It took David three hours to walk back to the Church of the Heart

Set Free.

⤳

The following afternoon, David was at home working on the next Sunday's sermon when he heard a knocking on his door. For a moment, it crossed his mind whether this day, this hour, was when he would be asked to face what Justin James, and Peter, and Paul, and so many others of the faithful had had to endure; but he pushed the thought away.

"General Lee!" he exclaimed when he swung the door open. "Come in, come in."

"I'm powerful sorry to disturb you, Pastor Gold, but I couldn't sleep a wink this past night, and couldn't eat a forkful all day, there's such a weight on mah mind."

"Sit down and tell me about it," said David, "and let's see if we can't cast your cares upon the Lord."

The General eased himself into a chair by the pastor's kitchen table and explained what had been going on since Luke and Lauren had come to each of the circle of friends with the news of Julia's note and the somber message of Psalm Fifty-Five.

"I never seen things so bad 'tween the five of us," he concluded. "Each of 'em thinkin' the worst 'a someone else. It's turned Isaiah quieter and more timid than ever, and I'm 'fraid Anne-Marie's taken to drink."

"And you say this has been going on for three weeks?" David inwardly groaned. How could this be taking place under his nose, and he not be aware? What a poor shepherd of his little flock! "I'm glad you came to me, General. It was the right—"

David's words were interrupted by the clatter of footsteps as Luke burst through the open door and into the room.

"Pastor Gold," he said breathlessly. "There's something I've got to tell you. It's—"

He broke off, noticing that the Bible on the kitchen table was open to Psalm Fifty-Five. There was an awkward silence.

"You know," he said.

"What you surmised was not entirely unreasonable, Luke," said David. "But you would have to assume that it was Julia's intention to sow suspicion and discord among her closest friends. The Psalms, like all of Scripture, are full of riches, and can be mined endlessly to the soul's delight. But the alchemy of doubt and mistrust can transform gold into lead."

The youth's face was white, and his eyes filled with tears.

"The Spirit speaks to you through the promptings of your conscience," David continued. "Ignoring it when you sensed that something was wrong—that was your only sin."

Luke straightened his posture and addressed the two men.

"What can I do now to make amends?"

"We got to get the gang together, boy," said the General. "Hash this thing out with Pastor Gold."

"That's right," David said. "Luke, search out Lauren and Isaiah. I'll find Mr. Polwarth and Anne-Marie, and we'll meet up at the church."

Luke briefly described where Anne-Marie was likely to be found, explaining that he'd come across her, despondent, not long before.

"All right," said David. "And Luke, buck up. I'm counting on you— from here on, I want you and Isaiah to spend every hour you can helping Edward Grimm, he's been carrying the weight of Black Canyon on his shoulders for far too long. Now, let's clear the air on Psalm Fifty-Five and get back to the work the Lord's set before us."

And with that the three went their separate ways.

~~

After searching in vain for half an hour, Luke began to hear the sounds of a commotion coming from the direction of Block 16. He began to walk there as the shouts and screams gathered in intensity, then broke into a run as he saw clouds of billowing smoke.

As he reached the corner of First and Stewart, a terrible scene came into view: a melee had broken out in front of the Church of the Heart Set Free, which was enveloped in flames. All the friends were there already, along with a few other members of the congregation who had come to see what was going on, and they were fighting a gang of ruffians whom Luke didn't recognize. He could see that David was trying as best he could to protect his flock and get them to leave the scene, but his words were lost in the din of battle and the roar of the fire.

Thud! Anne-Marie was wielding a bottle of gin like a medieval mace, and had already laid three of the enemy to waste. Isaiah lifted one of the smaller thugs up off his feet and used him as a human battering ram to upend several of the other assailants, while Mr. Polwarth took advantage of his diminutive status to dart among the combatants and throw himself at their knees.

A police car tore around the corner and screeched to a halt nearby.

"This is not a war we'll win by force of arms," David shouted, as he knocked two of the goons' heads together before they could get to Anne-Marie. "I'm ordering a full retreat!" He ducked before delivering a right hook which sent another of the enemy's men sprawling on the ground.

It was then that Detective Drake came up behind David, brought his cudgel down on the back of his head with all the force he could muster, and, for the pastor of the Church of the Heart Set Free, everything went black.

PART THREE

PERFECT IN WEAKNESS

Chapter Twenty-Nine
Turning Points

Sudden music from the radio on her night table jolted Joan awake from a deep sleep, and she hit the snooze button three times before remembering that Willie was coming over to meet her for breakfast at the Babylonian Buffet. She threw off the covers, slipped on the hotel bathrobe she'd draped over the back of a chair, pulled back the blinds so she could gaze at the dawn sky, and lit up a cigarette.

Then Joan remembered: to inspire her brother, she'd sworn to quit, and Daniel had prayed for her! But that hadn't stopped her from smoking half a pack before turning out the lights last night. Why couldn't she have read her Gideon's Bible, then sat patiently, in silence, waiting for the Spirit to make known to her the mind of Christ!

Daniel had asked that nothing but the will of God would be the master of her life. Amen, a perfect prayer! Once again, the words of the Apostle ran through her mind: *I do not understand my own actions. For I do not do what I want, but I do the very thing I hate.*

So, Joan thought, should she lie to Willie, if only to make him think that there was hope, that he, too, could quit? She looked at the beautiful burning tip of her Camel for a while before taking a long drag.

No. To forsake the truth now would be, as the pastor had said, to burrow her way into hell.

$$\sim$$

"Don't beat yourself up," said Willie, his plate piled high with breakfast burritos, butter croissants, and some scary-looking Asian concoction covered in seaweed.

He knew.

Joan was startled and relieved; she hadn't had the nerve to tell her brother when he'd first shown up and shot her that killer grin. But Willie could tell, just by looking at her, or by some trace, some smell that still somehow clung to her from the rest of the pack she'd smoked before showering and getting dressed and brushing her teeth. She would have told him, sooner or later, she thought, but he'd taken the decision out of her hands.

"I didn't make it twenty-four hours," said Joan. "It's like smoking's a part of me, it's become who I *am*. I'm a freaking cigarette."

"I warned you," said Willie. There was no "I told you so" in his voice; she could tell, looking at his ruined face, into his eyes—still beautiful, somehow—that his heart ached for her. "Nicotine's a monster, just can't compete with crank when it comes to puttin' on a show, that's all. Look, sissie, you're right 'bout me—I'm still a doper, though it's been years since I done ice."

"How'd you quit?" Joan asked.

"I can't hardly figure. You know, with meth, feelin' like I was bungee jumpin' off El Capitan, that was the least of it. It felt like there was *nuthin'* I couldn't do—you name it, fly an F-29, play the violin in Carnegie Hall. Everything revolved 'round me, I was the hub of flippin' reality, the center of the wheel. Total self-delusion, Joanie. And when I came down from the high, I'd get so paranoid 'n angry, I mean, worse than mom. That's how I lost Sugar, tell ya the truth. Fifty-one fifty, you bet."

"I'm sorry, Willie," said his sister.

"Yeah. How'd I quit crank? Just didn't wanna die, I guess. Who knows, maybe Jesus had somethin' to do with it, like Pastor Dan would prob'ly say. More power to Him if he did."

"He's in charge, Willie, He's the King. Maybe He wants you around. Maybe there's something He needs you to do."

"Oh, man," her brother chuckled. "Wouldn't that be sweet. I ain't had a delusion like *that* in a while!"

"Everything you described about what it was like on meth," Joan mused, "and my own struggles with smokes, it makes me think about what Pastor Dan was saying, that beneath the surface of things, there really are demons at work. It feels that way, doesn't it."

"I thought it's all just chemicals messin' with our brains. Said so on one of your shows, I saw your name in the credits. Producer: my sister, Joanie Reed!"

"Yeah, I know. But if you look at it that way, we're just, what, a bubble of accidental self-awareness produced in a swirling chemical stew by meaningless chance. In your gut, don't you believe that's a lie? It's like Dan asked my boss, Tim, even with all the crap you've dealt with in your life, do you *feel* it's been a meaningless existence?"

"Ah, hell, I dunno, I'm not that smart. Makes the whole thing even scarier, though—ya know, more hopeless—when ya bring demons into it, seems to me."

"I was thinking the same thing last night, Willie. But then I realized, they're just using us as pawns; their fight's against *God*. And, somehow, these demons and devils, these powers of the air, they've already been defeated at the Cross. So it's like we've already won, yet we're acting as if we don't know it." Joan frowned. "I'm not saying it right, it's coming out all garbled, I know."

"Nah, I get your drift," said her brother. "Hey, think your boss would wanna join us for breakfast?"

"Maybe." Joan tried to call Tim on her cell phone; when he failed to answer, she left a message telling him that she and her brother would be hanging out at the buffet. But she never heard back.

Willie and Joan went back for seconds, then talked for a long while over cups of coffee before going outside to smoke.

"How was it at your job last night?" Joan asked. "Did you see Mr. Osman again?"

"Oh yeah. The Oz man is my new best friend, maybe he's lonely or somethin', though I can't hardly imagine why. 'member the bronze bull I told ya 'bout?"

His sister nodded.

"So, Oz asks me to dispose of a pile of documents, right? Most guys, they'd say, put 'em in the shredder. Not him. He shows me how the bull's right side opens up, you throw crap in there, and there's a furnace 'a some sort that incinerates stuff lickety-split. But that ain't the in'erestin' part. Turns out there's all this tubin' inside, like on the outside of a trumpet or trombone, and the hot air blows through it and out'a the bull's mouth comes music. Sinatra, I think. Can't think of which song, all his kind'a sound the same to me."

"That is so weird, Willie."

"Yeah, and there's plenty more, but not worth talkin' 'bout."

The truth was, Willie just didn't want to creep his sister out. Last night, Oz had been in rare form, cracking jokes and practicing magic tricks. "Want to see some oldies but goodies?" he'd asked. Sure, why not. Osman rummaged through a chest, took out what appeared to be a walking cane, brandished it, then threw it on the plush carpeting that covered his office floor.

The cane transformed into a snake and slithered out of sight.

"Woah!" Willie had cried out. "We better find that thing before it scares the crap outta some secretary when she shows up in the mornin'."

"Don't worry about it," Osman had said, and asked Willie to bring him a cup of water. The casino boss bent over the glass, pondered it, then seemed to give it the evil eye. What a ham, Joan's brother thought to himself.

The liquid in the glass turned red before Willie's eyes; whatever it was, it was no longer water. He walked over to look more closely.

The water had turned into blood.

"That's gross, Mr. O," Willie had said. "Change it back, will ya, it's freakin' me out."

At that, Osman's face had turned dark.

"The dove's cages are filthy, William, see to cleaning them out, at once," he'd said, with a touch of anger in his voice.

Willie had shrugged and set to work on the cages. There was just no understanding the mind of a zillionaire tycoon like Oz!

⁓

When her brother finally left for work, Joan smoked one last cigarette and headed back to her room. It was all well and good that they were sharing stories and laughing together, but she was the older sister, she had a responsibility to lead the way. She'd let Willie down! If his successful sister, with all her advantages, couldn't give up smokes, what hope was there for him? Sure, she prayed for him, but didn't there need to be some balance between God's actions and the workings of her will? Wasn't that what Paul meant when he wrote, "work out your salvation with fear and trembling?"

Well, what about when you *don't* work it out? What happens when you fail?

She exercised in the hotel gym, swam laps to the point of exhaustion, then tried to call Tim again to see what he was up to. But there was still no answer.

That night, sitting in bed with her back against the headboard, Joan again visualized the final scene in John's Gospel.

The disciples, on the Sea of Galilee, with only an empty net to show for their efforts...

She changed the camera angles, modified the lighting, played it over and over in her mind. Extreme long shot of Jesus and Peter sitting together on the beach; then, a sudden close-up as the Lord asks, "Do you love me?"

She began to grow drowsy, and, sometime during that night, in her hotel room in Las Vegas, the producer/director lost control of the shoot.

The dark sky grew lighter; she heard the water lapping the side of the boat and felt the coolness of the early morning air. A hundred yards off, a stranger on the shore called out: "Friends, haven't you any fish?"

No, not one. "Cast your net to the right, you'll find some there." *Then, the miraculous catch, the net too heavy to haul in, and the beloved disciple clapping her on the back, pointing, shouting,* "It is the Lord!"

But what was this? Already the other disciples were on the beach, gathered with Jesus, sitting nearby the burning coals, eating bread and fish. Only Joan had been left behind.

She sunk to her knees in despair.

No! She dove over the side and swam with all her strength, but somehow, though she was a talented swimmer with a powerful stroke, there was a vicious current, taking her farther away from shore.

She struggled against it, made a bit of progress, and then was swept back by the riptide, far, far out to sea. She'd never make it.

So, at last, Joan stopped trying.

And that was when a strong hand grasped hers, and she felt herself lifted up like a small child who'd been gathered into her father's arms...

⁓

This time, Vicki was dressed in a tight-fitting t-shirt and jeans that seemed spray-painted on her skin. She smiled at Tim when he first got in the Porsche, then pulled out onto the Strip without saying a word. He tried to keep his eyes off her, not wanting to come across as just another lecherous, middle-aged jerk. This was a vulnerable young woman, understandably drawn to a successful, attractive, alpha male who shared her passion for science. He would treat her well!

Earlier that day, he'd imagined offering to be her mentor, perhaps over dinner and drinks. She'd be surprised and flattered; they'd clink glasses, and the conversation would go on long into the night, continuing in the luxurious privacy of his Emperor Suite at Babylon West.

Tim tried to ask Vicki a question, just to break the ice, but she had the top down on the Porsche, and her answer was lost in the roar of the engine, the blare of traffic, and the rushing of the wind. Shouting "what did you say?" seemed utterly uncool, so he lapsed into silence. Plenty of time for talk later! Once, she looked over at him from behind her mirrored glasses just as he was sneaking a sidelong glance; she laughed and reached over and stroked his cheek, her fingers brushing his lips and lingering for just an extra second, thrilling him with anticipation for what might come next.

Outside of town, Vicki turned onto a two-lane road that led them to a sort of no-man's land where the city ended and the desert began. Tim was increasingly puzzled about where they were headed, but figured he would score points by just going with the flow and enjoying the ride. Who knows, perhaps she had a romantic spot picked out for an assignation under the stars! But even he had a tough time imagining that the bleak landscape could serve as a setting for any sort of amorous interlude.

Finally, Vicki pulled off the road and killed the engine. In the sudden silence, he felt a shiver of fear for the first time, but shook it off. She looked around for a while, then pointed to something in what appeared to be merely a vacant stretch of land void of anything but sand and rock.

"Look," she said. "But don't stare, just relax your eyes."

Confused, Tim blinked a few times, then ceased trying to focus on any one thing. Gradually, he became aware of a shimmering of light perhaps thirty yards away, but when he looked right at it, it vanished from view. After a few tries, he learned not to look directly at the spectral image; and then, a few moments later, it resolved itself into something which, in that desolate location, made no sense.

Vicki got out of the Porsche, and Tim followed her toward what he could now see was a large wooden door set in a section of an old stone wall. At first, parts of the wall were transparent, but the closer they got, the more solid it appeared. When they reached it, she turned to him, put her hands on his shoulders, and whispered words, her breath warm and soft against his ear.

"I've brought you someplace very special," she said, "because I want you there with me. But it must be your choice to enter in."

She stepped back and pointed to a wrought-iron handle, and, without hesitation, Tim opened the door and stepped through to the other side.

Chapter Thirty
The Blue Room

"Want the doc to look at him?" Sergeant Stanton asked Deputy Drake. The two men were standing outside the holding tank of the city jail. David Gold lay stretched out on the floor near them, still unconscious, the back of his head swollen and sticky with dried blood.

"Nah. Just toss him in," Drake replied. "And this ain't no catch-and-release. I want him there three days. Anyone asks, the extra time is for bad behavior. But nobody needs to know about this, see?"

"Woah!" Stanton took the stogie out of his mouth and tapped its ashes onto the floor. Drake was a hard case, all right; men were usually turned loose the next morning. He made a mental note that the Sheriff was supposed to be back in *four* days; Stone and his deputy didn't always get along, might not be bad to have something on Drake if anything hinky went down, like the Feds getting wind of the C-notes they were collecting from the bootleggers who kept a river of liquor flowing through town.

The holding tank, better known as the Blue Room, had originally been designed to hold no more than two dozen prisoners, but, with the influx of riffraff since the dam project had been announced, it sometimes held more than one hundred. There were ninety-three men occupying it that evening, and the night was young! It was Las Vegas' answer to the Black Hole of Calcutta, a fifteen-by-forty-foot windowless cell, without plumbing, without features of any sort, just a concrete floor that sloped down into a sort of cesspool which Sergeant Stanton hosed out every few days. The Blue Room was highly effective as a deterrent; anyone who'd spent a night there would either go straight or leave town. Well, the sergeant figured, this Gold character must have gotten on Drake's bad side all right, poor bastard. No one had ever spent more than two days in the Blue Room, as far as he could recall, not when they were packed in there like *that*.

Gradually, David regained consciousness. He could see blurrily though half-opened eyes, and what he saw and heard and, most of all, smelled, made him think, *I must surely be in hell.* The stench of the Blue Room was overpowering; he shook off four men who were leaning against him and rose to his knees, wracked by dry heaves.

After a while, the intense nausea passed and he collected himself, trying to understand what had happened and where he was. Ah! His memory came back of the church, consumed by fire, and the riot taking place outside. He'd been taken prisoner; an armed guard sat, snoozing in a chair perhaps twenty feet away, on the other side of the iron bars which separated the holding tank from the rest of the station. David rose shakily to his feet and looked around as best he could; as far as he could tell, none of the other members of the church were there. The pastor said a silent prayer that none of the combatants in the melee had been seriously hurt, then spent a while observing the dynamics of the room.

Most men were crouching or standing, and any who had passed out or fallen asleep served as cushions for the rest. At any moment, some men were struggling through the mass of humanity to relieve themselves in the foul cesspool at the far end of the cell. Rations of bread and water came at infrequent intervals, but were being confiscated by a huge, muscle-bound man whom others addressed as Skull. He had a clean-shaven head with a pirate's skull and crossbones tattooed on his forehead. Food and drink were being consumed by him and his cronies.

All right then, he thought. If this is where the Lord wants me, after my utter failure leading the Heart Set Free, I'll just have to do my best.

"Excuse me," said David, shouldering his way through the crowd so that he could look Skull in the eye and get a measure of the man. "The bread and water needs to be shared equally by everyone in this room."

He'd spoken in a loud voice, and the din in the Blue Room was reduced to a few murmuring voices.

"Who the fwickin' hell are you?" said Skull, who spoke with a curious speech impediment.

"I'm David Gold. Come on, I'll work with you and your team and we'll get everyone fed."

"Hey, that's Pastor Dave!" someone shouted out.

Skull started to laugh.

"You weally a pathtah?" he asked.

"He's the one used to be a pug," said another. "Maybe you better watch out!"

"Watch out? Watch out foah what?" Skull raised himself to his full, imposing height. "Whatah you gonna do, pathtah man, punch me in the noeth?"

David rolled his eyes, silently prayed *forgive me, Lord, for what I am about to do*, and a moment later he was helping Skull to get up off the floor.

"You fwiggin' bathturd!" shouted Skull. "You bwoke my noeth!"

"It's not broken," said David, and he tore off a piece of his shirt and showed Skull where to apply pressure to staunch the bleeding. "Just lean against your friends there for a minute and you'll be fine."

The Blue Room had become utterly silent and still.

"The three of you, start passing out bread," said David, addressing Skull's posse. "And you guys, make the rounds with those buckets of water. Now, anyone needs to relieve himself—"

"Whatch'a mean, relief? Ain't no relief here, pastor!" someone shouted out.

"He means take a whizz awe take a cwap, ya dumb bathturd!" said Skull, who had apparently made a swift decision to become chief lieutenant to the room's new alpha male.

"Easy, big guy," said David. "But, yes, Mr. Skull is correct. We're all going to leave a couple inches of space either side of the seams in the cement which lead down to the, uhm, facilities, to make it easier for those who've got to go."

It wasn't long before everyone had had a crust to gobble and at least a slurp of water to wash it down.

"One more thing," David called out to the crowd. "Since we're spending all this time in close quarters, let's act like human beings.

Introduce yourselves to the men around you and shake hands. They're your neighbors. Treat them with friendship and respect."

Things went reasonably well for the next several hours, but sometime during the night, amid the growing stench and hunger and thirst, the usual cursing and griping in the Blue Room began to build into an angry roar.

"Hey!" shouted David, who'd had enough. "You guys think *this* is bad?" Perhaps half the room quieted down to hear what he had to say. "I got news for you. A man doesn't get his act together, things can get a *lot* worse."

"We need to hear that?" someone called out. "I heard enough bad news, don't need no more."

"I get that," said the pastor. "So, how about some Good News, in that case?"

"You got good news, I can use it, pal," said one man.

"Got that right," said another.

"Well, then," said David Gold, his face lighting up with a warm and confident smile, "let me lay it on ya, boys."

~

"Now y'all listen," said the General. "'cause I got sump'n important ta say."

He'd called an emergency meeting of Lauren, Isaiah, Mr. Polwarth, Luke, and Anne-Marie, and, since the church was now nothing but charred ruins, they'd convened on a wooden bench in the park by the railway depot on Fremont Street.

"But first, Ah gotta come clean. My—" the General paused, struggling with his words. "Well, dang it anyway, here's how it is. Ah ain't no general, and mah name ain't Robert E. Lee. It's Harold Merkle. Ah was a junior accountant on the general's staff durin' the War between the States. That's all Ah was."

There was silence for a few moments, and then Mr. Polwarth spoke up.

"So...do we call you Harry?"

"Men have died fo' less," Harold Merkle replied.

"I don't care what your name is," said Lauren. "You're our brother in Christ is all that counts."

"Amen," said Isaiah, and he was echoed by Luke.

"We're all in trouble," said Anne-Marie, "least, I am, anyway. I need your help, Mr. Merkle, and you've always been there for me."

"Well, all right then," said the retired accountant. "Thank y'all for that. Now, I got ta get somethin' off mah chest that's not so easy to say. Ah'm awful disappointed in the way y'all been treatin' each other these past few weeks—all 'a ya but for Ed Grimm, anyway, whose been workin' his tail off over in Black Canyon. I can hardly believe y'all, pointin' fingers at each other, harborin' suspicions, each behind th'other's back. Ah want each 'a ya to look deep inside: you really think any one of the folks sittin' here had anythin' ta do with the murder 'a Pastor James? Lauren, you believe your friend Polwarth sold the pastor out?"

Lauren, whose head was bandaged after she'd been hit by a brick during the riot outside the church, turned to the small man whose three-piece suit was now more tattered than ever.

"No," she said, her face beet red. "I'm sorry, Mr. Polwarth, for ever thinking such a thing."

"Polwarth," said Merkle. "Anythin' ya want to say to Anne-Marie?"

Merkel went around the table to make sure that all the poison was exposed, and finally came to Luke, who was looking increasingly distraught.

"It's all my fault," said the young man, fighting back tears. "None of this would have happened if I hadn't come up with the idea that Julia James was warning us of a traitor in our midst."

"Pull yourself together," said Anne-Marie. "You did nothing worse than the rest of us."

"I did learn this much, though," said Luke. "What Jesus meant, about the truth setting us free—it sets us free from the weight of our lies."

"I kin testify to that, boy," said the man who once called himself Robert E. Lee. "Look, we got one thing goin' for us, and that's bein' members of the Body of Christ, united in love—without that, we ain't but resoundin' gongs or clangin' cymbals."

"We got to put our heads together," said Isaiah. "Pastor Gold's behind bars, church is burnt to a crisp, and we ain't got two nickels to rub together 'tween the s-s-six of us. We need us a plan!"

"Pastor's got that covered," said Mr. Polwarth. "We just keep trusting in our Savior, the Everlasting God."

"We don't need a building," said Harold Merkel. "Wherever we meet, we're the Church of the Heart Set Free. Now, I'm goin' ta lead us in prayer for our pastor, and then Lauren, how 'bout you lead us in song."

Stars began to appear overhead as dusk darkened into night. After a heartfelt prayer for David, the six sang *Tis So Sweet to Trust in Jesus*, followed by *Blessed Assurance*, and then *Abide in Me*, and it was long past midnight before they bid each other goodnight and went their separate ways.

～

"You don't look real happy ta see me," said Sheriff Stone to his Sergeant outside the Blue Room. He'd startled the cigar-chomping Stanton, who'd been dozing in his chair and hadn't been expecting Stone for another two days. The Sheriff held a handkerchief over his nose and walked up to the iron bars to get a look-see at the action in the holding tank, which seemed more subdued than usual.

"Well I'll be damned!" He turned back to the sergeant, incredulous. "What the hell is Pastor Gold doin' in there?"

"You'll have to ask Drake about that," said Stanton. "He just told me to hold him for three days. Been in there for two."

Stone banged on the bars.

"Hey! Pastor! Come on over here."

A sea of human flesh parted to allow David to pass through.

"What can I do for you, Sheriff?"

"You look like crap, Gold, and your shirt's in shreds. I don't know what's going on here, but I'm springin' you for now. Stanton, open this damn door and let—"

"I appreciate the thought, but I've been told I was put in here for three days, and I'll serve out my term like all the rest."

A wave of cheers shook the Blue Room walls.

"Have you lost your friggin' mind?" asked Stone.

David shrugged.

"All right. Fine. Have it your way." The sheriff, eager to get away from the stench, wheeled around and walked off to find Deputy Drake.

The next morning, Sergeant Stanton made it clear that Pastor Gold would need to vacate the Blue Room, pronto. David asked for five minutes and shook hands with as many of the men around him as he could, inviting them to attend his church, though, he admitted, he had no idea where it would next meet.

Just as he was about to leave, one of the men, who'd been hauled in for public drunkenness while on leave from his job at the dam site, slapped David on the back.

"You're a good man, pastor. And hey, we could use a big guy like you, you ever get tired 'a preachin' 'n want a real job, bustin' yer butt on the Colorado River with the rest of us bums."

David smiled and was halfway out the door before he stopped in his tracks and turned around.

"Who would I talk to, if I did want a job?"

The man laughed.

"My cousin, Danny White."

David felt a jolt of adrenaline as he left the station and walked out onto Second Street to look for his congregation. The church, which of course hadn't been insured, had been reduced to cinders; he and his friends were pretty much broke; and the dam, as Edward Grimm had pointed out, was where there'd be the most souls to save.

It was off-limits to a pastor from Las Vegas—but not if he were a card-carrying member of the crew building the largest dam in the world, the colossus in Black Canyon.

Chapter Thirty-One
A Child of God

"Remember when we were driving through the high desert," said David, "south of Tonopah, those strange-looking trees you asked me about?"

David and I had been getting together for breakfast long before the sun came up ever since he'd been hired to work on the dam. We would talk about the Scripture I'd read the night before and about our successes and failures in living our faith in Jesus in our daily lives. Faith, he told me, meant nothing if it did not mean willing myself to be obedient to the Lord. I might fail today; but if I press on, the Holy Spirit will help me, until one day I am transformed into the image of the Son of God.

"Sure. The Joshua Trees—the ones that looked to me like they had their arms raised in surrender."

"Interesting. Actually, they were named by the Mormons who settled not far from here, because they reminded them of the Hebrews' commander, with his arms lifted up toward heaven in *prayer*. You're reading the Book of Joshua, so it came to my mind."

"But then, prayer is a sort of surrender, isn't it?" I asked. "Anne-Marie told me that during the war she'd heard a Scotsman preaching to the troops at a YMCA camp in Egypt. He'd said that when we pray in Jesus' name, we're praying in His *nature*. I had to think about that for a while before it made sense; and then I realized, it's just like you've been telling me: I have to surrender my nature, my ways, just give them up and hand them over so that my prayers can be like His."

David rarely praised me, but I could tell from the warmth of his smile that he was pleased. "You're right," he said. "And then every prayer, every request you make, becomes another way of saying, Your will be done."

"You know," he continued, "when the Hebrews arrived at the promised land, it wasn't just handed over to them—they had to fight for it against fierce foes every step of the way, with Joshua at the helm.

And though he was as good and brave a man as any, if they'd had to rely on *him*, they'd never have prevailed. The point of every one of the battles they fought was to teach them to trust in God. In fact, the name Joshua—in Hebrew, the same name as Jesus—means *God saves*. And so He does: from our foolishness, from our sins, from the darkness arrayed against us.

"Luke, make prayer, make the opening of your heart to God, the most important moments of each day. Pray, do whatever the Lord has this day set before you, trust in Him, and you cannot go wrong."

It was a blustery day in March 1931. In two months, work would begin on the diversion tunnels which would be drilled into the sheer canyon walls to send the Colorado River around the planned construction site, and then Isaiah and I would be hired on as well. After David set off for Black Canyon, I got down on my knees and prayed.

"Heavenly Father, guide my earthly father home to my mother and me; we have forgiven him, and I beg you, forgive him for his sins. I know you can harden hearts, so, if ever you soften them, please, soften his toward us, that he might love us again. And Father, it hurts that my mother has grown so cold toward me; I'm no longer the child she wishes me to be. Can you soften her heart, too? But how selfish I sound! Guide her heart to you, I'll say no more than that. Watch over David— Pastor Gold, I mean—and my friends, Lauren and Isaiah and Harold and Mr. Polwarth and Edward and Anne-Marie; and Julia James. And if it could possibly be your will that she and I might meet, how wonderful that would be. That is everything in my heart this morning, Amen."

~

"I preach with my hands," Edward Grimm told me, "because I haven't the gift of gab. It's like Mr. Polwarth once said, I'm dull as the boards I nail together."

We were in the squatter's settlement known as McKeeversville, not far from the dam site, helping to board up a tent for a young woman while she cared for her two infant children. A tent alone was scant protection against the fierce gusts of wind that covered everything with sand. Her husband was waiting in a long line of job seekers and would likely not return before dark.

"Do you know who St. Francis was?" he asked me. I shook my head. "You could do worse than to read about him some time. When I was a lad, my parents took me to a church with windows made of colored glass—they were like storybooks, showing the Lord and angels and saints. When the sun shone through them, Luke, you never saw such a beautiful thing in all your life. There was one window, showed a man preaching to the birds. That was St. Francis. Made an impression on me; right away, I knew he was the man I wanted to be. Always did like being out among the critters and beasts; oh, I've preached some mighty sermons to flocks of pigeons and gaggles of geese! But gather more than one or two of my own kind together and I'm tongue-tied. I've kept my homilies brief here in the desert, though, for there's naught but lizards, centipedes, tarantulas, scorpions, and snakes, and they're a skittish bunch."

The government had built cabins to house surveyors and engineers when the Boulder Dam project began, and it hadn't taken long before families began arriving, desperate for the jobs they'd heard were in the offing, and set up camp nearby. Most came with not much more than a mattress and change of clothes. A lucky few had gas lanterns and cooked on kerosene stoves, but some didn't even have a tent.

"I was a joiner, once upon a time," Grimm continued. "A cabinet maker. But out here, it's just rough carpentry that's called for. It's made me think that's the sort of carpenter our Lord must have been."

We were hunched down where there was some refuge from the wind, munching on the cheese sandwiches he'd packed for us. Isaiah and I had begun serving as Edward's helpers while we waited for our jobs at the dam; I worked from early morning until mid-afternoon and then Isaiah took my place, toiling alongside him until well into the night. I'd scavenge for scrap lumber, and then Grimm, treating each piece as though it were treasure, would improvise shelter, whether reinforcing a tent or creating a crude cabin for a family that had nothing else to protect them from the elements.

He never said much to the people we were helping, but sometimes, when they watched him work or thanked him when we were done, they'd ask him who he was or who we worked for. Edward would tell them that he was just a man trying to follow his master, Christ Jesus, who died to save us all from sin. Often, that would pretty much be a conversation-ender, but other times it got people talking and asking more questions. As time went by, if whomever we were talking to was young enough, he'd nod to me and I'd answer as best I could. Before we left, we'd invite anyone who would give us the time of day to join us that evening under the stars.

I'd return to McKeeversville each night after dinner. You could see its fires from miles away, for each family burned its own trash. There was no running water; it had to be hauled in, or else you'd have to filter water from the Colorado, which was thick with silt. There were two outhouses that everyone shared. One of the county workers put slaked lime in them once or twice a week.

Small kids ran about in dirty diapers, screaming; the wind blew sand in my clothes, my eyes, and my nose; and men came home with pale, scared faces, for there were thousands more men than jobs. Then Isaiah would get a campfire sending sparks heavenward, we'd muster up whatever food and drink we'd been able to procure, and Lauren or Anne-Marie would lead us in song. Not hymns, usually, more often just tunes everyone knew, like *Red River Valley* and *Clementine*.

There were times when I'd see David from afar off, a tall figure emerging from the darkness, and other times I only realized he was there when I heard his voice joining ours. He rarely preached, just introduced himself to people, one by one, and got them talking about themselves. Sometimes they'd ask him to tell his story, and when that happened the crowd would fall silent, and all you could hear was David telling tales of God's amazing grace, his voice strong and clear above the lonely howl of the desert wind.

~

One evening, we were cleaning up after almost everyone had gone home when David noticed a lone figure still sitting by the fire, the brim of his cowboy hat shadowing his eyes.

"That's quite a story you tell," said the man. "If it's all true. Which I s'pose it likely is."

"Good evening, sheriff," said David. "Didn't realize you were here."

"Just thought I'd check on what's goin' on in McKeeversville, 'n see what you're up to these days."

"Anything I can do for you?"

Stone stood up and walked closer to the fire to warm his hands.

"Wind's got a bite to it, don't it," he said. "You know, pastor, I'm just a small-town lawman. Vegas used to be a nowhere stop on the railway line, home to four, five thousand souls. But at this rate, we'll be at ten thousand next month, if we ain't there already, and what, fifteen, twenty thousand before long." He fell silent for a few moments and stood there gazing into the fire. "There's bad things headin' this way, Gold. Feels like dark clouds gatherin', with rumors of men who got their eyes on this town, men I'd just as soon shoot on sight. I guess what I'm tryin' ta say is, I'm in over my head. But there ain't nobody else wants this damn job, so here I am. Anyway, you got any prayers to spare, I could use 'em. I could use all you got."

"Let's pray together right now," said David, but the sheriff shook his head and began walking away.

"Nah, I don't know the words like you do. Foolish of me to ask."

"Not at all. I'll be praying for you, Sheriff Stone, count on it."

"Much appreciated," said the sheriff, and then, just as he reached the motorbike he'd parked nearby, he turned back toward David.

"You hear hide or hair of Miss James, make sure 'n let me know, okay? I don't want nuthin' happenin' to her like to her pa."

David nodded, and we watched as the sheriff drove away.

~

"Do you hear that strange singing?" I asked Edward Grimm. Off and on for the past half hour, I'd heard an eerie, high-pitched melody above the whistling wind.

Ed paused to listen, then frowned. "All these years of hammering, my ear drums are shot," he said. "I'm done with this tent, going to stretch my legs, be back in a bit. Take a break yourself, and then it'd be a good idea for you to scrounge us up some more wood."

I set off down one row of tents and pasteboard shacks, curious to know who was singing the plaintive tune. After five minutes of searching, I found the answer: a negro boy, perhaps ten years old, standing in the sand, his eyes closed, his face raised to the sky, crooning his odd, wordless song. I watched him for a while, and then he stopped singing and opened his eyes.

"Hello," I said.

His face was expressionless and he kept his eyes averted, but after a moment, he walked over to me and stood close by.

"You sing well," I told him. "Are there any words to that tune?"

He didn't answer, just moved even closer, so that his face was almost touching my chest.

"You must live here, I guess. Are your mom and dad around?"

That got a reaction from the mute child, and he tugged my arm and turned and headed off. I followed him to the far end of the shantytown, until he stopped in front of one of the tents and uttered an inarticulate, high-pitched cry. A moment later a man emerged.

"Lucas Jackson, where you been, playin' with your ghost friend again?" He turned to me. "He been botherin' you, son?"

"No, sir," I replied. "I was admiring his singing and wondered if he might be lost."

"Go on in, Lucas," said the man, but the boy stepped back and leaned his head against me.

"Well look at that!" The man laughed. "He doesn't much like bein' around anyone but his momma and me, but damned if he ain't taken a fancy to you. Name's Clarence Jackson, pleased to make your acquaintance."

"Luke Noongwook," I said, and we shook hands.

"Lucas and Luke, what do you know. He's one of God's babies," said Mr. Jackson. "Just a child 'a God. Hasn't ever said a word. Sings in his private language to tell us things like he's hungry, or he's off to play with his imaginary friend out in the desert. But you, you're real. Damn if he doesn't think you're his best pal."

"Well, I like him, too, I'd be glad to be his pal. I'm out here all the time, me and my friends from the church, Mr. Trueblood and Mr. Grimm, we can make your tent more secure against the wind, if you like. Wouldn't cost you anything, it's just something we do."

"Wind's about driving us out of our minds, Luke. I'd be thankful to take you up on that offer, as long as I could help out, too."

"Of course." I made a mental note to add the Jackson tent to our list. "Have you had any luck getting a job to work on the dam?" There wasn't any other reason a sane man would be in McKeeversville.

Clarence grimaced, then sat down cross-legged outside his tent and offered me a box to sit on.

"I've been trying. White folks are gettin' hired first, and probably last, too—look around, it's all white faces 'bout as far as the eye can see, 'cept for you and some Navajo I've met. Maybe you're Navajo yourself."

"No, Athabaskan. I'm from the Alaska Territory," I explained.

He laughed hard hearing that, which caused Lucas to walk over and touch his father's face.

"You sure took a wrong turn somewhere, son! Oh my. Alaska territory. Well, if they aren't hiring colored folk here, I might have to try my luck up north, who knows."

"I'm going to tell my pastor about the trouble you're having, Mr. Jackson, he works for Six Companies now. I've got to get back to work, though, and Lucas is welcome to come along with me. Aside from boarding up your tent, is there anything else I can do for you?"

"No, that's all—" He stopped in mid-sentence and looked at me, chewing his lip. "Well, you showing up kind of like an angel, I will ask you something after all, though it might sound crazy. I'd give anything for a fiddle—it'd be for Lucas, it's the one thing he can do, plays that fiddle like you wouldn't believe. I want his momma to hear him play again before she passes on, Luke, and she doesn't have much time. I wouldn't bring it up to you, it weren't for that."

"I am so sorry, sir!" I felt foolish and incompetent, at a loss for words in the face of something so dire as a man facing the impending death of his wife. "Do you need us to find a doctor? Surely there's something that can be done."

He smiled grimly and put his hand on my knee.

"No, no. Charlene's got a disease of the nerves I've seen a few times in my practice. There ain't no cure. Started with her right foot, last year; all of a sudden, she couldn't lift it. Then her whole right leg, then her left, and now her hands are no good. Pretty soon she'll have trouble talking, then breathing. And that's how it'll end. When she's gone, I had the courage, I'd take Lucas with me to the top of Black Canyon and jump, 'cause without her, we're lost."

"You can't do that," I said, horrified.

"'course I *can* do it. What you mean is, I *shouldn't* do it, and you'd be right. I should pick up my cross and carry it like a man, that's what you mean."

I looked down, mortified.

"If it's at all possible, I'll find Lucas a fiddle, Mr. Jackson."

"I know you will, son," he said softly. "And I'm sorry, takin' out my irritation on you, no excuse for that. I trust you with Lucas, any time you want to take him along with you, that's fine with me."

Lucas looked heavenward and uttered one of his high-pitched ululations. His father chuckled.

"That's his way of saying twenty-three skidoo. He becomes a bother, don't worry, the boy knows how to find his way home."

"Understood, sir."

I knew a spot where I could get past the perimeter with a small wheelbarrow and gather up some scrap lumber, so I set off with Lucas in tow.

~

By the beginning of May, with the great construction project about to begin in earnest and the pace of hiring picking up, a great tide of humanity was flooding into Black Canyon, fleeing the Depression and the Dust Bowl and desperate for jobs. Many of them were setting up camp on the Hemenway Wash, where the Colorado River first entered

Black Canyon. We all called the settlement Ragtown, because, like McKeeversville, it was a shantytown where hundreds of families sought shelter in tents, cardboard boxes, anything they could get their hands on to shield themselves from the wind and from the steadily increasing heat.

People washed their clothes in the river and hung them on the mesquite bushes that seemed to be the only vegetation which thrived in the sandy soil. Dysentery was rampant; there wasn't a time when I didn't see men, women, and children lined up to use the outhouses, or running to get behind a large rock. But the worst of it was the ants. If you had fashioned yourself a table, you put the legs in old tin cans filled with water or they'd be swarming your food in no time flat.

At the bottom of the Hemenway Wash was a general store that I'd heard had been set up by the boatman who'd been ferrying folks up and down the river for years, and one day I decided to venture in with Lucas by my side.

"How much for a quart bottle 'a milk, a loaf of white bread, and a pound of butter?" a woman in a threadbare dress asked the shopkeeper.

"Well, what were you used to paying back home?"

She thought for a moment.

"Twelve cents for the milk, ten for the bread, and twenty-nine for the butter. That's what they cost me in Rapid City."

"All right," said the man behind the counter. "Then that's what I'll charge you."

She began counting out change, and it became painfully obvious that she barely had a dime to her name.

"Tell you what, m'am," said the shopkeeper. "You keep that for now. I'll ring up a receipt as an IOU, and you pay me whenever your husband gets work."

"I can't hardly begin to thank you, sir," the woman said softly.

"I'm from Chicago," said the next woman in line. "Used to cost me three cents more for milk and a couple more for bread, but I'd gladly pay the extra if you could give me credit like you did her. My Charley used to be vice president of the First Federal Bank on LaSalle Street, I'm sure he'll be hired here fast as you can say Jack Robinson."

The shopkeeper accommodated her as well, then turned to me.

"I'm buying two pieces of penny candy for my friend Lucas, and paying cold cash," I said, plunking two coins down on the counter.

The man laughed.

"Well, much appreciated, young man, that'll come in handy, the way things are these days. I'm Murl Emery, and you are?"

"Luke Noongwook."

We shook hands.

The two women having left the store, I added, "What you did just before, Mr. Emery, I think that's what the Lord would have done, too."

"The Lord? Oh, you mean Jesus, don't you. Well, about that, I couldn't say. It isn't real complicated, though. Must be three dozen families arriving in Ragtown every day, maybe a thousand a month. Sometimes their cars break down miles from the Valley and they walk here, carrying everything they got on their backs, show up more dead than alive. And there ain't no one whose job it is to feed them or help them in any way. The Feds sure as hell don't give a damn. Six Companies, they figure, one job seeker dies, there's plenty more to take his place. In life, Luke, sometimes you look around and you realize, there's something needs to be done, and no one else is going to do it. You want to sleep at night, you do it, all on your own if need be."

"Mr. Emery, these days I'm working with Ed Grimm, shoring up shelter over in McKeeversville and here in Ragtown. But I get off around two, and I could help out at your store, doing whatever you needed to have done, up till around six o'clock. Wouldn't have to pay me a dime."

He looked me over appraisingly.

"Oh, *that's* who you are, the fellow from up north, works with the church folks. Well, you look sturdy enough, and I can always use a hand. Tell you what, you're serious, I've got a truck full of supplies from Vegas needs to be unloaded and shelved in the storage shed out back."

"Yes, sir, it'd be my pleasure. Long as I can have my friend Lucas here hanging by me, he won't cause any harm."

"No, that's fine." Murl smiled, and then his face grew dark. "Shoring up shelter, you said. There isn't going to be shelter enough, pretty soon, no matter how many boards you hammer in place. The heat bounces off the cliff walls, concentrates in the bottom of Black Canyon—ain't for nothing this place is called Hell's Hole. Here it is, only the first week of May—look at the temperature, Luke, and it'll do nothing but get hotter for the next hundred days."

I looked over at the large thermometer Murl Emery had hung just outside the store.

The mercury was just over one hundred and four degrees.

～

Early one evening, perhaps half an hour before the time when I'd head over to meet Isaiah and help get the campfire going, I felt Lucas tugging on my arm.

"You want me to come with you? All right. Where to?"

Lucas only uttered one of his high-pitched cries and set off at a fast pace while I jogged to keep up behind him. Pretty soon we had passed by the last tents of McKeeversville and were heading out into the desert toward an upward sloping area marked by an outcropping of large rocks.

"This where you play with your imaginary friend?" I wondered as we reached the bottom of a steep incline. Lucas stopped and let loose a plaintive wail. And then my blood ran cold.

An answering tune was coming from somewhere above.

Lucas tugged at me eagerly and we scrambled up the hillside. At the top, we made our way around a narrow ledge to the other side of a huge boulder. There, leaning against the rock wall, was a young woman, and though she was terribly thin, and so deeply tanned by the sun that we could have been brother and sister, and had cut her hair as short as a boy's, I knew at once I was face-to-face with Julia James.

Chapter Thirty-Two
The Absence of God and the Urgency of Love

When Joan awoke early the next morning, she tried to hold on to bits and pieces of the dream in which she'd jumped from the disciple's fishing boat to swim to shore. But the harder she tried to recall what she'd dreamt, the more it slipped away. Well, she thought, it must have been a good one, for though the fleeting images seemed strange enough, they had left her with a blissful sense of peace. She got out of bed, slipped on her bathrobe, and turned on the little coffee maker by the minibar. As soon as the coffee had brewed, she poured a cup, opened the blinds, and stretched out on a couch close to the window to enjoy watching the darkness transform into dawn. Could she see the changes as they occurred, the precise moments when the sky grew lighter? No, there was just an awareness that somehow, in the previous instant, a faint streak of rose or gold had appeared on the eastern horizon.

Ah, but to properly contemplate the break of day, one last thing was needed! What greater pleasure was there than the morning's first smoke? Joan reached for the lighter and pack of Camels she had set on the end table next to the couch.

But her hand froze before she could touch the cigarettes.

From somewhere far away came something like the sound of many waters, cascading, tumbling waters, and then they crashed upon her, rushing rivers went coursing through her, and oh, it was good, it was beyond any pleasure she had ever felt, only that wasn't it, it was beyond words, beyond feeling, and *oh Lord let this last forever, let this never end.*

As suddenly as they had come, the waters left. She had no idea how much time had gone by, only that the sun had risen and chased away the darkness, and that her face was wet with tears, her body soaked with sweat. But this Joan knew: the Holy Spirit had reached inside and ripped the smoking out of her, lifted the smoking from her, washed her clean.

She left the pack on the table; no need to strip them or flush them

232

down the toilet. Still stunned, she found her cell phone and dialed Willie.

Her brother answered after several rings, his voice still groggy with sleep.

"Wake up, Willie," she said. "Or do you want to make yourself coffee and call me back?"

"Uh-unh, hold on a sec. Bunny was just sleepin' with one 'a his ears about up my nose, lemme toss him outta my bed." Joan heard a dull thud. "'kay, all set. Whazzup?"

"I don't smoke anymore," said Joan.

"You quit again? That's great, sissie, more power to ya."

"No, you don't understand. I didn't have anything to do with it, nothing. I couldn't do it. It was done for me, by the Lord."

She felt sheepish for a moment, hearing how it sounded to confess the truth, and then thought, *that's the enemy, going right to work.*

"Yeah?" said Willie. "Well, better yet, then. But don't get over-confident—you know how it is with that nicotine demon, he's like a damn boomerang. So, how long you been off the smokes?"

"This all happened just minutes ago. But I'm telling you, whatever else lies in wait for me, I don't smoke anymore. Honest, you could light up right in front of me, and it wouldn't faze me in the least."

"Okay," said Willie, but she could tell that her brother just didn't get it. "Think the Almighty could work some 'a that magic for me?"

"Oh, gee, of course He can. Will He, though? I don't know. I don't begin to understand why He did this for me."

But even as she said those words, the thought came to her: she'd been given this gift that she might be a witness who would testify to the power of the living God at work in the world. And if not a witness to her brother, then to whom?

But what to say? She felt utterly unprepared!

"He's already died for you, Willie," Joan found herself blurting out. "Do you really need more than that? God became a man, and suffered and died on the cross to free us from sin—from smokes and drugs, swindles and lies, from all the crud that encrusts our lives—and all we need do is turn to Him, trust in Him, stop being control freaks who kid ourselves that we're in charge. Because we're not. If we're not serving the Lord, we're serving the other side. I'm still serving sin, I know it, but, man alive, brother, what I wouldn't give to call myself a slave of Christ!"

"There's lots'a Sundays I show up and listen ta Pastor Dan, Joanie."

"That's great, but it's not what I'm talking about."

"Well, whadda ya want from me, then?"

"It's not what I want, it's what the Lord wants. And He wants everything, He wants all you've got."

She could hear Willie breathing on the other end of the phone. *He's probably zoning out, scratching Bunny's ears. I'm all over the place*, she thought. *I'm blowing it, big-time. Those are words that work for me, not for him.*

"Look, the two of us always wanted a father," she said. "Well, think of the best father you can imagine, and then realize this: God is all that, and so much better yet. And He's right there for you, waiting for you, closer than your own breath."

"Imagine a good father? I'm not sure I can even do *that*. I mean, do you know any good fathers? My old boss, Judson, he's been married three times, has four kids he don't hardly see. *He* thought he had the best dad, sissie, till he was maybe twelve, thirteen years old. That's when it turned out his pops had another family on the far side of the state, 'n all those long business trips he'd been takin' weren't nuthin' but lies."

Joan winced. *Did* she know any? Her stepfather, Lonnie, had been the devil himself.

"I think our dad was a decent father, Willie. If only he hadn't died so young! I wish you remembered him."

Had he been a good father? Joan wondered. She remembered him, suddenly, holding a gun to her mother's head after she'd struck Joan for some trivial offense, like spilling oatmeal on the floor. Willie had been in his highchair, screaming, couldn't have been more than two years old back then. Well, however crazy things might have been, her dad had made her feel safe, that was for sure.

"There's a picture I used ta have," said Willie, "don't know what happened to it, but I can remember every detail, anyhow. Dad, in t-shirt 'n jeans, couldn'a been more'n twenty, standin' next'a his bike. He had a Thunderbird, just like Brando in *The Wild One*. Looked wicked cool; you say he was a good father, I believe ya. But it's a piss-off, ain't it? Why the hell then did God take him away?"

"I don't know," Joan said helplessly. "I wish I had the answers. I can only tell you, I'd given up trying to quit smoking—it was impossible, I could no more quit than fly to the moon. You know it, Willie, you never thought I could quit. I think the Holy Spirit worked this miracle for me so that somehow I could help show you the way to Him. Look, it won't kill you to get down on your knees and pray. Tell the Lord whatever is in your heart, ask Him about our dad, reveal your deepest longings and fears. Will you do that, for me?"

Her brother laughed.

"Might get my face slapped, I revealed quite so much as that. But, hell, Joanie, sure, for you, I'd do that 'n a whole lot more. I mean, you stayin' in touch with me, when I don't got no one else—" His voice trailed off. "'cept Bunny, that is."

"I love you, Willie."

"Love ya, too, sis."

Joan sat staring at the phone for a while after they'd hung up, then took a shower, making the water as hot as she could stand and letting it pour over her while she leaned her head against the shower wall and prayed.

~

So entranced was Tim by Vickie's voluptuous innocence, and by her desire for him, that it did not strike him as especially strange for an oaken door to have appeared in the desert waste. Nor was he startled when he stepped through and found himself in an elegant elevator car, dimly lit, with mirrors on all four sides.

Vicki followed him in, pressed a button, and down they went.

"Where are we—" he started to say.

"Shhh," she said, and then put her arms around him, and kissed him, at first softly and then harder, and her body was melting into his so that he could feel every one of her curves, and his very hunger for her was itself a greater pleasure than any mere satisfaction he had ever before received.

Look at that, Tim thought, catching a glimpse of himself endlessly reflected in the four mirrors—quite a handsome dude, in excellent shape, really, and still with a fine, full head of hair! Small wonder such an intelligent, gorgeous girl as Vicki wanted him. Something seemed wrong with how long it was taking for them to reach their destination— the structure must be some sort of inverted skyscraper, he reasoned, reaching one hundred, two hundred stories below the surface of the earth—but a sense of danger only added to the thrill. Wasn't this what it was all about, abandoning all caution and giving oneself up to passion, to being swept up in the terrible, beautiful madness of love?

The kiss went on and on, and still the elevator plunged ever downward.

~

"Henry Mencken, Mr. Faber," said the studious-looking man with the slick hair parted in the middle, "Your reputation proceeds you. We've been eagerly awaiting your arrival."

Vicki had excused herself when they'd finally arrived, explaining there was something she needed to do, and introduced Tim to a younger woman, Catina, who would attend to him in her absence. The new girl in turn had led him to this Mr. Mencken, who, she said, was the master of ceremonies at a "samovar" taking place in the next room.

"You've an advantage over me, it seems," said Tim. "This was all a surprise arranged by Ms.—" he paused, realizing that he didn't even know his lover's last name—"by Vicki. I have no idea what's going on."

"Hmm?" said Mencken. "Really. Well, come along, you'll soon see, it's right up your alley. Lucretius has just finished presenting his paper, *On Atheism and Divine Indifference*, and we're on to question-and-answer. This should be quite interesting—the agnostics get along with the Epicureans well enough, but some of the hard-core atheists love to give them a hard time. Follow me!"

Faber smiled; evidently, the girl had meant to say "seminar." He and Catina followed the emcee into what turned out to be a vast amphitheater, and then another thought flashed through his mind.

"Henry Mencken, you said—do you mean H.L. Mencken, by any chance?"

"Yes, of course," said the man, who sounded somewhat annoyed.

How amusing, thought Tim. Leave it to Oz to hire actors to play the greatest atheists and skeptics of all time! This must be his way of showing me his ideas for my ten-part series, *God is Not the Answer*. Well, he had to admit, the casino magnate might be an amateur, but he'd come up with just the sort of whimsical touch that could win a larger audience. Indeed, done right, this could be Emmy material!

"Next question, please," called out Mencken, and a number of hands eagerly waved. "Yes, Aristophanes—" he pointed to a man seated in the third row, wearing a t-shirt and jeans—"the floor is yours, by all means."

One of the emcee's assistants ran over and handed the Greek playwright a microphone.

"I always enjoy listening to you, my friend," said Aristophanes. "But please, come clean with us, if only just this once. Admit it: your belief in the gods is purely pro forma, is it not?"

Lucretius, who had been leaning forward against the speaker's podium, straightened up, took off his wire-rim glasses, and sipped from a bottle of Evian before deigning to answer.

"My point, dear Ari—and it's one which, I might add, I've made more than a time or two before—is that to debate a matter that can neither be proved or disproved is simply a waste of time. What difference if the gods exist? Everything can be explained by the meaningless motion of atoms in the great void. What gods there may be are quite indifferent to what happens here; they are neither to blame for our afflictions, nor to praise for the small victories in our lives. Our actions neither anger nor please them; for just as *apatheia* is our ideal, so surely it is theirs."

This last line brought a smattering of applause.

"I must say, though, that some of you make rather egregious misuse of materialism. The world about us may be random and chaotic, but our own response to it need not be so. My friend Friedrich and I have argued this point a time or two." Someone elbowed a dour-looking, shabbily-dressed man with a dark walrus mustache who had been dozing off in one of the back rows. "This noble philosophy can never be an excuse for immorality. No, for shame! That it is in our interest to lead a virtuous life ought to be self-evident to everyone in this room."

With that, the speaker picked up his lecture notes and left the podium to a mixed chorus of cheers and boos.

"Lucretius, ladies and gentlemen!" said Mencken, trying to stir up some applause. "That concludes this week's seminar, see you all next Thursday, when our guest of honor will be my friend, Art Schopenhauer, lecturing on *The Absence of God and the Urgency of Love*. I for one can't wait!"

He turned to Tim as people began to get up and leave the room.

"Come, I'll introduce you to Lucretius. I've been trying to get him more involved in our publicity efforts, and that is, after all, exactly where you come in."

Mencken brought the two men together and then excused himself to attend to other matters.

"If you don't mind my asking," said Tim, after the two had shaken hands, "if you're supposed to be Lucretius, why are you wearing khakis and a UNLV sweatshirt? Wouldn't a toga be more in character? Or perhaps you do the rehearsals in street clothes."

The Roman poet looked at him, nonplussed.

"This is 2011, and we're not at a frat party," he said. "So why would I be wearing a toga, for goodness sake?"

Tim was not sure what to say to that.

"Are you planning on using any sort of accent?" he asked. "Seems an upper-class British accent works well for playing the ancients, though of course it makes little enough sense."

Lucretius only stared at him, then looked at his watch.

"Look, I wouldn't mind hearing a bit about these publicity plans H.L. has been telling me about, but, frankly, there's some primo blow in the next room, and I'm supposed to meet Shaw there right now. You want to come along, do a few lines, that's fine with me."

"Wait a minute," said Tim. "You're trying to tell me that you're a Stoic—"

"Epicurean," the other corrected him.

"—and yet you're into coke?"

Lucretius shrugged.

"If good blow's available, I partake; if not, I do not mourn its absence." He looked at his watch again. "Let's go, or Shaw'll have snorted it all himself."

"Shaw? George Bernard Shaw?"

"Who else? Now, you coming or not?"

"Wouldn't miss it for the world," said Tim, and he and Catina trotted down the hall behind Lucretius, who was walking at a brisk pace. The hallway walls were mirrored and lit with a dim, rosy light, the sort that would make a dead man look like he was in the bloom of good health. Faber glanced at the young woman, who stuck close by his side. Her face was heavily made up, her eyelashes almost ludicrously dark and thick with mascara. Not the type he usually went for, but still, she was cute, there was no denying that, and he felt a stirring of desire.

Lucretius knocked on the door of the next room, then pushed it open, and he and Tim and Catina entered into the darkness within.

Chapter Thirty-Three
Water, Fire, and Blood

"Hello, Luke Noongwook," said the frail young woman to whom Lucas had led me. He scrambled over next to her, and she drew the boy close to her and gently stroked his hair while he looked up toward the sky.

"He's listening to angels," she whispered.

"Hello, Julia James," I said quietly, and she gave me a wan smile. "Did you ask Lucas to bring me here?" My mind was swimming with questions I wanted to ask.

"No," she laughed, "he found you for me all on his own."

"I know you from the photo Lauren showed me. But how do you know my name?"

"Oh, I've had my eyes on you ever since Lucas told me about your meeting. You know, you're not the most observant fellow. There were times I was so close, you should have felt my breath on the back of your neck. If I'd been the enemy, your goose would have been thoroughly cooked. So, you see, I know much more about you than your name. I know you work hard, and I know you've a quick mind, and a good heart, and value others above yourself. And that you're a handsome young man, in your way."

I was too stunned to think before I spoke.

"You're not embarrassed to talk like that? I mean, I've thought about you ever since the stories I heard from Lauren and Isaiah, and especially since I saw your photograph, but I could never have dreamed of telling you that just minutes after we first met."

"But you just did, didn't you? Anyway, why would you ever be ashamed of speaking the truth? That would be like being ashamed of Christ."

"How does that follow?" I asked. "Surely some things that are true are shameful nonetheless."

"You're speaking of *facts*," Julia replied. "I'm speaking of truth. Is there anything in how you've thought of me which you would be ashamed to admit before the Lord?"

"No," I said, and was surprised and grateful to realize I'd spoken no lie.

"Of course not. So neither of us have cause for regret when the hidden is revealed." Lucas gave voice to one of his eerie melodies, and Julia laughed. "He wants to know if I'll marry you," she explained, before singing to him in return.

"What did you tell him?" I asked.

"None of your beeswax! You have to actually ask a woman before she'll give you an answer, you know. You don't have much experience in love, clearly! You're not a worldly man at all, are you."

"No," I admitted, crestfallen that, just as my dream of meeting Julia had come true, I'd spoiled everything by revealing my naivety.

Julia sang again to Lucas, who reached up and touched her face.

"I told him I was only teasing you," she said. "I'm glad you're not worldly; our Father's Kingdom is not of this world. I haven't much experience either, really—there were only two years when I wasn't by my father's side, and I've never sought the company of young men. At least, not until Lucas told me of you."

I blushed, and hoped my skin was dark enough that it didn't show.

"But this is foolishness," she said, with a sudden sharpness. "I'm too odd a girl, I shan't inflict myself on any man, or on children who might fear their own mother, for there are tongues of flame that come and dance in me, that burn me from the inside and scorch my mind. When I was young, I came home one day and told my father I'd heard our neighbors saying I was *touched*. Do you know what he did? He swept me up in his arms and said, 'Yes, darling dear one, touched by God.' Then a shadow passed over his face, and he muttered, 'And yet, He's given you too much of heaven's fire.' 'But poppa,' I said, 'surely the Lord makes no mistakes.' I had him there, didn't I, Luke! 'That's true,' he admitted, and he stroked his beard. 'Only, He's given you a gift that's a heavy cross for such a little one to bear. We rejoice in our sufferings, and fill up in our flesh what is still lacking in the afflictions of Christ; only, Lord, let me bear the pain, and not my Julia, who is so small. Still, Your will be done, not mine.'

"Can you imagine how much I miss him?" she continued. "I've

wondered terrible things—whether my father's murder was in some way an answer to his prayer. For I've been baptized with water and with fire, but there is also the baptism of blood; did he take upon himself what was meant for me? But that couldn't have been an answer from God, for nothing evil ensues from Him."

Julia fell silent, as though contemplating this thought.

"I *can* imagine how much you miss him," I told her. Troubled by the pain she'd revealed to me, and eager to establish common ground between us, I told her my own strange, sad story while she leaned back against the rock wall, stroking Lucas' nappy hair. "Sometimes I wake in the deep of night, fearing that my father is forever lost, that he'll be doomed to hell," I said, after finishing my tale. "I can't bear to think it, Julia—to think of him eternally separated from God. Sometimes it about drives me mad."

"I don't believe anyone can be separated from God," she told me, "for in Him we live and move and have our being. You mustn't worry over matters you can't control—that's no different than worrying about the morrow. But you must pray for him, Luke, pray for your father morning, noon, and night, pray for him with all your heart. Trust in the One who sets all things right, and remember the Lord's words: *And I, when I am lifted up from the earth, will draw all people to myself.*"

"Yes, but what if my father never—" I caught myself before saying any more. "There I go, fretting about what should be left to God. I need to learn how to pray without ceasing—how I'd like to ask Timothy if he ever learned!" A quiet came over me, and I sat down on a nearby ledge and listened to the high, thin sound of Lucas' song.

"The pain you suffer from those tongues of flame, Julia," I said after a while, "does that happen when you're told that the rains are coming, and the dry riverbeds will be filled?"

"Some pain is itself a joy," she answered. "Those visions are like that."

"There's something I need to tell you," I said, and related the story of what had happened after Lauren had shown me Julia's quotation from Psalm Fifty-Five.

"Ah, I'm to blame," she said, sorrowfully. "I'd been thinking of King

David, who wrestled so often with the desire for revenge; I yearned to be free of those demons, and to be a dove of peace. Luke, when I witnessed my father's murder, it stirred the fires inside me, it became like a cauldron in my brain."

"You know who the killer is? Does he know you know?"

"Oh yes, he knows. He will not rest until I join my father in the grave."

"What a monster! No wonder you fled to the desert!"

She shook her head.

"You don't understand. I didn't flee out of fear for my own life, but for his. More than anything, I thirsted for vengeance to be mine. I didn't trust myself to be near here; I travelled by train and by foot, north toward Tonopah, where the desert meets the mountains and the stars blaze like torches in the night. I joined the Joshua Trees in prayer, and begged the Lord to put out the raging fire in my heart. I lived in the hollow trunk of a dead tree, and my companions were the desert woodrats who lived there, too, and ventured out at dark to forage. They're collectors, you know, and brought me many gifts. And night lizards would join us, tiny creatures no bigger than my little finger, green and blue and every shade of gray and brown. I meant to stay there for forty days; I stayed until I saw a vision of my father, telling me to go, and I knew my lust for vengeance was no more."

"But who is the killer? And what are you going to do now?" I asked, so transfixed by Julia's story that I didn't stop to think she would already have told me if she'd wanted me to know. "Surely there is some way that I can help. I have been tested more than once and have no fear of danger."

"It might be wise to fear," she said, and gave me a grim smile. "There may well be a time when I need your help; but for now, for your own good, I shan't tell you more."

A thought occurred to me that made me wince.

"Pastor Gold asked me to let him know if I ever heard anything about you. I know he's concerned for you, Julia, and I can't keep anything from him ever again."

She looked down and nodded.

"I understand. Tell the pastor what you know, even where we met this time. I won't reveal my hiding place, so your ignorance of my whereabouts will be nothing but the truth."

"But how will I see you again?"

"Lucas will find you. Now go, both of you, for the flames inside me are leaping and dancing. Go now!"

Lucas uttered a high, mournful wail as he took off running, and I followed at his heels.

~

By the end of May, David and I were both working on the tunnels that would divert the Colorado River so that the dam could be built on dry land. Neither Isaiah nor Clarence had yet been hired, although Trueblood's Indian heritage got him a promised job as one of the high scalers, the men who would dangle from ropes hundreds of feet above the canyon floor, pack dynamite into the stone walls, then swing out of the way before the blasts went off. Several Navajo were waiting for those jobs to begin in another year or two; no white folk had as yet expressed much interest in that line of work.

There would be four diversion tunnels, each one fifty feet in diameter and extending through four thousand feet of solid rock. Someone had come up with the idea of creating a two-story steel frame on top of a ten-ton truck; these were the jumbos, each carrying thirty men who worked the liners, jackhammers supplied by air and water lines, all drilling away at once. It was the only way the tunnels could possibly be completed on time.

I was assigned to work as a nipper on a jumbo, handing drilling steel to the men who worked the liners. When thirty holes had been drilled, each about ten feet deep, the men would pack them with primer using a long stick. They were using mercury fulminate, and if a man wasn't careful, the primer would go off in his face. They'd place dynamite in front or behind the primer and bring the wires out, tie them in place, and get the jumbo backed away before the shoot.

It took one ton of explosives to extend a tunnel fourteen feet into the canyon walls. We used an awful lot of dynamite.

The hiring boss, Danny White, had taken one look at David and brought him on as an oiler, one of the men who moved in after a blast to muck out broken rock with power shovels and hand tools. Before long, he was made a Cat skinner, operating a Caterpillar tractor for his mucking crew. He worked graveyard on the weekends, so that after a short nap he could preach on Sunday mornings by campfires at Ragtown and McKeeversville and under an oak tree in the park by the railroad depot in Las Vegas. Sheriff Stone, who collected motorcycles, loaned him a 1928 Indian Big Chief with a sidecar, and I learned every bump in the road as he drove us back and forth during the next several years.

After we'd hired on with Six Companies and established ourselves as good workers, David took me with him to see Danny and explained that we were looking for my father. "His name is Victor or Taliriktug Noongwook, " he told the hiring boss, "but he might well be using another—if you come across any man with the initials VN, or TN, I'd be much obliged if you'd let me know."

I gave Danny one of my few remaining pictures, and he pinned it to a corkboard and told us he'd keep my father in mind.

~⟫

After work one day, as I was approaching McKeeversville, I saw Lucas from perhaps fifty yards away. He was staring at the heavens and singing, as he did so often, but there were three men nearby, mocking him, and one of them was throwing stones at the boy.

"Nigger boy's too damn dumb to duck," the man laughed, as the stone struck Lucas in the face.

I broke into a run, but before I could get there, a woman tore into the three, knocking two to the ground and bringing a knife up to the stone-thrower's throat. Then she sliced off the man's belt so that his pants sagged down, and brought the knife down next to his crotch.

It was an ulu knife.

"You're not a man," said my mother, "so perhaps it would be best if

I relieved you of the burden of your manhood. Do you not agree?"

"Get this crazy bitch away from me," he cried out to his companions, but in a few bounds I was in front of them, with my hunting knife unsheathed.

"Move an inch and you're dead men," I said.

"Apologize to the boy," said my mother. The man gaped at her, frozen in fear. "*Now!*"

"I'm sorry, kid," said the bully. "We was just foolin', honest we were."

Lucas came over, his eyes still lifted upwards, stroked the man's face, and then scampered off.

"Now leave," my mother commanded the three men, "and never trouble the lad again."

I looked around; quite a crowd had gathered, including Edward Grimm, whose eyes I had never seen open quite so wide.

"Mr. Grimm," said my mother. "I've come to volunteer my services. I have some skill with woodworking myself, yet no one has ever asked me to help."

"Uhm," said Edward. "Mrs. Noongwook, I'd, uhm, be delighted, we can always use another hand."

"Mother," I said, but she kept her gaze on Grimm.

"Well," said Edward, "I suppose I'll be getting back to work now."

"Thank you, Mother," I said, and went over and put my arms around her. After a few moments, she turned and put her arms around me, too.

"Well, I'll be heading off, then" said Edward. "Join me anytime, no rush."

The crowd slowly drifted away. Lucas found his way back and leaned against the two of us, singing softly, and we stood there like that for a very long time.

Chapter Thirty-Four
Eternal Life

"Here's something else I don't get," I said. "How John gets to call himself—or someone, anyway—'the disciple whom Jesus loved.'"

My mother and I had built a shack in Ragtown, and five of us had gathered there for dinner one sweltering evening in late June. Mother and David were peeling carrots and potatoes and tossing them into a kettle that was bubbling on a kerosene stove, while Edward and Isaiah and I looked on, our stomachs grumbling in eager anticipation.

"I mean, does God really love some more than others?" I continued. "And how could He have said He loved Jacob but hated Esau? I'm just not seeing how Esau was all that bad. His Son told us to even love our enemies, so how can the Father, who *is* Love, hate?"

"Ah, you remind me of my young self," said David, smiling. "A lot gets lost in the translation of the Hebrew, Luke. Loving Jacob and hating Esau is a way of saying that God *chose* Jacob over Esau. In that sense, the Hebrews might have said that God loved Abraham and hated the rest of the world!"

"Keep peeling," said my mother, who was considerably faster than the pastor when it came to wielding a knife.

"That makes sense," I said, "but it doesn't address my question about the 'beloved disciple.' Did Jesus really have a favorite?"

"With these big, clumsy hands of mine, I need to focus," said David. "I'll just listen while the rest of you figure it out."

"It seems to me that Jesus showed infinite love for *everyone* by dying for us on the Cross," I said. "That's what throws me for a loop."

"Well, m-m-maybe it's like this," said Isaiah. "Maybe you can show more love for someone who loves you back—you know, do more things with 'em, have more fun. Someone's runnin' away from you, can't hardly h-h-hug 'em or anything, not like if they was runnin' towards you."

Knowing of his love for Julia, Isaiah's words made me feel like a louse. Was it a kind of lying not to have revealed to him that I'd met her?

It didn't seem that anything would be gained by such an admission—or was that only an excuse?

"That's a good point, Isaiah," I said. "I can't love my father in the same way when it seems he doesn't want me to find him."

Mother had recently written to Chinook Ray, who'd responded that he'd heard not even a rumor of her husband's whereabouts.

"I don't know," said Edward Grimm. "When I'm out among the winged creatures, and those that creep and crawl, my heart swells with yet larger love and compassion because they can't love me back—at least, not in any way that I recognize as such. I've wondered whether God thinks of us much like that. Don't the weak and pitiful—the unloving and seemingly unlovable!—need us yet more than those who have been blessed with the power to love?"

"Do you mean, Mr. Grimm, that love is something undeserved, like a gift of grace?" asked my mother. I was startled, thinking she'd been absorbed in preparing our meal.

"Well, yes, Yura, at least God's love, in any event."

"It seems to me you are correct," my mother went on, "for God showed His love for us while we were still sinners. But, as Mr. Trueblood's words suggest, our responses to His love allow Him to use us in different ways. The beloved disciple had such strong faith: he believed at the empty tomb, and then on the fishing boat he alone recognized Jesus from afar off. Therefore, gentlemen, I think Pastor Gold has already supplied the answer. Was not the beloved disciple *chosen* by Jesus, charged with looking after Mary as though he were her very own son?"

"Persuasively put," said Grimm.

"Lay it on us!" said Isaiah. "Ain't that the t-t-truth."

"Mother," I said, this being yet another occasion when I spoke before I thought, "I had no idea you were so well versed in Holy Scrip—"

"Do you think you are the only one with eyes to see and ears to hear?" she said, looking up from her work for the first time.

"She's a book or two ahead of you in the Old Testament, Luke," said David, as he tossed a potato he'd been whittling for a considerable time into the fire.

"Just peel the skin, please, pastor," said my mother, "we can ill afford to waste good food."

～

Two days later, Lucas handed me a note before swiftly scampering off.

The waters will flow tomorrow evening. Start at sunset, where Tumbleweed Trail begins; torches will mark the way.

I had told David of my meeting with Julia, though not of my feelings for her, and although he thought she was making a terrible mistake by staying hidden in the desert, he was glad he'd be able to communicate with her through me.

"Try to convince her to trust me, and let me—let all of us—help her," he had told me. "I know what it feels like to be alone when those you love have died before your eyes, and you feel like nothing more than a hunted beast." He was surely talking about his time in the Great War, and for a moment he paused, lost in thought. "That's when prayers can seem like a message in a bottle, tossed into a limitless sea, when all the time you've been whispering right into God's ear."

That night, David spread the word and about a dozen of us gathered the next evening at the trailhead on the outskirts of McKeeversville. A torch was clearly visible in the distance as we started off with our pastor in the lead. Anne-Marie, Lauren, and Polwarth were there, and Isaiah carried Mr. Merkle on his back. Mother and I were to be baptized, along with a very large man with a clean-shaved, if somewhat misshapen head, and several of his friends, who occasionally grumbled and fought amongst themselves, though the big fellow, whom I came to know as Mr. Skull, did his best to keep them in line.

"Don't emboweth me, you mawahns!" he'd say to them under his breath, giving one or the other a powerful smack upside the head to make sure they got the point. He and his contingent had been regular participants at Sunday services, though whether his associates' attendance was entirely voluntary was a matter of some debate.

Julia had placed twelve torches, each one or two hundred yards apart, and after a mile of hiking we arrived at a dry arroyo. The sky had turned dark with clouds earlier in the day, and we'd heard the sound of thunder associated with the brief, monsoon-like rainstorms that sometimes bring a few moments of relief from the intense summer heat. But all we saw upon our arrival was a barren ravine that had been carved into the rock.

Then came a sound, though at first it was only a vibration, a shaking of the earth. Soon, it became a distant rumbling, and next a roaring, and finally an explosion of rushing, foaming waters tearing around the far bend. We watched in awe, and even Skull's friends fell silent.

David waded in when it seemed safe to enter, and motioned for my mother to join him. After each baptism, Lauren sang hymns out into the desert night:

"My God, accept my heart this day,
"And make it always thine,
"That I from thee no more may stray,
"No more from thee decline.
"Before the cross of him who died,
"Behold, I prostrate fall;
"Let every sin be crucified,
"And Christ be all in all."

Mine was to be the last of the baptisms that evening. Was I ready to die, I asked myself, to die into my Savior's will, into His love, into eternal life?

David motioned for me to come quickly, for the ephemeral river was already beginning to recede. Let me die well, I thought, and be reborn from above, a son of God.

When David brought me up from the swirling water, I could hear Lauren singing,

"Be Thou my vision, O Lord of my heart
"Naught be all else to me, save that Thou art.
"Thou my best thought by day or by night
"Waking or sleeping, Thy presence my light."

Her melody was eerily echoed by Lucas, who must have followed us, and was hiding somewhere in the darkness.

⤳

The next day, my small friend found me as I left work and led me to a lonely spot on the cliffs, high above Black Canyon.

"Were you there?" I asked Julia. "Did you see?"

"Of course, Lucas and I saw everything," she said, smiling. "How could you even ask me that!"

"You're not well!" I exclaimed, seeing the dark circles under her eyes. "These visions you have when a storm will fill the arroyos, they hurt you, don't they."

She put her index finger against my lips.

"Shush. Do you think pain is always so dreadful? There are agonies you thank God for, terrible and beautiful, as I imagine the pain of childbirth would be. The waters come and go so quickly, don't they, so very quickly, Luke. Sometimes I think of the vanishing rivers as though it were my own blood that was draining away, as though I were being poured out for the Body of Christ. And blessed am I if that is true!"

We hungered to know everything about each other's lives. I told her of the times when my father had let me come with him to gatherings at the home of the Angakkuq; how I'd loved to lean against him, close my eyes and grow drowsy as the men talked, the fireplace crackled, and the stars wheeled across the sky. I told her tales of the tundra, of hunting moose and caribou, of watching the swooping and soaring of peregrine falcons, golden eagles, and red-tailed hawks.

Sometimes we simply listened to the whisperings and rustlings within the great silence of the night.

One day, I was awakened in the small hours of the morning by Lucas' strange singing outside our Ragtown shack, and he led me again to the perch overlooking the canyon. I sat close to Julia and learned to see the shades of rose and gold that glimmered within the dark shadows on the cliffside before sunrise.

We shared the dying of the sunset and the resurrection of the desert dawn.

Above all, we shared our love for the Word.

Eternal Life

One night, I told her of the discussion we'd had about the beloved disciple the week before, and how my mother's remarks had set me meditating on John 3:16: *For God so loved the world that he gave his only Son, that whoever believes in Him should not perish but have eternal life.*

"I'd even heard that verse before I became a Christian, I'd seen it on signs carried around by odd-looking people on city streets, though I didn't know what it meant. So I feel like I've known it forever. But when I thought about the words, I realized their meaning is not so obvious as I thought at first."

"How so?" Julia asked me.

"Well, what exactly does it mean to believe in Him? Simply to acknowledge that He exists? Even the demons did that! But John also wrote a letter in which he said, *'whoever does the will of God lives forever'*—and since 'living forever' is the same thing as 'eternal life,' the *doing* of God's will must be the same as *believing* in Him. Which must be why David—Pastor Gold—always says obedience to the Lord comes before everything else. We believe with our actions, with putting forth our own will to join with God's."

"Luke, I'll live my life trying to do the Lord's bidding, or gladly die trying."

"And I with you!" I exclaimed.

Unlike Julia, however, I had as yet only a glimmering of what it might mean to *count the cost.*

"So, you think you understand John 3:16 now?" she asked me, playfully. "Then what does the Apostle mean by 'eternal life'?"

"No mystery there; that same verse from his letter—1 John 2:17— says we 'live forever.' Surely that's the meaning of 'eternal life'!"

"Ha! You're confusing an *attribute* of eternal life with its essence. Really, he made it so clear in the seventeenth chapter of his Gospel—"

"Wait a minute! Don't tell me." I called up an image of the first page of the chapter in my mind, then blushed when I realized what was written in the third verse. *"'This is eternal life, that they know you, the only true God, and Jesus Christ whom You have sent.'* You're right! I'm quite the simpleton, it would seem." I thought for a moment. "Yes, and there's 1 Timothy 6:12, *'take hold of the eternal life to which you were called.'* So, eternal life is a *kind* of life, it's the life God wants us to live."

"Which means you and I can live it right now, Luke! But wait a minute yourself, just how much Scripture do you have in that head of yours?"

"That's just how my mind works, Julia; when I see or hear or read something, it gets filed away in my brain, and all I need to do is rummage around till I can call it back up. God made me that way, for some reason."

"I'll hardly need a Bible, then," she said, and leaned her head against my shoulder, "if I've got you nearby."

"Well, I don't have it *all* memorized, not yet."

"Why not?"

"I've gotten a bit bogged down in the Old Testament. My mother has evidently got the jump on me there."

"Hmm, that will never do. Why don't you start reciting Genesis, and we'll see how far you get."

"Okay," I said. "But tell me, when you read *In the beginning*, doesn't it make you think about what came before? Before the beginning, I mean. It's unfathomable, I know that, but still, I *want* to fathom it. All I can imagine is a great, dark stillness. Strange, isn't it, to think of a time when there wasn't a yesterday, just an ever-present *now*. Gives me a lonely feeling, somehow."

"There wouldn't have been any loneliness, though," she said. "For there was always God, and His Son, and the Holy Spirit besides."

Julia shivered suddenly, though it must have been over one hundred degrees, and I put my arm around her.

"Are you all right?"

"It will pass," she whispered. "Just hold me, Luke."

I hugged her tightly, and we sat in silence for quite a while and watched the rising of the harvest moon, a great golden ghost floating up into the sky above Black Canyon.

Chapter Thirty-Five
The Last Farthing

Tim awoke, naked, in a bedroom lit by the same dim, rose-colored light that seemed to prevail everywhere in the subterranean world to which he'd been led. For a moment, he couldn't remember how he had come to be there, and then memories began flooding back. After Mencken's strange seminar had ended, he and Lucretius—and someone else, he was pretty sure—had entered into a dark parlor, where George Bernard Shaw had greeted them brusquely, then set about pouring shots of what the playwright insisted was the only Irish whiskey worth drinking, a peated single malt from County Galway.

Tim couldn't remember how many shots they'd downed, but figured he must have snorted at least three or four lines of coke, for he could feel the dried blood in his nose, and his head ached the way it always did after doing too much blow.

But what was this? A naked woman lay next to him under the sleek satin covers. Ah, of course, Catina. After the coke, they'd started talking and she'd proudly told him she was in training to learn the secrets of sacred sex, to become a temple prostitute like her mentor, Vicki, whom Mr. Osman had announced would be the star attraction at the Shrine of Marduk atop the Etemenanki, the Tower of Babel. At first he'd seethed with jealousy and anger at having been played for a fool; but then, with Shaw's peated whiskey and the Bolivian marching powder setting fire to his brain, the thought of other men having their way with Vicki had begun to excite him. They'd left the Roman and the Irishman and retired to the privacy of an adjacent chamber, where, in a canopied bed, he'd had his way with Catina, thinking of Vicki all the while.

What a night! If only it didn't feel like someone was pounding an anvil inside his brain. He sighed and looked over at his sleeping companion. Much of the heavy makeup she'd been wearing was gone, and the thought came to Tim that she looked like a sweet, innocent young woman.

Suddenly, he was filled with a feeling of dread.

He pulled back the covers. The soft, unlined face, small breasts, and narrow hips—he was looking at a mere girl! In disbelief, he shook her shoulder, at first gently, then harder.

"Wake up! Please!"

"Hmm?" Catina said drowsily, then smiled and reached out to touch him. "Are you upset with me? I pleased you, didn't I? I can please you again."

He shrank back in horror.

"How old are you?"

"I'm not a *child*," she replied, pouting. "It's been two years since I first began to bleed."

"NO!" He scrambled off the bed and gathered up his pants and shirt. "This can't have happened. I can't have slept with you, it can't be true."

Was he going mad? Tim dressed hastily and ran barefoot out into the hall, the girl's anguished wail cutting him like a knife. He tore down the empty passageway, confused, with no sense of where the elevator which had brought him there might be found. He tried door after door and found them all bolted shut.

"Mencken!" he shouted. "Lucretius! Aristophanes! Shaw!"

No one answered. He was alone but for his own image, endlessly reflected in the mirrors that lined both sides of the hallway walls.

Can I be dreaming? he thought. No, this sort of brain-crushing pain didn't happen in dreams. Tim tried to keep a rising sense of panic at bay. I'll retrace my footsteps, have Catina show me the way out of here.

After walking countless hallways and trying a hundred, then two hundred doors, he realized he was searching in vain. All right, he was a smart man, surely he could figure out some method of escape. Ah, the ceiling, of course! As dim as the light was, he could make out the sort of panels used in most commercial offices to provide access to electrical wiring and ductwork. They seemed about five or six feet over his head; he just needed a chair or table to stand on.

But after hours of searching, Tim had found nothing he could use to climb up, and sank to the floor in despair.

"Help me, please," he heard himself murmur. But to whom was he talking? His reflection mocked him from the mirrored wall. There was something curious about the figure in the mirror—he had never looked so good! He was handsome, dashing, freshly shaved, his cheeks rosy with health, his eyes bright and hair perfectly coiffed—

But that's impossible. He touched his face and could feel stubble, reached up and felt his hair in wild disarray. Tears streaked his cheeks, but the perfect face in the mirror only looked back at him with an idiot's grin.

"No! You're a lie!" He rose to his feet and pounded on the mirror. "You're not me! That's not who I am! Damn you! DAMN YOU TO HELL!"

The hallway lights flickered for a moment, and then, after the blow that had accompanied his last words, a spider web of cracks began to spread across the mirror, obscuring his reflection. In desperation, he dug a fingernail into one of the cracks and tried to pry out the glass. Eventually, a piece broke off, and then another. He had only expected the mirror to be a thin layer, but to his astonishment, the chunks he was removing went two or three inches deep into the wall.

He removed as much as he could, creating a narrow ledge about five feet off the floor. If he could hoist himself up to stand on it, he'd be able to reach the panels! Tim placed the fingers of both hands on the ledge and winced. It was impossible to avoid the pieces of razor-sharp glass that remained despite his best efforts to break them off. Still, there was no other way, so he took off his shirt and tore off strips to wrap around his hands.

"Jesus Christ!" he cried out in agony as he pulled himself up onto the ledge. He had spoken the name of the Son of God as an expletive, in response to pain; but there it was, nonetheless, echoing down the empty hall.

The strips of shirt hadn't offered much protection, and the jagged glass was now also cutting into the soft flesh of his feet. He crouched on the ledge, blood dripping from his feet and hands, breathing in through his nose and slowly exhaling through pursed lips, trying to slow down the wild beating of his heart. After a few minutes, he rose cautiously and reached up to touch the ceiling panels.

Yes! They were easy to push out of the way, revealing a space about two feet high between the ceiling and the flooring above. He'd just have to haul himself up again using his wounded hands. Tim gathered his strength for the effort; above all, he must not fall back onto the floor!

With a great groan, he hoisted himself up and began to crawl forward to see what he could find, leaving a trail of blood behind him. His first thought had been to see if he could find another human being by looking down into one of the locked rooms, but the more he considered that, the more uneasy he became. What if there were some sort of insane conspiracy against him, if he were being held prisoner in this nightmarish place?

After a long time, making his way slowly through the narrow horizontal shaft and pausing periodically to turn onto his back and examine what was overhead, he raised his head and yelped in pain as it struck against a hard piece of metal. Groaning, he turned over to see what he'd come up against.

It was the bottom rung of a ladder.

His eyes strained in the gloom. The ladder seemed to climb up the side of a vertical shaft which rose he knew not how high, but after a few moments, he made out something which made his heart skip a beat: a tiny dot of light. Might the ladder be on the outside of the elevator shaft, and lead him to back to the surface of the earth?

There was only one way to find out. He unwrapped his hands and examined them; the cuts looked ugly, and several of his fingers were badly swollen. He couldn't see his feet, but there were sharp, burning pains in his heels and several toes. Could he actually climb all the way to the top? Tim tried to think how many floors he might have descended with Vicki, but he'd been oblivious, absorbed not so much in their kiss as in the ecstasy of thinking himself as the man whom a beautiful young woman desired. In any event, there was no question of going back. He'd rather fall to his death then return to the hallway and the presence of that hideous creature who had stared back at him from those mirrored walls!

He rewrapped his hands. His mouth was desperately dry, and,

before climbing, he leaned forward to lick some drops of moisture that clung to the rusted metal rails.

Somehow, I'm going to do this, he thought.

Somehow.

～

"William! Quit your dallying and come out here!"

Ah crap, Willie thought to himself. He was crouched down in Oz Osman's private bathroom, secreting a gallon-sized baggie filled with capsules behind the plumbing under the sink.

"Some things can't be rushed!" he called out, and reached over to flush the toilet for good effect. "Be there in just a minute!"

Willie tore off a strip of duct tape from the roll he'd brought along and began taping the baggie to the far underside of the sink. No way anyone would find it there!

His old boss, Judson, had shown up the previous night with a new girlfriend, Miyako, a skinny Japanese chick with scary eyes and a few too many rings piercing her nose and lips. They'd just gotten back from northern Mexico, where they'd been collecting peyote which Miyako set about boiling in water. Judson had opened a cardboard box containing an elegant tea set.

"Kyusu with clay filter," he'd explained proudly. "This girl's amazing, isn't she?" He'd gazed at his girlfriend adoringly while she went about preparing what he called an "authentic Japanese tea ceremony."

Willie had frowned; Bunny seemed less than enthusiastic about the young woman, and had decided to hide under some dirty laundry that was lying on the floor.

It turned out that this wasn't a purely social visit. Willie had noticed that there were fewer and fewer bones in the dinosaur graveyard, for Judson had been forced to sell two excavators and a trencher to pay his mounting bills.

"These are A-plus-plus buttons we're using, man," Judson had said, as they'd all sipped their tea. "But we're not just trippin' here, Willie. Look at this." He'd reached into the cardboard box and pulled out the bulging baggie. "Pure mescaline sulfate, buddy, the real deal. Bought it from a spooky Indian dude, had to promise him it was strictly for sacramental use to worship the Great Spirit. This is gonna get me set back up in business, pal! Then I can hire you back along with all the dirt jockeys, the whole gang. I ran into Biggie the other day, he's been outta work since oh-seven. Four years, man! Got a beard down to his knees and holes in his shoes, made me want to cry like a baby, seein' that. There's laterals and lines in our future yet, my boy! Just need you to hold on to this for me until I figure out how to get top dollar. I don't think the cops have been shadowing me—" he edged over to the window and cautiously peered out—"but can't be too careful. You're clean, right? No one's going to mess with you."

Willie grunted with satisfaction as he finished taping the baggie. Maybe agreeing to help Judson hadn't been the brightest idea, but Biggie and his wife, Lola, had five kids to feed. And who knew how long this crazy gig with Oz was going to last?

"WILLIAM! What's taking so long?"

Willie flushed the toilet again.

"Sorry, boss, I'll be right there!"

You told your sister you would pray, he thought to himself. You promised. Ah geez. It was true, though. And here he was, already on his knees! But what to say?

"God, if you're up there—well, yeah, you're up there, I do know that much, but if you're listenin' ta me, I mean—help me get my damn act together, will ya?" He sighed. "You can tell I'm not real enthusiastic about that notion, huh, don't even much know what it means. Well, lemme ask ya for somethin' I really do want: protect my big sister, Lord, be with Joanie, keep her from the smokes, and guide her to ya, 'cause I know that's what she wants with all her heart. That's it: Amen, 'n thanks for listenin' to a washed-up ol' doper like me."

"Okay, here I am," said Willie, as he marched up to the casino magnate's massive mahogany desk. "What do you have for me to do?"

How long had Tim been climbing the rungs of that interminable ladder? Had hours gone by, or days? He had no idea. For the longest time, his hands and feet had been ablaze with agonizing pain, but now they were mostly numb, just lumps of meat, and making sure he had a tight grip on the rails and foothold on the rungs had become terribly hard.

Sometimes he wrapped his arms around the ladder as best he could and allowed himself to sleep.

"Hey!" he shouted as a bat woke him from his nap. "Get away from me, you winged rat!" Damn it! Waving away the flying rodent had almost caused him to fall. Get back to climbing, he told himself, and then looked up and gasped.

The light he'd been climbing toward was now only perhaps fifty yards above. Tears streaming down his cheeks, Tim laboriously reached up to grasp the next rung, and then the next, and the one after that, until he reached the top.

But what he found there filled him with disappointment and despair. He'd desperately hoped that the light had come from outside, that he'd be able to exit out into the world, feel sunlight on his face and breathe in fresh air; but it was nothing but a bare electric bulb.

The bulb illuminated a huge, corroded pipe. Tim pulled himself up onto a small concrete platform that allowed him to examine the pipe more closely, and, after a moment, he saw that there was a handle attached to what appeared to be an entry hatch. He reached up and tugged, but the hatch was so rusted that he couldn't get it to budge.

On either side of the platform, the pipe disappeared into a solid wall. This was the end of the line; he'd either have to get into the hatch or all the agony of his climb would have been in vain.

A chunk from the stone wall lay at the edge of the platform, a few feet from him, and Tim cautiously made his way over and bent down to pick it up. His fingers were so numb that at first he bobbled it, but finally he grasped the chunk, stepped back to the hatch, and pounded it with all the force he could muster.

Please let this work. But was there anyone to whom that thought was directed, or was it only sent out into the void? He grasped the handle, screamed every curse he knew as his muscles strained to make it budge, until finally the hatch swung open with a great groaning, and Tim climbed up to enter into the pipe.

Halfway in, he stopped and began to violently retch. There was nothing to come out, but for the better part of a minute he heaved and heaved. This was a sewer pipe, carrying human excrement and who knew what else! A dead animal, bloated, hideous, impossible to identify, floated past him. He moaned in misery. It would be easier to give up and die!

That's not an option.

The thought, unbidden, came into his mind. Tim closed his eyes, cursed that he'd ever gotten out of bed to meet Vicki, cursed he'd ever talked to her, cursed every decision he had ever made that led him to this miserable moment in his life.

Then he dove into the slowly flowing, fetid water and began to swim.

When his arms grew too weary, he let the current carry him. The muck was in his nose, and when he raised his head above the water to breathe, a few stinking drops entered into his mouth, and he'd gag and fight to keep his mind from slipping into a dark, panicked madness.

Every few minutes he looked around to see if there were any exits out of the pipe; for hours, there was nothing to be seen, and then, abruptly, he noticed a thin strip of faint light off to his right. He struggled to turn around and swim back against the current so he could check out the source of the light.

Tim caught hold of a railing and hauled himself up. The light was indeed the outline of a hatch. The wild thought came to him that the pipe had been built in a great circle, and he had only returned to the same place from which he'd started hours before. He put his shoulder against the hatch and pushed, shouting to distract himself from the pain.

It swung open, revealing a concrete cavity. But as Tim stepped out of the pipe, his heart began to beat wildly, and he sank to his knees and sobbed with joy. From above his head came the clear and beautiful sound of passing cars!

"Help!" he tried to shout, but his voice was no more than a hoarse croak. He looked around; four dots of light were visible overhead.

It was a manhole cover, reachable by a short metal ladder affixed to the wall.

~

"Momma! Look!"

"What is it, honey?"

The woman was walking toward Fremont Street, holding her five-year-old's hand. Why didn't these casinos offer better daycare, anyway? She'd be drinking Seven and Seven and playing keno instead of hauling Junior from here to kingdom come!

"An angel, momma! Over there!"

The woman tried to see where her child was pointing. Angels? Who knew what the kid was picking up at church on Sundays!

"That's just a beam of sunlight passing through dust stirred up by the traffic, honey."

"Noooo, momma!" The little boy began sniffling. "It's true, it's true!"

"Oh my God!" the mother gasped in horror. Something —whether human or animal she wasn't sure—had shoved aside a manhole cover and was crawling up onto the street and into the gutter, something reeking and awful, covered in mud and feces, leaving a trail of slime and blood.

"Let's go, Junior. *Now!*"

"Bye-bye, angel, bye-bye!" the boy called out forlornly, and waved before being dragged off.

From perhaps ten feet in the air above Tim Faber, the angel waved back.

To Tim, oblivious to angels, and to mothers and children and the traffic racing past, the feel of the baking hot sidewalk was sweetness and life itself.

"Thank God," he murmured, and promptly passed out.

Hovering above him, the angel smiled. While not able to peer as deeply into the hearts of men as some of his peers, the angel took Tim's words as merely a worldly expression of relief. Still, if they were empty words, the angel thought, that which is empty can yet be filled. And so fill it he would.

"Thank you, Ancient of Days!" sang the angel.

"Thank you for the heavens, fretted with fire,

"For the salt seas below, teeming with life,

"For the earth's verdant fields, fragrant with fruit;

"Thank you for your mercy in sparing this man;

"Thank you, Heavenly Father,

"Lord and Savior of all creation,

"Almighty and Everlasting God!"

Chapter Thirty-Six
Settling Up

I was on my way to a prayer meeting in McKeeversville after work one evening, when I heard Lucas singing somewhere nearby. A moment later he appeared from out of the shadows and began tugging on my arm.

"What's the matter, buddy?"

I knew from the jagged rhythm of his song that he wasn't taking me to Julia. Instead, he led me off into a trackless desert waste where scorpions were just beginning to stir from their daytime slumber. After a while we came to an area where the sight of a few thorny greasewood shrubs and a scattering of silvery sagebrush were a welcome relief to my eyes.

Lucas, who had been softly crooning, suddenly went silent. In front of us were two men stretched out on the ground. One lay on his side, mumbling "gilly" over and over, his face blistered and burnt from the sun. The other, a much larger man, was on his back, his sightless eyes glazed over in death.

Both of us carried water bottles, and I put mine to the smaller man's lips while Lucas tried to give water to his unfortunate companion, then gave a shrill, sad howl and closed the man's eyes.

"Never mind me," the lone survivor whispered after he'd had enough of a swig to be able to speak, "just make sure Gil's okay. Ol' boy got me outta so many scrapes, saved my sorry butt more times than I kin remember, been doin' that ever since we was kids, tearin' up Chi-town somethin' fierce. He don't talk much, but most folks don't say nothin' but nonsense, anyways. I ain't taken good care 'a him all these years, but that's gonna change, you kin count on that."

A memory came back to me from six years past of Billy Goat Gibson and his friend Gil. Some dentist had done a poor job of repairing the front teeth Miss McSorley had knocked out with her shotgun barrel, leaving Billy looking sadly snaggle-toothed.

"Mr. Gibson," I started to say, and his eyes widened.

"We know each other?"

"Just met briefly up near Seattle, back in twenty-six. I'm sorry, sir, but your friend—"

"Was I ever up Seattle way? Can't 'member worth a damn no more. Yeah, William Gibson, that's me, pleased ta meetcha. You know, ol' Gil, been over thirty years now, never did learn his last name. He's just Gil, that's all he is." He tried to sit up, but didn't have the strength. "Car broke down on the main road, we been walking all day till we couldn't walk no more. Gilly, you drink up, hear me? You drink up good!"

"Sir, I'm so sorry, but Gil didn't make it. The sun was too strong, Mr. Gibson, he's passed on."

"What the hell you talkin' 'bout?" he said, with a fierce, hoarse anger. "Gilly! Damn it!" He shoved my water bottle away from himself and toward his friend. "You drink up, you big dumbie! There's jobs here for the takin', I'll get us both on the payroll, 'n it'll be high times then! I let you down, Gil, but that's all done with, you hear me, 'ol boy? Hell, I'll give you *my* last name, you want it, you can be Gil Gibson, what you think of that?"

He began crying, and Lucas came over to stroke his forehead.

"What the hell that nigger boy doin'?" he said weakly, but didn't shrink back from Lucas' touch.

I said a brief, silent prayer that we could get Mr. Gibson help in time.

"Lucas, run back and get your dad or Isaiah to help us bring Mr. Gibson and his friend to the hospital." I was hoping David had his Big Chief and sidecar so we could get to Las Vegas.

"Please, don't send the boy away," Gibson whispered.

"All right." I handed Lucas my water bottle. "Keep him drinking and I'll go as fast as I can."

Though David and Isaiah weren't around, I found Clarence and we hurried back as quickly as we could. But from fifty yards away I could hear Lucas singing a high, mournful melody, and knew that we were too late.

Settling Up

On July 26th, 1931, four women died of heat prostration. All that summer the temperature stayed above one hundred twenty from nine in the morning until nine at night. Murl Emery had been right; it seemed every day was hotter than the last, and on that day the mercury outside his store reached one hundred thirty degrees.

David, Clarence Jackson, Murl, and I were in the store, talking about the challenges we faced trying to keep people alive.

"I was able to find one of the women's husbands," David said. "Young couple in their twenties, only married a few years. He works swing shift in the tunnels, and he'd done his best for her, left her with a thermos of ice water before going to work. They've got a German Shepherd, smart as a whip, and sometime early that evening she must have realized she was in trouble, so she tied a note around the dog's neck and told him to find Williams, the ranger, whom the dog knew well. Note just asked for him to come and take her down to the river so she could cool off. That young woman knew she was burning alive. But she'd been dead an hour by the time the dog found him."

"That makes at least seventeen deaths from the heat in the past month," I said. "Thirteen men on the job and then the women today."

"Oh, there's almost certainly more'n that," said Clarence, who'd been a doctor in St. Louis. "Folks are getting' carbon monoxide poisoning in those tunnels you're diggin', pastor. Turns into pneumonia pretty easy, and that's most likely how they die. Someone passes on from pneumonia in the hospital, no one thinks it's got much to do with the dam."

"Six Companies likes it that way," said Murl. "They don't have to pay death benefits if a man doesn't croak right on the job. I'm with you, Clarence, the number's higher for sure. Thursday last, I get this call, man sounded like the world was coming to an end, and he wasn't far off the mark. Took the next boat down to the upper portals, and I tell you, they were hauling men out of the tunnels like cordwood. Those fellows were alive, but they'd been gassed pretty bad. I laid them on the bottom of the boat any way I could, delivered them to a truck that went on into Vegas. How many made it back, I haven't heard."

"Most did, but it can get grim in the tunnels from all the diesel exhaust, that's for sure," said David. "Makes my skin crawl when blue halos start showing up around the wall lights. I've had the men stop a couple times, but often it's only when you get outside and start gulping fresh air that the sickness gets you."

"Easy-doughs just don't give a damn, do they," said Clarence.

"Not much, it seems," David replied. "Some men—or their wives— tell me, since I'm a pastor, I ought to quit over the way men are being treated here. Make a public statement, complain to the Feds, embarrass the top brass. Maybe they're right, but to my mind, it's more important to show folks I'm here with them, hauling out muck, taking the same risks, suffering whatever they suffer, right by their side."

"You'd be just another whiner, pissing in the wind, if you quit," said Murl.

"Yeah, you got that right," said Clarence. "But that doesn't mean there ain't things we can do. Ever since Sunday, when you were sermonizing on how we're s'pposed to be salt 'n light, I've been thinking. All those men, dying from the heat—the bosses got them drinking water, but that's only half the battle. Human body tries to cool itself off by sweating, and you boys, working when it's a hundred-twenty, a hundred thirty degrees, water's pouring outta you like Niagara Falls. And here's the thing: *salt's* going along for the ride. You're losing a shaker a day, I'd wager. Word for it is *hyponatremia*—you ain't got the sodium in your system your body needs, muscles start to cramp and your brain tissues swell. I was Six Companies and didn't want half my workforce droppin' dead, I'd make salting the food mandatory, have the men salt their damn cornflakes at breakfast if that's what it takes."

"How about I get a meeting with the big dogs and you come with me, tell them what you just told us?" David suggested.

"Nah, I'd just be some uppity nigger causing trouble. You tell 'em. It ain't all that terribly complex."

"All right." David turned to Murl. "You have a few pounds of table salt I can buy? We can distribute it through Ragtown and McKeeversville tonight. Payday's Friday, I can pay for it then and settle up on the rest of the church's bill."

"Sure," said Emery. "Luke can haul five pounds out from the back. But as to the bill, your wife was in here just this morning, paid off what you owed."

"My wife?" David said, nonplussed. "I'm not married, Murl."

"The lovely lady who's always by your side, I just assumed— well, hell, I've put my foot in it, I guess."

Clarence and Emery both laughed.

"Oh, you mean Yura," said David. "Mrs. Noongwook helps out with just about everything these days, she's sort of become my right hand."

It was the first time I'd ever seen him blush.

~

"Did you run the whole way?" Julia asked me when Lucas brought me to her later that evening. "I've never seen you so soaked in sweat!"

"Just practicing something before Lucas found me," I said, mysteriously. "It's a surprise I want to show David—and you, of course, but only when I'm ready. I can have secrets, too, you know!"

"You're feelings are hurt, aren't they. I'm sorry I haven't been able to tell you where I spend my nights, but it really has been for your own good. Are you terribly angry with me?"

"Horribly. But I'll let bygones be bygones if we can read together from the Song of Songs."

"Fair enough!" She leaned her head against my chest for a moment while Lucas scooped up her well-thumbed Bible and held it out for her to grasp.

"My part's in my head already," I said. "We don't need to share."

"Show-off," said Julia. "It was going to be an excuse to sit close, but that's your loss. Now, we'd just finished the fourth chapter, where I said: *"Let my beloved come into his garden and taste its choice fruits."*

"I came to my garden, my sister,
    my bride," I recited in return.

"I gathered my myrrh with my spice.

"I have eaten my honeycomb with my honey;
  I drank my wine with my milk.
"And then their friends say, *Eat, friends, drink,*
  And be drunk with love!"
"I slept but my heart was awake," Julia read.
  "A sound! My beloved is knocking:
"'Open to me, my sister, my darling.
  my dove, my perfect one,
"'for my head is wet with dew,
  My locks with the drops of the night.'"

"How perfectly appropriate! If you'd had your wits about you, you could have uttered those lines when you first arrived— 'dew and drops of the night' being ever so much more pleasing than mere manly sweat."

I moved closer to her on the pretext of looking at the notes at the bottom of the page.

"When my father used to talk of the day that I'd meet a man, fall in love, and have children of my own," she continued, "I'd pretend to laugh, and I'd tell him, poppa, that will happen when the stars fall from the sky! Now, sometimes I wonder whether *I'm* star-fire that fell from the sky. Whether I'm not where I'm supposed to be, but just a burning ember, far from home."

It hurt my heart when she talked that way, but I worried that if I told her so she'd no longer confide in me. So, lacking confidence, I only talked around the edges of the truth.

"That reminds me of language in John's Revelation," I said. *"And the stars of the sky fell to the earth, as the fig tree sheds her winter fruit when shaken by a gale.* Figs don't ripen once they're shaken loose, I know that because our friends had a fig tree when I was living near Seattle. But you're still ripening, and you know it. This *is* your home, for you're connected to the vine, the True Vine, and the proof of it is the fruit you've borne and yet will bear."

"I want what you're saying to be true," said Julia, and leaned her head against me. "The passage you quoted, that was from the opening of the sixth seal. But just before, when the Lamb opens the fifth seal and the martyrs cry out, asking how long they must wait till their blood is avenged by their Sovereign Lord—that's always bothered me. We've been told to forgive, time and again, told by the Lamb of God Himself. Yes, vengeance is the Lord's, but to yearn for God to strike the blow is still to yearn for vengeance. Does forgiveness then end at death? Or will the martyrs be properly rebuked?"

"They're only told to wait until others join them," I said, after thinking for a moment. "But forgiveness *must* last beyond the grave, for we're to love even our enemies, and to love is to forgive, it's eternal life itself."

"I think you're right," said Julia, "despite Revelation's hundred-pound hailstones and seas of blood. I think what Jesus revealed to John is that forgiveness and love aren't always gentle and sweet, that they can be terrible, they can come like a trumpet blast that shatters the heavens, they can cut like a double-edged sword. At least, I hope that's true; for, at last, I know what I have to do. Luke, I pray there's no desire for revenge left in me; let these fires that burn within purify me, let them be like the live coal with which the angel touched the prophet's lips."

"You've decided what to do about your father's murderer! Whatever it is, let me be part of it, I can't bear the thought of you taking that on by yourself."

"Never fear, you've a role to play. I know you don't want secrets from your pastor, and I'm proud of you for that, so I won't tell you more. But it will come soon."

For a moment, everything in front of me—Julia, the cliffside, the mighty river far below—faded from view and was replaced by the vision I'd had weeks before, when David drove us from Tonopah to Las Vegas. Once again, I was staring from a far distance at an elegant, evil man and a malevolent giant towering over David, who was on his knees beside the body of a lifeless girl.

I could not see her face.

Please, Lord, I prayed, *let this be a mere phantasm, let it not be your will, and above all, let it not be Julia James.*

The vision faded, and we sat together in somber silence. Sometime after moonrise, Lucas came over and put his head in Julia's lap, and she ran her hands through his hair until he fell into what seemed a blissful sleep.

~

"Tell Monroe I'll pay for this no later than the end of next week," Murl Emery said to the fellow who'd just arrived with a truckload of goods he'd ordered from Las Vegas. It was Friday evening, and I was helping out at the store.

"Sorry, Mr. Emery, but this time he told me to collect before I unload."

"For Pete's sake, Roy! How long have we been doing business together? Hang on, I'll talk to him myself."

Murl picked up the phone, listened to it ring nine or ten times, then slowly hung up.

"All right. Do what you got to do. I know it isn't your fault."

Roy mumbled his apologies and left.

"We've got quite a line out there, Mr. Emery," I said. "What do you want me to do?"

"Nothing we *can* do but serve people till the shelves are bare. Less you got any other idea."

"No, sir," I said, as he went back behind the counter and greeted the next person in line.

"What can I get for you?" he asked, a little more brusquely than usual, and it was only then that I noticed something unusual: while our clients were normally women, almost everyone in line this evening was a man.

"Not a thing sir, I'm here to settle our bill. Pruitt, twenty-three dollars and forty-six cents; my wife Maggie's been here a time or two." He laid the bills and change down carefully on the counter.

"Names Grayson, and I owe ya thirteen bucks and change, but let's call it fourteen even," said the next man. "Don't know what we would'a done, you hadn't been there for us, Mr. Emery. Can't thank ya enough."

"Nine dollars twenty-seven."

271

Settling Up

"Thirty-four and sixteen cents!"

I ran out to see if I could get to Roy before he took off.

It was a payday to be remembered, for the line outside waiting to settle up with Murl must have been a hundred yards long. Years later, Emery told me that all but two of the countless IOU's he'd issued had been paid back, and he was pretty sure those were owed by two of the men who'd lost their lives building Hoover Dam.

Chapter Thirty-Seven
Ten Thousand Charms

"It's the damn President, comin' ta kiss babies and shake hands with us workin' stiffs!"

"Hah! Lot you know—car like that, gotta be John D. Rockefeller, more likely!"

"Rockefeller, hell, that ain't nothin' less'n the king of France!"

Anyone in McKeeversville who wasn't on shift was gaping at the long, sleek, low-slung limousine that had just braked to a halt by a scattering of shacks and tents. I recognized it in a heartbeat as Jack Johnson's 1930 Duesenberg Phaeton, and moments later the former champ himself emerged from behind the wheel.

"Ain't never seen a nigger chauffeur wearin' duds like that!" muttered someone behind me.

Johnson was especially resplendent in a blue-and-white-striped gaberdine suit and panama hat.

"Sorry to disturb you fine folks on such a splendid day," he said, wiping his face with the handkerchief from his breast pocket. "Would anyone know the whereabouts of a certain Mr. David Gold?"

"The preacher man? His butt's a thousand feet deep in the tunnels right now, watch'a want with him?"

"Private matter, sir. Well, then, does anyone know a couple 'a Eskimos, young man and his mother, Dirk and Flora, last name's something like Nunchuck?"

"Mr. Johnson!" I called out, and made my way through the crowd. "Luke Noongwook. What a surprise! I know David would love to see you, but he's working the four-to-midnight shift. Will you be able to stay?"

"Young master Luke!" Johnson accepted my proffered water bottle and took a swig. "Thanks kindly. No, I'm just here making a delivery." He turned to the car. "Irene, honey! Bring my gift for the boy Dave and Luke called me about."

Irene, a plump white woman with a kind face, winced just a bit as she came out into the one hundred and twenty-five-degree heat. She was carrying a violin case, which she handed to me.

"It ain't a Stradivarius," Johnson continued, "but my friend Arturo—Italian with the mustache, conducts the New York Philharmonic—said it wasn't half bad. Wish I could stay, but we got to get to Phoenix this evening, I need to sign about a thousand autographs to pay for this thing."

"Woah Nellie," someone called out, "that there's Jack Johnson, in the flesh!"

"Hey, champ, me and my buddies'll part with a sawbuck if ya could see clear ta punch our Gaffer in the nose!"

Irene hugged me while her husband waved to the crowd. I gave her my water bottle before they got back into the Duesenberg and took off at high speed, leaving a great cloud of dust in their wake.

Although, like most of the others, I was coughing and clearing the sand from my nose and eyes, I set out with fiddle in hand to look for Lucas' dad, my heart filled with joy.

~

"Well ain't this the living end!" Clarence said when I handed him the violin case and explained who it was from. He opened it, took out the beautiful, burnished fiddle and wiped a tear from his eye. "Can't hardly believe it! I don't know what to say, Luke, but to thank you and the pastor from the bottom of my heart."

"I'll pass that on to Jack Johnson, sir, since it's his doing."

"The man's a brother to me now," said Clarence, "I tell you true. Can't wait to give this to Lucas when he gets back, he's been gone for a while."

"I won't say a word if I see him first, sir," I said, bid him goodnight, and began walking toward home.

After I'd gone about half a mile, Lucas appeared by my side, strangely silent, and motioned urgently for me to follow. It was early in the midsummer evening, and the sun wouldn't set for another hour. He led me away from the canyon and out into the desert to a hilly region spotted with pricklypear cactus, a full mile past the end of Trespass Trail. There he stopped, sang briefly, and pointed to something close by that at first I couldn't make out.

"Welcome, Luke," said Julia, stepping out from what I now could see was the opening of an old mineshaft set into the hillside. She sang something sad and lovely to Lucas, who hesitated for a moment, then touched my face and sped off.

"I've sent him home," she explained. "The man who murdered my father received a sealed message from me through Lauren a short while ago. There's little doubt but that he'll come tonight." She took me by the hand and led me a few feet into the mine. "Don't walk anywhere without me. We're standing just in front of a trapping pit which I've covered with a thin layer of dirt. It's taken me weeks and weeks, but now it's done. When my father and I lived in Western Montana, one of our neighbors was a farmer who dug these to catch wolves. It's nearly twelve feet deep and almost as wide as the shaft, with smooth walls, there'll be no way for him to get out without the rope ladder I've got curled up against the back wall. But there are no sharpened stakes at the bottom, for we very much want him alive."

"All right, but surely now you'll tell me who the man is!" I exclaimed.

"You really don't know?"

Of course I had my suspicions, but I paused and thought over the events since we'd arrived in September of the previous year.

"Ever since I saw the detective, Drake, strike David with such force on the day the church was set on fire, and saw the merciless expression on his face, I thought he might be the one."

"Yes, of course," said Julia. "But he was only the instrument of my father's murder; the real question is, whose bidding did he do? That's why I must be the one who traps him. I don't know whether the sheriff was involved, but I don't trust him to get to the bottom of things and make sure justice is done. I'm going to keep Drake in this pit until I hear the truth come out of his mouth. Then we'll contact the authorities in Reno. I'm quite sure he'll try to kill me when he comes; you'll be a witness to it, and to any confession he makes. When a man like him, a small, mean, coward, gets hungry and thirsty enough, I believe he'll talk. And the Spirit will guide us in knowing truth from lies."

I wasn't sure which question to ask first.

"How can you be sure he'll come? Won't he assume you're lying in wait to gain revenge?"

"The message says that I forgive him—and that is true, for forgive him I must!—and that I want to tell him so, face to face. I wrote that he has nothing to fear from me—truth again, for it is only a man's evil, his madness, that causes him to fear the truth. But it matters little if he believes what he reads; he'll come because he wants to silence the only witness to his crime."

"He knows you know?"

"He saw me that morning, Luke."

"He's armed, and he'll try to kill you. I can stop him, of course, with this—" I pointed to my hunting knife—"but if you want him alive, what's your plan for assuring he'll fall into the pit?"

"We'll be at the rearmost section of the shaft—you can see how terribly dark it is back there. You'll follow me, staying close to the wall. We can easily see someone silhouetted against the opening to the outside, and even if he comes late, it's a moonlit night. He can't see us, but he'll hear me welcoming him in."

"Your voice gives away your location, what makes you think he won't shoot the moment you speak?"

"I very much hope he does," Julia replied calmly. "You'll be a witness to attempted murder at that point. There're barrels at the back that provide some shelter, and the sound of my voice will give away nothing, for words echo off these stone walls. He'll move forward to finish the job."

"I'm not so sure as you that this makes sense," I said. "But I'll be by your side, regardless."

"Much as I'd like that, it will be better for us to be on opposite sides of the shaft, just in case something does go wrong."

We clung to the damp stone and made our way to where the horizontal shaft ended about twenty feet from the entry. Two large oaken barrels were set against the opposing walls, which were only about ten feet apart.

"I've set a searchlight near the ceiling," she said. "This string controls it. It's terribly bright, and should blind and confuse him, in case it comes to that. One way or the other, he's going in the pit."

We prayed together and then settled in, waiting for Drake to show up. One or the other of us kept an eye on the entrance, but after a while we began whispering back and forth to pass the time, and I told her the somber story of Billy Goat Gibson and Gil.

"I believe he was beginning to repent of the things he'd done wrong in his life," I concluded. "Some of them, anyway. It took his friend's death to make him do that, and his own, I suppose, for he must have known he was near the end. But was that enough? Might he yet be saved?"

"What does it mean to you, Luke, to say a man is saved?"

"That he's rescued from slavery to sin—saved from death and into eternal life."

"Yes, saved from the delusion that God is not his perfect, loving Father, the wellspring of his life. The other evening, you told me that eternal life is the knowing of God, becoming like Christ, living the Life we were meant to live. *That* is what it means to be saved. So, if the perfect Father sees a man in the process of turning from his sin and becoming more like His Son, however feebly at first, would He not be filled with joy? Wasn't Mr. Gibson akin to the prodigal, just beginning to lift his eyes from the trough and wishing for a better life? Darling, would the Perfect Father let bodily death end a journey from darkness to light?"

I smiled in the darkness, thrilled to hear the word *darling* coming from Julia's lips. But our conversation came to an abrupt end as a dark form appeared at the entry to the mine before ducking back out of view.

"Miss James! If you want to talk, come out where I can see you!" Drake called out.

"I've reason to fear you, sir, but you've nothing to dread from me. There's no weapon in my hand, and I've no wish to see you harmed. Come in so that I can talk to you with peace of mind."

Perhaps a full minute passed. Finally, the detective, crouching and keeping low to the ground, moved cautiously inside. My heart skipped a beat; perhaps Julia's plan would work, after all!

And then everything began to go wrong.

"Julia! Take cover, he's drawn his gun!"

It was Isaiah Trueblood, who came running toward Drake, knife in hand. The detective spun around and fired, his gun roaring like a cannon in the mine shaft, and I heard the awful sound of our brave friend groaning in pain.

My mind filled with rage. I jumped up, trusting that the darkness would hide me, and ran along the wall, but, though I didn't fall, the pounding of my footsteps caused the flimsy covering over the trapping pit to come loose, and the rocks and dirt crashed down, revealing what we'd had in store for Drake.

"You lying bitch," he said, "you'll join your father in the grave."

I could see the flash from the muzzle of his gun, and a bullet ricocheted off the stone wall, just inches from my head. The next moment I was upon him, my hunting knife unsheathed. Julia had wanted him alive, so, instead of going for the kill, I struck the gun from his hand. As it clattered to the ground, I realized I'd made a terrible mistake; thin as he was, the detective was much the taller and stronger man, and he grabbed my right arm with both hands and began turning my own blade against me.

Julia came running along the wall, but, just as she reached us, Drake delivered a powerful kick that sent her tumbling down into the pit. Try as I could to push back, the blade was moving inexorably toward my throat, until, just as I felt the tip begin to press against my flesh, I was deafened by a new explosion and spattered with gore. The detective's nearly headless body fell against me before I shoved it away and dropped to my knees, shaking, then crawled over to the edge of the pit.

"Julia!"

"I've only had the wind knocked out of me, see to Isaiah!"

I turned toward the entry and saw the sheriff lay his shotgun against the wall and kneel down by our friend. It only took a minute to run back and lower the rope ladder for Julia, then join the two men at the front of the mine.

"Take a swig 'a this, Trueblood," said the sheriff, producing a flask that I presumed was filled with liquor. "It'll ease the pain."

"No sir, I ain't gonna meet my maker with whiskey on my breath."

"You damn fool kids should'a trusted me," Stone said, looking at us angrily as Julia made her way to Isaiah's side. "None of this would'a happened."

"Julia," said the wounded man, who was breathing in hoarse, bloody gasps. "Lemme look on you, girl. Make dyin' easier. I been watchin' Drake, followed him here, wasn't gonna let nothin' happen to you. But looks like I messed up bad."

"You didn't mess up, dear Isaiah," she said, stroking his brow. "And you hang on, I'm not letting you go, not like this."

"I'm gut-shot, angel, there ain't no hope." Bubbles of blood were forming on our friend's lips as he spoke. "But it's okay, 'cause my prayers've been answered, I got to see you again before I die."

"You're going to be all right, Isaiah," said Julia, fighting back tears.

I put my arms around the two of them as the sheriff looked on helplessly.

"Gonna meet the Lord, sweetheart, ain't that somethin'! And listen to *me!* I ain't stutterin', not even once, no, not any more. You hear?"

"That's right," I said. "You're talking as clear and crisp as ever a man that walked this earth."

Isaiah laughed weakly and then began coughing up blood.

"Gonna look right at Jesus and tell Him I do love Him so," he said, his voice now barely a whisper. "Gonna walk right into His arms." He fell silent before struggling once more to speak. "You take care 'a my Julia, Luke, take care 'a her good."

And then he was gone.

~

"I had a dream last night," said my mother. "A dark dream."

All of us who'd known Isaiah were gathered the next day at Woodlawn Cemetery in Las Vegas. Even the sheriff was there, wide-brimmed hat in hand; it turned out he'd suspected the deputy for some time, and, like Isaiah, had followed him into the desert on that terrible night.

Our friend's coffin had been lowered into the grave, and David had spoken a eulogy, but none of us much wanted to leave.

"I was back in Nenana," she continued, "watching the Angakkuq as he slowly danced 'round a great fire that spat points of flame toward the heavens. They were like fireflies, like the souls of the dead. I thought of Raven—the evil one, the shape-shifter, who can take the form of scorpions and snakes, or of barren rocks and choking dust. Or of men; men like Drake. So I grew very afraid. But I awoke with the dawn and felt the presence of Anirnialuk, the Great Spirit, which is our word for God the Father of Christ Jesus, He who hovered over the deep waters, in the formless blackness before the coming of the Light. And I feared no more."

"Lucas wants ta pay his respects, y'all don't mind," said Clarence Jackson.

The small boy took his new fiddle from its case, tucked it under his chin, and began sending a mournful melody soaring high above the oak trees. Lauren and Anne-Marie sang while Lucas played the hymn that has ever since been close to my heart.

> *Come, ye sinners, poor and needy,*
> *Weak and wounded, sick and sore;*
> *Jesus ready stands to save you,*
> *Full of pity, love and pow'r.*
> *I will arise and go to Jesus,*
> *He will embrace me in His arms;*
> *In the arms of my dear Savior,*
> *Oh, there are ten thousand charms.*

Chapter Thirty-Eight
Icons

It was always the same dream.

Daniel, in his childhood home on Hacienda Drive, was awakened suddenly by the smell of smoke and burning rubber and by the popping and crackling of light bulbs exploding from the heat. Where to go? The only escape, the only way out, was up, up to the safety of the roof, up through the crimson sea. And ah, at last, there was the Savior, walking toward him on a sea of fire! Then the boy looked down to see his mother and father, their faces death-masks melting in the maelstrom of flames. But where was the Lord's outstretched hand? Instead, He was looking at Daniel with darkened brow.

"Woe to you who saved yourself and left those who gave you birth behind! For whoever wants to save his life will surely lose it in the end..."

The sound of his cell phone ringing woke the pastor from his dream, and he stumbled out of bed, a tired, middle-aged man, neuropathic pains blazing in his feet and hands.

Whoever wants to save his life...

Why couldn't you have taken me, too, Lord? he thought, and then forced himself to answer the phone.

"Hello? Daniel, are you there?" Joan asked after there'd been a few moments of silence. "It's Joan Reed, returning your call."

He was frozen, staring incredulously at a bottle of Blue that was lying on its side on the bedroom floor, open and half empty. Much of it seemed to have soaked into the carpet, and its thick, sweet smell pervaded the room.

"Just a moment," he said, and bent down. He could see it and smell it, but as he reached out to grasp the bottle it vanished from sight.

"I'm sorry, Joan," he said, straightening up slowly. "I've gotten into the habit of taking afternoon naps and wasn't quite awake. But I'm so glad you called! Are you and Tim available to go see Uncle Luke? We found the letter—well, Elena did, actually—and he's feeling well today."

"Tim's nowhere to be found, but I'm ready right now. I'm a bit worried about him—my boss might not be the most responsible man in the world, but it's not like him to just disappear without a word. I'm pretty sure he hasn't answered his cell phone or room phone or responded to email for the past three days."

"Some men go on binges when they get here and just shut the real world out," said Daniel, though he had an uneasy feeling about Tim. "But don't worry, I'll follow up after our meeting and make sure Mr. Faber's all right. It's just a question of putting the word out—there are members of my congregation who know most everything that goes on around here."

Much of which I'd rather not know, he thought, unless it were the only way of helping the Lord to save a soul.

~

"A couple days ago, when you were talking about your marriage, I asked whether you thought your friends were right when they said you'd be a fool if you ever took your husband back," said Daniel, as he and Joan drove in his dusty pickup down Las Vegas Boulevard. "And you said it wouldn't matter if they were."

"Oh, there was a full moon that night, most likely. And then the conversation went elsewhere—I don't recall you ever said what *you* thought."

"I think that if you'd be a fool, you'd be just the right sort. Paul called himself a fool for the sake of Christ and exhorted the Corinthians—and through them, all of us—to imitate him. Joan, we live and love for the sake of Christ, and we're the sheerest fools for love if we follow all that the apostle laid out: suffer long, bear all things, believe all things, hope all things, endure all things. Not advice you'll find in many self-help books, is it."

"No, it's not. Goes against the grain, against common sense."

"Oh, Jesus will play utter havoc with your common sense! It's in following Him in the hardest things that we first understand what it means to take a leap of faith. Someone once said that it requires a dash of divine madness to become His disciple. Perhaps so. Certainly, by the logic of the world, the saints must seem quite mad."

"I don't much care what others think, not anymore, anyway. It's academic, though, for Jesse's been gone for a more than a year now, and I don't kid myself that he's ever coming back."

"He may or may not," said Daniel, "but no one ever went broke betting on the unpredictability of men, as they might say in this town. And here we are," he added, pulling into Luke's driveway. "The answers to your questions await; I only hope you won't be disappointed."

"Never fear," said Joan, smiling. "I don't think your Uncle Luke could disappoint me if he tried."

The old man was sitting by his library window, covered by blankets. Once again, she was struck by the contrast between his dark eyes and the pure whiteness of his shoulder-length hair.

"Good afternoon, Uncle," said Daniel. "You remember Joan Reed?"

"Of course," he said, "from Science Cable TV. On the trail of my friend Georges. I'll turn the music down in a moment, but listen along with me, this is my favorite part."

She remained silent, listening to the swoops and soars of a solo violin until they faded into silence.

"Thanks so much for taking the time to see me, Professor. Such beautiful music! Was it the Bach Chaconne, by chance?"

"It was indeed."

"My ex might not have been good for much," said Joan, glancing at Daniel, "but he did teach me to appreciate the classics, I'll grant him that. Such a performance! I'm curious who the violinist was."

"Just an old friend whom I dearly loved," Luke replied. "It takes some getting used to, when you become as old as I am, how one friend after another leaves you behind. How could we bear it if not for our faith in the restoration of all things, friendships not the least. The Lord has told us that there is no marriage in heaven, you know, and once those were hard words, bitter for me to contemplate. But no more; for any bliss that is taken from us shall be replaced with joy increased a thousand-fold, of that I have no doubt. And the Lord is so good; not a day goes by that I don't thank him for Danny, who is like a son to me."

"As you are my father," the pastor said softly.

"You never had children, Professor?" Joan asked, moved by the interchange between the two men, before thinking to herself, *idiot—how could you be so rude!*

"No." For a moment Luke's face was like a mask; then he looked up at Joan, as if seeing her for the first time. "There has been a great change in you since the last time we met! Come closer, my dear." He reached out to her, and she grasped his hand. His skin was paper thin, with every vein exposed, but his grip was surprisingly strong. "You have been touched by the Lord."

Joan didn't know what to say and chose to stay silent.

"Have you ever seen two oxen in a field, yoked together side by side? When He says His yoke is light," Luke continued, "Jesus is not referring to a yoke he has fashioned for you, He means that you can share the very yoke He wears Himself: the doing of His Father's will. No greater honor can be given to man or woman than that."

He released Joan's hand and opened his arms to her. She hesitated for a moment, then knelt down and put her head against his chest, and for a short while he stroked her hair. Much to her embarrassment, she found herself crying.

"I'm sorry," she said, "I don't know what's come over me!"

"Ah, you couldn't give me a more precious gift than these salt tears," he responded. "I'll take them with me when I go."

"You're not 'going' anytime soon, Uncle," said Daniel, "it's been years since I've seen you so full of life. There's no need for such ominous thoughts."

"Ominous? A fine pastor you are, to describe a man's passage to Jesus with such a word!"

"Touché." Daniel laughed. "There is, however, something about the Talbot that I've been meaning to ask you. That jiggling I've seen you do when you shift into third gear—perhaps Jesus might delay your departure just a bit, till you teach me the trick."

"No need to shift past second, Danny, what worldly destination could merit such a rush? Rise, dear woman," he said to Joan, "sit on the couch by my nephew, and we'll talk of Georges Lemaître. But first, tell me your understanding of the mystery."

For a few moments, Joan had felt the same sense of security and comfort that she'd known in her father's arms. Now, as she got to her feet, a grown woman twice her father's age when he'd died at only twenty-six, she felt a calmness and confidence, and something else, something she could only call love.

This, she thought, must be what it means to know oneself a child of God.

"All right," she said, pausing to collect her thoughts. "Tell me if I go astray. In 1917, Einstein realized that his general theory of relativity implied a universe that was either expanding or contracting, whereas, for countless centuries, scientists and poets alike had envisioned an unchanging cosmos. Unaware of any evidence for a dynamic universe, and finding the idea repugnant, he modified his equations to leave the heavens serenely static.

"Then, ten years later, your friend Georges Lemaître, an obscure young Belgian priest whose theories Einstein had already dismissed with scorn, published his own solutions to the great man's equations—a complete model of an expanding universe, supported with tantalizing scraps of evidence gathered from astronomers he'd visited in the United States. When an object is moving away from us, its light is shifted to the red end of the spectrum—sort of the optical equivalent of the Doppler effect, as I understand it, where we can tell from the sound of its siren whether an ambulance is moving toward us or heading away—and the light from most other galaxies seemed to be showing a red shift. They were moving away from us, just as Lemaître's model predicted! Then, a few years later, he added to his model, and proposed that the cosmos had a beginning, when it burst into being from a single quantum, a point in space.

"An expanding universe that began like a blaze of fireworks, creating the stuff of stars, forming the galaxies and sending them whirling apart—this was one of the most revolutionary theories in the history of science! Yet today, when people speak of the expanding universe, they refer to *Hubble's law* and the *Hubble constant*. Many even think of Hubble as the father of the Big Bang theory—but he only provided the data which supports Lemaître's model!

"And that brings us to your friend's 1927 paper. No one paid it any attention until several years later, when the data supporting expansion became overwhelming, and it was translated into English and published in 1931. But several of the most important paragraphs—the ones describing 'Hubble's law' and 'Hubble's constant'—were missing! And that is what brings me here, Professor Noongwook. Who prepared the translation, and who deleted those paragraphs?"

"Bravo, Miss Reed." Luke gave Joan a warm smile. "Your understanding is essentially correct. But surely, with all the research you've done, you must have a theory of your own."

"Well, I know of a Canadian astronomer who believes the paper was edited to assure that Americans would get all the glory, and a mathematician who thinks Hubble himself had a hand in it. But I've read up on Edwin Hubble, and, as huge an ego as he had, I don't believe he was such a small man as that. But would others have taken such a drastic—even dastardly!—action without Hubble's prompting? I don't buy it. So, it seems I'm stumped."

"Your instincts are excellent." Luke chuckled and handed Joan a single sheet of paper. "This is a copy of a letter Georges sent to the editor of the journal in which the translation appeared."

It didn't take long to read. Stunned, she read it again, repeating two lines out loud.

"'I join a French text with indication of the passages omitted in the translation. I made this translation as exact as I can, but I would be very glad if some of yours would be kind enough to read it and correct my English, which I am afraid is rather rough.' So it was Lemaître himself who translated his paper, and left out those paragraphs! But why?"

"Georges and Edwin were not strangers; they first met in 1925. If fame meant so much to the American, eh bien, Monsieur Hubble had done excellent work measuring the red shifts of many nebulae, let him have the public accolades—c'est pas grand chose! What Georges cared for was that the world would marvel at the handiwork of his Heavenly Father, at the majesty of the cosmos created through Christ Jesus."

"So," said Daniel. "What do you think? Will your viewers be content?"

"There could be no more satisfying—and humbling—answer to the riddle," said Joan. "Thank you, Professor. Will it be possible for us to disclose the existence of the letter when we air our show?"

"Yes, of course, anyone who looked hard enough could have found it long ago. I'm so very glad it pleases you."

"How did you come to meet Georges Lemaître?" Joan asked. "You must have been quite young —were you studying astronomy at the time?"

"I knew nothing of astronomy before I met Georges and Milt—Milton Humason, I should say, who was Mr. Hubble's right-hand man. I met them through Danny's grandfather when they came to Las Vegas in 1933, the year when Einstein confessed to the world that Georges had been right all along."

Joan was transfixed. There was no record of such a trip in any of the histories she'd read!

"Professor, I don't want to ask anything that might seem disrespectful to Monsignor Lemaître, but I must tell you, I came across a report filed by a Las Vegas policeman, a Sheriff Stone, who claimed that organized crime figures had, as he put it, 'a hit out' on your friend—that they'd placed a bounty on Georges' head. Though, listening to myself speaking out loud, it sounds like pure madness."

"Not at all," Luke said grimly. "It might well be true."

"Is there anything you can tell me? I'll be honest, our best hope to tell the story of Georges Lemaître to as large an audience as possible is if we have something just a bit lurid to promote, and an underworld connection to the priest who proved Einstein wrong just might do the trick."

"That's quite all right, Miss Reed—there is, after all, nothing hidden that shall not be revealed. But if I'm to tell the story properly, I must paint the picture and fill in a bit of background. So, let's make ourselves comfortable, what do you say?"

Luke called for Elena, who brought in a tray of ice tea and a platter of Pepperidge Farm cookies, and then he began to speak.

~

"We've hit the freakin' jackpot with this one, cap'n," said the young man known as Maggot. Wanting to be called Viper, he'd once paid a drug-addled dentist to sharpen several of his teeth down to fine points; but, finding himself frequently drawing blood from his own tongue, he'd had them capped with metal, and now resembled nothing so much as a vampire with braces.

"Watch'a got there?" asked Cap'n Hook, whose left arm ended in a stump to which he affixed an assortment of metal devices, his favorite being a rusty meathook.

"Lookit—fat with Benjies!" Maggot gleefully waved Tim Faber's wallet above his head, then began to disgorge the hundred-dollar bills.

"You know the effin' rules," said the Cap'n. "Don't take nothin' till we've shown it to the boss."

"The boss, the boss, my ass! What we need *him* for? I wuz on my own, gimme fifteen minutes and I'd be floatin' on China White."

"Yeah, well you ain't on yer own, Maggot. Now give it here."

As the younger man pouted and began to pull away, the Cap'n dealt him several bone-jarring blows with his right hand before spearing the wallet with his hook.

"Don't go anywhere," he advised his associate, who lay sniffling on the ground. "I'll be back."

It was a brisk twenty-minute walk to the boss's office, which was in a far back room behind a pawnshop. Walking down the long hallway to see the boss always made the Cap'n uneasy. All those creepy pictures of old geezers on the walls—he knew what a *con* was, but what the hell was an *icon*, anyway? And the countless candles, casting flickering shadows on the wall! There was something about the boss that was just, well, weird, like making them attend Sunday services. What was *that* all about?

"Pwesent da goods, Hook."

The Cap'n had never quite gotten used to the boss, a hulking man in his forties with a do-rag around his clean-shaven head, his body covered with tattoos which, as he had once explained, marked the "stations of the cross." Whatever that meant! He handed over the wallet, then watched as the boss rifled through it and withdrew a card that Tim had been carrying around for several days.

"Uh-uh." The boss shook his head. "We ain't takin' a dime fwom dis one. I told ya, fwends 'a pathtah Dan are off-limit. My gwampa 'n his was betht pals. They were waw hewoes, the both of 'em, didj'a know dat?"

The Cap'n's heart sank.

"But boss, please. It's been hard times, what with the recession 'n all. We gotta think about the troops' morale."

"The twoops?!" It was never a good sign when the veins on the boss's head were popping out. "The twoops? The twoops do what I thay, if they're fond 'a their lives. You got dat, Hook?"

"Yes sir," said the Cap'n.

"Yeth thir what?"

"Yes sir, Mr. Skull."

"All wight, den. Where'd you find dis?"

"Maggot stumbled across some guy lying unconscious just off 'a Fremont."

"Bwing him here, pwonto."

"Yes sir, Mr. Skull, but I gotta warn you, he's messed up pretty bad. Smells like a rat that up and died after eatin' his way to the center of a crap sandwich."

"Just bwing him. Now!"

Skull rummaged about for a while before finding a garden hose and carrying it outside. Eventually, Maggot and the Cap'n arrived, muttering oaths as they carried Tim between them.

"Set the poor bathturd down," he told them, "and buzz off."

It took a good ten minutes to hose Tim off sufficiently. The executive producer of Science Cable TV sputtered, opened his eyes briefly, then groaned in horror as he looked up at the fearsome countenance of the man standing above him and promptly swooned.

Wonder what your thtory ith, Skull murmured. He took out his cell phone and dialed Daniel's number, but when it went immediately to voicemail he shrugged and hung up. No matter; he could use some exercise and would deliver the man himself.

He took a deep breath, hoisted Tim up onto his back, and set off for the Church of the Heart Set Free.

PART FOUR

MORE LOVELY
THAN THE DAWN

Chapter Thirty-Nine
The Prodigal, Homeward Bound

In January 1933, two hundred miles north of Las Vegas, there was a catastrophic roof-fall at the Belmont mine. Lenny told Jake to gather everyone he could to clear debris, but he hadn't much hope; there were several tons of rock blocking the way to the men trapped in a stope off the Desert Queen, one of the mine's two vertical shafts, and he doubted that they had survived the collapse. This would surely be a matter of recovering the bodies of the dead.

The unlit cigar tasted foul in his mouth, and he threw it away before taking out a new one to chomp on. Well, they'd give it all they had, no matter the odds. He only wished that big fellow was there to help out—what was his name? Oh yes, Gold, a miner doesn't forget a name like that! The preacher-man. Lenny looked around, and, seeing no one in sight, got down on his knees to pray.

Sometimes you just had to try everything, no matter how far-fetched!

$$\sim$$

"We're dead men," said the man who called himself Victor Midnight. It was difficult for him to talk, for several of his ribs had been broken by the heavy beam that was now pressing down on his chest, and he felt daggers of pain with every breath.

"I know what dead is," said Hugo, who'd been working next to Victor when the roof collapsed. "I was dead for years before I found the Source of Life. Before I found Jesus Christ."

"Sweet for you," said Victor. "But I'm an evil man, my friend, there's no good in me at all. The truth is, I left my wife and my son for a woman whose money I spent on drink and gambling and whores, and when every penny was gone, I left her, too."

He laughed bitterly, suddenly aware of a large silver nugget lying only inches away.

The Prodigal, Homeward Bound

"Twelve years ago," said Hugo, "I was released from prison after serving time for armed robbery. No one would give me a chance, no one would hire me but one woman, whom I served for the next six years. How well she treated me! And do you know how I repaid her? By stealing her money and leaving her for dead. There, now you better know the man who'll share your tomb. What matter the past? There is only one thing that matters: do you know the Lord?"

The last beams that were restraining the rocks just a few inches above their heads creaked loudly, and both men flinched.

"My grandfather had once been a priest," said Victor, who now could speak only in a whisper. "He'd lost his faith, but still asked my father to have us baptized when the missionaries came to our town. There were years when I went to mass every week. But what good is that now? What a mockery, to ask God for mercy only when the jaws of hell are opened wide!"

"What good? All the good that flows from the wounds of our Savior, from the very heart of God. Listen to me, Victor Midnight: perhaps you are the thief on the cross next to Jesus, and the life you think so real has only been a dream."

"A dream..." murmured Victor. "But my wife, my son; who will show them the way, who will lead them through life? Better I had never been born!"

"You must put your faith and trust in the Lord, and leave them to Him. Repent of your sins, Victor, and give yourself to the Son of God."

There was blood seeping from Victor's mouth and ears, and his eyes dripped crimson tears.

"Will you do that?" Hugo asked.

His friend could no longer speak, but managed to nod his head.

"Look," said Hugo, "I think there's just enough about me that we can share the Lord's Supper. This last crust of bread from our lunch—" he placed a few crumbs on Victor's tongue, and on his own—"this is His body, broken for us. And here, you see, we thought we'd drunk it all down, but there's yet a sip of wine." Hugo let a drop fall on the dying man's swollen tongue, and then on his own. "This is His blood, shed for us. Have mercy on the souls of two sinners, dear Savior—"

Victor blinked a few times. How strange; for it was no longer Hugo's face above him, but that of another man. And in that man's gaze was a fierce kindness, and in his eyes was a terrible love.

You're asking everything of me, thought Victor, when I have so little left to give. But what I have is Yours.

Do not be afraid, Taliriktug Noongwook, said the Man of Sorrows, and then, with a great groaning, the last supports above them gave way.

Chapter Forty
The Telegram

The day after Drake was buried, I asked Julia to marry me.

"You said you don't want to inflict yourself on any man," I told her. "But sharing your agonies and sorrows is something I choose to do. How could love shrink back or turn away when its object is afflicted and in pain? I will only run faster toward you, cling to you tighter, love you all the more!"

"I fear you don't know what you're saying." She looked away. "I've sheltered you, dear Luke. Do you know, sometimes the fires that rage inside my body, inside my mind, they burn so hot, there are times I've stripped off my clothes and gone out into the desert night to see if the cold light of the moon would give me some relief. What right do I have to bring children into the world to such a mother? Marrying me would be a terrible mistake. Far better to forget me and find another girl."

"I'm not a coward," I said with some anger. "I asked you to marry me, and you owe me an answer, not advice on how I should live my life. Do you love me, Julia, and will you be my wife?"

She put her hands on my shoulders, gently kissed me on the lips, then leaned her head against my chest.

"You know I love you. Of course I want you to be mine. But if one day I saw that you were unhappy and regretted being my husband, it would break my heart." She looked up into my eyes. "I will promise you this: if, three years from this day, you still want me, then I will be yours, I give you my solemn word. Can you bear to prove your love by waiting so long?"

This was both the best and worst of news: Julia James would marry me! But *three years*—over a thousand sunrises, a thousand sunsets...

"If I had to," I said, "I'd wait a hundred years."

"No need for that, darling Luke. The time will pass quickly enough if your heart is true."

And so Julia became my fiancée, though we told no one, thinking that such a long engagement would only prompt questions we preferred not to answer.

For the rest of 1931, and all of the following year, our lives were as calm and uneventful as the times allowed. My mother had indeed become David's right hand. He was pushed to the limit by his job in the tunnels while he continued to preach in Ragtown, McKeeversville, and Las Vegas, and to minister to the poor, hungry, and desperate who flocked to Black Canyon in search of work.

"She's an angel sent by the Lord," he said more than once, and, if he noticed me nearby, would hasten to add, "as you are, Luke. I'd be lost without the two of you."

There were no more deaths from heat prostration. Six Companies was grateful for the advice that David had passed on from Clarence Jackson, and, though they wouldn't hire him, made a modest contribution to the church. David asked the good doctor to work with Ed Grimm and tend to the sick, though we could only afford to pay him a pittance, and from then on I'd often see him and Lucas making their rounds.

On Sundays, Lucas tucked himself in alongside me in the sidecar of the Indian Big Chief and played his fiddle at all of our church services. There were no schools for the children who ran about in the two tent cities, so Julia began to teach classes. My mother held Bible-study and prayer meetings for the women and girls. David and Julia and my mother and I had meals together almost every day. Life was hard, but it was good.

And then, in January 1933, everything changed.

—◦—

"Good morning, Sheriff, will you have breakfast with us?" asked my mother, as Stone appeared at the door of our Ragtown shack.

She, David, Polwarth, Julia, and I were enjoying a rare feast of flapjacks and scrambled eggs.

"Just a cup of joe, Yura, thanks." He settled down on one of the crates we used for chairs and unfolded the Las Vegas Evening Review. "Thought you'd want to see this," he said, handing the paper to David, who read the front-page story aloud.

"Sunday, January 22nd: Fire ravaged the estate of one of Las Vegas' most eminent citizens, Mr. Sebastian Bale, reducing his sprawling mansion to smoldering ashes. 'Most terrible thing I ever seen,' said Oscar Gantry, Bale's gardener, one of the few who survived the blaze. 'Wish I could forget the screams and the smell as the boss's men came running out, their clothes and hair on fire. But I'll tell you the worst, it was looking up at Mr. Bale's office window on the second floor and seeing him standing there, looking out, stock still, like a human torch, all swallowed up in flames. What gave me the chills was, seemed like he was burning without being consumed, if you get what I mean. But then I turned and ran, and I guess there wasn't nothing left of him, soon enough.' The Las Vegas Police Department is conducting an ongoing investigation, and has pronounced the blaze as being of 'suspicious origin.'"

"Your words, Sheriff?" asked Polwarth.

"Yeah, got a silver tongue, don't I."

"Got to admit, it feels good, seeing God's justice delivered like that," Polwarth added.

"*God's* justice?" David asked. "I hope you're right. But somehow I'm not so sure."

"If it was God's idea," said the sheriff, "he delegated the work to someone who used Molotov cocktails loaded with diesel fuel."

"What's that tell you?" queried Polwarth.

"That the perpetrator wasn't concerned about covering his tracks. Most arsonists, they'll start the blaze near a fuse box or fireplace, try to make it look like an accident. Not this guy. He *wants* people to know."

"To know what, exactly?" I asked.

"That something wicked this way comes," said Julia, softly. Her face was pale, and I reached for her hand, which was cold as ice.

Sheriff Stone turned to her, his eyebrows raised.

"My thoughts, exactly, Miss James. I told you, Pastor, there's dark cloud's gatherin', bigger fish than I know how to handle got their sights set on Las Vegas. I've asked Reno for help, but it ain't comin' any time soon. I guess I'm just sayin', take care."

"Your warning's appreciated," said David, "though I doubt there's anything much we can do other than keep trusting in God; it's gotten us this far, and it's going to have to get us the rest of the way. But hold on a second—look at this!"

He put the paper down on our makeshift dining table and pointed to a picture at the bottom of the front page that showed two men standing side by side. The first was a youthful fellow, dressed in black and wearing a clerical collar. On his left was a rumpled, middle-aged, mustached man with wildly disheveled hair.

"That's Albert Einstein!" I said.

"The smartest egghead in the world," said Polwarth. "But who's the priest?"

"I know him," said David, with some excitement. "Georges Lemaître, we fought together in the Great War, in Flanders Fields." He quickly scanned the brief article below the photograph.

"They're in Pasadena, California, at the California Institute of Technology. Dr. Einstein has admitted that he was wrong about the universe—"

"Sounds like kind of a big mistake," said Polwarth.

"—and Georges was right all along. Seems my friend is saying that there was a moment of creation, when the universe began like a great burst of fireworks!"

"Pretty much how I imagined it," I said, "after God said, *Let there be light!*"

"How far away is Pasadena?" asked David.

"250 miles from here," said Julia. "If Dr. Einstein and your friend would hop a freight train, they could be here in six or seven hours!"

"Well, I don't know about your arsonist," said David. "But it's no coincidence, your bringing this paper to me this morning. Thank you, Sheriff! I'm glad I'm working swing-shift today, because I'm going to drive to Las Vegas to send a telegram to Georges. Whether he'll remember me, I don't know, but I'd give anything to see him again."

It seems Lucas must have been nearby, for we suddenly heard his eerie, high-pitched song.

"He wants to know if he can come with you," Julia explained.

"What do you say, Yura?" David asked my mother, who had been listening quietly since the sheriff's arrival. "Let's the three of us go into town, we'll be back before lunch."

"All right," she replied. "If you'll entertain us with stories about Georges and the war, I suppose we can break from the schedule, just this once."

~

There was a telegram waiting for David when he came off shift that night, but it wasn't from Georges Lemaître. He came straight to our shack and woke us, though it was after one A.M. When my mother saw his face, she asked me to read it and tell her what it said.

FOUND THE MAN YOU'RE LOOKING FOR STOP I.D. READS VICTOR NOONGWOOK STOP MINING ACCIDENT, DECEASED STOP BODY HELD AT LOFTON'S IN TONOPAH STOP REGRETS STOP LENNY STEVENS

We rode with David in the Big Chief to Las Vegas, where we woke Sheriff Stone to borrow a car which the exhausted pastor let me drive to Tonopah. It was exceedingly strange, travelling through the high desert once again on a moonlit night. Was this real, or was I dreaming? Was the man Lenny had found truly my father? Perhaps someone had stolen his wallet and was carrying his ID!

David slept during the five-hour trip, and neither my mother nor I said a word.

The sun was just breaking over the eastern horizon when we arrived at Lofton's Funeral Parlor, and we went in search of breakfast, since it didn't open until nine. It was a somber meal, mostly untouched.

Mr. Lofton found us waiting when he opened the doors, and he ushered us into a back room where a body lay on a table, under a sheet.

"We did the best we could," he said, "but you must understand, the man was badly hurt—"

"How did he die?" my mother asked, her voice low and flat.

Lofton hesitated, then cleared his throat.

"Crushed by falling rock. It's all too frequent in the mines."

She strode to the table and pulled back the sheet.

Despite the swelling and abrasions and the beard he'd grown sometime in the past eight years, there was no doubt: there was my father, at long last.

"Taliriktug," my mother said, looking down on his battered face, "your arms were not strong enough when luck ran out. No one's are. You needed your son's, you needed mine."

Then she fell silent, her face a pale mask, void of emotion.

I had thought I was ready to face my father's death, but I saw then that I had never really believed it possible until his still, stiff body lay stretched out before me. In my memory—the remembrance of a thirteen-year-old boy—he had loomed so large; but I was taller and broader-shouldered than this man, and all I could think was, I should never have rested, never have attended school in Seattle or waited in Las Vegas.

"Father," I cried, laying my head on his chest, "this is my fault! I should have kept looking until I found you!"

"Do not embarrass me, Uukkarnit," said my mother. It was the first time in years that she'd used my Athabascan name.

"Luke," said David, putting his hand on my shoulder, "you and Yura did everything humanly possible. These terribly hard moments are what put us to the test. Now, this moment, is when you must put all your trust in the Lord."

"Trust Him to do what?" my mother asked. "To send his father's soul into the depths of hell?"

"Yura—"

"Please, don't speak. I don't want to hear it. Mr. Lofton!" she called out, and the proprietor, who had retreated into the hallway, reentered the room. "I will pay to have my husband cremated, and will return for his ashes."

"As you wish, ma'am. If you would like, I can show you some lovely urns—"

"Enough. A box will suffice, the simplest you have. Now good day." She began walking to the door, and, without stopping, said, "Let's go home."

The Telegram

We drove back to Las Vegas in grim silence. Had my faith been tested and failed? All my prayers—how many thousands, or tens of thousands, had I lifted to God in vain? My worst fears had been realized. What did trusting in Him even mean at this point?

We arrived at our shack at half-past three; both David's and my shift started at four.

My mother began to open the passenger door, then turned to the pastor.

"Don't forget, you're to meet Edward and Clarence in the morning," she said.

"Never mind that," he said. "Can I talk to you when I get off tonight?"

"I've made a decision," said my mother. "I'm going to take Taliriktug's ashes back to Nenana. I've still got some money, I can make my way. Luke, you've got a life here with Julia and David and the church. But Alaska is my home; I can't stay."

"Yura," said David. "How will I get along without you?"

"You've still got Luke, and Edward, and Clarence is a brilliant man, he can do everything far better than me."

"That's not what I meant," said David, his voice breaking.

The two looked at each other for what seemed a long while.

"I'm sorry," said my mother, "but I must go," and she turned and walked away.

Chapter Forty-One
The Seven Sisters

"Mother," I said, following her into our home after David drove off, "how can you leave?"

"There comes a time when mothers and sons part ways," she said, beginning to pack her things. "Of course you must stay; I know that you love Julia, and the love she has for you shines from her eyes."

"But what of David's—"

"Do not talk of what you do not understand," she said sharply. "You father should never have left Nenana, and that is where I, too, belong. Let us not argue over what must be."

One of Murl Emery's suppliers was bound for Reno and San Francisco, and the next day she rode along with him. From there she would take the train to Seattle, where she planned to stay briefly with Asaaluk and Ray, earning enough money from her carvings to take the S.S. Yukon back to Alaska.

In one day, I had lost both mother and father, and the desert around me was mirrored by a bleakness within my soul. How could I carry on, I thought, were it not for Julia and David? But it stung me to think this, for surely solace should first have come from my faith!

To the contrary, thoughts of God, and of His wrath and justice, were filling me with dread.

~

"Not only do I see my father in my memories, I can breathe in his scent of smoke and sweat," I said to Julia and David over breakfast the next day. "I loved when he'd come home and sit by the fire, and I'd rest my head against him while mother carved walrus ivory into the shapes of wolves and bears. He taught me the patience of the hunt; we never joined the men who set out in the spring, but waited for fall, when the caribou were plump and their hides sleek, and he taught me to lie in wait for hours, however stiff with cold, until the moment was perfect, and only then our shots rang out!

"How then can I be at peace, not knowing my father's eternal fate? What bliss could there be in heaven, knowing my father was suffering the torments of hell?"

"My own father chose to walk an evil road," said David, "so I understand what you're saying all too well. But Luke, your love for your father is as nothing compared to the Lord's love for him. God is good and just and perfectly fair, and His Spirit is always at work, revealing the Lord to men. What your or my father's fate will be, I don't presume to know. But we can pray, and we can hope."

"What is gnawing at your mind, though," said Julia, "is that his life was cut short. You think *you* could have saved him, if only you'd have found him and pointed him toward the Light. But then time ran out."

"Well—" I hesitated. Was that the truth? "Yes, I knew what was at stake. How could I rest?"

"Jesus did not tell us to spend every moment searching for one man, even a father, however loved; He told us to make disciples of all the nations, which is what you're doing tirelessly here in Black Canyon. He said that *He*, the shepherd, would not rest until he found His lost sheep—even if only one had strayed. Time ran out for *you*; but I cannot believe that death, the enemy which our Lord defeated at the Cross, is any obstacle for Him.

"I could not have asked for a better, more loving father than my own," she continued, "but our Heavenly Father is a thousand-fold greater yet. Jesus said that blessed are they who have not seen, and yet have believed; but still, He appeared to Thomas and let him place his hand into His open wound. The Bible tells me that our Savior wants all men to be saved and to come to a knowledge of the truth, and so I believe that He reveals Himself to every man. Whether a man might then turn from Him, in the full knowledge of His glory, I can scarcely imagine, for he would then be no different from the demons and would have willed his own damnation. But you have told me enough, darling, that I cannot imagine your father was such a man."

"How I would like to believe that a man might still repent, even after death!" I said. "Yet, 'it is appointed unto men once to die, and after this the judgment.'"

"Judgment, indeed," Julia replied. "A man might well be made to repay the last farthing owed. The Psalmist wrote that *unto thee, O Lord, belongeth mercy: for thou renderest to every man according to his work.* Surely the judgments God renders are merciful because, however terrible, they serve to bring men back to Him.'"

One truth rang out clearly: that it would be well worth it for a man to suffer the worst of torments, if only it led him to despise his sins and turn to God! But was it too much to hope that my father might yet repent, even after death?

I turned to look at David.

"I can't go as far as you, Julia," he said, "for I preach the urgency of accepting Christ in this life. Yet God is rich in mercy, and it would take a cold heart not to hope for those we love. But I hold onto this above all else: the day will come when the Lord will wipe every tear from our eyes, and no fears, no anxious thoughts will plague us! Luke, in the knowledge of His perfect lovingkindness, may your heart find rest."

I would be still, I told myself, and know that He is God; and in that, I found some measure of relief.

～

"Look—this is sweet news," said David the next morning, handing me a telegram he'd received shortly before.

OVERJOYED AT THOUGHT OF SEEING YOU AGAIN, MON CHER AMI STOP GOD WILLING HOPE TO ARRIVE DAY AFTER NEXT STOP JE T'EMBRASSE STOP GEORGES

It was good to see David smiling so broadly, for my mother's departure had been a blow to him, and, though he tried to be joyful, I'd seen a sadness in his eyes that mirrored my own grief.

"Georges went through far more than I did in the war," he said, his face suddenly serious. "It had a great effect on me, seeing the depth of his trust in the goodness of God in the midst of sheer madness. Don't be ashamed of your doubts, Luke. My time in the trenches was no more of a test than what you are going through now—and woe to him who has never wrestled with doubt, when the greater tests come! But if we face doubt honestly and bravely, our faith will emerge all the stronger."

Three days would pass before I'd meet Georges Lemaître. We'd expected him to come by train, but his arrival, much like Jack Johnson's, was heralded by the sounds of a commotion as a Studebaker pulled up in the middle of Ragtown on a blustery January afternoon.

"It's one 'a them damn Bolshies, come to org'nize us!" someone cried, as two men emerged from the vehicle.

"Man's carryin' a violin, you eejit," said another. "Them musicians is *all* long-hairs."

"Get a load of the next fella—somebody must be dyin', 'n called for a priest!"

As I made my way over, I could see Father Lemaître and Albert Einstein, their faces showing much the same amazement as those of the crowd which gaped back at them. The driver of the car, a serious-looking, bespectacled man who, like Georges, looked to be about David's age, got out next.

"Hi, folks," he said. "Hope we're not disturbing anything. Can anybody tell us where to find Pastor David Gold? Or perhaps point us toward his church?"

"His church? You're parked on it," one man remarked. "That stretch 'a sand's where they gather and sing hymns 'n such on Sunday mornings."

"Big Dave's workin' day shift," another offered. "Should'a got off by now, prob'ly home showerin' off the sweat. I'd tell ya ta make yerselves comf'table while yer waitin', but that's pretty much imposs'ble out here."

"Hello!" I called out, making my way through the crowd. "I'm Luke Noongwook, I work with Pastor Gold."

"Milt Humason," said the driver.

"Pleased to meet you," I said, and then turned to Georges. "I'll go tell him you're here—I know he can't wait to see you, Father."

"Thank you, young man," said Georges, and we shook hands. "Allow me to introduce you to Dr. Einstein."

The great man nodded at me morosely.

"This is perhaps not the most picturesque of landscapes or salubrious of climates, eh, Georges?" he muttered.

Gusts of winds were whipping us with sand and playing havoc with Einstein's hair.

"*Alors*, Herr Professor, where is your sense of adventure?" the priest responded, laughing.

"Please," I said, "follow me; my home is exceedingly modest, but you'll be out of the wind and can help yourselves to hot tea."

"I am not much for strong drink, but not entirely a teetotaler—might I hope for *ein kleines Glas Schnapps?*" Dr. Einstein asked wistfully.

I knew that Schnapps was hard liquor and told him that, unfortunately, I kept no alcohol.

"Never fear, Professor, this will warm you right up," said Humason, producing a hip flask.

"Ach, I have tasted your moonbeam—"

"Moon*shine*," said Lemaître.

"—and it is a wonder I am yet alive. *Nie wieder!*"

When we got to the shack, Milt assured me he could work the kerosene stove and went right to work with the tea kettle, so I ran off to find David.

We arrived back at my home to find a small crowd had gathered outside. David had been telling me the story of how he'd first met Georges, but, as we made our way through to the front door, several of the bystanders—our fellow tunnellers and their wives—glowered at us and held their index fingers to their lips.

"Shush!" whispered one. "We're listening to the bee-yoo-tiful music."

They were indeed. Inside, Dr. Einstein was playing Lina, the violin he carried everywhere, pausing frequently to let Lucas repeat what he'd just heard. To my ear, my young friend's notes sounded as rich and warm as the professor's.

"Has he a teacher?" Einstein asked.

"No sir," I answered. "My friend Lucas taught himself, I believe."

"*Ach du lieber, dieser Junge ist ein Genie!* I would teach him the Mozart sonatas, but perhaps you have no pianos or pianists in this wilderness of yours; so, I think it shall be the partitas of Bach. *Ja, er wird sie schön spielen!*"

Georges introduced David to both of his companions, but Dr. Einstein gave David only the most cursory of handshakes before returning to his violin.

"Surely you and Herr Gold have much to talk about," he said to the priest. "The Great War, ja? Only go somewhere, and leave us musicians in peace!"

And so we left.

"I'll do a bit of exploring off the beaten path, if you don't mind," said Milt Humason, as we set off for Julia's Ragtown abode. David had graciously suggested that she join us, and I thought the sheltered overlook where she and I had often gazed down on Black Canyon would be the best place for conversation.

"It was Milt who measured the red shifts for Monsieur Hubble," said Lemaître, after Humason disappeared from view. "He is a bit of a cowboy, that one—they tell me he dropped out of school after the eighth grade and drove mules up and down the mountains after that. But I think there is no one else who could have made such extraordinarily difficult measurements, and done them *avec une précision exquise.* It is thanks to him that we have the evidence of the expansion of the universe. I must tell you, David, I heard tales of his killing a mountain lion, and there is a small arsenal of weapons in the trunk of his car that would have been most useful to us in the war. So you see, Dr. Einstein and I had no fear of highwaymen on our way here."

David and I had hauled wood along with us in our backpacks, and we built a fire, nestled in the overlook and safe from the wind. At Georges' urging, David told him of the journey he'd been on during the eighteen years since the two had parted ways. Julia and I smiled at each other as the two men traded verses from the Psalms, their words sounding like music in the winter night against a counterpoint of crackling flames.

"You are a fortunate man," said Lemaître. "*En effet, un homme béni par Dieu*, for you have been called to serve Him in no small way. My work is my passion, yes, and I hope brings Him glory; but yours wins souls."

"I can scarcely compare the two," said David. "From the newspaper reports, it seems you've proven the story of creation told in Genesis, and even Albert Einstein admits you're right!"

"Ah, Albert wants nothing to do with creation, *mon ami*. But I must correct you, my work has no bearing on the Bible; I have too much respect for God to make him a scientific hypothesis."

"But, as a physicist *and* a priest," David replied, "aren't you the perfect person to unite faith and science?"

"There are two ways of arriving at truth," replied Georges. "The way of science reveals the truths of the physical universe, while the way of faith reveals the truths of man's salvation. But they are separate paths, you see; as a young man, I simply decided to follow them both."

"I don't understand why the paths must be separate," I said, unable to resist speaking up. "The universe is God's creation. Doesn't your theory solve what would appear to be a conflict between religion and science—one which might cause some to lose their faith?"

"I thought much like you when I was your age," said Georges, regarding me with both seriousness and warmth. "*Mais non, ça ne marche pas;* to try to find science in Scripture is like trying to extract theology from the binomial theorem. But conflict is an illusion, *mon jeune ami*, which vanishes when one adopts a more symbolic exegesis. There is no reason to abandon the Bible because we now believe that it took perhaps ten thousand million years to create what we think of as the universe. Genesis teaches that one day in seven should be devoted to rest, worship, and reverence—all of which are necessary for salvation.

"Science sees through a glass darkly and gropes its way to understand God's works; at any moment, its 'truths' are merely our latest and best hypothesis to explain the physical world. But the Word of God reveals eternal, unchanging Truths—truths of our salvation, truths of God's grace.

"You wish for a unity of science and faith? It comes at the moment a scientist—or a student, such as perhaps each of you," he said, looking

309

at both Julia and me, "solving an equation, or observing a photograph of a galaxy, entrusts his work to God, and places it in His hands. A man remains a child of God when he puts his eye to the microscope, just as much as in his morning prayers. When he thinks of the truths of faith, he knows that his knowledge of microbes and moons will be neither a benefit nor a hindrance to approach the inaccessible light; and, as for any man, to enter the kingdom of heaven, he would need to have the heart of a little child."

I felt that a new world was opening up to me and silently thanked God for allowing me to hear George's words that evening.

The men talked as the fire burned down and a crescent moon rose, stark white in the coal-dark sky.

"I fear the blood we shed in the war will not yield a lasting peace," said Georges. "Only yesterday the news came from Germany that Herr Hitler has been appointed chancellor."

"I haven't heard of him," said David.

"A man far worse than the Kaiser, it would appear. Evil is at work in the world, and yet, no more so than when our Lord walked the earth. You know, it was not long after we returned from the trenches that Mr. Yeats wrote 'things fall apart; the center cannot hold; mere anarchy is loosed upon the world.' I admire the music of his poetry, but his despair is born of a feeble faith."

"Indeed," said David. "The center always holds, for the center is Jesus Christ. And still, when I think of your expanding universe, the galaxies fleeing one from another, I feel a great loneliness. Maybe it's an echo of what happens here on Earth—the dead leave us behind, friends grow apart, and love doesn't last; we wake to find our world an emptier place."

"But why this sudden sadness, cher ami? Here we are, reunited after so many years! Surely that refutes your theory of, shall we say, interpersonal entropy?"

"Ah, it's nothing," David replied, "just a passing sadness."

But I knew what he meant; my mother had set off for Alaska, Julia and I had both lost our fathers, Isaiah was gone, and Lucas' dear mother, Charlene, was not long for this world. I gripped Julia's hand tighter and, though I'd meant to pray silently, found myself speaking out loud

"May our eyes stay fixed on Jesus, the author and perfecter of our faith, the center of all things."

"Amen and amen," said Georges.

"Father Lemaître, if I may," said Julia, "I've read that the most complex mathematics is food for your soul, and it is only by solving Dr. Einstein's equations that you came to understand that God designed the universe in a way entirely different from how men had always thought. And you are a priest who quotes the poetry of King David and even of Yeats. So, tell me, please, what you see when you look into this sky stretched out above us, laced with stars?"

Georges looked surprised for a moment, then laughed and raised his eyes to the heavens.

"I see the constellations my father pointed out to me when I was a small boy. Look, there, the Pleiades, a favorite of mine—follow the belt of the hunter, Orion, past that bright star, Aldebaran, and there they are. The Greeks said they were sisters, the seven daughters of Atlas, the titan who holds up the sky."

"Yet I only see six," said Julia, after gazing at the stars for some time.

"Ah well, it is said that Merope, youngest of the sisters, was wooed by Orion. But she married Sisyphus, who was a mere mortal, you know, and so became mortal herself and faded away."

"I'm proud of her," said Julia, "for choosing love over life."

"Georges!" we heard Mr. Humason calling. Dr. Einstein was hungry, he informed us, and we returned to my shack for a meal that Milt had already prepared on the kerosene stove.

Later that evening, I walked Julia to the cabin she shared with Anne-Marie, and when we reached her door she turned and hugged me close.

"You know that I'm the seventh sister," she whispered. "But it's not true, that bit about fading away. No, darling Luke, I told you, I'm star-fire that fell to earth. And landed here, safe in your arms."

We remained outside, joined in that tender embrace, for the longest time.

Chapter Forty-Two
The Night of Falling Stars

Despite his fondness for Lucas, the desert was not much to Dr. Einstein's liking, and so the three men bid us farewell the next day. Georges and Milt lingered over breakfast with David and me and promised to return by themselves in mid-April. The priest's talk of two paths to the truth had fired my imagination; I thought of it while I toiled in the tunnels, and I talked of it with Julia when I was done with work. David had set me on the path of revelation, of God's Word, and he had led me to the Psalmist's words of praise:

The heavens declare the glory of God; the skies proclaim the work of His hands.

There are no coincidences, Julia said, only the sovereign workings of God, the prowling of the devil, and the striving of our own free will. The Lord had brought Father Lemaître into my life for a reason, and I found myself hungering to explore the work of His hands, the better to see His glory.

There was no public library in Las Vegas, but I sought out the science teacher at the high school, who loaned me a battered copy of *In Starry Realms*, an astronomy text published twenty-three years before. I read it over the next two days, sleeping for only a few hours each night. In 1910, men thought of the Milky Way as the entire cosmos; just two decades later, we knew it to be only one island in a limitless ocean! How the Lord was blessing mankind with new insight into the wonders of His creation!

Men were turning from God and blaming their doubt on science, but astronomy was revealing heavens of unspeakable majesty, heavens that declared His glory and shouted His praise!

I ingratiated myself to the editor of the Evening Review, who granted me access to their archives of back issues. The text I'd been reading spoke of six planets which revolved around the sun, but I'd learned of eight in school, and soon enough found a headline from 1930 that heralded the discovery of a ninth:

Illinois Farmboy Finds Long-Sought Planet 'X'!

I read about Clyde Tombaugh, who was only three years older than me when he discovered a new world that God had long ago set spinning in the vastness of space, and I read about the contest to give it a name. I'd never have dubbed the ninth planet *Pluto*, god of the underworld, but rather Gabriel, or Michael, or perhaps Abraham, whose descendants would one day be more numerous than the stars!

Was the Lord calling me to study the skies? I knelt down on the floor at the Evening Review and prayed for guidance, much to the amusement of the staff.

⁓

That night, Julia and I bundled up against the cold and lay on our backs looking up at the night sky and talking for hours.

"It's not much of a mystery, when you're called," she said. "You can fight it, but then you'll only end up kicking against the goads or getting swallowed by a whale. Now, whether it's your *own* fancy, masquerading as God's will, that's another question. There's a Psalm you can pray to get to the bottom of that, of course. Go on, I know you've learned them all by heart—or have I stumped the Bible answer man?"

"That's too easy!" I laughed. "But it's what I wish for with everything in me: *Search me, O God, and know my heart: Try me, and know my thoughts; and see if there be any wicked way in me, and lead me in the everlasting way.*"

Our talk turned to her own calling, and I listened with both fascination and dread.

"Because of my gift," she told me, "we travelled all through the desert states—West Texas, New Mexico, Arizona, Nevada, never settling anywhere until Las Vegas.

"We'd be staying in some roadside inn, when the Spirit would come upon me like a torrent, and I'd know there would soon be streams of water in the dry and empty land. My father and I would set up a tent in the nearest town, and you should have heard him, speaking truth to anyone with ears to hear, telling them that they're dead in their sins until they turn to Christ. Oh, how he preached repentance and the love and mercy of Almighty God! Word spread, people would be waiting for me, for the girl who knew when floods would rage through the arroyos, and could lead them to rivers in the wasteland to be baptized, new men, new women, reborn from above."

"But you suffered every time. I think your father settled here because he couldn't bear to see you in pain; he hoped that if you settled down, the visions would come to an end."

"Ah, Luke," she said, and leaned her head against me. "Who with the love of God in her heart would not choose to suffer so?"

Julia's last vision of the racing waters had been for my baptism eighteen months before. I wanted to ask her if she missed the feeling of the Spirit coming upon her, missed the excitement of the crowds, the thrill of helping to win souls for the Lord. But I kept silent, afraid of what her answer might be. I was glad the visions had stopped, and not simply out of concern for her well-being; I wanted her all for myself.

~

Georges Lemaître and Milt Humason came back on April 16th, checked into a hotel in Las Vegas, and drove out to Ragtown that night. After dinner, while the priest and the pastor went for a walk, Milt taught me seven-card stud, which we played for matchsticks, and all the while we played, we talked. I learned he loved horses and fishing, and he was keen to hear my tales of hunting in Alaska and of my father's skill as a musher and his heroic race to deliver diphtheria vaccine to Nome in '25. Soon enough, I told him of how Georges' words had sparked my interest, and of what I'd been reading, and the passion that was growing within me for the stars.

"Planet X, that's a sore subject," he said, with a wry smile. "When the news came of Tombaugh's discovery, I went back and looked at photographic plates I'd made back in 1919, and there it was, plain as the nose on your face. I missed it; Clyde didn't. And you know what? Good for him!"

Milt set the cards down.

"I can see you're fascinated by all this. If you're asking me whether you can become an astronomer, well, sure, why not. I never saw the inside of a high school, and Tombaugh never went to college. But it's a long, tough road. You want to know what I have going for me? Sheer persistence and an inventive mind. And I'm color blind, which makes my night vision better than most. So, tell me, Luke, what is it you've got?"

"From what I've read about it," I replied, "I have an eidetic memory; once something's in my head, it doesn't leave. Also, mathematics comes easy to me, though I've never had a chance to find out how good I am. And while I stumble sometimes, I'm devoted to the Lord Jesus Christ."

"A photographic memory would come in handy, there's no doubt about that," said Milt. "As to math—or the Lord, for that matter—I need to get you with Georges, he's the master in both those departments."

Father Lemaître began working with me the next morning, assessing my knowledge of calculus and seeing how quickly I grasped more advanced ideas. By late that afternoon, he closed the notebook we were using to perform calculations and looked at me intently.

"You have the mind for science, I am convinced; it is only a question of whether this is a mere flirtation or the beginning of a lifetime love. I would be happy to recommend your acceptance to the California Institute of Technology, where my name is not unknown and a scholarship might perhaps be available. Now come, we'll join David and Milt for dinner, and I hope Miss Julia will join us as well. Then perhaps we shall all do some gazing at the stars."

～

"Look up at the *Voie Lactée*," said Georges, after we'd taken an after-dinner stroll and settled into the lookout over Black Canyon, "the Milky Way Galaxy that blazes above our heads, and tell me what you see. Be precise; I am not looking for poetry."

"I see a hazy band of light stretched across the length of the sky," Julia offered.

"It's ten or twenty degrees wide," I added, "and the stars seem distributed fairly uniformly throughout."

"*Eh bien*," said the physicist-priest, "not too terribly bad. So, what then can you tell me of the shape of this galaxy we find ourselves in—and perhaps of our location within it?"

We gazed and thought in silence for a while.

"It must be relatively flat," I said at last. "For, if it were a sphere, then the haze of stars would appear throughout the sky, not only in what is, after all, a fairly narrow band. And I suppose we must be more or less in the same plane as the majority of stars, for if we were much above or below, the sky would not appear to be split in half, and one side of the night sky would be far brighter."

"Well done," said Georges. "Our galaxy is indeed a flattened disk, with spiraling arms, and we are on the disk plane, Luke, as you said. Now I will tell you something that men have only known for a bit more than ten years: our sun is nowhere near the center of the Milky Way, but exiled to the outer reaches of one spiral arm. It appears that our Lord has placed us on a rather small planet, circling what is only a middling star. How far we are from the galactic core! When I first heard this, I wondered, how might our world appear to one looking out from the grandest star-castle in the very center of that great city of light?"

He motioned to the heavens and smiled at us.

"And the answer that came to me, you know, is that we would not look much different than Nazareth must have seemed when viewed from Rome. So, you see, my paths are separate, yes, but from each I learn humility, and in each I behold the magnificence of God."

For a while, Georges talked of astronomy, and then, finding we knew little of the constellations and less of Greek mythology, he told us more of the stories his father had told him about the gods and heroes pictured in the stars.

"Look to the north," he told us. "You see what looks like a 'W', yes? That is Cassiopeia, who boasted that she was the most beautiful of women—fairer even than the gods! So, Poseidon, ruler of the seas, this angered him greatly, for he was quite sure that none were more beautiful than his nymphs. In his rage, he brought forth a monster, a leviathan, to ravage the seas. Well, you can imagine that men pleaded with Cassiopeia, but, in her vanity, she would not admit any fairer than her! Therefore, the gods decreed that her only daughter, lovely Andromeda, be sacrificed to the sea monster Poseidon had unleashed."

Georges showed us how to find the constellation Andromeda before continuing his tale.

"So the beautiful maiden was chained to a rock at the ocean's edge and left to await the monster's arrival. But do not despair! Look where I am pointing now: there is our hero, Perseus, arriving in the nick of time to slay the beast, free Andromeda, and take her home to be his bride."

He looked over at David.

"You are perhaps wondering why I chose to speak of this myth? I will let your pastor hazard a guess."

"I know nothing of Greek myths," said David, "but it strikes me that your story is a foreshadowing of Christ. Cassiopeia's pride was the primal sin, putting herself before God, no different than Adam and Eve. Her daughter then paid the price, chained to the rock, facing an awful and certain death, as we do, too, prisoners of the ruler of this world. But, glory be to God, His Son has rescued us, defeating death and freeing us from slavery to sin! We, His church, are set free to be the bride of Christ."

"Just so!" said Georges. "And now I will tell you one last tale. You have heard of Orpheus and Eurydice, perhaps? He was the son of Apollo and Calliope, the muse, and he played his lyre so sweetly that even the wildest of beasts was charmed. The constellation Lyra is his lyre, and it is quite easy to find, for it contains Vega, one of the brightest of stars. You see—" he pointed "—yes, right there. Now, Orpheus fell desperately in love with the nymph, Eurydice, who adored him in return, and the two were soon wed. But when she was out among her fellow nymphs, a shepherd, smitten by her beauty, gave her chase, and as she ran from him she stumbled upon a serpent and perished from its poisonous bite.

"Orpheus, beside himself with grief, sought out Pluto, ruler of the underworld, and so entranced the dark lord with his music that he was granted permission to take his beloved Eurydice with him to the world above. But there was a condition, of course; as she followed him, he must not look back until he had left the land of the dead. Up and up and up they climbed, in utter silence, through the cold blackness of Pluto's realm, closer and closer to the light and warmth at the surface of the earth. Then, just before reaching his goal, Orpheus, concerned that his wife's strength might be failing, glanced behind him; and as he did so, the beautiful nymph was pulled back into the stygian depths. He reached out for her, in vain; and though she died a second death, Eurydice had only the tenderest affection for her husband, for she knew he bore her a very great love."

We were silent for a few moments, contemplating the story and looking up at the stars.

"I tell you this sad tale of Orpheus and his lyre," said Father Lemaître, "because the night after next, if you gaze up at Lyra, you will see a shower of meteors—the Lyrids, they are called; and who knows, perhaps they are the tears of the gods."

~

"You're walking so slowly," I said to Julia, as I accompanied her home later that evening. "Are you all right?"

She stopped, placed her hands on my shoulders and looked up into my eyes.

"Luke, I don't want to wait any longer, let's be married as soon as possible, tonight if David would do it! I've not been afflicted since the time of your baptism, that's a whole year and a half—so you see, I'm a fallen star whose fire has quite gone out. I want to make you breakfast when you come home from a night of peering up at the heavens, and have your babies, and I want us to live a terribly normal, happy life. Oh darling, I'm sorry I didn't say yes right away—yell at me, tell me what an idiot I've been, only say you still want me for your wife!"

"You're a woman of the wildest extremes," I said smiling, my heart filled with joy. "But since we've waited this long, let's take one more day to invite our friends and be married on the night of falling stars."

"Well, of course you're right," said Julia, and she hugged me and leaned her head against my chest. "But I'm entirely too excited to sleep;

let's at least tell David, even if we have to wake him up. Oh, how I wish Lucas was here!"

Our pastor's lights were out when we arrived at his shack, but I roused him by pounding enthusiastically on his door.

"You two!" he said, when he appeared after a moment. "Is something wrong?"

"No, no, something is wonderfully right. We want you to marry us the day after tomorrow, and to give us your blessings, for you're practically a father to us both."

"And I assure you, this is no rash decision," Julia added, "for we've been secretly engaged these past eighteen months."

"Ah, well, it's not really been much of a secret," David said, laughing. "You've been through a lot in the last few years, both of you, as have we all. I do think you're good for each other. *Two are better than one*—" he paused and looked at me, smiling.

"*...because they have a good return for their labor,*" I said, continuing the quote from Ecclesiastes. "*If either of them falls down, one can help the other up. And if two lie down together, they will keep warm. But how can one keep warm alone?*"

"Indeed," said David, "there are cold days of the soul when a dozen woolen blankets wouldn't help. But what pleases me most is that I know you place God first, above even each other; *and though one may be overpowered, two can defend themselves, for a cord of three strands is not quickly broken.*"

We invited everyone we knew.

Lucas was my best man, and he played his fiddle while Lauren sang *Blessed Be the Tie That Binds* along with Anne-Marie. Harold Merkle had grown very frail, but Mr. Polwarth devoted himself to his friend, pushing him everywhere in a second-hand wheelchair that David had procured. Murl Emery was there, as was Mr. Skull and his men, who came bearing gifts—none of which, the big man assured me, were purloined. Still, throughout the ceremony and the celebration, they kept a wary distance from Sheriff Stone.

Clarence Jackson came too, carrying his beloved wife, Charlene, who had lost the use of her arms and legs and could no longer speak.

The Night of Falling Stars

"I want to show you something," he said, placing his wedding ring alongside his wife's so that together they formed a sideways figure eight. "Look: this is eternity. This is the infinite fullness of love."

"*Place me like a seal over your heart, like a seal on your arm,*" I said, as we'd made this verse from the Song of Songs a part of our vows.

"*For love is as strong as death, its jealousy unyielding as the grave. It burns like blazing fire, like a mighty flame,*" Julia responded.

So we were wed; and all that night, the stars of the sky fell to earth, one by one.

Chapter Forty-Three
The Leap

"Show me a man who says that he has never been beset by doubt," said Georges Lemaître, "and I will show you a liar."

David, Milt, Georges, Julia, and I were once again talking late into the night, sitting around a fire we'd built in the sheltered overlook at the edge of Black Canyon.

"Still," I said, "I feel guilty—or stupid!—for finding myself so troubled by these handful of passages of Scripture. Abraham and Isaac, for example. I believe my father was tempted by Satan to abandon his wife and son. But for God to ask—no, to *command* a man to kill his child, even as a test of faith, as you have said, Pastor Gold, to make the point that we cannot put anything before Him? It seems needlessly cruel."

"There are passages so difficult," said Julia, "that I have decided to leave them as mysteries."

"I would gladly do the same; but I am told to love the Lord my God with all my heart and soul and strength and mind, and the terrible pain of such verses is that they place a stumbling block in the way of love. Am I failing the test that Abraham passed?"

"Does this sound at all familiar to you?" said David to Georges, before turning to me. "I understand your anguish all too well; we had many such discussions in 1915, while bullets whizzed above our heads."

"*Oh la la*, for shame," said Father Lemaître, "for the most part, we conversed in perfect safety while my leg was on the mend. But I must tell you, *mon ami*, I agree with our young friend Luke, your exegesis fails to entirely satisfy. God, being omniscient, could have had no doubt of Abraham's faith; *ainsi*, something more must have been intended." The priest fixed me with his intense yet gentle gaze. "To us, child sacrifice is not only an utter horror, but a freakish aberration; but in the days of Abraham, a god might demand the offering up of one's son or daughter at any time. Yes, it was a test, only not that God might learn of Abraham, *but Abraham of God*. In this way was the character of the

Almighty revealed: that He is no Moloch, but *He Who Provides*, who is ever giving us all we need. And this also Abraham came to understand: that through our faithful obedience, God's blessings flow to us and to all the nations of the earth."

We talked of other hard passages in Scripture, and, while there was much I learned, not every explanation put my heart at ease.

"I'll tell you what I know," said Julia, when I expressed my dissatisfaction with both David's and Georges' interpretation of the conquest of the Canaanites. "That I trust utterly in a God who is light, and in whom there is no darkness at all. And if I don't see the light in something that Scripture tells me is of God, then I put it aside, and I am still, and I know the day will come when the truth I cannot yet perceive will be made clear."

"Julia," said David, "yours is a beautiful faith. But there are those of us who must struggle with doubt for a time, like Jacob, who wrestled with the angel and received his wound. And we must be willing to be wounded in our struggles—as you have been—for there are wounds that make us wise, that ready us for battles yet unfought, even wounds that heal."

"Indeed," said Father Lemaître, "wounds that make us one with Christ, who alone enables us to weather the darkest nights of the soul."

That night, I resolved to take a final leap of faith in God's goodness, in His infinite lovingkindness, and hold on to my faith in Him, no matter what.

⟶

Our two friends bid us farewell the next day, promising to return in early July before Georges returned home to Belgium. Julia's and my thoughts soon turned to whether I ought to apply to the California Institute of Technology. The thought of leaving David in the lurch was painful, but he insisted that it would be the purest foolishness not to follow through on Georges' suggestion, and that God would raise up others in the church to fill the gap.

Julia said that she would get a job once we'd moved to Pasadena;

if there were no opportunities to teach, then she'd wait tables or do whatever came along. We decided to put off having children until I was out of school, but still, it was impossible to resist imagining what they might be like.

"I hope we have a girl who looks just like you," I told her on more than one occasion.

"Only after a little boy who's the very image of his daddy," she'd reply.

We'd name him Justin, after her father, and his sister would be Yura.

"You have stolen my heart, my sister, my bride," I would quote to her from the Song of Songs, for Julia was my rose of Sharon, my dove, my flawless one. She told me that, before our marriage, she'd often lain awake deep into the night; but how soundly she slept in our days together, her head against my chest, the better to hear the beating of my heart. I'd fight off sleep just to treasure those moments, and breathe in her scent, which was like star jasmine borne on the desert wind.

So we loved, and dreamed, and made our plans; and all the while, another man was making his.

Chapter Forty-Four
A Consuming Fire

For the newlyweds, the month of May was blissfully mild, but the mercury began rising several degrees every day by the middle of June, and by July it rarely dipped below one hundred until long after sunset. Six Companies put on quite a fireworks display on the Fourth, but, midway through, Julia told Luke that she wasn't feeling well and asked if they could go home.

When he touched her hands, they were cold as the Arctic waste.

"Do you think you're pregnant?" he asked.

"No, it's not that," she replied, and then, when they were inside their front door, she kissed her husband tenderly and hugged him close. "I love you, darling Luke," she whispered. "We are forever, you know, together in Christ, and nothing can ever change that."

"Tell me what's wrong!" he implored her, for a moment feeling terribly afraid.

"I'm sorry," she said, "it's really nothing, just a woman's passing mood. Come, let's go to bed, you'll hold me, and everything will be fine."

But that night she hardly slept at all.

~

The next morning, Luke and Julia and Lucas were having breakfast with David when a visitor entered through the unlocked door.

"Davey Gold!" said the man, who spoke with a Brooklyn accent. "What kind 'a crap-hole are you livin' in these days?"

He was a good-looking man with blue eyes and dark, slicked-back hair, dressed in a tan linen suit, white fedora, and brown and white spectator shoes complete with spats.

"Hello, Ben," said the pastor.

"Hello, Ben? That's all you got?"

David was silent, his face expressionless, his eyes fixed on the man who'd walked in.

Ben wiped a thin film of sweat from his forehead with a silk handkerchief. "These two yours?" he asked, motioning to Julia and Luke.

"Neighbors," said David. "They were just leaving to go to work."

A man, elegantly dressed, reeking of evil, Luke thought, remembering the vision he'd had nearly three years before. For a moment his heart raced wildly; and then, suddenly, he was calm.

Faced with darkness, he would show no fear.

"I am Luke Noongwook," he said. "Who are you?"

"Ben Siegel," said the man, grinning widely. "Boy's got better manners than you, cuz, someone'd think you were raised in a friggin' barn."

David's cousin was one of the founders of Murder, Inc. and a friend of Meyer Lansky and Al Capone. The press referred to him as Bugsy Siegel, though no one called him that to his face and lived.

"Lemme give you some advice, kid," said Siegel. "That last name's gotta go. You ever been to the movies?"

Luke offered no response, but Bugsy continued, oblivious.

"Some 'a my best friends' is Hollywood stars—just the other day I wuz havin' highballs with Charlie Farrell and friggin' Louis B. Meyer comes by, asks me to take a screen test, can you believe it? Anyway, Clark Gable, he was at my dinner party in L.A. last week, I'll lay you ten to one his name used to be Clark Noongwook before they made him change it. It's all about PR, kid, ya gotta wise up.

"And you, dollface," he continued, looking at Julia. "You ought'a put on a few pounds, that skinny-ass flapper look's gone out'a style."

"You have business with me, Ben, let's discuss it in private," said David.

"Oh, I got business with you, all right," said Bugsy. "However, I'm gonna go get some breakfast in Vegas, seein' as the odds of a decent meal in this Crapolaville 'a yours is less than zero." He paused, noticing Lucas, who was staring toward the ceiling, mouthing the words to a silent song. "But first, maybe the crazy nigger kid can shine my shoes. There'd be a dime in it for him, what do you say?"

David pushed back his chair and stood up, a full head taller than Bugsy Siegel.

"That's enough, Ben. Whatever you're here for, it's between you and me."

The gangster looked up at him and gave the pastor his broadest smile. At the same time, two other well-armed men stepped inside.

"Touchy, ain't you," said Bugsy. "Relax, big guy. Although, funny thing is, see, there's bigger than you out there, did you know that? Yeah, funny indeed. Anyhow, stick around, I wouldn't go anywhere, I wuz you. I'll be back soon enough."

The two gunmen smirked at David, then followed their boss out into his Ford Deuce Coupe.

"He's my cousin," the pastor explained, watching the men drive away. "I'm sorry to have put you through that. I was on a path to doing something terribly stupid and sinful a few years ago; I was going to throw a fight to a man, and Ben would have made money by betting on it, and then given me a cut. By the grace of God, I came to my senses at the last minute and never showed for the fight. My cousin didn't lose a red cent from it, he's just here to give me a hard time. None of this involves you, but he's got a notoriously bad temper, so just steer clear of me for a while, that's all. It's a family matter, really; there's nothing for Ben here in Ragtown. I'll humor him, and he'll soon enough lose interest and be gone."

David wasn't sure that he believed his own words, and neither Luke nor Julia looked convinced.

"I'm not afraid of those men," said Luke. "I don't much like the thought of you dealing with them alone; I'd rather be by your side."

"No! That's out of the question," David said sharply. "This is *my* business, is that clear? Luke, get to your shift, *now*, and let them know I won't be in today. And Julia, take Lucas, go to McKeeversville and just stay there with Clarence, out of sight."

The pastor walked outside with his friends and hugged each in turn.

"I'm sorry," he told them, "it's going to be enough for me to deal with my cousin, I don't want to be worrying about the three of you.

Now go and do as I said."

From a bluff about a hundred yards away, Bugsy Siegel was looking at the foursome through binoculars and laughing.

"Awfully fond 'a your neighbors, ain't you, cuz." He handed the field glasses to a man next to him who hadn't accompanied the others to David's home. "Focus in on the skinny dame and little black Sambo there," he said. "He got real defensive about the kid, I think that's our best bet if you wanna rumble; but worst case, get the girl, then meet us at that spot we spec'd out up the road. And don't mess up, see, or you'll find yourself right back at the loony bin I sprung you from."

"No, boss," said the man, a look of distress crossing his face. "I no mess up," and he rose to his full seven-foot four-inch height and began lumbering toward Lucas and Julia.

"Come on, you lugs," said Busgy, "let's go back for Gold."

Siegel's gunmen looked at each other and rolled their eyes. Ever since the arson job they'd pulled on the Bale gang, clearing the way to take over the casino action in Vegas, the boss was acting even more bugged-out than usual. There was money to be made, and yet here they were in the hottest part of the desert, wasting time on some two-bit preacher!

What had gotten into Bugsy, anyway?

~

Julia kissed Luke goodbye as he set off for Black Canyon, then took Lucas by the hand. After they'd gone a short distance, he looked at her quizzically and reached up to stroke her cheek.

"Ah, dear one," she said. "There's nothing I can hide from you."

Inside her, the fires were raging once again.

Lord Jesus, she silently prayed, *this is so terribly hard to bear. Yet not mine, but your will be done; only please, help me to be brave.*

Suddenly, everything within Julia's field of vision faded from sight, as though veiled by a dense fog, except for Lucas and another figure, a monster of a man, striding rapidly toward them. She kneeled down and put her hands on the small boy's shoulders.

"Look at me," she said, and he gazed steadily into her eyes. "You must do as I say: run home, run like the wind, like you've never run before, and don't look back." She kissed him on the forehead. "Now go."

Lucas tore off, and she turned toward her nemesis.

"So," said Julia James, looking up into the giant's cruel, brutal face, "are you the one who will baptize me with blood?"

~

David was hardly surprised when Bugsy returned with his men.

"Lost my appetite, cuz, so let's talk. Where's your church, by the way? Oh, that's right, you don't have one, that's what I heard." He laughed sardonically. "I'm imaginin' it's Sunday mornin', some ol' grannie's sittin' on a rock just to rest her bones, 'n there you are, yammerin' in her face; yeah, be a sure sign there's a God if he'd send a howlin' wind to drown out your voice."

"Ben, you're angry with me because I skipped out on the fight, and I don't blame you. But I know you wouldn't have paid Carter Jackson before hearing he'd taken a dive. Look, I'm sorry, cousin, more than I can say."

"Hey, he's sorry," Bugsy repeated to his two gunmen. "Well okay then boys, let's vamoose."

He turned as if to go, then spun around, his face red with rage, kicked David's dining table over, sending the plates clattering onto the floor, then smashed a chair against the wall, reducing it to splinters. Siegel retrieved his fedora, which had fallen off during the tantrum, brushed it off, then checked his hair in the mirror and carefully repositioned his hat at just the right jaunty angle.

"I ain't angry with you 'cause you skipped, I'm angry 'cause you're dumber than a rock. Makes me wonder if we're really flesh and blood." Bugsy took out a silver cigarette case, then snapped his fingers, and one of his men hopped forward with a light. He took a deep drag, exhaled, then leaned back against the wall and regarded David with a contemplative gaze.

"Pastor Dave," he said after a while, drawing the words out so that they dripped with scorn. "I ask you, what would our Bubbe Gold say, suckin' her tea through that sugar cube she held between her teeth, huh? *Oy vey iz mir,* that's what she'd say. *Feh!* Probably spit right in your face. Hey, come to think of it, these hobo hicks know you're a New York Jew? Hmm? No, I can tell, they don't know crap.

"I'll tell you a story, heard it from one of my Texas boys, maybe you'll think it's funny, maybe you won't. There's this couple, see, down in Houston, this sheik and his Sheba, and they're goin' at it every night like guys 'n dolls do; 'n I don't wanna shock you or nothin', but it's entirely possible they weren't hitched, hadn't even said their I do's. But anyhow, men bein' men—'cept for you, I mean—after a while, the guy gets bored with this Betsy, so one morning he kind'a eases himself outta bed and tells the broad he's goin' out for a pack 'a cigarettes. And he don't ever come back. Well, this poor dumb Dora, she's waitin', and waitin', and hours are goin' by and then days, until finally she gets up outta bed and pulls on some clothes and says, 'Who'd 'a thunk he'd have to go all the way to Dallas for smokes!'"

Siegel cackled, then took a last drag, flicked the cigarette to the floor and ground it out under his shoe.

"Do you get it, cuz? See, all you Christers, you Jesus lovers, you remind me 'a that dizzy dame. It's what, goin' on two thousand years later, and you're still waitin'? Your guy ain't comin' back, Davey boy, wake up 'n face the music."

David, who had kept himself still and calm, felt a muscle twitch in his jaw.

"Tell me what you want, Ben. If it's the money you could have made, you can see I don't have a dime to my name."

"Yeah, I'll bet ol' granny put her false teeth in the collection plate, and after that she wuz all tapped out." Bugsy scowled. "I should be upset, you thinkin' I'm just all about the moolah. But that's okay, I gotta remember you're none too bright. You wanna know what I want? Okay, I'll tell you: you're gonna fight that match you wuz 'sposed to lose."

"I'm done with boxing, and after all this time, who would bet on me, anyway?"

"Oh, hell, no one. But you're not gettin' it. This'll be a private showing, see, just for me 'n the boys. Only, Mr. Jackson, he's the no-show this time, 'cause it seems he kind'a lost his head, so to speak, at the hands of my new guy. Yeah, I got a dandy of a pug, cuz, he's undefeated, everyone I've sicced him on is pushin' up daisies."

Please, Lord, David prayed, *guide me, I don't know what to do.*

"I'm not a boxer anymore, Ben. I don't fight. If that makes me a coward in your eyes, so be it."

"You don't fight, huh?" said Bugsy, as he motioned for his goons to hustle David into their car. "We'll see about that."

~

As soon as Lucas knew he was out of sight, he doubled back and peeked out cautiously from behind the side of an adjoining house. He noted the direction in which the giant had set off with Julia, and then, seeing Siegel and the others taking off in the Deuce Coupe, ran swiftly back to David's home, retrieved the keys to the Indian Big Chief, hopped up onto the driver's seat and tore off for Black Canyon.

Six Companies had set some old railroad crossing gates at the entrance to the dam site, and the security guard manning them was just settling into a pleasant snooze when the roar of a motorcycle jarred him awake. He rubbed his eyes; it looked like there was a tiny black kid driving Pastor Dave's Big Chief!

"Hey! Stop!" he called out, then dove out of the way seconds before Lucas came crashing through the entry gate and barreled on, swerving out of the way of the astonished construction workers, until he reached the area where he knew his friend was helping to build the dam's foundation. Then he threw back his head and howled a high, shrill siren song.

Hearing Lucas' cry, Luke dropped his tools and ran to the boy's side. It took only a short, sad melody for him to understand what had transpired and where.

"I'll take the Big Chief," he said. "Thank you, dear friend—now go home and stay safe until my return."

Luke headed for the spot Lucas had last seen Julia and her captor; he'd hunted enough big game in Alaska that he was confident he could follow the giant's tracks.

Lucas, however, had no thoughts of going home. He looked around the construction site, then dashed over to a delivery van which had been left in idle while the driver got out to ask directions. The entry security guard was talking with an angry supervisor when a loud honking attracted their attention: with Lucas barely tall enough to see over the steering wheel, it appeared that a driverless van was bearing down on them at high speed! They dove out of the way as the vehicle crashed through the exit gate with its driver intent on alerting the sheriff.

But much would happen before Lucas would find Sheriff Stone.

~

The gangsters drove about a mile down Trespass Trail before leading David out of the Ford at gunpoint. They climbed a small hill, then descended to a sheltered area where someone had placed rocks defining a square about the size of a boxing ring.

"It ain't Madison Square Garden," said Bugsy, "but then, you never fought there, did you. Never made it to the big time. Well, that's all right. I got a soft spot for losers. Good ones, anyway." He barked out a short, angry laugh. "Nah, not really. What do I always say, boys?"

"The only good loser's a dead loser," they replied in unison.

"You a good loser, Davey? You lose gracefully, with style? Tip your hat to the pug standin' over you, lettin' his sweat drip down 'n mix with your blood?"

Siegel abruptly drew a revolver and held it to his cousin's face.

"Get down on your knees, pal."

David knelt down, expressionless, keeping his gaze fixed on Bugsy's eyes.

"You know what I think, Davey boy? I think you're a bad influence on the fine up-and-comin' metropolis of Las Vegas. I been investing here, see, which is why I bumped off that loud-mouth who used to do the preachin' in these parts. So what do you think when I learned that my own dear cousin had shown up to take his place? Was I a happy man when I heard that, boys?"

"No, boss."

"That's right, I was not. So, you're gonna fight this morning, cuz, 'n it's gonna be the fight of your life. Look over yonder—" he pointed to where the giant was just coming into view perhaps two hundred yards away, walking along the ridge of the hill, and congratulated himself for having planned the brute's entry for maximum effect. "Golem's his name. But, you bein' David 'n all, let's just call him Goliath."

David glanced at the behemoth, though he couldn't yet tell that he was carrying Julia in his arms. He's young, the pastor thought, bulked up with muscle, and well over seven feet tall; must weigh upwards of three hundred pounds.

"I'll give you an out, buddy, if you're startin' to crap your pants. All you gotta do is tell me that Jesus ain't your man."

David spit in the gangster's face.

Bugsy took out his silk handkerchief and wiped himself off.

"You'll regret that," he whispered into the pastor's ear, and kissed his forehead with lips cold as ice.

Only then did David see whom Golem was carrying.

⟿

Why hadn't she understood before, Julia wondered, *how beautifully the fire burned!* She marveled at what she saw, looking inward toward the white-hot heart of the inferno: a great melting away of regret and sin and sorrow, all the detritus of life, the bits and pieces that had never come together, now fusing into something that shone like diamonds. Like the Pleiades on a moonless night! She would show them to Luke as soon as she could.

And ah! Ah! A voice was calling to her from out of the darkness, the sweet cool darkness, bidding her come to where her Savior waited on the far shore, in a bright land free of pain.

〜

"She's got nothing to do with this," said David, trying to still his mind and stave off panic. "You want a fight, Ben, all right, I'll give you one, I'll take your man on, only let the girl go."

"I dunno, cuz, seems to me like you're just going through the motions. I need you properly motivated, see. I'm thinkin' I gotta light your fuse. You know, you want a horse to run his best, you gotta dig your spurs into his side."

Bugsy nodded to the giant, who gave him a savage grin and then, to David's horror, twisted his captive's neck and cast her lifeless body to the ground.

But only a husk dropped to the desert sand, for Julia had long since escaped.

Seeing his young friend murdered was more than David could bear; in a frenzy of rage, he lunged toward Bugsy, seeking to maim him, kill his cousin if he could before they shot him dead, but Golem was too quick and blocked his way. He felt as if he'd run into a stone wall, and then he was being pummeled, his ribs cracking from the man's body blows, his face a bloody mask.

Everything began to slow down in his mind. *You ever fight a tall man,* Jack Johnson had asked him in a Paris café, in another life, a million years before. *Tell me, Jack,* he thought, *tell me what to do.* And the champion grinned at him and repeated the words he'd said at Les Deux Magots: *surest way to knock a man out is a mighty jab to the jaw, thrown from below. Tall man's brains bounce around and he passes out cold for the count.*

Summon all your strength, he told himself, for one last punch.

But it was no good, he was too old, too slow, too weak, and it was Golem who delivered a savage blow that sent David to his knees.

"Hold up, big guy," said Siegel. "How you doin', cuz? Had better days? Hey, where's your boy Jesus when you need him?"

David looked to where Bugsy's voice was coming from, for his eyes were nearly swollen shut.

"Listen to me, you son of Satan," he said. "You can kill me, kill my friends, but know this: the Day of the Lord is coming. He will have His day of vengeance, for my God is a consuming fire, and His sword will devour and drink its fill of your blood."

"What do you say, boss?" asked Golem.

Bugsy nodded and pointed his thumb down.

"Finish him off."

In the moment that followed, there came a silence, broken only by something that sounded like the far distant whine of the winter wind. It was the sound of a smooth river rock flying from the hilltop, where it had been expertly released from a sling; for this was the skill that Luke had been practicing, the surprise he'd been planning for David for the past three years.

The rock hit the giant squarely between the eyes and bounced off.

"Hey! That hurt, boss," said Golem, and then his eyes rolled back into his head, and he fell face first onto the ground.

With a wild cry, Luke leapt from the hilltop and knelt beside Julia's body, then turned to Bugsy with his hunting knife in hand, but David stopped him, covering him with his body before the gunmen could shoot.

"That was impressive, kid," said the mobster. "It's actually kind of a shame I'm going to have to kill you now."

"If there's any killing going to happen, Siegel," said Milt Humason, standing ten feet behind him, on the ridge of the hill, "it's going to be me killing you."

The sound of two shotguns being cocked followed those words.

Bugsy turned around slowly to see Humason and Georges Lemaître, their weapons trained on him.

"Who the hell are you?" he asked.

"Just call me the angel of death," said Milt.

"Yeah? Then we're well acquainted." Bugsy stared quizzically at Lemaître's collar and grinned. "Woah, Padre! Careful! You really know how to use that thing?"

"If you want to know badly enough," said the priest, "you will find yourself in hell with the answer."

"Hey, that's not bad, Padre, not bad at all."

"Shut up, Siegel," said Milt. "One more wisecrack and I'll gut-shoot you just to enjoy watching you die. Now, you and your men, drop your guns."

Bugsy seemed about to respond, then stopped, and the light went out of his eyes.

"Go ahead, boys, drop 'em. I'm bored with my piece 'a crap cuz, anyway."

"Luke," Milt called out, "pick up their pistols and give one to David, then pat those jokers down. We'll keep them covered while Lucas is getting Sheriff Stone; we met him on the highway when we were heading to Ragtown, and he brought us here before setting out for the station in Vegas."

"Don't worry," said Bugsy. "They got nothing on us, see, the killer bein' dead along with the girl. My lawyer'll have us out in no time flat."

"He's got a point, David," said Milt. "It would do the world good if we sent all three of them to an early grave right here and now."

"No," said the pastor, getting wearily to his feet and wiping the blood from his face. "That's not our call."

It was two hours before the sheriff arrived with two men and a Black Maria, and Lucas followed soon after. Luke sat on the sand, cradling Julia in his arms, and when one of the deputies asked if he could take her body he shook his head no and tightened his grip.

"I'll carry her home," he said, and motioned for Lucas to follow.

"It's near a mile in the noonday heat, son," said the sheriff, but Luke would have it no other way.

Chapter Forty-Five
Lightning from Heaven

As Skull's grandson was trudging down Las Vegas Boulevard with Tim Faber slung over his shoulder, Daniel was waking up and looking at a text message that had just appeared on his phone:

Got something: be at Hacienda and South Valley at ten.

He looked at the clock by his bed; nine-fifteen, he'd been up most of the night with pain racing through familiar pathways in his face and hands. Daniel got out of bed, started for the bathroom to take a quick shower, then turned back and looked around his bedroom. The phantom bottle of Blue which normally haunted the first moments of his waking was nowhere to be seen.

"Thank you, Lord," he murmured, and dropped to his knees to spend a few minutes in prayer.

The message was from a young man who called himself Monstro, leader of a gang the local media referred to as the Feral Youth. They were children who'd been abandoned by parents who had come to Las Vegas and lost themselves in a sea of gambling and alcohol and sex. But the kids who survived had found each other and gathered into a roving band that lived on the fringes of the city, in the shadows.

It was Daniel's hope to bring them into the light.

"The geek in your tweet, I seen him," Monstro said when Daniel arrived. He was about seventeen, tall and skinny, with long, lank hair that he kept brushing back from his eyes.

"Good work," said Daniel, who'd used his Twitter account to see if anyone could help him locate Tim Faber. "Where at?"

"Dude!" Monstro said with disdain. "Show me some love."

"Bring in the whole posse," said the pastor, "and there'll be all the cream of mushroom soup your little hearts could desire."

"Preacher-man, puh-leez. Your soup's good, but it ain't *that* good. You want what I got, lay on the green."

Daniel sighed, then took out his wallet and peeled off five twenties.

"Right direction, but you ain't there yet, dude," said Monstro. "Trust me, it's worth it."

"Take this. If you're for real, there's a hundred forty more in my wallet, and that'll have to do. I know you don't take checks."

The youth snatched the money.

"Day before yesterday, I seen your boy with that killer bitch from Bab West—the one goes by Vicki."

Victoria Savage, thought Daniel. He'd heard stories about her.

"But it's *where* I seen them, that's the good part. It was at the Dark Portal, dude."

"Come on, the Portal is Las Vegas legend," said Daniel, but he felt his pulse quickening, nonetheless. "Don't waste my time. Give me some reason to believe you."

"Believe what you want, Dan the Man. I've had the Port staked for a while, 'cause when it shows up, there ain't nuthin' more chill in all of Vegas. It's a door, a freakin' big ol' wood door in a stone wall with nuthin' on the other side of it, and it's just floatin' there, like a mirage or somethin', but I've gone up and touched it, man, and it's for real. Thing is, ain't hardly no one sees it, I seen cops walk right by it like it wasn't there at all. But Vicki and the Faber dude, they opened that door and walked in and poof, they were gone. Ain't there now or I would'a showed you. What're you lookin' at me like that? Play fair, Big Dan, I been tellin' you true."

Monstro held out his hand and Daniel gave him the rest of the bills in his wallet.

"Text me when you and your friends can come over for a meal," said the pastor of the Church of the Heart Set Free. "I'll arrange it so no one else is there, seeing you're such a shy, bashful lad."

"Yeah, maybe," said the leader of the Feral Youth, and in a matter of seconds was out of sight.

Daniel stood there for a while, closed his eyes, and tried to clear his mind. His grandmother Yura had taught his father to pray the Psalms, and his father had taught him in turn.

Give light to my eyes, Lord, he prayed, *or I will sleep in death, and my enemy will say, "I have overcome him," and my foes will rejoice when I fall. But I trust in Your unfailing love; my heart rejoices in Your salvation.*

Lightning from Heaven

Then the pastor set off for Babylon West.

⌇

Oz Osman was not in a good mood. The director of his Cerberus Security Division had just sent an urgent message to let him know that the all-but-impossible had apparently taken place; one who had willingly entered the Dark Portal had escaped! How that fool Faber could possibly have managed it, Osman had no idea, but he was fuming and had just sent Willie Reed to hand-deliver a sealed envelope pronouncing the director's doom.

Email and texts were all very convenient, but some matters still required the old-fashioned, personal touch.

"Excuse me, Mr. Osman," came his secretary's voice over the intercom. "Pastor Gold is here to see you."

"Ah, well, very good." Osman's mood began to lighten. This was most serendipitous! Or could it be that the preacher was somehow behind Faber's escape? But how? No matter; either way, the time was ripe to bring things between them to a head. "Send him in."

He leaned back in his overstuffed chair and gave Daniel a hideous, leering smile as the pastor entered the room.

"Friar! To what do I owe the pleasure of your company?"

"Spare me your frivolity. I don't know who you are, though I'm beginning to suspect the worst. I'm here for Tim Faber; deliver him to me, now, I command you, in the name of Father, Son, and Holy Ghost."

Osman wiped tears of laughter from behind his dark glasses. Excellent! It seemed Gold had no idea that Faber was on the loose!

"Ah, me. Did they teach you that at seminary? Bless your soul, so to speak. You know, this pleases me immensely. I thought at first the woman would be your undoing—for your fondness for each other was quite evident when you brought her and that idiot fellow here last week. But then I realized, no, the man, *he's* the prize, for it's his soul that's in play. And I was right."

Daniel stood there looking at the casino magnate, counting on Heaven to guide his tongue.

338

"My Lord beheld Satan fallen as lightning from heaven," he said at last. "As you, too, shall one day fall."

"Perhaps not today, though, eh?" Osman said with a sneer. "You're a nasty one, though. Lucky for you, I've a most magnanimous nature, and am prepared to forgive all. Since you want Mr. Faber so badly, very well, he's yours. There's only one thing you need to do."

He reached into a drawer of the credenza behind him and placed a magnum of Johnny Walker Blue on his desk.

"All I ask is that you drink my health."

There it was, the real thing, the bottle that had taunted and teased him for so long. Daniel stared at it, suddenly aching with a fierce thirst, while Osman poured whiskey into two crystal glasses.

"Drink up, Deacon Gold!"

Daniel stood stock still, eyes fixed on the bottle, his hands balled into fists.

"Oh, come, come, friend, surely you will not scruple to save a soul!" Osman waited a few more moments, then rose to face the pastor and slowly removed his wrap-around glasses.

"Look," he said, and his breath was cold as ice. "Look deep within my eyes."

Daniel lifted his gaze to find he was peering into two pools of fathomless darkness; and then, within their black depths, he noticed something, something spinning, like a pinwheel from hell...

"Drink," said Osman softly, like a man might speak to a woman he wanted to seduce. Oh yes, not for nothing had he been known as the foremost hypnotist in Las Vegas! "How you've longed for the sweetness, for the only elixir that stops your pain. Drink."

He watched as Daniel reached for the bottle and grasped it with both hands.

"You prefer not to trouble with glasses? All the better! Go ahead, drink, my friend, drink your fill."

Slowly, his arms and hands trembling as though engaged in a great struggle, the pastor raised the bottle to his lips. Osman chortled with glee. But wait, what was this? The fingers of Daniel's hands were growing white, a vein throbbing in his forehead as he squeezed the bottle, tighter and tighter...

The smile faded from Osman's face.

A line of hairline cracks began to run down the length of the magnum. *No, this isn't possible, no man is that strong...*

Suddenly, the bottle shattered into a thousand pieces, and Oz Osman's great mahogany desk was covered in shards of glass and whiskey and Daniel Gold's blood.

"Tell me your name," the pastor demanded. "Reveal yourself for what you are!"

"You want to know what I am?" Osman snarled. "I am the night wind that fanned the flames that sent your father and mother to their graves, the white-hot blaze that gave you the face of a freak and fried your nerves, the torment you feel upon waking and the agony that keeps you from sleep at night. But my name?" He spat and placed the dark glasses back over his eyes. "Our name is legion, oh man of God."

"No," said Daniel, "you are the chaff the wind blows away, you will vanish like smoke, melt like wax. I never needed you; if God so wills, He'll deliver Tim Faber into my hands." He turned and walked out of the office, leaving a trail of blood that dripped from his palms.

"You'll regret this," murmured Osman. He dipped his index finger into the pool of whiskey and blood on his desk and put it to his lips, then reached for his phone to call Joan.

~

Willie Reed hadn't gotten all that far with the sealed envelope when Judson's number showed up on his cell phone.

"Yo!" said Willie, curious to learn what luck his old boss might be having in moving the mescaline sulfate he'd taped to the underside of the sink in Oz's private bathroom.

"Listen to me, man," said Judson, talking in a breathless whisper. "I've got big-money buyers, but they're mean mofo's, I kid you not. I need the buttons, buddy, and I need them now, or these bad boys are gonna think I was jerkin' them around."

Really, thought Willie, what a drama queen!

"How 'bout I swing by this evening, bro, the boss just sent me off to do something impor—"

"*Willie!*" Judson squeaked. "Drop everything, man, or my ass is grass. Just bring me the beans."

Willie knit his brows in frustration, grimaced, looked at the envelope he was carrying, and sighed. No way he could leave ol' Judson hanging out to dry! Worst case, I get fired, he thought, which wouldn't be all bad, anyway, it was getting creepier and creepier working for Mister O.

~

The pastor called Joan's room from the lobby but got no answer, then called her cell phone several times before leaving a message.

"Joan, this is Daniel. It's urgent that you check out of Babylon West as soon as possible—book yourself anywhere else, or, better yet, meet me at the church. And don't, under any circumstances, have anything to do with Mr. Osman. I'll explain when I see you. Take care."

"Sir?" asked a valet, who seemed unusually nervous. "Would you like us to call a doctor?"

Daniel looked up to see a crowd gaping at him. His hands were soaked in blood, and a crimson trail marked his path.

"No," he said, "but I'm sorry for the mess."

Then he took off his shirt, tore it into two halves, bandaged himself as best he could, and set off for the Church of the Heart Set Free.

~

Joan had just come back to her locker at the hotel fitness center when she received Osman's call.

"You must come to my office immediately, Joan," he said. "It's about your brother Willie, I'm afraid."

Joan felt a sickening feeling in her stomach.

"Please, tell me, is he all right?"

"This is not a matter for phone calls. Come at once!" said Osman, and he hung up.

He's overdosed, thought Joan, as she ran to take the elevator to the mogul's office on the top floor. No, it didn't sound like that. He's been caught stealing, more likely. *He can't go back to jail again*—the thought of her brother locked up was more than she could stand. I'd do anything for him, anything, she thought, to make up for his wounded past...

"Tell Miss Reed to come right in when she arrives," Osman told his secretary over the intercom. His office was rather a mess, but that hardly mattered now; he turned to his credenza, flicked a switch on the control panel, and began whistling a favorite tune while one of his walls slid open, revealing his most prized possession.

The pastor will pay dearly for his insolence, he thought. Of course, he could have struck Gold down right then and there—but what pleasure in that? No, the revenge of Oz Osman would be exquisitely sweet! Yes, man of God, what will become of your faith when all those whom you care for die a hideous death, one by one? He looked at the bank of monitors to his left; yes, the cameras were operating. He would make sure the preacher saw the terror in each of his friends' faces before they died.

And then it would be his turn.

～

When Joan entered Osman's palatial inner sanctum, which occupied almost the entire top floor of Babylon West, at first her brain couldn't process what she saw. The smell of whiskey was in the air, Oz's massive desk was strewn with fragments of glass, and the carpeting was stained with blood.

She fell to her knees and vomited her breakfast onto the floor.

"What has happened to my brother?"

"Oh, you're his keeper, are you? Well, don't fret, he's fine—for now."

She tried to scream, but no sound would come out. Osman's long hair, normally tied back in a pony tail, was loose, cascading over his shoulders. But what struck Joan dumb with terror was the monstrosity behind him: an enormous, gleaming bronze bull, its eyes glowing red, its side open to reveal a raging fire within.

"You know of the brazen bull, do you not? An invention of Perillos of Athens, who built it for the tyrant Phalaris. For torture and execution of those deposited within, without equal; but you have not yet begun to appreciate how marvelously it is designed."

Turns out there's all this tubing inside, she remembered Willie saying, *and the hot air blows through it and out'a the bull's mouth comes music. Sinatra, I think, can't remember which song...*

"Oh, how Perillos expected to be handsomely paid!" Osman continued. "The victims' screams, he told the tyrant,will come to you as the very tenderest, most melodious of sounds. How I laughed when he was the first to be consigned to the flames! And how I roared when Phalaris himself was overthrown and fed to the bull!"

The man's insane, she thought, and tried to calm her racing mind. Why was I taking those Krav Maga lessons, if not for this? He's fifteen, twenty feet away from me, she thought. If only I can get close enough...

"Tim and I have been impressed with your plans for the tower, Oz," she said, slowly standing up. "We would love to collabor—"

"Shush!" he commanded, removing his glasses. "Look, Joan Reed— look into my eyes!"

She was looking into the darkest night sky she'd ever seen, no moon, no stars, no faintest glimmer of light; and yet, something was there, after all, spinning in the blackness...

He had underestimated the pastor, but this woman would be like all the others, no match for his powers.

"Come to me, woman! Come, and feed the brazen bull, as so many have fed it before. Now, *walk!*"

Joan felt herself beginning to move forward against her will, step by step, until she was just in front of the fiery opening in the bull's side, and only inches away from her tormentor. *The move I've practiced so hard that my muscles ached, now is the time, now, and it will be this maniac who'll be tossed in the flames.*

But it was no use; her body was not her own to command.

～

"Hi, Petunia!" said Willie, flashing Osman's secretary one of his killer smiles. "I'm just here to pick up somethin' I forgot."

Petunia couldn't help smiling in return—Mr. O's new assistant seemed a bit of a loser, but who could resist the man's charm?

"Your sister's here," she said. "I'm sure it's fine if you go on in."

For a moment, as Willie passed through into Oz's office, time seemed to stand still. He took in the scene: the blood, the bull in full blaze, the unmitigated evil in Oz Osman's depthless eyes, and the sister he adored.

Dear Lord Jesus, he thought, *do with me as you will, only spare my darling Joan.*

Then he began to charge.

"In the name of the Prince of Darkness," called out Osman, "in the name of all that is unholy, I command you to stop!"

To command a weak-willed stumblebum like Willie Reed should have been child's play, but something more than Willie was coming at Oz. *How could this be?* It seemed to him that Willie had become a white stallion, swifter than leopards, more fierce than evening wolves, flying like an eagle swift to devour, and in Willie's eyes burned a holy hatred and in his heart a sacred love.

Not for the first time, nor for the last, the thing which had once called itself Sebastian Bale, and now Oz Osman, realized that it had gambled and lost. For it had never dreamed that in facing Willie Reed it would be facing the most powerful force in the universe, the power of self-sacrificial love. And so it turned to run, but too late, for Willie was upon it, and his momentum carried them into the furnace, into the belly of the beast, and the great bronze door clanged shut.

"*NO!*" Joan screamed in horror, and she tugged on the handle with all her might, clawed at the door, and then sank in hopeless grief to the floor.

At first, all she could hear was the sound of the flames; then, gradually, there came music, at first like a whisper, and then like a whistle, a humming, but soon enough it was a full-throated song roaring from the bull's mouth. Willie had been spot on, it was Sinatra, all right, singing *My Way*. She knew there'd been a good reason she'd never liked that song.

Joan cried and cried, but then found herself laughing through her tears, for she was so proud of her brave brother, and certain that he was safe, and free, free at last, wrapped in the Lord's strong and gentle arms.

Chapter Forty-Six
More Lovely than the Dawn

"My faith in God is unshaken," I told Georges, a few days after Julia was buried next to her father. "I *know* He's there, and yet now, when I need Him most, He seems so far away. It's like my faith is only an *idea*, one that doesn't ease my pain or the loneliness of a future that looms like an endless Arctic night."

"I know something of how you feel," said Lemaître, "for I lost many dear friends in the Great War. But there is another who knows your sorrow far better—even your distance from God. *My God, my God, why have you forsaken me?* Never were two closer than the Father and the Son, never a separation more wrenching. The Lord well knows your suffering; that is why we are told to *come boldly unto the throne, and find grace to help in time of need.* Turn to Him, for your faith is no mere idea, but a relationship with the living Lord."

No one approached the throne more boldly than King David, David reminded me, and for a long time, never a day passed when he and I didn't meet to pray the Psalms.

O Lord, heal me, for my bones are in agony. My soul is in anguish...
Precious in the sight of the Lord, is the death of his saints.

I spent hours talking with Georges the night before he and Milt returned to Pasadena.

"You don't have to worry about feeling lost," Lemaître told me, "as long as you are following Him. Abraham had faith and was sent out he knew not where. Moses' first vision of God was in the light of the burning bush, but he was never closer to the Almighty than on Sinai when he *drew near unto the thick darkness where God was.*"

"The two paths to Truth seem quite different in this regard," I replied. "On one, more faith might lead us into what seems like blackest night; while on the path of science each new discovery casts an ever-expanding light."

"In this you are quite mistaken, my young friend," said the priest.

"Often enough, the greatest discoveries open up new vistas shrouded in darkness. What is more, God has set a limit to our knowledge, as though He were saying, beyond this you shall not look, you shall not know. I see this in the microcosm, in the new quantum physics you will soon study, as well as in the world writ large; for when we imagine the beginnings of our universe and come to the day with no yesterday, there science must stop."

The notion that there is a *limit to our knowing* somehow helped me in my grief, though I wasn't sure why until David and I talked.

"The two paths are separate for Georges," he said, "yet I marvel at the beautiful way that they're intertwined. When man thought there was no limit to what he could accomplish with his own mind and hands, look at what God did: toppled the Tower of Babel, destroying our delusions of self-sufficiency and reminding us of our utter dependence on Him. We can't save ourselves, and thanks be to God that we don't have to."

Perhaps in this life I would never know the mystery of His ways; but everything I *needed* to know about God was revealed in Jesus Christ.

I could not yet feel His presence, but I placed myself in His hands, to do with as He would.

⌇

I began to work on my application to the California Institute of Technology, knowing that Georges had already written a letter singing my praises.

For weeks I held on to Julia's clothes, not wanting to part with anything that reminded me of her. Then I thought, if these material things remain important to me, death has won a victory, however small; so I gave them all away, for there were still many families camped in Ragtown who were in need.

At work, I became one of the high scalers, the men who dangled from ropes high above the dry riverbed and blasted away the canyon walls. We had thick ropes attached to our safety belts, which we tied to metal stakes before we dropped ourselves over, with jackhammers and steel tied to an extra rope alongside. We'd drill holes where engineers had marked the wall, pack them with powder and shoot them off, then pry away loose rock and let them tumble seven hundred feet to the canyon floor.

"Luke, you crazy injun," someone would shout, "we're done, come on up." But sometimes I'd linger for just a few more minutes, enjoying the feeling of the wind, watching a hawk wheel and dive in the azure sky, and talking to Julia in my mind.

After work, I'd help David or Clarence or Ed Grimm, then listen to Lauren teach Lucas hymns that he'd play on his fiddle. Afterwards, he'd accompany me home and play the Bach which Dr. Einstein had taught him, until I would finally fall asleep.

Bugsy had been right; his attorney was able to get him and his men released after only five days in the Las Vegas jail. By an odd coincidence, however, Mr. Skull and his crew, who had been on their best behavior for quite some time, managed to get themselves arrested just after the mobster was brought in. Sheriff Stone threw them in the Blue Room along with Siegel and his gunmen and then gave Sergeant Stanton the rest of the week off.

"He did not enjoy a pleasant stay," was all that the sheriff told us.

"It's a foretaste of the justice that may one day roll down upon Ben Siegel," said David when he heard the news. "Nonetheless, our first duty is to pray for him."

"I just can't do that." I told him. "I understand it in my head but not in my heart,"

David had planted the seed, however, and I wrestled with the thought of praying for the man responsible for the murder of my wife. Up to that point in my life, the Lord's command to pray for my enemies had only been words on paper; now I was understanding their full and awful import. Would I, too, leave Him because He spoke hard words? There was no money to ask me to forsake, as He had asked of the rich young man. *This* is what he was asking of me: simply to pray for a man whom I wished to see burning in hell.

"I understand Jonah," I told my pastor. "The thought of a man like Siegel making a last-minute conversion to escape the judgment he deserves, when I don't even know the fate of my own father's soul—it's more than I can bear."

"Do you think the Lord is so easily fooled?" David asked me. "He knows us better than we know ourselves, He sees into the hidden chambers of our hearts. I know full well the desire for revenge, Luke, but it's the worst part of me, not the best, not the man reborn from above. There is nothing that could glorify God more than for the worst of sinners to fall to his knees and repent, for He whom we worship takes no pleasure in the death of the wicked, but that the wicked turn from his way and live."

I decided I would pray for Julia's killers even though my heart was not in it, hoping that, through this act of obedience, the Lord would change me from the inside.

And, over these long years, so He has.

~

The sheriff said that it would be prudent for us to have security at our weekly services in Ragtown and Las Vegas, so he became a regular attendee, pacing around the perimeter of the crowds that gathered to sing hymns and hear David preach. Soon enough, though, he began attending Bible Study several evenings each week, and it wasn't long before his full-throated baritone joined in the singing on Sunday mornings.

One day in early September, David roused me from sleep in the predawn darkness, poured us cups of coffee from his thermos, and talked while he cooked breakfast.

"It's been three years since Bale's men burned down the church," he said. "We've made do with tents against the sun and rain, and firepits to warm us in the winter. And it's been good; we showed that the Heart Set Free isn't a building, it's the people in it, the Body of Christ. But there's also a sense in which we've been running scared, thinking that when you've got nothing, you've nothing to lose.

"Well, I don't want to run anymore." He looked at me and smiled. "We're going to build a church."

"Really!" I exclaimed. "We should go wake up Ed Grimm, he's the most skilled craftsman we've got."

"He'll have a chance to get involved," David said, "along with Lauren and Polwarth and Anne-Marie and everyone else. But Ed and the others have got plenty to do; when I say we, I mean the two of us. You and me, we'll do most of the work."

The idea made me happy, yet uneasy at the same time.

"Is this just to give me something to get my mind off Julia? Because I don't want to stop thinking about her, I don't ever want to forget."

"No, it's not that," he told me. "I just want to build the church with you, that's all. We're each other's family, Luke; if you were my own son, I couldn't love you more."

I looked down and fought back tears and told him it sounded like a good idea.

So we started making plans, figuring that if we worked hard enough in our spare time we ought to have the church rebuilt by the summer of '34.

Where would the money come from? That was simple enough: we prayed.

"Pastor Gold," said Jacob Arliss, who'd been providing lumber to construct the workers' homes in Boulder City, which was taking shape nearby. "I was dead in my sin before I heard you preach. Whatever you need, it will be an honor for me to provide."

"You know, my Maria was the church-goer, not me," said a local flooring supplier. "But when my love was at death's door, and you came every day and read to her from the Good Book, and prayed, I told God one day I will show this man that Raul Vasquez knows how to repay a debt. And sir, that day has come."

There were many more who provided materials and tools, and no shortage of volunteers when a job was more than David and I could handle by ourselves. We had no need of money to build the church.

~~

In April, I received a letter from the California Institute of Technology informing me that I had been accepted as a student, with a full scholarship including room and board, starting in the fall. I sank to my knees and praised God, found Lucas and David to tell them, and wrote a letter of thanks to Georges.

It was a brief, blissful moment in a time of great loss.

Later that month, Clarence's beloved wife Charlene at last succumbed to the disease that had robbed her of movement and speech. Though I had learned to interpret the messages my friend would sing, that night Lucas gave voice to a new song, lovely and mysterious, and I sat with him and his father while he sang until dawn.

That May, Harold Merkle passed away in his good friend Mr. Polwarth's arms, and we buried him next to Isaiah Trueblood. Then Lauren, who had been baptized in the Catholic church as a child, surprised us by announcing she was leaving to join a convent in Carmel, California, to take her vows as a nun.

One by one, the people in my life were slipping away.

There came a night when I could not sleep, and I walked to the overlook where Julia and I had passed so many hours. Sometime after midnight, the sliver of a crescent moon rose over Black Canyon, ghostly pale against the fierce brilliance of the stars. I tried to remember the stories that Georges had told us of the constellations, but as I gazed at the heavens I was seized by the loneliness David had spoken of when he thought of the universe Lemaître had described, with its galaxies spinning away, flying apart, leaving an ever-expanding void, a vast desert of cold, empty space.

And yet...

There were two paths to truth, the priest had explained, and not all truths are of equal importance. The one gives us a glimpse of the machinery behind the scenes, backstage; the other tells us the plot of the play. Here, there, everywhere was the beating heart of God, the Consuming Fire, a blaze swallowing up the darkness, filling every emptiness, expanding faster than space. At that moment, I felt the presence of His Word incarnate, the living Lord, my King, and I bowed my head and wept.

Then something else became utterly real to me, as tangible as the desert sand beneath my feet: Julia and I were only parted for a while, for she lived in life eternal with the Risen Lord. I knew that His love was stronger than death, that He would not rest until my father, too, was drawn to Him. And every doubt was banished, and my heart was set free to soar with joy.

~

By the middle of June, the church was far enough along that David decided we could begin worshipping there. In the twilight of a Saturday evening, with the first service set for that Sunday morning, I went to look at our work. As I entered, I saw the pastor kneeling at the altar rail, praying from the Psalms and offering thanks to God. How much he meant to me! *I've never told him that I love him*, I thought, and resolved to do so that evening.

Not wanting to interrupt his prayers, I stepped back outside, sat down on the front steps, and closed my eyes to meditate. I'm not sure how much time passed, but I was startled awake by drops of water splashing onto my face.

They were my mother's tears.

We were both at a loss for words. I stood, embraced her, picked her up in my arms and spun around, and then I pointed through the open doorway to where David still knelt in prayer.

She walked up behind him and placed her hands on his great, broad shoulders. For a moment he was motionless, and then, without turning, he placed his hands on hers.

"Yura," he said, softly. "Tell me you're here to stay."

"Can you forgive me?" she asked.

And then he rose and took her in his arms.

"Only seventy times seven times," he told her, "and then a thousand more besides."

"I hope I will not need so much forgiving as that," said my mother, and she ran her hands over his face and looked up joyously into his eyes.

He could see me, standing in the doorway, and smiled.

"Yura Noongwook," said the man who would become my stepfather, "do you think you could be a pastor's wife?"

"Only yours, David," she replied, and hugged him yet tighter. "Only yours."

Chapter Forty-Seven
The Song

When Daniel arrived at the Church of the Heart Set Free, he found Tim stretched out in the vestibule, loudly snoring. A note had been pinned to his sodden shirt, which read, *Lost Soul?* It was signed with a crudely drawn skull.

He bent down and gently squeezed the sleeping man's shoulder.

"Tim, it's Dan Gold. Wake up, man."

Faber snorted and sputtered, opened his eyes wide, then closed them for a while before squinting at the pastor through two narrow slits.

"Is he gone?" he whispered.

"Who?"

"That maniacal Mr. Clean."

"Oh, Skull—you had nothing to fear from him. Come on, let me help you up; a hot shower, change of clothes, good food, some bandages on those wounds, and you'll feel like a new man."

"A new man, that's funny," said Tim, sitting up and looking around. "This is a church, isn't it!" he exclaimed, and Daniel nodded. "Then I'm not going anywhere. They won't come after me here."

"The walls of a church are no protection from whomever or whatever may be after you," said the pastor, "only the armor of God. But, for now, you're safe with me, Tim. Come along."

"I'm not going back to the hotel," Faber said adamantly, slowly rising to his feet. "Osman is a madman."

"He's worse than that, I'm afraid. No, we'll steer clear of Babylon West, I'm taking you to my Uncle Luke's. His housekeeper, Elena, is also his nurse, and she can tend to us both."

"Do you want to talk about what happened?" Daniel asked as they drove in his pickup, but his companion was silent, his eyes fixed on the middle distance. *The man's still in shock,* thought the pastor, and they drove the rest of the way in silence.

As they came to the front door, the two men found Luke up and about and waiting for them in the entryway, leaning on his cane.

"Elena!" the old man called out. "I've two patients for you to attend to! It appears my nephew and his friend have had the worst of it in a brawl."

"Thank you, uncle," said Daniel. "Tim is not much taller than you, would you mind if he borrowed some of your clothing after getting cleaned up?"

"Be my guest. In fact, the guest room's available if you'd like to rest, Mr. Faber. I'll leave you two to Elena now, please join me later, if you care to."

After Tim had bathed, the three men had lunch together in the dining room while Mozart violin sonatas played in the background.

"I know what it means to be weary unto death, Mr. Faber," said Luke as they finished the last of Elena's fruit tarts and sipped coffee. "And that is the look in your eyes. I suggest you take me up on my offer, and make yourself comfortable in the empty suite upstairs. I live in the library these days, myself. Stay as long as you like."

Tim looked up from his plate for the first time and forced a wan smile.

"I *am* tired to the bone," he said. "I'd like very much to stay here for a while, if it won't be too much of a bother." Then, turning to Daniel, he added, "Joan and I were supposed to return to New York tomorrow, but I can't go back to work, not just yet. I'll be taking at least a short leave of absence; would you tell Joan when you see her?"

"Of course," said the pastor, and then, taking out his cell phone, saw that he'd missed several of her calls.

~

"It's fortunate that Mr. Osman had cameras taping everything that went down in his office," Detective Connors told Daniel and Joan after they'd spent hours answering questions at the headquarters of the Las Vegas Police Department. "Otherwise, there'd be no way we could let you leave town, Miss Reed. But the tape bears out both your stories."

She stood up and smiled at them. "So you're free to go. My condolences on the loss of your brother, ma'am; he was a true hero."

"Thank you," Joan replied just as the precinct sergeant appeared.

"I'll warn you," he said, "the reporters are out in full force, this sort of story's catnip to those guys. It's gotten so I can predict the headlines: *Casino Magnate Foiled in Murder Plot, Flambéed in His Own Dastardly Deathtrap*. Mark my words, Will Reed will be a famous man come morning."

With her back to the sergeant, Detective Connors rolled her eyes and mouthed the word "sorry," then walked the two to a side door where they'd be less likely to be bothered by the press.

When they left the station, Joan admitted that she hadn't eaten since breakfast, and the two decided the closest Denny's would be the only fitting place to honor Willie and make sense of all that had happened. Daniel told her what he knew of the evil that had departed—for a season—and of his own battles with the darkness. Joan talked of her brother and only wished she had more memories to share.

"Willie would hate being in the papers," she said. "And he'd get a pretty good laugh out of being called a hero. You know, I doubt he ever paid much attention in church, but he knew himself a sinner, and had a simple faith in God, and I just know that he's with Jesus."

"They'll be no theology tests on Judgment Day," the pastor concurred. "Just this: did we trust in the one perfect hero who ever walked the earth? These victories of ours, they may seem to take place in the physical realm, but they're spiritual nonetheless. That's why, when we abandon ourselves to Him, the outcomes of our actions hardly matter—whether worldly success or failure, even whether life or death—for He's already fought the battle and won. In the worst of times, if our spiritual eyes are open, we'd see what Elisha saw, the hills teeming with an army of angels riding chariots of fire."

When Daniel drove Joan to the airport the next morning, they lingered a bit, talking in the drop-off zone.

"Tell Tim he can take his time getting back to New York," she said, "I'll hold down the fort. And I'm going to tell the story of Georges Lemaître in a way that will make your uncle proud."

"I've no doubt of that," he said. "You've been blessed in extraordinary ways, you know. Now go and live your faith."

"I will," Joan replied, and, stepping out of the pastor's pickup, headed off to catch her plane.

⁓

"Leave Mr. Faber to me," Luke told Daniel, who could tell by the look in the older man's eyes that this was not a matter for debate. In truth, Luke wasn't at all sure what he was going to do or why it was right for him to take charge, only that it had come to him in prayer as what he must do.

On the second day of his stay, Tim wandered into the library, attracted by the beauty of the music the professor was playing on his old-style phonograph, and they spent much of the first week listening to the Mozart violin sonatas.

"Do you care for Bach?" he asked Faber.

"Well, sure, though I'm hardly an expert on classical music."

Luke decided to start out with the Brandenburg concertos, and, when he could see Tim was sufficiently delighted, introduced him to Bach's works for solo violin, which he had on a set of 78 RPM records that, he explained, were recorded "by an old friend, long ago."

When they'd finished listening to the six sonatas and partitas, Tim was silent for a while and then softly asked, "Can you play them again?"

Over the next few days, they listened to the works for solo violin and for solo cello as well as some of the organ preludes and fugues.

"This music, it's a glimpse of the infinite," Luke said, pleased that his guest appeared to have been moved. "It articulates those things we would most like to express—joy, sorrow, veneration, desire—but for which we cannot find the words."

Tim said nothing, but returned to the library each day to listen to the music his host played.

One night, Luke had a dream: he was a young man in Alaska, hunting for Dall sheep with his father on the slopes of Denali. He hoped to bring home several sets of curled horns for his mother to carve and was running quickly through a steep, unfamiliar terrain, till at last he realized he was lost and fell to his knees, panting for breath. "Father!" he called out, but Victor was nowhere to be seen, and all he could hear was the echo of his own voice brought back on the wind.

Yet he was not alone.

"Don't be concerned, darling, for your father is already home," Julia told him. "And your mother needs no ram horns, for she is at work right now on a great block of wood."

"That's fine for them, but what should I do next?" Luke asked her. "Tim Faber's been given over into my care."

"You're lost without me, aren't you!" she laughed.

"It hasn't been easy," he said, laying his head in her lap.

"Well, let's see," she mused, stroking his hair. "Between music and the Word, there's the poetry of song, is there not? When one is beautiful enough, a man can't help but join in. So, there you have it: just teach Mr. Faber the finest song you know."

"I'll do my best," he said, and woke to find himself bathed in the pale moonlight flowing in through his library windows.

❧

"These old eyes make reading a chore," said Luke, truthfully enough, as they finished off the last of the breakfast Elena had prepared. "Would you mind terribly if I asked you to read to me?"

"Not at all, it's the least I can do," said Tim.

When they went into the library, he accepted a slender volume from Luke and settled down to read an elegant edition of the *Song of Songs*.

Faber fell silent after he finished reading, and Luke waited patiently for him to speak.

"*Love is as strong as death*" he said, at length, reading from the book. "So poets would have us believe, anyway. Do *you* believe it, professor?"

"I know it to be true," his host replied.

Tim turned that over in his mind. "Would you like me to read it again?" he asked. "I'd probably do a better job the second time round."

That evening, as they dined together, Luke said, "So much of the greatest human expression—whether in music, or poetry, or prose—is about *longing*. We yearn for this or that, only to find, once it's within our grasp, that it was not what we were looking for at all. Finding that which will finally satisfy our restless longings is the aim of life."

When they'd finished dinner, he asked Tim to drive him into the desert.

"It's been ages since I've gotten away from the lights of Las Vegas and seen the stars," he explained.

"Gladly," Faber replied. "You've got a car, I take it?"

"Yes, the Talbot. Danny had it tuned and left the keys here, though I've given the vehicle to him. So let's take advantage, shall we?"

"You want me to drive an antique, which must be worth a fortune, out into the desert at night? Are you kidding?"

"Do I seem like a jokester to you?" Luke asked, with eyebrows raised. "Don't worry, the road will be paved. Most of the way, anyhow."

It took Tim a good twenty minutes to get comfortable with the clutch, but the Talbot ran smoothly, and within an hour they had driven part of the way up Mt. Charleston and onto a side road, to a spot sheltered from the city glare. Faber put the top down, and they leaned their heads back and looked up into a night sky electric with stars. The Milky Way sprawled across the heavens, its beauty barely dimmed by the light of the rising moon.

"I know you're a believer," Tim said. "Everything you've been telling me, about music and poetry, and having us drive out here tonight—it's all about God, that hasn't been lost on me. And maybe there have even been times I've wanted to believe. Yet—it's not so simple."

"Perhaps it's simpler than you think. But tell me what you mean."

"Well, look, we're men of science, we speak the same language. Put it into words I can understand, lay it out for me, show me, step by step, that God exists."

"I can't do that the way you want me to, Mr. Faber. As scientists, we deal in facts; we weave theories to explain them and adjust our theories when presented with a new and better set of facts. But there is no jigsaw puzzle of facts that you can assemble which will prove His existence, no formula, no fine-spun logic that will convince you that He is the very source of your being. You'll find God in the realm of Truth, and Truth must be experienced to be understood."

"How is it that you're distinguishing between truth and fact?" Tim asked.

"Water is composed of one atom of oxygen and two of hydrogen—that is a fact. However, you do not understand the *truth* of water until your throat is parched with thirst, and finally, at long last, you've had a chance to drink your fill. And consider light, which sometimes behaves like a particle and sometimes like a wave; those are facts. But when you are searching in the darkness for something precious, and finally strike a match ah, now, you know the truth of light."

"So what does that mean—that I need to wait for a revelatory experience?"

Luke studied Tim for moment or two. *The man's been through something life-changing,* he thought; *the hound of heaven is on his trail.* "Are you sure you haven't already had one?" he asked.

"I'm not entirely sure of anything these days," Tim replied.

"Well, there's much to be said for waiting," Luke told him. "And watching, all the while."

The two men gazed heavenward for a while longer, then drove home in a contemplative silence.

⌇

The next morning, Tim walked over to a large framed mirror in the library and observed himself closely.

"Look at that," he said. "I'm a balding, middle-aged man, that's a fact. And not a good man at all, if truth be told." He laughed. "Well, what do you know, I do believe I've grasped the distinction between truth and facts!"

"Indeed you have," said Luke, with a smile.

"So, professor, I suppose you'll tell me we're to be lovers of truth, no matter the pain and whatever the cost."

"It sets you free," Luke replied.

"Ah," Tim murmured, "sometimes quite literally so."

He turned to his host and hesitated, gathering the courage to speak.

"I know next to nothing of God or heaven, but perhaps something of the devil and hell. Both of which are a great joke among my kind; some fellow in red tights, using a pitchfork to stir a pit of burning sulphur while he listens to the howling of the damned. And there *are* howls, that part's true enough, though I only heard my own; for the most part there were just the murmurings one hears at an afternoon seminar amid the learned discourse of reasonable men. And silence, terrible, deathly still silence." Faber faltered for a moment, and blushed. "I'm sorry, I shouldn't have started in, this is all just a jumble of confused nonsense after all."

"There's something you want to tell me," said Luke, "that I would very much like to hear."

Tim sat down and stared at the floor, then raised his eyes to Luke's and told his strange, dark tale.

⌒

"I don't know," said Faber, when he'd finished relating all that had transpired since his arrival in Las Vegas. "Perhaps I was drugged and these were only hallucinations; they already seem unreal. Only, if it was all a fantasy, it was one in which I saw my own wretchedness and lies, and somehow that knowledge has become the most valuable thing I possess."

"Of course it has," said Luke, "because to know ourselves as we really are is the first step on the path to knowing God."

"Do you think it's possible to believe in hell and not in heaven?" Tim asked. "The devil seems entirely more plausible than God; and, really, it's *his* punishment that I deserve."

"But there is no place that is not ruled by our sovereign Lord," his host replied, "and His punishments are as merciful as they are just, for they serve to turn our hearts to Him. A wise man once wrote that '*there can be no such agony for created soul, as to see itself vile—vile by its own action and choice. The severest punishment that can be inflicted upon the wrong-doer is simply to let him know what he is; for his nature is of God, and the deepest in him is the divine.'"*

Luke was silent for a moment and let Tim absorb his words.

"There is a deep ache within you, my friend" he added, speaking with a gentle warmth, "that surely goes beyond what's happened in the past few weeks. Let me help you to carry your burden, that together we might bring it to Christ."

Faber stood up and walked over to a large globe of the earth on Luke's desk and spun it slowly, stalling for time.

"I don't understand myself," he said at last. "I betrayed my wife, Teresa—Tress—not once, but many times, and then left her after sixteen years, divorced her to be with a woman whose face has faded from my memory. We were eighteen when we met, and we were married within the year, and I'll tell you something that might give you a good laugh: Tress is the only woman I ever loved, and I love her still, more than I can say. I can't explain my own actions, let alone excuse them; somehow I turned my life into a nightmare which I've been trying to forget."

"Better to come awake," said Luke. "Please, sit by me and tell me about Tress, tell me everything about her that you love."

Tim talked, and there were times he wished that the *Song of Songs* was written on his heart, for the bridegroom in the poem had given voice to all that he longed to express.

"I would give anything to make up for what I did," he said, "if that were even possible, and to tell her of the depth of my regret."

"Then you must do so."

"I can't."

"Why not?"

"*Because it's too late,*" said Tim Faber, his voice like a cry of pain. "Because she's gone, because she died suddenly three years ago, and I will never see her again, never have a chance to beg her forgiveness, never have a chance to set things right."

And then Luke understood, and he thought, *Ah, Lord, this is why you've kept me alive all these years, why you chose me to help this man. Grant me the wisdom to lead him the rest of the way.*

"Tim," he said, "answer me from the deepest part of your soul: do you think that everything beautiful about Tress was only an accident of mindless nature? That she is utterly gone and has simply ceased to exist?"

"No," said Tim, his voice barely louder than a whisper, "no, that can't be true."

"Of course not. You know, as I knew when I lost my dear Julia long ago, that the good things of God can never be destroyed. In Tress's very absence, when you listen to the still, small voice of truth, you know that a loving God exists."

"But how convenient, that I should believe because I long to atone for the pain I inflicted on my wife!"

"No, you believe because it's *true*," said Luke, and there was a power in his voice that belied his years. "What first leads us to the Truth? For one man, fear of Hell; for another, an ardent desire to set wrong things right. And, praise God, there is One who *has* atoned for our sins, yours and mine and every man's, and who one day will set *all* things right.

"Tim, last night you wanted me to prove to you that God exists. Today, I will do better than that; I will introduce you to Him who is *the radiance of God's glory and the express image of His person*: our Lord and Savior, Jesus Christ. We meet Him in the pages of the Gospels, and if you will read to me again, we'll begin with the Gospel of John."

That night, Tim knelt by the side of his bed, and, for the first time in his life, he prayed.

"Lord, I want with all my heart to believe in You, but I am filled with the doubts of a foolish and prideful man, I can't do it on my own! Please, I beg you, give me the faith to believe all that is in Your Word."

Tim gave thanks for the love he'd received from Tress and for all who had ever tried to help him in his blindness, and then he crawled into bed and fell into a deep and restful sleep.

⁓

In the days that followed, the two men read through the four Gospels together, and Luke talked of how the words of Scripture had transformed and shaped his life. At the end of Tim's second week at his home, he picked up the receiver of the old rotary phone hanging on the wall of his kitchen and called his nephew, explaining that it was important for him to come as quickly as he could.

"Of course," said Daniel, and fifteen minutes later Elena ushered him in.

"I need you to drive us into the desert in your pickup," Luke told him. "Our friend would like to be baptized, and there is a river in the desert that will soon start to flow, near the end of Trespass Trail."

For a moment, Daniel was too stunned to speak.

"My uncle has been keeping me posted, Tim, but, still—well, this is wonderful and amazing, praise God! But uncle, perhaps we should use the church, for the sky is perfectly clear."

"Look again," said Luke, and when the pastor walked to the window, sure enough, he saw that dark clouds were gathering in the southeast.

"How did you know—"

"It is an unexpected gift we've been given," said his uncle, "and that's all you need know. Quickly now, we must leave at once, for the arroyo will not stay full for long."

The wind began to rise as they set out, and the sky had grown black well before they reached the Trail.

"Are you sure this is necessary?" Tim asked, as thunder rolled through the desert, lightning wrent the heavens, and the truck's windshield wipers fought a losing battle with the rain. "It would seem a shame for us all to perish on my account."

"Hush," said Luke. "You've nothing to fear."

"A superb opportunity to trust in the Lord," Daniel muttered, as he squinted and swerved to keep them on the road, and, sure enough, by the time they pulled to a stop at the Trail's end the rain had ceased.

"I've heard legends of these baptisms from my father," said the pastor, "but never thought I'd be performing one myself. Where do we head from here?"

"We'll walk," said Luke. "You can carry me, Danny, it's just a half mile to the east."

It took a half hour to trek through the wilderness. When the three rounded the corner of a canyon wall and came to the sight of a river flowing calmly through the barren desert, they fell to their knees in awe and thankfulness, and Daniel led them in prayer. Tim opened up a folding chair that he'd carried for Luke to sit on, set a change of clothes nearby, and waded into the water with Daniel Gold.

In a few minutes, it was done; he'd been baptized in the name of the Father, Son, and Holy Spirit, and he climbed back onto dry ground and stretched out in the sunlight which had just begun streaming through the clouds.

The next thing that happened caused him to sit up and gasp, for he saw Luke rising from his chair, only this wasn't the old man, it was a youth barely out of his teens, who in two bounds was at the water's edge. Standing there to greet him was a slender young woman with short dark hair, and behind her, joining the two lovers' hands, a third figure, a man whom Tim knew at once, a man in whom was all of wisdom, light, and love.

"Look," he whispered to Daniel, who was standing next to him in the sun.

"At what?"

"*Right there*," Tim said, incredulous, but the three figures were already fading from his sight just as the river was starting to recede.

"What is it?" Daniel asked him, and the newly baptized Christian quickly explained what he'd seen.

"Uncle!" the pastor called out, and he ran over to where Luke was sitting, slumped over in his chair. He knelt and felt for a pulse, then picked up the man who'd been like a father to him for nearly forty years and cradled him in his arms.

"Let's go home," was all he could bring himself to say.

~

The two men dined together that evening, and Daniel talked of his uncle before bringing the conversation around to what Tim had seen.

"Listen to me," he said, "and listen well. You were granted a spiritual vision, and there's a reason for it. You must always remember what you saw this day, you must burn it into your mind, your heart, your soul. For there may well come a time when your faith will be mocked and you yourself ridiculed; when your strength has left you, and you're broken, and all of Scripture seems only empty words. *Remember what I am telling you this night:* you press on. You leave the past, with all its shame and all its false glories, you leave it far behind you, and with your eyes fixed on the goal He has set before us, *you press on.*"

"I will never forget," said Tim, and, for the rest of his life, he never did.

~

Late one night, two weeks after she returned from Las Vegas, Joan was sitting at her kitchen table, copying some favorite verses from the Psalms into a notebook and debating whether to make herself a midnight snack, when her cell phone rang.

It showed a number that she never thought she'd hear from again.

"Hello," she said quietly, after hesitating for a just a moment or two, but the only sound at the other end was a stifled sob.

"Please, don't hang up," her former husband managed to say at last.

"I won't," she said. "It's all right, you don't have to talk."

They listened to each other breathing for a long while before Joan decided what to do.

"Jesse," she said. "Do you love me?"

Chapter Forty-Eight
Epilogue

Jesse saw Joan's willingness to take him back as an extraordinary act of forgiveness and nothing less than a miracle in his life. They were remarried by Daniel three months later at the Church of the Heart Set Free.

In 2013, Joan began having trouble moving her right foot and soon could walk only with the help of a cane. That year, she was diagnosed with ALS, the same disease that had afflicted Charlene Jackson eighty years before.

"I'm sorry," said the neurologist after he'd delivered the fatal diagnosis. "Since there are no effective treatments at present, my advice is to enjoy your life while you can; take a trip to Hawaii or wherever you've always wanted to visit, and go ahead and eat what you love, cheeseburgers or whatever else."

"Thank you," she replied, "I know you mean well."

"All right then. My staff will be in touch about hospice care. Do you have any questions for me before you go?"

"Only one," she replied. "Do you know our Lord and Savior, Jesus Christ?"

That night, Joan and Jesse talked of how best to spend their remaining days together. Perhaps they should move from their tiny Jersey City apartment, her husband suggested, to some peaceful retreat far from the madness of New York.

"No," said Joan. "For the first time, I really get what Hamlet meant when he said that he could be bounded in a nutshell and count himself a king of infinite space. Besides, I see a form of resurrection every morning, and what better reminder of God's grace!"

From their apartment, they looked out east over the Hudson River, and sunrise often bathed their bedroom in shades of pale yellow and rose.

"We have a long and wonderful reading wish-list," she continued, referring to the works of Oswald Chambers, C.S. Lewis, and George MacDonald, "and twenty-four months without terribly much else to do. We'll begin and end each day with Scripture, and throughout we'll pray the Psalms."

Jesse had some money saved up, and he quit his job to be with his wife. They sat side-by-side and read together until reading was too difficult for Joan, and then he read to her. However hard life became, they both felt blessed to have had the chance to spend such precious time together.

A few weeks before she died, Joan told her husband that she had something important to tell him.

"When this is over," she said, and he had to bend down to hear her hoarse, soft voice, "I want you to write a book about what happened four years ago when Tim and I went to Las Vegas. Write about us, and Willy, and Daniel Gold, and his uncle Luke. Start with Daniel; he'll help you, I know he will, because it's a story that ought to be told. Do this for me, Jesse. You have the talent, just let the Holy Spirit guide your pen."

He knew that Joan was giving him a project to keep him from feeling quite so terribly lost and lonely after she was gone, and it made him love her all the more.

I know this, dear reader, because I, that once-faithless husband, am the author of this book.

Joan had asked me not to tarry after her death, but to begin work as soon as possible, and the next day I called Pastor Gold.

"Come to Las Vegas," he told me. "I'll tell you everything I know; but, more than that, I've got some things I want you to see."

What he shared with me were the diaries of both Luke and his grandfather David, and I read them over and over during the next several weeks.

"Almost everything's changed, of course," Daniel told me as we set out one morning to visit some of the places about which I'd been reading. "Luke once showed me the Canyon overlook where he and Julia spent so much time, and it's still there. But Ragtown and McKeeversville are only memories, and there's a housing development where the old church used to be."

"It's the rivers in the desert that I'd give anything to see," I told him.

"I'm sure," he responded. "But you've witnessed the Living Water in the wilderness of your own life, have you not?"

Indeed, Joan had been a mirror of the Lord, drawing me to Him, and with every breath I take I feel His presence and know God's grace.

⸻

David and Yura were married in the summer of 1934, and the birth of their son, Nathan—Luke's half-brother, and Daniel's father—followed the next year. Anne-Marie and Polwarth were married a few months after their pastor, for the remaining two members of the six Musketeers had fallen in love and were inseparable for the rest of their days. Their one child, Justin, now in his eighties, is the strong, Godly patriarch of the Polwarth clan. He moved to the East Coast after college, made a small fortune by the 1980s through hard, honest labor, and has devoted himself to supporting Christian causes ever since.

⸻

"You've got an eight-year-old son," Yura said in a voice raw with emotion, "and you're no longer a young man."

"I know that all too well," said David, and she could see in his eyes his great love for her and for Nathan; but in them she saw also a grim resignation.

It was the summer of 1943. Luke had volunteered after Pearl Harbor and became one of the scientists working on the development of radar in a Navy facility in San Diego. Now David, after long and ardent prayer, had come to the conclusion that he could not stay out of the fight.

"You've read to me often enough from Isaiah," said Yura, after a long silence. *"Here am I; send me.* So, I understand. I won't make this any harder for you, my love."

Though he had just turned fifty-one, the pastor was able to enlist as an Army Chaplain with the help of an old friend from his boxing days who had risen to the rank of major general. In June 1944, he was with the second wave of U.S. troops to land once the Normandy beaches had been secured.

After six months of steady progress pushing the Germans back toward the Rhine, the Allied forces were stunned by a Nazi counteroffensive launched in the Ardennes forests. The Germans soon surrounded the critical crossroads at Bastogne, and, though General Patton had vowed to break through to relieve the town by Christmas Day, December 25th dawned with his U.S. Third Army nowhere in sight. Inside the besieged town, when Brigadier General Anthony McAuliffe was asked to surrender or face certain annihilation, he responded to the German Commander with one word—NUTS!—and some of the bloodiest fighting of the war commenced.

The few *Schnellbombers* that the Luftwaffe could still send into the skies wreaked havoc over Bastogne, and Chaplain David Gold found himself in the thick of the action, caring for wounded soldiers and terrified Belgian refugees who had swarmed into the city as their last refuge. Among the structures to collapse from the bombardment was a three-story building which had been serving as the aid post for the 10th Armored Division. Its ranks having been decimated, the 10th was being led by a non-commissioned officer with a curious speech impediment, a man who had become a legend since storming ashore at Omaha Beach. Massive, foul-mouthed, and fearless, he was revered by his men, who referred to him with the utmost respect as Sergeant Skull.

Clouds of dust had turned day into night. The chaplain and the sergeant, who had both been thrown to the ground by the blast, saw flames and heard moans and cries for help coming from every direction.

"Please," said a nurse, "We've got to evacuate the aid post or those men will burn to death in their beds."

David and Skull picked themselves up from the rubble, looked at each other, and ran together into the blaze. Nine times the big men emerged from the fiery building, bringing twenty-eight soldiers to safety.

But from their tenth venture into the inferno, they never returned.

The Ardennes American Cemetery is about an hour drive from

Bastogne. Its graves are arranged in the form of a Greek cross, and each is marked by a white cross inscribed with a soldier's name. A very few bear the gold five-pointed star of the Medal of Honor; among them are those of Chaplain David Gold and Sergeant Augustus Schull.

~

"Whatever happened to Luke Noongwook?" asked one of the old-timers at a meeting of the West Coast Astrophysical Society some years ago. "He had shown so much promise early on, and that eidetic memory of his was positively unnerving."

"I was a colleague at Caltech," said another. "His students liked him well enough, I'll give him that, but as to research, well, he never did amount to much."

It was true; by the world's standards, Luke's career was a great disappointment, if not an outright failure, for he'd come up with no theories, discovered no comets or black holes or X-ray stars. But the standards of the Kingdom of Heaven are a different matter by far.

After David's death, Luke spent as much time as he could in Las Vegas, driving there whenever his work with the Navy allowed. The boy who had lost his earthly father at thirteen had found his Heavenly Father and gained a loving stepfather in David Gold. Now he in turn became like a father to young Nathan, and then, after his half-brother's death, to his nephew Daniel.

Luke was a source of infinite consolation to Yura, and mother and son worked with the pastor whom David had hand-picked to shepherd his flock while he served overseas, until Nathan assumed the pastorship in 1965. The native Alaskan woman had come to call the desert home; in the aftermath of her husband's death, it seemed that the Spirit was transforming Yura, as though she was being forged by the consuming fire of God's love. Her sometimes cold and taciturn demeanor melted away, and she became a beloved leader at the church and a second mother to countless young women who fled from prostitution and addiction to her strong, welcoming arms. Truly, Luke thought, as he drove back to Pasadena late one Sunday night, she herself was water

Epilogue

flowing in the barren land.

⟿

One evening in the spring of 1987, Luke drove to his nephew's Las Vegas apartment after repeatedly failing to reach him by phone. He rang the doorbell several times, waited a few minutes, then tried the handle and found it unlocked. Once inside, he turned on the lights: soiled clothes were strewn about, the sink was filled with dirty dishes, and it seemed that trash had been accumulating for weeks. Luke opened the windows to let in some fresh air, then set about cleaning up and emptying every bottle of booze he could find.

Two hours later, Daniel returned home.

"What are you doing here?" he asked his uncle, incredulous. "Are you out of your freakin' mind?"

Luke could smell the whiskey on his breath from across the room.

The hulking twenty-seven-year-old had been a star linebacker for the UNLV Rebels, then gone on to earn a masters degree in divinity at a university in Southern California. There was a part of him that loved to spend time in Scripture, but another part argued that he was only trying to please his uncle and his grandmother Yura, whom he knew had dreams that one day he'd take over the pastorship of the Heart Set Free. Well, that gig hadn't done his father much good, had it now, he'd think to himself, hanging out at bars where UNLV alumnae would come by to slap him on the back and talk about old times.

During the past three years, he'd been working on a framing crew to earn money so he could drink. It was to ease the pain from the nerve damage he'd suffered in the fire that had killed his parents, he told himself. But Luke knew better, for his nephew's true anguish was a matter of the heart.

"I love you too much to let you throw your life away," said Luke.

"You shouldn't'a come here and done this," said Daniel, and he stormed across the room, his hands balled into fists. "You had no right!"

"You want to hit me, go ahead, take a swing," his uncle said calmly, holding his ground.

The two men stood inches apart, staring at each other for what seemed the longest time. Then a great weariness seemed to come over Daniel; his shoulders slumped, his hands relaxed, and the anger faded from his eyes.

"I want to stop drinking," he said softly. "But I don't know how." He fell to his knees and leaned his head against the man who'd been a father to him for the past fourteen years. "I don't know how."

Luke stroked his nephew's hair, then got down on his knees alongside the young man.

"I will be with you in this," he said. "All the way. But, more important, another is with you who is far mightier than me. We'll pray to Him, and we'll seek His help with all our heart, all our strength, Danny. He will not let us down."

Luke spent the night at Daniel's apartment and cooked him breakfast the next morning.

"I'm flying to Guatemala this weekend," he said while flipping pancakes, "and I want you to come with me."

"Central America? Sounds hotter than Vegas. But I suppose it's as good a plan as any if I'm not drinking."

"Lucas is coming, too," said Luke, knowing Daniel was especially fond of his uncle's best friend. "I'll be straight with you: it's dangerous where we're going," he added, and then thought to himself, *though only to the body; the life you've been living is death to the soul.*

Daniel shrugged.

"All the same to me. So, what'll we be doing there?"

"Claiming the body of an old friend of mine, a woman named Lauren McBride. I just heard from the U.S. Embassy yesterday morning; she hadn't been close to her family, and it turns out she'd listed me as next of kin. Lauren is the woman who talked your grandfather into coming to Las Vegas back in 1930, and Grandma Yura and I went along for the ride. She left town a few years later to join the Sisters of Compassion and has been with their mission in Guatemala for quite a long while. We stayed in touch through letters over these five decades, though I hadn't heard from her in nearly a year."

"I'm sorry, uncle—I'm guessing from your comment about danger that she didn't die of old age."

"I don't know how she died," said Luke. "I haven't been able to get the Embassy to give me a straight answer. But we'll be meeting with one of the Sisters, the woman who's taking her place, and I intend to find out."

Sister Sofia Morales, a small, wiry, middle-aged woman, picked up the three men at the airport in a mud-spattered Jeep. Over dinner that evening, she briefed them on the situation in Guatemala.

"For over thirty years, our country has been riven by a bloody civil war," she explained. "The military dictatorships do everything they can to crush the indigenous Maya people and others among the rural poor, who fight back as best they can. Both sides are ruthless, don't get me wrong; but the government death squads have been perpetrating a savage genocide which has so far taken nearly two hundred thousand lives. They target students, teachers, intellectuals, and anyone involved in promoting social justice. But there is nothing that the dictators fear more than the Gospel of Jesus Christ. That Sister Lauren was teaching the Maya children to read and write, and giving witness to the glory of God, made her a marked woman. Her school was burned to the ground and she was murdered for her faith; I will tell you only that it was not an easy death."

"If you're going to take her place," said Daniel, "surely there must be someone who can provide protection to assure you won't meet the same fate."

"You imagine a United Nations army will defend every schoolhouse?" Sister Morales responded. "One or two bodyguards will not stop the death squads, Mr. Gold. I simply go to do my duty; His will be done."

"Has the school been rebuilt?" asked Daniel.

"No. I will figure that out when I get there."

"In that case, I propose to come with you. Building is what I do, Sister, I'd like to lend a hand." He turned to Luke, suddenly unsure if he'd gone too far. "Uncle, what do you say?"

"I've never shied away from pounding nails," Luke replied, sickened though not surprised by the news of Lauren's fate. "Lucas, are you in?"

But that was a strictly rhetorical question.

In her will, Lauren had requested that she be buried close by the Maya people she had loved and served, so Luke ordered a tombstone carved for her grave and arranged for her body to be transported with them back to the village where she'd lost her life. The foursome spent a week planning and purchasing supplies and then set off for the highlands.

The streets of Ixilnango had been crowded with villagers, but, as the jeep drew closer, the people vanished behind closed doors and drawn blinds.

"They think that death will follow us," said Sister Morales. "I cannot blame them."

Luke and Lucas dug a grave in the village cemetery nearby that of a priest who'd been martyred twelve years before, while Daniel and Sophia examined the ruins of the old schoolhouse. They buried Lauren McBride later that day, and Lucas played *I Will Arise and Go to Jesus* as he had for Isaiah Trueblood so many years before.

That night, Luke sat by Lauren's grave, thinking of her and meditating on how his life had changed since that first trip to Las Vegas. Thank you, Lord, he prayed, for this angel who long ago told me to leap over the chasm of doubt and trust in your goodness.

These words were inscribed on her headstone:

Lauren McBride

1910-1987

Now I rejoice...

Col. 1:24

In the weeks that followed, they had little contact with the villagers, who hurried past them and averted their eyes when any of the Americans attempted a greeting. Then, with the framing complete and the school beginning to take shape, there came a day when a truck pulled up and four heavily armed men emerged, dressed in black, who smoked cigarettes and watched them work.

"Just keep at it," Luke whispered to Daniel.

"Yes," murmured Sister Morales. "And pray."

Lucas, however, took out his fiddle, and, standing between the construction site and the soldiers, began playing a Mayan folk song he'd overheard not long before. Translated into English, the words go like this:

There is a love that never dies,
that cannot be killed,
that heals all wounds.
How we long for this love,
and for the end to all our tears.

"Viejo idiota," one of the armed men sneered.

Something happened as Lucas played: at first, it was only the children who emerged from their shuttered homes, but then their parents followed, and their grandparents, until at last the entire village stood by the fiddler and sang as one.

The leader of the men in black shrugged his shoulders, waved his hand derisively at the crowd, ordered his men back in the truck, and drove away.

With the help of the townspeople, the school was finished within a month.

Daniel Gold never drank again.

There are some who say that the Age of Miracles ended when the last of the Apostles passed away, but they were not present when Lucas Jackson played his fiddle in the village of Ixilnango on that sun-drenched afternoon.

~

Tim Faber returned to New York in the early fall of 2011, armed with the sure conviction that there should be no conflict between religion and science and eager to live his faith while continuing as Executive Producer of Science Cable TV.

His optimism would prove to be naïve.

"I'm going to talk straight with you, Faber," the CEO said after calling Tim into his office. "It was your calling out and taking on the God crowd over the past ten years that gave us an edge. Without that, we're just one of a thousand stations competing for advertising dollars, and I'm not going to let that happen. So I need you to pick back up on that documentary series, *Why God is Not the Answer*, or there's no future for you here."

"I can't do that," said Tim, feeling like the world was crumbling around him.

Which it surely was, praise be to God.

After losing his job, Tim became depressed, and grew ashamed of his depression—after all, shouldn't the love of God bring continual joy? He was equally ashamed of the doubts that sometimes assailed him while lying awake in the small hours of the night. Nevertheless, he followed the advice Daniel had given him, praying the Psalms and pondering the strange and wonderful ways in which he had been blessed.

Tim's old friends and connections turned him a cold shoulder, his phone calls went unanswered, the resumes he sent out were tossed into the trash. He had never been a saver, and, as the money he'd won on the slot machine at Babylon West gradually ran out, he found himself wondering how he would make ends meet.

"Do not be anxious about anything," he read, opening the Bible to Paul's letter to the Philippians one morning, "but in everything by prayer and supplication with thanksgiving let your requests be made known to God."

He will supply my every need, Tim thought, even if only in the life to come.

He moved into a much smaller apartment in a less expensive part of town and began spending more time in Christian fellowship and prayer.

One day, the pastor at his church introduced a guest speaker from The Salvation Foundation, which supports missionaries all over the world. The man showed a brief documentary film about their efforts, and afterwards Tim went up and introduced himself.

"What you're doing is thrilling," he said. "But, I'll be honest, the video you showed could have been so much better—it doesn't do justice to your work."

"You could do better, I suppose?" said the speaker, a bit taken aback.

"Yes," said Tim, "I've been doing this sort of thing for twenty years. If the Foundation could give me access to the raw footage, I'd be happy to show you—just as a volunteer, it wouldn't cost you a cent."

A meeting was set up for Tim to make a presentation, and the more he thought about it, the more excited he became. An idea began taking shape in his mind; he didn't merely want to make films, he wanted to be part of the Great Commission itself. Perhaps he could volunteer to take part in missions and then make documentaries about them which could be used for fund-raising by the sponsoring church!

The day came when Tim appeared in a large conference room before several of the senior managers of The Salvation Foundation at its headquarters in midtown Manhattan. He told them a bit about his background, explained the shortcomings of the film he'd seen, and laid out the vision of what he'd like to do.

"We could start with the re-do," he concluded, "and if you like that, then perhaps move on to my other ideas."

"And just how much will this cost us?" asked the director of marketing.

"Nothing," Tim responded. "I'm willing to work free of charge."

If the work was God's will, he thought, then He would somehow provide.

"He's saying that," said the executive vice president, "because he wants on the inside. Get real, everyone—haven't you ever watched Science Cable TV? For as long as I can remember, Tim Faber has been the enemy of everything Christian, ruthlessly attacking what we stand for, taking no prisoners. And now we're going to link our name with his?"

"Yes, we are," said a small, elderly man sitting toward the back, and, though he spoke softly, his voice instantly silenced the room. "I trust this man, and I'll take full responsibility."

"What's *he* doing here?" the executive vice president muttered under his breath.

The old man rose and made his way over to Tim to shake his hand.

"Mr. Faber, I'm Justin Polwarth, chairman of The Salvation Foundation, and I'm awfully glad something prompted me to drop in on this meeting, for I like what you had to say. Only there's to be no talk of working free of charge; the worker is worthy of his wages." Then he turned to address the others. "I'm not sure how this meeting began, but we shall end it in prayer—a prayer of thanks to God for Mr. Faber, who once was lost and now is found."

When I last heard from Tim, he was in Ghana, on his third mission trip, a man at peace and ever grateful for God's amazing grace.

～

In 2008, for five terrifying seconds that seemed to last forever, Detective Nora Connors of the Las Vegas Metro Police Department was convinced that she was about to die. She was thirty-four, living with Zeke, a blackjack dealer and sometime bartender who raced dirt bikes on weekends. The two were swingers and heavy drinkers, and God, if he wasn't dead, was nothing but the punchline to a bad joke.

It was a sweltering August evening, and Nora was chasing a meth-head high on bathtub crank down a blind alley off Paradise Road. He was trying to clamber up a chain-link fence; she reached up to grab him and he fell back against her, and then they were wrestling on the ground, and he had her gun and was holding it inches from her face.

Move, she thought as the punk pulled the trigger, his finger moving in slow motion. But it was as though she were rooted to the ground.

Click.

A misfire. And still she was frozen!

Cling-clang. A clattering came from some garbage cans behind them, and the tweaker's eyes grew wide with fear. He threw the gun away and fled.

A long-haired, bearded bum appeared from out of the darkness. She gaped up at him and he laughed and then bent down and kissed her forehead.

"You're loved," he said before shuffling off into the night.

It was hours before she could stop shaking.

"What's wrong, babe?" Zeke asked when he came home around midnight, for she was still shivering under the covers.

"Just a cold or something," she answered, not wanting to talk about what had happened, though she couldn't say why.

Epilogue

"Guess you don't wanna play tonight, huh," he said.

"Guess not," she replied, and pulled the covers up over her head.

The next day, on her way into work, a sign outside of Holy Redeemer Baptist Church caught her eye. On it, the pastor had posted three words:

YOU ARE LOVED

Silly coincidence, she thought. But all that day, memories assailed her of the meth-head, and the gun aimed at her, point-blank, and the hobo with his tattered clothes.

"You okay?" asked her captain. "Seem out of it today."

"Must be coming down with something," she said.

You're loved, the man had said. Really? What would it feel like to be loved, she wondered. To feel safe. To not have to chase after thrills that always fail to satisfy.

She drove past the church, parked for a few minutes, then drove around the block and back and forth several times before heading home.

"I'm working Sunday morning," she told Zeke that evening.

Her boyfriend rolled his eyes.

"Yeah, well, as much fun as you been lately, that don't make much difference to me."

Nora sat in the back row during the service that Sunday, her mind racing, only catching bits and pieces of what was said. But she enjoyed letting the worship music wash over her, and she lingered after most of the parishioners had left.

And that was when Sarah, the pastor's wife, noticed the pale, lonely woman sitting alone against the far wall. She went over and introduced herself and said she was so glad that Nora had decided to come to their church.

"I think I need a new life," Nora told her, and then, much to her embarrassment, she found herself crying. "I'm sorry, I'm so lost I don't know up from down. Do you think you can help me?"

"I know who can," Sarah replied, and that day Nora learned from her about the love of Father, Son, and Holy Spirit.

"It's an awful lot to take in," she said as they parted, blowing her nose and dabbing at her red, swollen eyes.

"Don't worry," said Sarah, hugging her warmly. "There's no rush. The Lord has called you to Him; only trust Him, and He will guide you. About your boyfriend, though—do you need a place to stay tonight?"

"No," said Nora, who was planning on moving out and staying with another female officer until she could get her own place. "He knows better than to mess with a woman who carries a Glock 17."

Nora learned much from Sarah and her husband, and she grew in faith and understanding over the next three years. Still, she felt that her life was only a shadow of what it ought to be; *I'm thirty-seven,* she thought to herself, *childless and unmarried, in a city filled with scuzzballs and liars and cheats. Maybe what I need is a change of scene.*

She put in an application to the police department in Des Moines, Iowa, the city in which she'd grown up, and flew out for an interview. The chief loved her and told her it was just a matter of timing and paperwork, she'd hear from them in the coming weeks.

The next day, Nora was assigned to the most sensational case anyone in the department could remember: the fiery deaths at Babylon West. The tapes secured from Osman's office bore out the story told by Pastor Gold and Joan Reed, but something bothered Detective Connors.

"I want a detailed analysis of whatever DNA traces were gathered from inside the brass bull," she told the crime lab. Then she asked the boys in the computer lab to see if they could find older tapes that had been stored on the casino magnate's hard drive. *This couldn't have been the first time that freak tried to take a life,* she thought; *he's done it before.*

While Nora waited for the results, she contacted Daniel to see if there was anything more he could tell her about Oz. Or at least that was the excuse she told herself, for the truth was that the pastor's calm, gentle confidence had made a powerful impression on her. And she'd never seen a man with shoulders quite so broad!

They met late the next morning in his office at the church, and Daniel answered all of Nora's questions as best he could, which didn't take long.

"I'm hungry," he said. "Do you think we could continue this at the Denny's across the street?"

Epilogue

"Actually, I didn't have anything more about Osman to ask you," she said, her face reddening.

"All the better," said Daniel, with a smile that made Nora's heart skip a beat. "So, would you join me for lunch?"

～

Nora's instincts were right; the trace remains of a host of missing persons were indeed found within the brass bull—though, strangely enough, not the remains of Oz Osman himself—and, for a brief while, all one read about was how the city of Las Vegas had been saved by the late Willie Reed.

Not long afterward, Detective Connors received an excellent offer from the Des Moines police department and turned it down, for she and Daniel had fallen deeply in love and were married a year to the day after they first met. Nora retired from the force two years ago, after giving birth to a baby boy who they named after Daniel's grandfather David.

And what of Pastor Gold today?

You will find him, dear reader, at the far end of Las Vegas Boulevard, preaching to the lost and lonely, the hopeless and heavy-laden, declaring the Kingdom of Heaven and the glory of Christ Jesus at the Church of the Heart Set Free.

THE END

Afterword

This section is provided for readers who would like to learn more about the historical characters featured in *Hearts Set Free*, and the times in which they lived.

Jack Johnson

I first learned of Johnson as a teenager when I watched a movie called *The Great White Hope*, starring James Earl Jones. A good way to get a handle on this complicated and controversial man is by reading both his autobiography, *Jack Johnson—In the Ring—And Out*, and Geoffrey C. Ward's outstanding biography, *Unforgivable Blackness*.

Georges Lemaître

Though the Belgian physicist-priest is arguably among the greatest men in the history of science, he is virtually unknown to the general public. Anyone intrigued by Lemaître and the science discussed in this novel would do well to read *The Day Without Yesterday: Lemaître, Einstein, and the Birth of Modern Cosmology*, by John Farrell. It is one of the best books of popular science published in the past twenty years. For those who want to dive deeper, Dominque Lambert's *The Atom of the Universe: The Life and Work of Georges Lemaître* is the definitive biography. Several lines of his dialogue on pages 309 and 310 can be found in that book.

Credit for solving the mystery of the missing language in the English translation of Lemaître's 1927 paper goes to Mario Livio, who published the solution when he was an astrophysicist at the Space Telescope Science Institute. His brief, fascinating write-up can be found here: http://imgsrc.hubblesite.org/hvi/uploads/science_paper/file_attachment/69/pdf.pdf

Milt Humason

The real-life Humason could well have played the role given to him in *Hearts Set Free*. Ronald L. Voller's biography, The

Muleskinner and the Stars: *The Life and Times of Milton La Salle Humason, Astronomer*, is thorough and well-written.

Hoover Dam

Much has been written about the great dam which looms in the background through most of *Hearts Set Free*. An excellent history of Hoover Dam is provided in Michael Hiltzik's *Colossus*. For those wanting an intimate, first-person account of what it was like to be there in the 1930s, there is no substitute for reading *Building Hoover Dam: An Oral History of the Great Depression*, by Andrew J. Dunbar and Dennis McBride. The transcripts of Murl Emery recounting his experiences were especially valuable to me, and are the source of some of the words he speaks on page 266 of this book.

Bugsy Siegel

If there is one place where I played fast and loose with history, it is in placing Siegel in Las Vegas in 1933. However, I had little interest in the historical Bugsy, who was merely a pretentious thug. Those interested in better understanding demons would be well advised to consult the Old and New Testaments.

Unattributed Quotes

The unidentified Scotsman quoted on page 221 is Oswald Chambers. His works—transcripts of his lectures edited and published after his death by his devoted wife, including the devotional, *My Utmost for His Highest*—are masterpieces of Christian thinking.

The "wise man" whose words appear on page 361 is another Scotsman, the 19th century novelist, poet, and minister George MacDonald, of whom C.S. Lewis famously remarked "I know hardly any other writer who seems to be closer, or more continually close, to the Spirit of Christ Himself." When my late wife was diagnosed with ALS, we did indeed spend much of her last two years immersing ourselves in MacDonald's luminous writing, which brought us ever closer to our Lord.

About the Author

According to Daniel Gold, "Jess Lederman writes about the struggle, passion, and adventure of faith, about the Truth that transforms lives. Currently, he's at work on *Fire*, a novel set in Las Vegas in 1955. And if you think the legion of demons who possessed Oz Osman were up to no good back then, too, well, you might just be right!

You can find out more about Jess, read his blog posts, and sign up for the newsletter he'll be starting by visiting his website, jesslederman. com. If you have questions or comments about his writing, please email him at jess@jesslederman.com. He answers all his emails!

If you liked *Hearts Set Free*, we'd appreciate if you'd post a review on Amazon. They really make a difference! To review the book, scroll down to the Customer Reviews section and click the button labeled "Write a Customer Review." And thanks!

Made in United States
North Haven, CT
09 February 2025

65609144R00238